P9-CND-173

ALLIED

ALLIED

AMY TINTERA

HARPER TEEN
An Imprint of HarperCollinsPublishers

HarperTeen is an imprint of HarperCollins Publishers.

Allied

Copyright © 2018 by Amy Tintera

All rights reserved. Printed in the United States of America.
No part of this book may be used or reproduced in any manner
whatsoever without written permission except in the case of brief
quotations embodied in critical articles and reviews. For information
address HarperCollins Children's Books, a division of HarperCollins
Publishers, 195 Broadway, New York, NY 10007.

www.epicreads.com

ISBN 978-0-06-239666-2

Typography by Torborg Davern
18 19 20 21 22   PC/LSCH   10 9 8 7 6 5 4 3 2 1

First Edition

ALLIED

ONE

EMELINA FLORES WAS no one's hero.

Smoke filled the air. Distantly, she heard someone laugh. The sound was manically gleeful, and Em knew it was her sister, Olivia. She didn't turn around to confirm.

The flames licked up the white pillars at the front of the governor's home. It was a large, cheery two-story home, the first thing that greeted visitors to the town of Westhaven. There was no reason to destroy it.

Except that it pleased Olivia.

Em glanced over her shoulder. Olivia Flores stood a few paces away, the flames illuminating her delighted face. Her dark hair blew in the wind. Beside her, Jacobo grinned at the flames he'd created. He could also use his Ruined magic to make rain and extinguish the flames, but that wasn't how this game was played.

Behind her, about a hundred Ruined huddled together. They were all the Ruined left in the entire world. They'd had more just a few weeks ago, in Ruina, when they thought they could return to their home and live in peace. But Olivia would never find peace.

Aren stood next to Em, both of them a safe distance from the fire. He nudged her arm and nodded at something ahead. She followed his gaze.

The people of Westhaven were fleeing. Some carried bags and rode horses, but most were on foot, running away without a single belonging. Hundreds of them streamed down the street, all headed east. East was Royal City, and the castle. East was Cas—King Casimir.

It was not the first time Em and Olivia had taken over a town and driven the human inhabitants away. But it was the first time they'd done it in Lera.

Em looked at Olivia again. Her sister saw the humans, but she made no move to stop them. She caught Em's eye and made a face like, *Are you happy now?*

Em nodded like she was. She'd always been good at lying.

"There are people in that house," Aren said, pointing to where a woman's face was pressed to a window, mouth open like she was screaming. Em couldn't hear her at this distance.

"Olivia blocked the doors." And Em was no one's hero.

Em had suggested the Ruined invade Westhaven, the town west of Royal City. It was far enough from the castle to keep Cas safe, but not so far that Em couldn't reach him if she needed.

She'd studied Lera when making her plan to steal Princess Mary's identity and marry Cas, and she knew the surrounding cities well. It took only a day to reach Westhaven on foot from Royal City.

"Come on," Olivia said to Jacobo. "Let's go make sure the rest of the buildings are empty." She strode past Em and Aren.

"No more fires," Em said quietly.

Olivia paused, glancing over her shoulder. "Sorry?"

"No more fires. We need somewhere to sleep."

"Whatever you say, sister."

Jacobo turned so he was walking backward. He grinned at the fire again. "I'll put that one out in a while, before it spreads. But let's not rush."

Because if he rushed, the people inside might survive. He stared at Em like he was challenging her to bring up that point.

"Fine," Em said.

He turned around and walked with Olivia down the dirt road that curved into town. Ahead of them, the windows of homes and buildings were bright against the night sky, candles and lanterns left lit as the inhabitants fled.

The Ruined trickled after Olivia and Jacobo. Mariana bit her lip as she passed Em, obviously looking for a plan or direction. Mariana had once thought Em was inept as well as useless; now she always looked to her for guidance.

Em had nothing.

A scream drifted out of the house. The woman had disappeared from the window, perhaps giving up after realizing Olivia had tied the bigger windows shut, winding pieces of rope through the handles. Em hoped she'd gone to get a chair or something to try to break it.

"Em," Aren said softly.

"Go with the Ruined," she said, and took a step toward the house.

"Do you want help?" he asked.

"No." She wouldn't ask Aren to help with a fire. They'd both been caught in the flames that destroyed the Ruina castle—their home—but only Aren bore the scars, his dark skin covered in them from the waist up to his neck. The scars she'd acquired in the Olso castle fire were far less serious. They only covered her left arm and some of her torso.

Em glanced back at Aren as she walked toward the house. He was ignoring her order to go with the other Ruined. He stood rooted in place, watching her. Perhaps he was curious if she was actually going to save those people.

She was curious herself.

There was a door on the west side of the house, a heavy box in front of it. She pushed the box out of the way and stuck her hand in her coat. She turned her face away as she grasped the door handle with her coat-covered hand and flung it open. She quickly stepped back. Smoke poured out of the open door.

"Hey," she said, her voice barely a whisper. She cleared her throat. A quick scan of the area confirmed only Aren was nearby. "Hey! Is there anyone in there?" she called again, louder.

A figure appeared in the smoke. It was a woman, a white

cloth pressed to her mouth. She coughed as she darted out of the house. A small child trailed behind her, his mouth also covered by a rag.

The woman collapsed into Em, a mess of tears and hysteria. Em stumbled backward and the woman's hands found nothing but air. She hit her knees. She immediately turned and grabbed her son. Tears streaked down his cheeks.

"Are you all right?" she practically screamed to the boy. He coughed and nodded. She clutched him close to her chest and turned back to Em. "Thank you. Thank you . . . so . . . much." Her sobs made it hard to talk.

Em rubbed her thumb across her *O* necklace, her sister's necklace, but quickly dropped it when she realized her sister would not approve of what she was doing.

"You need to leave," she said. "Now."

The woman stood on shaky legs and scooped her son off the ground. Her cheeks were smudged with soot, and she blinked at Em through watery eyes. She was clearly trying to figure out who Em was.

"Emelina Flores," Em said.

The woman sucked in a breath. All of Lera knew who Em was. The girl who had killed the princess of Vallos and impersonated her in order to marry the prince. The girl who had partnered with the kingdom of Olso to launch an attack on Royal City and invade Lera.

"You rode with King Casimir to take back Royal City," the woman said.

Em's eyebrows shot up. She'd done that as well, just two days ago. News traveled fast.

"Go to Royal City," Em said. "Ask for an audience with the king. They'll give it to you if you tell them you have a message about me."

The woman nodded, wiping the tears from her face. She squared her shoulders, as if happy to have been given a task.

"Tell Cas—King Casimir—that we're here."

The woman nodded with more enthusiasm than was necessary. "I'll tell him you saved me."

Em wasn't going to ask for that, and she felt both embarrassed and proud as she imagined the woman relaying that to Cas.

You'll make the right decision.

He'd said those words to her just a day ago, the last time she saw him. He'd been so confident she would choose him that she wouldn't let her sister destroy everything. She almost wished she could see his face when he discovered he was right.

He would probably be smug. And unsurprised.

"Tell him I will find a way to get a message to him, eventually," Em said.

"I can take it," the woman said eagerly.

"I don't have a plan. Maybe don't tell him that part. Or, do. I don't know."

The woman squinted, some of the confidence slipping from her expression. Em knew the feeling. She'd lied to Olivia—and to Aren, and to everyone—when she said she had a plan of what to do next. In reality, she had had no idea.

"Just tell him he's safe for now. But I need time to figure out the next step."

The woman appeared reassured. "I will."

Em pointed east. "Go."

The woman stepped forward, tears filling her eyes again as she closed her fingers around Em's arm. "Thank you so much. I'll tell everyone you saved me."

The woman turned and ran. A disbelieving laugh escaped Em's lips.

Emelina Flores, the girl who killed the princess, the girl who destroyed Lera, the girl who rode with the king to put it back together.

Emelina Flores, the hero.

No one would believe it.

TWO

"THE RUINED DO not have *horns*." Cas tried to keep the exasperation from his voice, but it crept in anyway.

The man in front of him gave him a deeply suspicious look. "I've seen paintings."

"The artist took some liberties." Cas shifted on his throne. The Great Hall was full of Lera citizens lined up to talk to him. The room was sometimes filled with tables for dining, or featured musicians at the back wall so people could dance. But today the hall was empty, tables cleared out, only a blue rug running up the center of the room that stopped at Cas's feet. His guards stood on either side of him and mingled with the people, checking baskets for weapons.

He'd insisted they take a few days for the people of Lera to bring their questions about the Ruined to him, and the guards were doing their best to keep him safe in the process. Cas thought the number of guards in the room was excessive, but just recently he'd been stabbed, shot by an arrow, and poisoned, so what did he know?

Two hours in, and he was starting to doubt this plan. Most of the people of Lera had never even seen a Ruined, and the rumors had not been kind to them. An alliance with the Ruined felt unrealistic at best.

"Are you sure?" the man asked, still skeptical about the horns. His wrinkled face was scrunched up like he'd have to rethink every idea he'd ever had. Or he thought Cas was insane. The latter was more likely, actually.

"Positive. I have met many Ruined."

The man must have known this—everyone knew Cas had married Emelina Flores, that Olivia had killed his mother, and that he'd spent time with the Ruined in Vallos after being poisoned by his own cousin—but he still didn't seem convinced.

"Thank you for coming," Cas said. The man opened his mouth to say more, but two guards swooped in to show him to the door. The guards around him were much more stiff and serious than Galo, Cas's best friend and captain of his guard. Galo had asked for a few days off to travel north and check on his family, and Cas had agreed.

"Would you like to take a break?" Violet asked. She stood next to him, greeting people as they came in and introducing herself as the governor of the southern province. Violet put people at ease, with her pretty face and calm smile.

"No. Let's keep going. I want to at least get through everyone in the room."

She nodded and beckoned for the guards to let the next woman come forward. She bowed her head as she approached, her light hair falling over her shoulders as she did it.

"Is it true the Ruined can kill you with just one look?" she asked as she straightened.

"That is true," he said. "Some of them can. But I think it's more important that they chose not to, don't you think?"

And so it continued for an hour, the people asking questions and Cas trying his best to answer them. Some of them were outright hostile, like the woman who yelled that Cas's father and grandfather and great-grandfather would be ashamed that their descendant defended the Ruined. Considering Cas's father was dead as a direct result of his Ruined policies, he couldn't muster up much of a reaction to that.

He spent a lot of time actively trying not to think about his dead mother and father. He'd had time to slow down and really think about what had happened to them since returning to the castle. He was occasionally overwhelmed with grief, then with guilt, for missing people who had murdered so many. It was better to just not think of them at all.

Luckily most of the Lerans who had come to talk to him were kind enough not to bring up the late king and queen. Few were supportive of his ideas about the Ruined, but there were some who were just curious, and it gave Cas hope. The Ruined and

Lerans wouldn't be best friends anytime soon, but perhaps they could be in the same room without killing each other.

"There's one more," Violet said when Cas finally rose from his throne. "But I think you should take this one in private."

The guard led them out of the hall. The Grand Hall was on the second floor of the castle, which hadn't been damaged by the Olso invasion weeks before. The first floor had blackened walls and some rooms that were nearly totally destroyed. But the second floor was still bright and merry, the walls painted red and green and blue and purple—a different shade every time you turned a corner.

Cas's office was also on the second floor, an office that had technically been his father's but was rarely used. The late king had preferred to take meetings in his private library, where there were comfortable chairs and a view of the ocean. Cas liked the small office, tucked away in the west corner of the castle.

A young woman waited in front of the office door with four guards. Her clothes were dark with dirt or soot, but her face was bright like she'd just scrubbed it clean. A little boy stood next to her.

"Your Majesty," the woman said with a bow of her head. "Thank you for seeing me."

"Of course. Please come in." He opened the door to the office and swept inside. A large wooden desk was to his left, shelves of books stretching up the wall behind it. Directly in front of him was a tall window overlooking the west entrance of the castle with four chairs and a small round table in front of it. As usual, a jug of water and a pot of tea were on the table, along with some breads and sweets. They were replenished several times a day, though Cas never saw the staff member do it.

He gestured for the woman and the boy to sit. The little boy scurried to the table, eyeing the pastries.

"Please, help yourself," he said. The woman nodded to the little boy. His eyes lit up, and he grabbed a tart and plunked down in one of the chairs.

The woman extended a tin to Cas as he sat. "It's cheese bread. I know it's your favorite."

"Thank you," he said with a smile, even though it would have to be thrown out. He wasn't allowed to eat anything that wasn't prepared under strict supervision of a guard, or was prepared by Cas himself, which always gave the kitchen staff a laugh.

The guard took the tin from Cas's hands. Three guards had followed them into the office, including the one hovering over his shoulder.

"What can I do for you?" Cas asked the woman.

"I've come with a message from Emelina Flores."

Cas's eyebrows shot up. "Violet," he said quietly.

"Please wait outside," Violet said to the guards.

"Your Majesty—" the hovering guard began.

"I will call if I need you," Cas said firmly. The guard obviously wanted to argue, but he quickly shuffled out of the room, taking his two friends with him. Violet looked at him questioningly, and he motioned for her to stay. She closed the door and walked across the room to join them.

Cas turned back to the woman. "Where did you see Emelina Flores?"

"Westhaven. I am—was—a maid in the governor's household. The Ruined have taken over the town."

Cas already knew this. He'd sent soldiers to follow the Ruined and they'd reported back just yesterday about the Ruined's movements.

"Emelina said you're safe for now, but she needs some time to figure out the next step. She'll get another message to you eventually."

A smile twitched at Cas's lips. He'd already assumed as much, but it was nice to hear.

"She saved me," the woman said. She gestured to her son. "Both of us. The Ruined lit the house on fire and trapped us inside, but she saved us."

"I'm not surprised," Cas said. "She's not what people say."

The woman nodded enthusiastically. "She's not. I've been telling people."

"Good. Keep doing that." He paused, cracking a knuckle. "How . . . how was she? Did she look all right?"

"She seemed well. Taller than I expected."

He chuckled. "Yes."

"I don't think the other Ruined knew what she was doing when she saved me. She waited until they left."

He nodded. There was no way Olivia knew Em had rescued this woman. Olivia was probably the one who lit the house on fire. "Do you have a place to stay?"

The woman shook her head, worry crossing her face as she glanced at the little boy still happily eating his tart.

"We have shelters set up." He turned to Violet. "Will you have someone take them to the kitchen for a meal, then to the shelter?"

"Of course, Your Majesty," Violet said.

"Thank you for bringing the message," Cas said to the woman. Violet opened the door to relay instructions to the guards.

The woman bowed to Cas again as she left. The boy trailed after her, his eyes round as he stared at Cas. His mouth was now smeared with cherry.

Violet shut the door. Cas strode across the office to his desk and flopped down in his chair. "How long until my next meeting? And what is my next meeting, by the way? Have they narrowed down candidates for my secretary? You shouldn't have to know all this."

Violet walked to his desk and sat down in one of the chairs placed in front of it. She'd been indispensable in the fortress, and had proved to be an even more powerful ally as they worked to secure Cas's power as king. "Yes, they have a couple of candidates. You'll meet with them soon. And your next meeting is in half an hour with me and the new governors. They've found Jovita."

Cas looked up quickly. "They found her? When?"

"We just received word. A few soldiers are following her, discreetly, like you asked. But she's amassed an army of hunters and former soldiers who betrayed you—a small army, but it's bigger than when she left Lera a few days ago."

"And you think this army . . . is to attack me?"

"You, and the Ruined. Perhaps not in that order. She's headed west, which is worrying us."

"Why?"

"Because there's nothing west, except the jungle. Until you get to Olso."

He took in a sharp breath. "You think she's going to make a deal with August."

"We can't be sure. She could just be planning to hide in the jungle for a while. But our messenger said she's showed no signs of stopping yet."

Anger bubbled in his veins, more intense than he had expected. Jovita had already lost to the Ruined once. She'd sent hundreds of Lera soldiers to Ruina to be slaughtered by them. She'd lost to Cas, too, when the majority of Lerans had aligned behind him. But she refused to accept defeat, even at a point when Lera was in danger of being attacked by Olivia.

"Would they be able to kill her? The soldiers who are following her?" Cas asked. The words popped out of his mouth so suddenly he was almost surprised to hear them.

Violet appeared surprised as well. "I'm sure they could, if you gave that order before she reached the Olso border."

He should have killed her himself, when he had the chance. He'd told Em that he would, then he'd hesitated until it was too late. He would have saved himself a lot of trouble by just getting rid of her.

The thought startled him, and he looked up at Violet to see

her wearing a slightly alarmed expression. His anger must have been apparent.

"We'll discuss it at the meeting," he said, dropping his eyes to his desk.

"Sure." Violet stood. "Is there anything else?"

He kept his gaze on his desk, pretending to examine a list of refugees in Royal City shelters. "Is it possible to find out—for sure—if Jovita was the one who poisoned me at the fortress?"

"We could certainly try. You don't think it was her?"

"I do, but she always denied it. I'd like to know for sure."

"I will see if anyone has information."

"Thank you." Perhaps it would be easier to order Jovita's death if he knew, definitively, that she had tried to kill him. Surely that would help ease the uncomfortable feeling in the pit of his stomach. She deserved to die. He just needed to be certain of it.

THREE

GALO WAS A fantastic, diligent, and admirable man. At least according to his parents. The praise was unexpected and, surprisingly, unwelcome.

His father beamed at him from across the dinner table. Galo had only been home a few hours, but already he'd seen his father smile more in that time than he had in his entire life.

His mother placed a tray of fruit for dessert in the middle of the table, putting a hand on Mateo's shoulder for a moment as she did it. Galo had never brought home a boyfriend before, and his parents seemed thrilled with Mateo. But they seemed thrilled by everything Galo did at the moment.

"Will you be making any changes to the guard now that you're back in the castle?" his father asked.

"Um." Galo shifted in his seat. He was most taken aback by his father's exuberance over his job as captain of the king's guard. He'd been a perpetual disappointment to his demanding father, and when Galo had left three years ago to join the guard his father had said something along the lines of *I guess you won't be able to find anything better.*

But now Galo had the highest job of any guard in the castle, and even his father couldn't find something to complain about.

"I haven't thought about it much," Galo lied. "We're still adjusting."

"This is delicious," Mateo said, chewing on a mango and clearly trying to save Galo from this conversation. He knew that the last thing Galo wanted to talk about right now was the job of guarding Cas. It was part of the reason Galo had come home.

"There's plenty more if you want," Galo's mother said with a smile. It was true—the kitchen was well stocked with food, the house untouched by war. Galo's parents weren't wealthy, but they'd always had enough to eat and a comfortable home.

He hadn't been sure it would still be standing. He'd left Royal City yesterday fearing the worst, actually—that his home was gone and his parents were dead. But the Olso warriors had never ventured very far north, instead focusing their resources on the two largest cities, Royal City and Gallego City. His hometown, Mareton, was the same as it had always been. The people there wouldn't have even known there was a war going on if it weren't for messengers bringing word from other parts of the country.

"I've heard the Ruined are still in Lera," his father said. "The king isn't really going to let them stay, is he?"

His mother leaned forward and lowered her voice to a whisper, like there was someone who was going to overhear and judge her. "I don't wish them ill, but I really think they should go back to where they came from. They just don't belong here, you know?"

Galo had been wrong—the last thing he actually wanted to talk about was the Ruined. His parents had never hated the Ruined, but they'd also never spoken particularly kindly about them, and Galo found himself feeling uneasy. The extermination of the Ruined had always made Galo uncomfortable, but now that he knew them, it was embarrassing to hear his parents speak about them in such careless ways.

"King Casimir has a close relationship with Em—with Emelina Flores," he said. Cas had made it clear he had no intention of hiding his affection for Em. "And they don't have a home to go back to."

"Surely they can rebuild," his mother said. She took a piece of fruit from a plate that had been hand-painted by Galo's grandmother. It was easy to tell the Ruined to rebuild their entire lives when they'd lost nothing themselves.

His father seemed to read the expression on Galo's face and quickly changed the subject. He asked a few more questions about the last few weeks—Cas's poisoning, their trip to Vallos, the march back to Royal City—until Galo caught Mateo trying to hide a yawn, which Galo used as an excuse to retreat to his room.

He said good night and took Mateo's hand to lead him to

the back of the house, where his room was. It was small and bare, with only a bed and a wardrobe. He didn't come home much.

Galo sat heavily on the bed with a sigh. Mateo kicked off his shoes and flopped down on his back next to him, running a hand through his dark curls.

"Your parents like me," Mateo announced.

"Everyone likes you," Galo said with a smile.

"Well, yes. But your father disapproves of everything you do, so I thought that might extend to me." Today was the first time Mateo had met his father, but Galo had told him stories.

"Apparently he doesn't disapprove anymore," Galo muttered. "Is it weird that all the praise made me uncomfortable?"

"Yes." Mateo gave him a hard look. They'd had this conversation before.

"I'm just saying that Cas got captured and stabbed and poisoned recently. Maybe I'm not actually that good at being a guard."

"Would you stop it with that?"

"Remember when Aren said I wasn't doing a good job? He kind of had a—"

"Who cares what *Aren* thinks?" Mateo interrupted. "That guy is the worst. And the entire guard is to blame for Cas being captured. You can't keep taking responsibility for that. Plus, you weren't even there when he was stabbed."

"Because I let him get captured."

Mateo made an annoyed noise. "And Jovita didn't let you

near Cas when she was poisoning him. There was no way for you to stop it."

"Because I let him get locked up." Galo scooted back to lie down next to Mateo.

Mateo rolled onto his side, draping an arm over Galo's stomach and resting his head on his shoulder. "Not everything is your responsibility, Galo. You don't have to save the whole world."

"I have to save Cas, at least. It's my job."

Mateo snorted. "Please. You have to save everyone. It's your most endearing and most annoying quality."

Mateo might have had a point. It was even how they had gotten together—Galo had helped Mateo save his brother from being shipped off to join the hunters. Galo had barely known Mateo at the time, but Galo had taken the risk anyway. Of course, Mateo's dimples had also played a role.

"Besides, you've saved Cas. He's back in his castle, protected every minute of the day. You succeeded."

Galo wasn't so sure. Cas was alive thanks to Em, not him. Thanks to Aren, of all people, who helped them get out of the fortress and away from Jovita without a fight. Everyone on the guard knew it, and Galo had noticed the way some of them stopped talking when he entered a room. He knew many of them thought he wasn't qualified to be captain of the guard, that Cas had just picked him because they were friends.

Galo hated to admit it, but maybe they were right. He was already overwhelmed thinking about all the things he needed to do as captain, and half of them he wasn't even sure *how* to do. Cas's previous captain was dead, as was the last captain of the king's guard. Captains usually had at least a decade of experience, not three years of service and convenient connections to the royal family.

Not to mention that Galo hadn't planned on being a guard forever. There were good parts to the job, but it was often dull and repetitive. He might have quit in his first year if it weren't for his friendship with Cas and the fact that his father would have never let him live it down.

He slid his arm around Mateo's shoulders and gave him a squeeze. "I think I'm going to step down," he said quietly.

"Don't be an idiot," Mateo said affectionately.

"I'm serious."

Mateo lifted his head with a start. "You're really considering stepping down as captain?"

"Yes. I think I'm going to ask to leave the guard entirely."

Mateo sat up, a baffled look on his face. "I think that's an overreaction."

Galo sat up as well, crossing his legs and leaning back against the wall. "There are people who could do better. And Cas needs the very best right now."

"Is this some sort of weird reaction to your father being proud of you? You shouldn't give this up just because of him."

"It doesn't have anything to do with him. It's about what's best for me, and Cas. They're rebuilding the guard; it's the perfect time for a new captain to step in. I can be of more help elsewhere right now."

"Where?" Mateo asked with a frown.

"I don't know. But doesn't this"—he gestured around the room—"make you feel strange? That both our homes were fine, like nothing ever happened?"

"Strange like relieved? Yes."

"No, like . . . we got incredibly lucky. Buildings in Royal City are gone, everyone who lived in Gallego City is still displaced, all of the people in Westhaven had to run for their lives, and the Ruined lost everything. I hadn't even thought about it before, but Cas said Em went back to the site of the castle in Ruina, the place that used to be her home. It burned to the ground. The entire country burned to the ground."

Mateo just stared at him.

"I just feel this incredible sense of guilt, and I don't know where to put it. But I know that staying on the guard isn't the best choice right now."

"Now is the time you *should* stay on the guard. Nothing is safe."

"It's better to do it now, when there's a break from the madness." If the past few months had taught him anything, it was that the quiet times never lasted long. There was always more danger right around the corner.

Mateo gave him a look like he still didn't understand. Galo hadn't expected him to. He'd been a guard for three years; Mateo had only joined a few months before Em arrived and everything crumbled. He hadn't been around for the boredom of the years that had come before, the ones Galo hoped would come again.

"What are you going to do instead?" Mateo asked.

"I have no idea."

FOUR

EM HAD RESCUED three more humans since the fire. It was getting ridiculous.

Two she'd found hiding in a barn. They'd screamed when she discovered them, screamed again when they spotted her necklace and figured out who she was, then stared in confusion when she told them to shut up and run. She wasn't sure they would make it very far.

The other was simply wandering down the road like an idiot, and she'd turned him around and told him to go back to Royal City. He'd smiled and agreed, then patted her on the head.

It had been a weird few days.

Em walked out of her bedroom and through the quiet house she was sharing with Olivia. The house was one story, with a large seating area, kitchen, and dining room visible once you walked through the door. At the back of the house were three bedrooms and another room that had been turned into an office. From what Em could tell, the people who lived here were teachers. They had walls and walls of books, and the office was full of textbooks and papers and essays.

Em walked into the dining room and slid into one of the chairs. She put her cheek on the large wooden kitchen table and spread her arms out on top of it. She always ate breakfast alone, at this big table. It sat eight, yet it was always just her. She was surprised Olivia hadn't secured her own house away from Em, but perhaps she figured this one was so big that they could avoid each other.

A yell sounded from outside. Em didn't move at first. Screams weren't unusual. They hadn't been for over a year, but they were especially common with Olivia around.

She considered just going back to bed. She couldn't be responsible for what she didn't see.

She stood, slowly. That excuse would never work. She didn't even believe it.

Em walked to the door and stepped outside. Their house was on Market Street, in the middle of Westhaven. At the end of the street were a bunch of shops and food carts, now abandoned and looted by the Ruined.

Olivia stood on the street, surrounded by about twenty Ruined. They were all on horses, ready for a journey.

Em looked around at the Ruined. They were the ones who

had clearly aligned themselves with Olivia—Jacobo, Ester, Carmen, Priscila, and several others who were very powerful. It wasn't surprising that they'd chosen Olivia. Em had barely spoken to most of them since she became queen. They were never going to follow a useless Ruined.

"Going somewhere?" Em asked.

"Yes." Olivia mounted her horse.

"Are you coming back?"

"Of course," she said shortly.

Olivia didn't look well, despite the days of rest and quiet in Westhaven. Her olive skin was splotchy, her dark hair limp and thin. Em wasn't sure if Olivia wasn't sleeping, or if the constant use of her magic was finally catching up to her.

"She's going to attack the town to the south," a voice said from behind Em. She turned to see Aren walking to them. He stopped next to Em and looked at Olivia. "Fayburn. Right?"

She just stared at him.

"I heard Jacobo and Ester talking about it last night."

Olivia sighed loudly, and cast a disapproving cast at Jacobo and Ester.

"What?" Ester didn't look the least bit ashamed. She was several years older than Em, with a long, pinched face that frequently looked annoyed. Or perhaps that was just how she always looked when Em was around. She'd never made a secret of her disdain for useless Ruined. "Is the plan a secret? Do you need Em's permission?" The words were a challenge, which Olivia clearly recognized. She squared her shoulders.

"Of course not."

"What's the plan? Attack random humans for fun?" Aren asked.

"Keep underestimating me, Aren. I'm sure that will work out so well for you in the end," Olivia said. Aren stiffened. He and Em both knew better than to underestimate Olivia.

"I'm going to take over every big town between here and Gallego City," Olivia said. "Starting with Fayburn."

"That's"—Em pictured a map of Lera in her head—"at least five towns, maybe ten, depending on what you consider *big*."

"Perfect. I plan to invade each one and kill most of the humans. Maybe you can draw me a map, Em. You know Lera so well." She said the last sentence like a dare. Sometimes Em was sure Olivia knew that Em was no longer on her side. Other times, she was certain Olivia would never suspect that Em—or any Ruined—would betray her. Not on such a large scale, anyway.

"What's the purpose of that?" Em asked. "Just to kill everyone?"

"No. The survivors will run to Royal City. Then we'll take over towns to the north, until we have them all trapped in Royal City. The south is half deserted now anyway, so we'll worry about that later. Then all of northern Lera will belong to the Ruined, and we can decide what to do about Royal City later. Perhaps we'll let them live there for a while. They could be useful." She gestured at Aren. "Aren's found a good use for humans, after all."

Em's stomach twisted into knots. Olivia could conceivably murder thousands if she was free to carry out that plan.

"We don't have enough people," Em said. "Once we leave

here, the humans will likely just come right back."

"I think we can spare a few Ruined who will travel between our conquered cities. People will learn what happens if they go back to a Ruined city." Olivia's lips twisted into something like a smile. "Besides, Casimir doesn't have much of an army these days, does he? Isn't his cousin still trying to take the throne from him? And they surely haven't heard the last from Olso yet. Those warriors never retreat for long."

Em swallowed. Olivia was right, unfortunately. Cas couldn't fight *three* enemies at once. It was the perfect time for the Ruined to swoop in. It was the sort of scenario their mother had dreamed of.

"It's a good plan, isn't it?" Olivia asked smugly.

"It's a risky plan."

"All the best ones are. You taught me that."

The knots in her stomach tightened. Em *had* taught her that. Olivia was free because of Em's risky plan, because she killed a princess in cold blood and planned to kill many more. King Salomir was the one who kidnapped and enraged Olivia, but Em certainly hadn't set a good example since.

Em reached for her throat, where the necklace with the *O* charm—for Olivia—used to hang around her neck. She'd put it in a drawer a few days ago, and she kept forgetting and reaching for it.

Olivia's eyes followed the movement.

"I put it away," Em said quietly. "It was how people recognized me. I'd prefer to be more discreet." It was the truth, but only part of it. The necklace had become a constant reminder of her sister. Em preferred it out of sight.

Olivia turned away before Em could see her expression.

"You can come if you want," Olivia said, her voice light. "But I know how emotional you get, watching humans dying. I guess you have more in common with them than the Ruined these days, don't you?"

A few of the Ruined murmured their agreement.

Olivia looked back at Em and raised her eyebrows. She clearly wanted Em to come, if only to prove that Em couldn't stop them. She was right. Even if Aren came with her, the two of them couldn't stop twenty Ruined on their own.

"Let's go," Olivia said when Em didn't answer. She kicked the sides of her horse and started down the road. The other Ruined followed.

"What do we do?" Aren asked quietly as they watched them go.

"Nothing." Em closed her eyes and let out a heavy sigh. While she'd been fretting and feeling sorry for herself, Olivia had formed a plan. She'd organized her supporters and now there was nothing Em could do to save the people in Fayburn.

And this certainly wouldn't do anything to endear them to the people of Lera. Cas already had his work cut out for him, trying to convince his people that not all the Ruined wanted to hurt them.

"We need to find out for sure who's with us," Em said. "We need a plan to stop her."

"I know some. I can talk to Mariana and Ivanna and see who might be on our side."

"Good. Do it. Let's meet first thing tomorrow morning."

"Do we have a plan to tell them?" Aren asked.

"Not really. But I think I know where we need to start."

"Where?"

"Partnering with Cas and the Lera army."

FIVE

IRIA HAD SPENT three nights in a jail cell.

She'd arrived in Olso dirty and exhausted from the trip across the ocean, and had actually been grateful for the tiny lumpy bed in the cell. At least it wasn't rocking and jerking with the waves. She'd always hated traveling by ship.

But she'd only slept well the first night. The morning had brought warriors trailing in, one after another, to glare and yell at her. They didn't usually allow prisoners awaiting trial to have visitors. It seemed Iria was the exception.

The fourth morning she woke early, the sun not yet peeking in from the tiny window at the back of her cell. She sat on her bed and waited, knees pulled to her chest.

Today would not be a good day. Today, she stood trial for treason.

Outside, she could hear the sounds of the day getting started as the sun rose—murmured voices, horse hooves on the street, even the smell of fresh bread. There was a bakery near the courthouse, and some mornings the breeze carried the scent of bread all the way to her cell.

She'd grown up not far from here, and had visited that bakery several times. Mornings were chilly year round, and she had the first shift at school, so she'd often duck in before sunrise and eat a warm sticky bun before class. The owner, an older woman with a kind smile, would give her free hot chocolate sometimes, and Iria would sit at one of the stools by the window and watch warriors and judges and other government people stream into the courthouse.

She'd gone back to the bakery recently, when she'd been home briefly between her trips to Lera and Ruina. The kind owner had passed away and a perfectly nice young man had taken her place, but the rolls tasted different and they didn't sell hot chocolate anymore. And as she walked out of the bakery with her disappointing pastry, she'd thought of Aren, and wondered if he'd made it to Ruina, and if he had enough food. It had been her idea to bring the Ruined food when the king decided to send August.

She willed away thoughts of Aren as a guard stomped down the center aisle of the jail cells. There were at least twenty cells at this location, but Iria hadn't seen or heard any other prisoners. Perhaps they thought being a traitor was contagious.

Iria got to her feet as the guard stopped in front of her cell. The door slid open with a bang. Another guard appeared beside him.

"It's time," the first guard said. "Hold out your arms."

She did as he said, and the guard slapped handcuffs around her wrists. The chains rattled as she lowered her hands.

"Follow me." The guard stepped out of the cell and she trailed behind him. The other one was on her heels, and up ahead she could see two more in their white-and-red uniforms. Olso jails were not easy to escape from, but they clearly weren't taking any chances.

The cells were attached to the courthouse through a long hallway, and her heart thudded in her chest as they walked. She hadn't seen her family or friends since arriving back in Olso, and she was both dreading and looking forward to it.

They reached the end of the hallway and the guard pulled open the door. Iria squinted in the bright light as they stepped onto the marble floors.

She knew this courthouse well—the high ceilings, the bright white floors, the stained-glass doors that brought a blast of cool air every time they opened. Her father was a judge. She wondered if he still was, or if he'd been punished for her actions as well.

The courthouse was full of people, and they turned to stare as she walked by. Cas's mother, the former queen of Lera, used to be the most famous traitor in Olso. It seemed Iria had snatched that title away.

She swallowed down a wave of panic. She still wasn't entirely sure how she'd gotten here. Her family was highly regarded in Olso, and she'd had no trouble passing the exams to become a warrior. She'd beaten out stiff competition to win the honor of helping Emelina Flores execute her plan to take down Lera. Then the Lera castle had fallen, the Ruined agreed to partner with Olso, and Iria had been heralded as a hero. She could still see the pride in her mother's eyes when she'd come back from Lera, the first time. She had exceeded her expectations, and that was not an easy task with her mother.

And now, Iria was here. About to go on trial for treason.

Aren. His face popped into her head and refused to leave, no matter how many times she willed it away. She had betrayed her fellow warriors in the jungle for him. The choice was to let them kill Aren, or betray them, and that had not been a difficult decision. She hadn't given it a second thought before screaming the warning that saved Aren's life. She hadn't hesitated to run when he took her hand.

He, however, hesitated plenty. He was still in Lera—or back in Ruina, maybe—because he was too scared to leave the Ruined. Even when he was horrified and scared of Olivia, he chose her over Iria, because of the marks on their bodies. Because of the powers they shared. She could see the conflict in Aren's eyes, but still, he hesitated.

Not that it mattered now. Barring a miracle, she would rot in a prison for the rest of her life.

I'll find you. I don't care if I have to break into every prison in Olso. I'll find you. Aren's last words to her rang in her ears, spoken only a couple of weeks ago. She'd believed him at the time. She remembered thinking that of course the most powerful Ruined alive would rescue her.

But reality hit on the journey across the sea. As they put her in the cell. Aren had never even been to Olso. The Ruined were on the brink of war with Lera. She was not his priority, and to hope for a miraculous rescue from him would only bring disappointment.

A shout made her head jerk up, and through the front windows, she saw a huge group of people standing outside the courthouse. Most of them wore black and brown coats—fashion in Olso was much more understated than in Lera—and there were a few red warrior uniforms scattered among them. Some of the people held signs, and she craned her neck to read a few.

WE DEMAND VICTORY.

FIGHT THE RUINED.

A few of the protestors were trying to enter the courthouse, and guards were struggling to keep them back.

Iria felt a tug on her chains, urging her to walk faster, and she turned away from the protestors. The Olso warriors had suffered humiliating defeats in Lera and in their own country, and it seemed not everyone was ready to give up the fight.

The guard opened the door to the courtroom. The benches

to her left and right were packed but silent, and she had to blink away tears as she scanned the faces. Many were familiar.

She spotted her parents almost immediately. Her mother hadn't bothered to turn to see Iria enter. She stood rigidly, staring straight ahead. Iria's mother was not understanding about even the smallest of things, so she certainly wouldn't have any sympathy for a traitor daughter. Iria knew this, but it stung anyway. Her father was turned to watch Iria, tears in his eyes, disappointment and anger lining his face.

At the front of the room sat the judge, on a platform elevated slightly over the rest of the room. To the left of the judge was a woman Iria didn't know—a government official, probably—and to the right was August. *King* August now, since Olivia had killed almost his entire family. Of all the heirs to the Olso throne, Iria would have chosen August last.

The king wouldn't normally be present at a trial, but Iria was special. He watched her walk into the room, his face unreadable. He was already an unpopular king, since the people (rightly) blamed him for the Ruined attack on the Olso castle.

A long table was in front of the judge, where Iria was expected to stand during the proceedings. The guard left her at the table without removing the chains around her wrists.

Iria dared a glance over her shoulder. Just behind her was Daven, a boy she had dated briefly a couple of years ago. He glared at her with such contempt that she wished she'd been meaner when she dumped him.

She faced forward again. The judge motioned for the room to

quiet down and the hushed whispers around her faded.

"Iria Ubino," the judge said. "You've been charged with treason, murder, and colluding with the enemy. You may speak to these charges, if you wish."

She clasped her hands together to keep them from shaking. "I never murdered anyone."

The judge pointed to Iria's right. "Warrior Rodrigo, can you speak to those charges?"

Iria looked and found Rodrigo standing. He was a warrior she'd known well, before. He had been there when she escaped with Aren, when he and the other warriors killed the Ruined with no warning, no reason.

"Three warriors died when that Ruined, Aren, attacked us and left with Iria," he said.

Iria faced the judge. "And two Ruined died. The warriors killed them."

"As they'd been ordered to," the judge said.

"It was the wrong order."

"That is not for you to decide. You took an oath to always follow the orders of your leaders. Three warriors died because you did not. Do you have anything else to say with regard to the charges?"

Tears pricked her eyes. There was no miracle coming. She didn't know what she expected—understanding? Not about the Ruined. Not when Olivia had just burned down a good portion of the castle and killed the royal family.

She peeked at August. The only thing that could possibly

save her was a pardon from him.

He stared back at her. His gaze was steely, his eyes dark with the evidence of little sleep. He didn't even look angry, just . . . empty. Like he couldn't even bring himself to care. He would not help her.

"They were supposed to be our allies," she said quietly, turning away from August. She cleared her throat so the whole room could hear. "You sent me there to help them, and then you punish me when I do."

"Your loyalty should always be to us, not to them." The judge pushed some papers aside. "I've heard all I need to hear."

"No you have not!" A familiar voice rang through the courtroom. Iria turned with a start to find Bethania standing among the seated crowd, fists clenched. She was so angry that her wild dark curls were practically vibrating. Iria knew the stance well. Bethania was always clenching her fists in the year she and Iria had dated—they'd driven each other crazy.

"Quiet, please," the judge said.

"She served the warriors loyally for *years*," Bethania shouted. Iria had been a warrior for only four short years, but Bethania was prone to exaggeration. "You sent her on impossible assignments, ask her to make friends of the Ruined, and then punish her when she does just that? What kind of person would have stood by while their friend was murdered?"

"Will someone escort her from the courtroom, please?" the judge asked, pinching his brow with two fingers.

Two guards grabbed Bethania's arms and began dragging her

to the doors. She struggled against them.

"You're as bad as Lera if you do this!" she shouted. "You're cowards!" The guards pulled her out the door, her shouts fading as they dragged her away.

Iria rubbed her wet cheek against her shoulder. Given the stony stares of the rest of the courtroom, there were not many who agreed with Bethania. Even her parents just stood there silently.

"Iria Ubino, I find you guilty on all three charges," the judge said. "You will serve a lifetime sentence at Central Olso Prison." He glared at where Bethania had disappeared. "I would just like to point out that if you were charged with this crime in Lera, you would be sentenced to death. You should count yourself lucky to be a citizen of Olso, and I hope you will take this time to reflect on your crimes."

A few people clapped. The sound rang in Iria's ears as she ducked her head and closed her eyes.

"Let's go, prisoner," a guard barked.

She tried to hide her tears as they led her away.

SIX

CAS SPENT THE weeks after returning to the castle assessing the damage to the building. It wasn't nearly as bad as it could have been—the warriors must have extinguished the flames not long after he escaped. A lot of cleaning and repainting had to be done, and several rooms needed to be completely refurnished.

The royal suite, his parents' rooms, were apparently in perfect condition. He hadn't gone in to confirm for himself.

"The maid staff would like to know if they should start cleaning the rooms," Cas's new secretary, Xavier, said. He stood in front of Cas's desk, holding a paper and pen and looking at Cas like he didn't know this question sent panic shooting up Cas's spine.

"Um," Cas said, and could almost hear his father's annoyed

sigh. He would be so disappointed in Cas in almost every way, but he certainly wouldn't like his uncommanding tone.

"They have one of the keys, but they weren't sure if they should go in . . ." Xavier didn't finish his sentence. He knew Cas had the other key.

"Let's—" He cut himself off before saying *wait*. It was dumb to wait. He hoped that eventually Em would return; those rooms were supposed to be for the king and queen. He could at least have the suite cleared out and cleaned. He didn't have to move in right away.

"Tomorrow," he said, ignoring the burst of nerves in his stomach. "I will go through the rooms tonight, and the staff can clean them tomorrow. Ask them to box up all my parents' belongings and put them in storage."

Xavier nodded and wrote something on his paper.

"That's all for today," Cas said. "Have a good evening."

"Thank you, Your Majesty." Xavier bowed his head and walked out of the office.

Cas got up from his desk and followed Xavier out. Guards trailed behind him. He still wasn't used to having guards follow him everywhere, and he hoped Galo would ease up a bit after they got settled.

He dropped by his room for the key, then went directly to one of the doors to the royal suite. "I'm going in by myself," he said to the guards without turning around. He thought maybe he'd said it so he wouldn't chicken out again.

He stuck the key in the lock and pushed open the door.

He was entering through the sitting room that connected the king's and queen's suites, and it was darker and quieter than he'd ever seen before. The curtains were drawn, a tiny sliver of late-afternoon light dancing across the gray rug.

His parents hadn't used the sitting room much, and it was as pristine as ever, a blanket neatly folded on the couch, the bright red chairs so stiff it appeared as though they were brand-new.

He turned left, in the direction of his father's rooms. Sometimes the royal couple shared the rooms to the left, leaving the other rooms for special guests or children. But his parents had never shared a bedroom, as far as Cas knew.

He walked through the room that served as his father's closet and dressing room and pushed open the door to the bedroom.

The curtains had been left open, bathing the room in orange light. Cas's eyes skipped over the dresser, the wardrobe, the chair in the corner with a book open on top of it. He wasn't sure what he was looking for. Something to take with him? Something to remember his father by other than this legacy of death and war?

Maybe he shouldn't take anything at all. Was he allowed to miss someone who had destroyed so many lives? Was he allowed to remember the good things?

He walked to the dresser and pulled open the top drawer. There were cuff links and tie clips and a few other things inside, but nothing special. The second drawer was bigger, and Cas pushed aside some scarves to find a stack of leather-bound notebooks.

He pulled one out. He was almost certain his father wouldn't have kept journals—deep self-reflection wasn't his father's specialty—and he opened to find that he was right. They were sketches—of the castle, people Cas didn't know, and a younger version of his mother. He'd often seen his father doodling in these notebooks when Cas was younger. He said it relaxed him.

Cas found several sketches of himself, as a baby, then as a toddler, then at about age five. He was chubby-cheeked and smiling in the latter, and though it was just a pencil sketch, he looked very much like he did in the professional paintings they had hanging around the castle.

The pages were blank after that. His father must have given up the hobby at that point.

Cas grabbed all the sketchbooks, five in total, and tucked them under his arm. He didn't have the strength to search through all of them right now, but maybe he'd find some one day.

He went to his mother's room next. The scent of her perfume still lingered in the air, and the smell brought such powerful memories with it that he had to stop in the doorway for a moment. He closed his eyes and took in a few shaky breaths.

When the urge to crumple to the floor had passed, he stepped inside. His mother's room was more cluttered—bottles and creams spread across several surfaces, four different books open and scattered across the room, and various pieces of clothing tossed on chairs.

He knew what he wanted of his mother's, and he found it in one of the dresser drawers. It was her warrior pin, something she'd kept despite her obvious disdain for her home country. He also took a necklace and a ring he knew had been gifts from her parents when she was young. He tucked them into his pocket and quickly walked out of the room.

Relief flooded his veins as he headed for the door leading out of the royal suite. He'd been avoiding that for so long, and now he wished he'd done it earlier, just to get it over with.

He stepped out of the suite and into the castle hallway to find Galo waiting with the guards. Cas looked at him in surprise, some of the tension leaving his chest at the sight of his friend.

"You're back," Cas said.

"Just now." Galo's eyes skipped to the sketchbooks in Cas's arm. He murmured to the other guards that they could leave.

"Are you going to stop having them follow me around everywhere? It's really not necessary in the castle," Cas said as they walked away.

"I'll ask them to back off now that we're settled." Galo glanced at the doorway behind Cas. "Is everything all right?"

"They're cleaning it out tomorrow." He gestured to the notebooks. "Just picking up a few things."

Galo squinted at him, because Cas hadn't really answered the question.

"How was the trip home?" Cas asked, turning and walking in the direction of his rooms.

"Fine. Odd. I need to talk to you, when you have a chance." He said the last sentence in a rush, like he needed to get it out quickly.

"I have a chance now," Cas said.

Cas led them to his sitting room, and dropped the sketch-books on a table. He'd find another spot for them soon. Preferably somewhere he didn't have to look at them.

He sank into a chair and gestured for Galo to sit across from him.

"I'd like to resign as captain of the guard," Galo blurted out.

Silence followed that statement. Cas could hear the clock ticking behind him. "What?"

Galo clasped his hands together, his face more nervous than Cas had ever seen. "I'd like to resign as captain. And I'd like to leave the guard entirely, if you'll allow it."

"Why?" Panic flared in Cas's chest. Both of his parents were dead, his cousin had fled—she was probably plotting to kill him right this moment—and the girl he loved could only send messages to him through random maids she rescued. Galo was one of the only people he had left.

"I'm not qualified to be your captain," Galo said. "You only gave me the position because we're friends. There were dozens of other guards who would have been more qualified."

"Not anymore," Cas pointed out. A good number of guards were killed when Olso invaded the Lera castle. Many more were killed at the battle of Fort Victorra. They were in the process of recruiting more men and women to train.

"There are still plenty who are more qualified," Galo said. "I'd be happy to give you suggestions."

"Don't you think that knowing me well makes you the most qualified?" Cas asked.

"No. I think it's a hindrance, actually."

"How so?"

"I'm concerned with what you want. I let you sneak out of the castle—"

"That was a different time," Cas said. A safer time.

"Still, our friendship is not helpful to your safety. Obviously. You've recently been stabbed, poisoned, and taken an arrow in the shoulder."

"You weren't there for the arrow," Cas said.

"Because I lost you."

"I don't think we can reasonably blame you for Olso invading Lera."

"I was there for the stabbing and the poison." Galo raised his eyebrows meaningfully.

Cas let out a dramatic sigh and slumped back in his chair. "You're *one* person. You can't take all the blame."

"I'm not a good captain, Cas. I'm inexperienced. You need the best right now. It's the perfect time to change leadership, when we're putting the castle back together."

A little voice nagged at Cas, whispering that it was true. He had given the position to his friend. It was only weeks ago when they rode through the jungle and Cas offered him the job, but it felt like a lifetime. He was rebuilding his guard, and perhaps a change wasn't the worst idea.

"But you want to leave the guard entirely?" Cas asked.

"It doesn't feel like the right place for me." Galo clasped and unclasped his hands. "Honestly, I've never really liked being a guard. I joined because I didn't have many other options, and then I stayed because of you."

"Oh," Cas said, suddenly feeling very stupid that he hadn't known that. He'd assumed Galo wanted to be captain of his guard. He'd never even asked.

"I still want to help, though," Galo said. "I just don't think that the guard is the best place for me."

"Is there something you'd rather do?" Cas asked. "I have a lot of open positions at the moment." He smiled when he said it, but there was no humor in his voice.

"I will go wherever you would like me. I could join the soldiers, maybe. At least until we resolve the Olivia situation. I'm good with a sword."

"Maybe."

"In the meantime I can go to one of the shelters. I won't take up the guards' quarters."

"No, you won't. I'll have a room made up for you. How about Jovita's old room?"

"No, that not nec—"

"Don't argue." Cas said it firmly, and Galo snapped his mouth shut. "I'm actually quite eager to give that room away." He was still waiting to hear an answer about Jovita poisoning him, but the flare of anger still accompanied the thought of her. "Think about what you'd like to do. And come up with a few names for your replacement. You'll need to continue your duties until I've picked someone."

"Of course."

"And if you change your mind, you're always welcome back on the king's guard."

"Thank you." He said it stiffly, like it was an automatic response, not an option he would actually consider.

"I'm sorry," Cas said. "I feel like I should have known that you didn't like it."

"That's ridiculous. There's no way for you to know if I didn't tell you."

"Well, true." Cas laughed even though he still felt stupid. "Did something happen with your parents that made you want to leave now?"

"No . . . yes . . . I don't know." Galo leaned forward, resting his elbows on his thighs. "My father isn't usually proud of me, and he suddenly was, over something that I knew wasn't right for me. It made the decision easier."

Cas blinked, a little taken aback. "Your father isn't usually proud of you?"

"No. I never did that well in school, which was something he really valued. He saw my joining the guard as a last resort."

"Was it?"

"No. Staying in Mareton and working at the mill or in the fields was the last resort. Being a guard was several steps before last resort. And he knew that. He just didn't like making things easy for me."

"Oh. I'm sorry." Cas realized suddenly that Galo knew

everything about Cas's family, but Cas knew very little about his. "But now that you have his approval, you're going to give it up?"

"Well, it turns out I never wanted his approval." Galo gave him a sad smile. "I know you understand that."

"Yes." Cas leaned his head back with a sigh. "I really do."

SEVEN

"THERE'S STILL TIME to change your mind."

Galo dropped a shirt into his bag and looked up. Mateo stood in the doorway of his room, his arms crossed over his chest. He was off duty and wearing an old gray shirt that was frayed at the sleeves but clung nicely to his lightly muscular frame. Galo had always liked that shirt.

"I'm not going to change my mind," Galo said. He'd lost track of how many times he'd said that over the past few days. It wasn't just Mateo; the guards, the staff—they all thought he'd change his mind about leaving the guard.

Mateo blew out an annoyed breath. "Did they even find a new captain yet? Why are you moving out?"

"Cas is finishing the interviews tomorrow. And I'm not

moving out, I'm just going upstairs." He pulled the string tight on his bag and slung it over his shoulder. He didn't have much. He wore the clothes issued to the guard most of the time, and he'd brought very little from home. "You want to come with me?"

"I guess," Mateo grumbled, but a smile twitched at his lips as Galo took his hand and pulled him into the hallway.

Galo walked quickly away from the guards' quarters, hoping to not make a big scene. He knew half of the guards were happy to see him go, the other half angry he was deserting them. He didn't want to run into either at the moment.

He walked up the stairs and down the sunny hallway with Mateo. The door to Jovita's old sitting room was open, and Galo stepped inside.

Jovita had four rooms—a sitting room, an office, a bedroom, and a small bathing area. Galo had never been inside, and he walked slowly through all four rooms. They were huge, rooms fit for the woman who had been second in line to the throne, after Cas. Galo still felt weird about taking them. It felt like these rooms should go to someone important.

Mateo was perched on the edge of the bed when Galo walked back into the room. He pointed to the table in the corner of the room where a tray of tea and pastries had been placed. "They even brought you a snack."

Galo dropped his bag on the bed. "I still can't believe Cas gave me this room."

"Of course he did. It's a family room." Mateo flopped onto his back. "So what now?"

Galo sat down beside Mateo. It was a good question. He'd still be working as a guard for a few more weeks, to make sure everything ran smoothly for the new captain, but after that, he had no idea. He wasn't trained to do anything but guard the royal family, something he'd never particularly liked. And it turned out he wasn't even good at it.

"Did you write to your father?" Mateo asked.

"Yes. I wrote to both my parents and told them I was resigning from the guard." He glanced at Mateo, who just stared at him. They both knew he could have told them in person, but Galo had chickened out.

"You don't have to prove anything, Galo," Mateo said quietly. "No sensible person blames you for what happened to Cas. He's still alive because you realized so quickly that he'd been poisoned."

"I'm not looking to prove anything." It came out like the lie it was. "Can we stop talking about it?"

Mateo quickly sat up and got to his feet, annoyance written all over his face. "I'm going to go back downstairs."

Galo grabbed Mateo's belt loop and pulled him closer, until his legs bumped against Galo's knees. "I'm sorry. Don't go." He hooked his finger into the other belt loop. "I finally have a room of my own." The tiny two-person rooms were his least favorite part of being a guard, especially since meeting Mateo. He used to have a strict no-dating policy, since it was near impossible to sustain a relationship in that environment. But then Mateo had come along and all his old rules had gone out the window.

Mateo moved a little closer, putting one of his hands on

Galo's neck. "I'm worried you're going to leave," he said quietly.

"Where would I go?"

"I don't know. But if you're not on the guard you don't have to stay here and . . ." He shrugged, his eyes downcast.

Galo tilted his head up, brushing his lips against Mateo's. "I'm not going anywhere," he said quietly. "I promise."

Em sat on her porch, watching the sun come up over the trees. She'd woken earlier than usual and peeked into Olivia's bedroom to find her sister still sleeping. Olivia looked young and innocent asleep, and it reminded Em of mornings at home, when she'd run into her sister's room and jump on her bed to wake her up.

Em got to her feet and stepped off the porch. She walked slowly down the quiet road, the weight in her chest increasing with every step.

Olivia had come back from her trip to Fayburn happy and smug. Em hadn't asked. She knew everyone was dead.

She had a meeting with the Ruined shortly, and she'd spent all day yesterday trying to figure out what she was going to say to them. They all knew she hadn't been able to stop Olivia from going to Fayburn yesterday—that she hadn't even tried.

"Em."

She looked up with a start to find Ivanna standing in the grass in front of a small home. Her gray hair was braided and she was already fully dressed, despite the early hour.

"Are you headed to the meeting? It's a bit early, isn't it?" Ivanna asked.

"I was just taking a walk first."

"Can I join you? I was just about to head out for a walk myself."

"Sure."

Ivanna fell into step beside Em, her breathing a little faster and heavier than Em's. Em listened to it for several minutes in silence.

"Didn't you use to take walks around the castle with my mother?" Em finally asked.

"Yes. I always get up before dawn, and so did she. We often met and walked through the castle and into town."

"What did you talk about?"

"Nothing too important. Your mother didn't trust me."

Em regarded her with surprise. "She didn't?"

"Well, she trusted me as much as any Ruined, but no more than that. She had a small group that she truly trusted. With me, she usually talked about business or you and Olivia. Mostly you and Olivia."

"Do I want to know what she said about me and Olivia?"

Ivanna tilted her head. "Are you under the impression your mother didn't like you? That's not true."

"No," Em said softly. "I know she loved me. But sometimes I think about her, and what she expected of me, and it's too horrifying. I wonder if none of this had happened, if I would have ended up torturing people for her and Olivia, like she planned."

"That wasn't her only plan for you. I think she intended to use you to negotiate with Olso. She knew your strengths. I

wouldn't be surprised if things had played out a bit similarly—
with a marriage arrangement with August."

"She would have only let me marry him if we planned to kill
him soon after the wedding."

"Oh, for sure. But she would have gotten what she wanted
first."

Em didn't know if she would have agreed to marry August
for her mother. Maybe, if Cas had never been in the picture. Perhaps she would have married him and they would have conquered
Lera together. What a disturbing thought.

"She would never understand, me betraying Olivia," Em said.

"No," Ivanna agreed.

Em kicked a rock with the toe of her shoe. "She told me
something once. I think it was to make me feel better, about
being useless. But I've been thinking about it a lot lately."

"What's that?"

"She said that Olivia was going to be the most powerful
Ruined queen ever. The most powerful Ruined, period. But I
was the only one who had power over Olivia."

Ivanna looked at her expectantly, waiting for her to go on.

"Because Olivia can't hurt me. Or control me. She can control humans, and even other Ruined, if she really puts her mind
to it. But not me."

"True," Ivanna said.

"And that means . . . that means I could kill her. It would
be easy for me to kill her. She doesn't use a sword and none of

her strength is physical. I know that everyone knows that." Her words came out in a rush. She'd thought over and over about all the ways she could stop Olivia, and she kept coming back to the obvious—she could kill her.

"We do," Ivanna said gently. "But no one expects you to do that."

"I would save a lot of people, right? If I killed her?" Tears slipped down her cheeks. "There's no way we'll stop her before she kills more people—maybe hundreds, or thousands—and I could have saved them all if I just—"

"Em." Ivanna stopped, taking both Em's hands in hers. "No one expects that of you. Aren could probably kill her too. Would you ever ask that of him?"

"Of course not."

"Your mother used murder as a solution often. It's what Olivia always chooses. You've used it yourself. But you can choose to do things differently from now on."

Em wiped a hand across her eyes. "I still have to live with the fact that Olivia will kill people that I could have saved."

Ivanna shook her head. "You can't think of it like that. Olivia is responsible for her own actions. Do you blame Cas for everything his father did?"

"No," Em said quietly.

"And he doesn't blame you for what your mother did. There comes a time when we have to accept that people make their own choices, and we're not responsible for those choices, even if they're our family. You've expected Casimir to stand against his family's choices, even if it meant losing them. It's time to expect the same from yourself."

Em took in a shaky breath. She hadn't thought of it like that, but Ivanna wasn't wrong. She *had* expected Cas to turn away from Jovita, and his mother, when she was still alive, in order to do the right thing. She hadn't really even considered how hard that would be for him. It had seemed so obvious to her—his family had committed genocide, and Cas had to make it right. But now that she was faced with a similar problem in Olivia, she realized just how terrible it must have been for him.

"And don't forget that Olivia isn't the only powerful Ruined," Ivanna added. "Killing one Ruined won't solve our problems, not long-term."

"You're right," Em said quietly.

"I often am," Ivanna said lightly.

Em linked her arm through Ivanna's as they started walking again.

"Thank you," Em said. "I don't have a lot of people to talk to these days."

"I noticed. I'll be taking this walk every morning, if you'd like to join me."

"That would be nice."

They walked in a loop, until the sun rose higher in the sky, and they turned in the direction of Mariana's house. She'd taken up residence two blocks over, on a quiet street with matching houses.

Mariana answered the door with a smile, though her eyes nervously scanned the street behind Em and Ivanna.

"No one followed us," Em said. She looked Mariana up and down. She was wearing a soft pink dress that reached the floor, her arms bare. Her black hair was braided into a crown around her head, with the ends tucked into a bun at the nape of her neck. Her dark brown skin was radiant, and Em wondered if she'd done something different, or if she just hadn't seen Mariana well rested in a long time.

"You look lovely," Em said.

"Thank you." Mariana swung her hips so the dress swayed. "I found the dress in a box. I don't think whoever lived here wore it anymore, so I helped myself."

"It's beautiful," Em said as they stepped inside. Mariana was only a year older than her. If none of this had happened, she'd probably be wearing pretty dresses to the Ruina castle and dancing with Aren or some other handsome Ruined boy.

Aren sat at the dining table to her left, along with Davi and a few other Ruined. Ivanna and Davi were in their fifties, two of the only remaining older Ruined and part of the Ruined council. The entire Ruined council was present, actually, with the exception of Jacobo. He never left Olivia's side these days.

About thirty other Ruined were packed into the dining room, leaning against the wall and sitting on the floor. They'd only invited Ruined Em truly trusted, those who were horrified by what Olivia was doing and were willing to work with Cas.

Em slid into the seat next to Aren. His handsome face was

tight with worry, which had been his constant expression since Iria had been taken back to Olso.

"Did Olivia leave again this morning?" Mariana asked as she took a seat across from Em, in between Ivanna and Davi.

"She's still sleeping. She said she was going to train some of the Ruined today," Em said.

"They've been in that field behind the bakery," Ivanna said. "They bring out a few of the hostages for practice." Em rubbed her forehead. Olivia had taken several humans hostage, and locked them in the town jail. Since discovering that Aren drew power from humans, she'd been trying to do the same.

"I did get word that she's feeding them, at least," Patricio said quietly. He was a young Ruined, with the power to ruin the body, like Aren. Em had never known him well, but he was close to Mariana, and she'd vouched for him. Beside him was Selena, who Em remembered as a little girl, but she must have been about fourteen now. Her face was solemn, making her look even older.

"She needs them alive," Aren muttered.

"I'd suggest sneaking in to free them, but she'll just go get more," Em said. "I think we have to leave it for now."

"If we're not going to do anything to help them, then I don't understand why we're still in Lera," Davi said.

"Olivia will kill everyone if we leave," Em said. "You've heard her plan to conquer the north? At least if we stay, we can hold her off for a while."

"I'm sorry, but how is that our problem?" a young woman named Gisela asked. She leaned against the wall behind Davi and

Mariana. She was close to Em in age, with pale skin and straight black hair, and was often in motion, whether it was pacing, tapping her fingers, or tugging on her hair. She had the same power as Olivia and Aren, but Em knew she didn't have even half the strength that they did.

"You don't mind if Olivia kills all the people in Lera?" Aren asked.

"I *mind*, but I'm not ready to stick my neck out to defend them. They've never done anything to defend us." Murmurs of agreement rose up around the room.

"I know the people here don't deserve our help," Em said. "I know we can never fully forgive them for what they did to us. But we don't have to be the same as them. We can be better, and not let them suffer the same fate that we did."

Several people turned to Aren. They still did that sometimes: consulted a Ruined with power to back up what Em was saying.

"I agree," Aren said. He rolled his eyes as he said it, like he was tired of playing this game. "I'm not just leaving Olivia here to murder anyone she chooses."

Em gave him a grateful look. They'd had a serious conversation about leaving right after arriving, and Aren hadn't been convinced at first that they should stay. He wanted to go to Olso to break Iria out of prison. Em felt terrible asking him to stay, but he was the most powerful Ruined alive. Em needed his help to stop not just Olivia, but the Ruined loyal to her as well.

"But if half the Ruined leave, Olivia can't carry out this plan to invade all the cities," Mariana said.

"We're not half," Em said, looking around the room. Maybe a third of the Ruined were solidly with her. "And clearly Olivia isn't counting on your support anyway. Notice that she isn't training any of *you*."

"I guess you're right," Mariana said, chewing on her lip.

"What's your plan, then?" Ivanna asked. "You're going to stop Olivia from taking over Lera?"

"Eventually, yes," Em said. "I think if we partner with the Lera army, we stand a chance of fighting off Olivia. But for now, I'd like to get a head count of all the Ruined. I'm not sure how many we have total, so let's find that out. Then, if you guys are willing, I'd like to start finding out who would agree to work with King Casimir."

"Work how?" Mariana asked at the same time Gisela said "No."

Em looked at Gisela. "No?"

"No." She crossed her arms over her chest. "That's my answer about working with Casimir. No."

"We have to start thinking long-term," Em said, trying to keep the desperation from her voice. If she couldn't convince the Ruined to help Cas, he was doomed. "Are we going back to Ruina?"

"Why not?" Gisela asked. "It's our home."

Patricio scrunched up his face, a look mirrored by several other Ruined in the room. "Not really, not anymore. There's nothing left. They took our home."

"We'd have to start completely from scratch," Em said. "It

will take years to rebuild even half of what we had."

"You're suggesting we stay here instead?" Mariana asked.

"It's a possibility. But if we stay, we have to deal with the king eventually. None of this is ours." She gestured to the house around her. "Invading a town and stealing everything isn't a long-term plan."

"Olivia has a long-term plan," Gisela said. She raised her eyebrows at Em, as if to challenge her.

"A plan that includes killing everyone," Aren said.

"A plan to doesn't include working with someone who murdered all of our families," Gisela shot back.

Em swallowed a wave of panic. At least half the Ruined in the room were nodding in agreement with Gisela.

"What would convince you?" she asked quickly. "If you could have anything you want from King Casimir, what would you ask for?"

"Some people mentioned that the king should pay us reparations," Ivanna said. "And I have to agree. They took everything from us."

"Good," Em said. "That's reasonable."

"I'd like my parents back," Gisela said. "Ask him if he can give me that."

"We can't change the past—" Em began.

"I don't want money, I want my parents—" Gisela interrupted.

"You're being completely unreasonable," Aren cut in. "She's just trying—"

"One at a time!" Ivanna yelled over their voices. Gisela leaned back against the wall, a scowl on her face. Silence fell over the room.

"What if he gives up the throne?" Mariana finally asked.

Em looked at her quickly. "What?"

"It's his family that did this to us. Maybe someone else should lead Lera." She looked at Gisela. "Would that convince you?"

Gisela shrugged. "Maybe."

"I don't think I can ask for that," Em said. "I'm not even sure that's a good idea. He's sympathetic to us. We may not get so lucky with a new leader."

"If he's the only person in all of Lera sympathetic to us, this won't work anyway," Ivanna said.

Em swallowed. She had a point.

"It's not . . . entirely unreasonable," Aren said reluctantly. "There should be consequences for what his family did to us. But maybe he doesn't need to give up his throne entirely."

Gisela made an annoyed sound.

"We could ask that they strip some power from the monarchy," Aren said. "So that he has less authority as king." He looked at Gisela. "That's a good compromise, wouldn't you say?" She just shrugged.

"Would he even agree to that?" Mariana asked.

"I don't know," Em said.

"Is there any way we can communicate with him?" Ivanna asked.

"Em could go to the castle," Aren said, and Em looked at

him in surprise. "What? There are plenty of horses in the barns around town, and it would only take half a day to ride there."

"What will I tell Olivia?" Em asked.

Aren rubbed the back of his neck in thought. "Maybe go for more food? Or feed for the horses? We are actually running a little low on feed, I think." He glanced at Mariana for confirmation. She nodded in agreement. "If Cas could give you a wagonful, you could come back and say you stole it."

"Olivia will still be suspicious," Gisela said.

"She's already suspicious," Em said.

"We have to set up a way to communicate with them. You can go have an initial talk with Cas, then set up a way to talk in the future," Ivanna said. "None of this matters if they aren't willing to negotiate with us."

Dread settled into Em's chest. She'd been the one who convinced Cas to go back to Lera when he wanted to give up his throne. Now she was going to tell him they wanted to strip him of his power?

She glanced at Gisela. *Olivia has a long-term plan.* If Em didn't act, she might lose the few Ruined she had on her side.

She nodded grimly. "I'll go talk to Cas."

EIGHT

EVERYONE WAS LYING to Olivia.

Everyone who mattered, anyway.

Olivia stared at her sister. Em stood in the kitchen, stirring a pot of soup on the stove. Her stance was casual, like she'd just remembered something and wanted to mention it to Olivia.

"I'm riding out to find more feed for the horses," Em said, holding her sister's gaze. Em always had been a good liar. "First thing in the morning."

"By yourself." Olivia didn't say it as a question.

"I'll be wearing a cloak; no one will be able to tell who I am. And I don't need help."

"A bit risky just for feed, wouldn't you say?"

"We need the horses, Liv. I'm not going to let them starve."

Olivia blew out a frustrated breath. "Fine. Go." Part of her wanted to believe Em. Maybe they really did need feed for the horses.

Or maybe—probably—she was going to see Casimir.

"I shouldn't be gone long. A day, maybe."

"No problem," Olivia said with a flippancy she didn't feel. "Why don't you take Aren with you?" The words came out as a challenge. She couldn't take Aren with her, and Olivia knew it. Who would keep Olivia in check?

Em had the decency to look ashamed. She lowered her gaze to the soup. "I'll be fine on my own."

Olivia could send a Ruined to follow Em. If she told Jacobo right now, he'd stay up all night just to make sure he caught Em as soon as she left.

But Em wasn't stupid. She would be checking to see if she was followed, because she didn't trust Olivia anymore.

The feeling was mutual.

Besides, Olivia didn't need to confirm what she already knew. Her sister was a traitor. Olivia hadn't figured out how deep Em's betrayal went, but it would reveal itself in time. And Olivia wasn't worried about her useless sister.

Aren, on the other hand . . .

Olivia pushed back a swell of anger at the thought of Aren. He'd dared to use his powers on her, but that wasn't what really enraged her.

He could pull power from humans. He could use them to make himself stronger. Stronger than *her*.

And she couldn't do it. She'd captured a few humans to practice on, but so far, nothing but failure. It was infuriating.

She marched out the door, shoulders squared. No. She hadn't failed. If she simply kept trying, she would figure it out eventually.

"This is almost done, if you want dinner," Em called as Olivia stomped away.

"I'm not hungry." She let the door slam shut behind her.

She squinted in the late-afternoon sun as she walked the two blocks to the Westhaven courthouse. It was a tiny building, nestled beneath tall trees in the middle of Oak Street.

Inside, it was quiet, nearly deserted. Jacobo sat at the desk in the middle of the room, his feet propped up in front of him. He sprang up when Olivia walked inside.

"Olivia."

She liked how he said her name. His voice had a hint of reverence in it. Everyone should say her name the way Jacobo did.

"Hello, Jacobo." He was several years older than her, with dark hair and eyes like daggers. He was good-looking, in an angry sort of way. She hadn't known him well before she was taken. She hadn't paid much attention to him after coming back either, thanks to her preoccupation with the traitor, Aren.

But Jacobo was proving to be almost as powerful as Aren. He could rip trees from the ground and command wind so powerful a small home couldn't withstand it. It was a useful power, occasionally.

"How are the prisoners?" she asked.

"Fine. I fed them about an hour ago. Ester is in with them now."

"You don't need to stay, you know. They're not going anywhere." Olivia had the only keys, after all.

"I know," he said, then met her gaze. He'd been waiting to see her.

She smiled, pleased. "You can go now. I'll see you at dinner." She knew that he was disappointed. She'd seen the expression on his face several times lately, as he'd worked to prove himself to her.

It wasn't that she didn't like him, it was just that she didn't trust him—or anyone—anymore. The two people she'd trusted most in the world, Em and Aren, had betrayed her. She couldn't rely on anyone but herself.

That was just fine with her. There was no need to rely on someone else. She was the most powerful Ruined alive.

Jacobo's footsteps faded as he walked out of the building. She walked down the hallway and slipped through the door. The town only had six cells, three on either side of her, and from the pristine look of them, they weren't used often. Each had a small bed, a sink, and toilet, and bars perfect for keeping humans right where she wanted them.

The man to her left shrank back against the wall when she walked in. His arm was in a sling. A Ruined woman named Ester sat on the floor in front of the last cell, her gaze fixed on the man inside.

"What are you doing?" Olivia asked.

Ester didn't turn. "Practicing. I'm trying to make him see the ocean." She shook her head, her short dark hair swinging. "No, not just see it. *Feel* it. Smell it."

Olivia walked to the cell to see the man on the floor, eyes turned to the ceiling. He blinked very slowly, then shivered.

"I think you've about worn that one out," Olivia said. "His mind won't bounce back if you keep it up."

Ester sighed and got to her feet. "You're right."

"I don't mind, I just know you'd prefer to keep practicing. Can't practice if you drive him insane."

Ester smiled, briefly touching Olivia's arm as she walked past her. She didn't display the same devotion as Jacobo, but Olivia appreciated her disdain for humans.

Ester disappeared through the door, and Olivia sat down in front of the middle cell. A woman was curled up on the ground, staring at Olivia, but she didn't move.

"Come here," Olivia said.

The woman hesitated, but only for a moment. She sat up and trudged to the cell door, plopping down on the ground. Dark circles marred the skin beneath her eyes.

"Arm," Olivia ordered.

The woman stuck it through the bars. Olivia grabbed it and jerked it closer to her. The woman yelped.

Olivia put both her hands on the woman's arm and held tightly. Nothing. She squeezed a little tighter. Nothing. She could feel the woman's heart beating, could pinpoint every bone in her body, could feel the blood coursing through her veins. She could kill her with a quick look. But she couldn't figure out how to use the humans to fuel her own power.

She dropped the arm. "Are you all broken? What is wrong with you?"

There was certainly nothing wrong with *her*. If Aren could do it, she could do it. And she *had* to be able to do it.

She would never admit it to Em, but her sister was right when she'd called Olivia's plan *risky*. That was a kind way to put it, actually. *Insane* might have been more appropriate. It was nearly impossible to conquer ten Lera cities with only a handful of Ruined.

But not *completely* impossible. Not if she could learn to draw strength from humans, the way Aren did. Then she'd be unstoppable.

She jumped to her feet and stomped out of the room and down the hallway. There was a trick to it. She'd promised herself she wouldn't even speak to Aren, much less ask for his help, but she had to know how he did it.

She strode down Market Street, where some of the Ruined were gathered at the tables in front of the bakery. Jacobo sat with Carmen, and they stopped talking when she approached.

"Have you seen Aren?" she asked.

Carmen wrinkled her nose. She, like Aren, ruined the body, and she'd made her disdain for Aren well known the past week. Olivia was not impressed with Carmen's powers, but she did appreciate her attitude.

"I think he's in the gardens," Carmen said.

Olivia whirled around and walked down the block, to the small plot of land near the park. She spotted Aren as she approached the gate, on his knees, pulling weeds from in between the vegetables.

"What are you doing?" she asked.

He sat back on his heels, wiping his forehead with his arm as he turned to her. "What does it look like I'm doing?"

"*Why* are you weeding the humans' garden?"

"It helps to keep me from ripping your head off instead." He leveled his gaze with hers, as if daring her to try him.

Rage swelled in her chest. She was supposed to be a hero to the Ruined, and Aren dared to make her feel like she was doing something *wrong*. Like she was the bad one, just because she didn't like people who had murdered and exiled her people.

"Tell me how you do it," she demanded.

"What?"

"The humans. How do you pull energy from them?"

He shrugged. "I don't know. It just happened one day with Iria."

"Was she the only one? Did you try it on anyone else?"

He turned back to the weeds and yanked another one out of the ground. "She's not the only one. It worked with others."

Olivia angrily kicked a rock. Part of her had been hoping it was Iria who was special, not Aren.

"Tell me how you do it."

"I told you I don't know." He sat back on his heels and met

her gaze. "But even if I did, I'd never tell you."

She curled her fingers into fists. Her Ruined magic burned in her veins, and she let it loose. Aren's hand flew off the weed and straight backward, knocking him right in the face.

He shot her a venomous look. She smiled smugly and turned on her heel.

Her entire body froze. Every bone and muscle was no longer in her control.

"Careful, Olivia," Aren said.

A chill ran through her body as he released her. She wanted to turn and glare at him, maybe break his nose this time, but she was worried that shock was plastered across her features. She couldn't have controlled Aren's entire body. Just taking hold of his hand required intense effort.

But he'd done it like it was nothing.

Aren watched as Olivia stomped away from the gardens. He waited until she was out of sight, and then stood, grabbing his bag of weeds and tossing it in the pile with the others.

He started down the road. His house was to the west, which wasn't a coincidence. West was Olso. West was Iria.

He couldn't see Olso, of course. It would take days to cross the jungle by horse, and then he'd be faced with a heavily guarded border.

But still, Iria was west, and the first day they arrived, he'd headed west and almost just kept going. It had taken all of his willpower to stop himself from grabbing a horse and riding there. She was certainly in prison by now, and he'd promised to save her. He *would* save her.

But he couldn't ask Em to let him leave Lera right now. She needed him if she was going to stop Olivia from killing everyone. Olivia's priority was to take over Lera; Em's priority was to stop her. He knew Em wanted him to save Iria, but they both knew he had time. Olso didn't execute people.

Aren kicked a rock, wishing he'd protected Iria when he had the chance. If Olivia hadn't attacked him and Iria, he would have had the strength to stop the warriors.

If he hadn't been so stupid and left her, maybe she wouldn't have been taken at all. Iria was mad at him for trying to leave her in Lera, and he couldn't blame her. Maybe if he'd stayed with her, she would have been by his side the whole time.

Laughter drifted over from the bakery, and he glanced up. Olivia and Jacobo sat at the tables with Ester, Priscila, and a few other Ruined, which meant the humans in the courthouse were unattended.

He took a quick turn, looping around and taking the long way to the courthouse. He grabbed four apples from the produce stand, which he'd replenished himself that morning.

Oak Street was deserted, and he jogged up the steps and walked into the building. It was empty, the desk in the middle of the room bare, and the door to the left slightly ajar. He stepped forward and slowly pushed the door open.

Six cells stretched out in front of him, four of them occupied.

A woman to the left, and a man to the right. He stepped forward. Another woman, another man.

He didn't know what exactly he'd planned to say to them, so he just slipped an apple through the bars into each cell. The woman in the rear cell didn't roll over in bed. The other three humans stared, their faces full of venom. An apple didn't mean much when they were imprisoned and had their lives threatened daily by Olivia.

His legs felt shaky suddenly. He sank to the ground, his back to the wall in between the two women's cells. He drew his knees to his chest and rested his forehead on them.

Tears spilled down his cheeks. He couldn't rescue anyone. Not Iria, not the people in these cells, not the Ruined who were terrified of Olivia.

It had been easier when he hated everyone. Back when they'd first rescued Olivia, walking to the Ruina border with her and Em, discussing plans for the Ruined. Aren had thought they'd never see Cas or Iria or any of them ever again. Now he wasn't sure how he'd ever stirred up that much hate.

He tried to think of what his mother would say in this situation. Maybe: *Your gifts only take you so far. Use your head.* Or: *You can't control the actions of everyone around you, but you can control how you respond.* Or even: *Have faith, Aren. Do your best and everything will work out in the end.* None of it seemed right. Even his talkative, lecture-prone mother might have been speechless in this situation.

"Are you Aren?" a female voice asked.

He wiped a hand across his eyes as he peered over his shoulder at the woman in the first cell. She'd moved to the far left side, probably so she could see him. She sat cross-legged on the ground, the anger he'd seen on her face a moment ago gone.

"Yes," he said. He turned so he was facing her. "Have we met?"

She shook her head. "I heard her mention you to Jacobo. She said, 'Watch out for Aren. He may try to free them.'"

He scrubbed his hands down his face. "I can't free you. They have the only keys. I'm sorry."

"You're Ruined." She eyed the marks on his neck. "I thought maybe you were human when she said you'd try to rescue us."

"Not all Ruined are like Olivia." He closed his fingers around the bars of her cell. "Listen. Do what she wants. Things are . . . tense here. We probably won't be here for long. If you can hold out for a little while longer, I can try to get you out of here."

The woman leaned her head against the wall. "That honestly doesn't inspire much confidence, Aren." The man in the cell behind Aren laughed hollowly.

"I'm sorry," he said, the words getting stuck in his throat. "It's . . ." He wanted to tell her they were working to save all of Lera, that he had to be careful not to bring the full force of Olivia's anger down on them. But it all sounded stupid. It didn't excuse that he was leaving them here, maybe to die.

"I'm sorry," he said again quietly. He slowly got to his feet. "Do you need anything? I can bring more food if you want."

"Another blanket would be nice," the woman said. "It's cold in here at night."

"Me too," one of the men said.

"Sure," he said, relieved to have something to do for them. He walked out of the room, leaving the door propped open.

He found a room around the corner with linens and grabbed four blankets. When he walked back to the cells the woman was standing in front of her bars, her head tilted forward like she was watching to see if he'd really come back. She took a few steps back when she spotted him.

He held one blanket through the bars. She hesitated for a moment before taking it, her fingers lightly brushing his.

"Thank you," she said.

The shock of her touch vibrated up his arm. His Ruined magic stirred, almost like it wanted him to lean closer to her.

He took a step back instead. The woman was looking at her hand like she'd felt something too. She regarded him suspiciously.

He quickly distributed the other blankets and walked away from the cells. Tears burned in his eyes and he stopped as soon as he was outside. He braced his hands against his thighs, taking in gasps of air.

What use was it to be the most powerful Ruined alive if he couldn't save anyone? If he couldn't save Iria?

NINE

CAS TAPPED HIS fingers on his desk as he regarded the man in front of him. He was many years older than Galo, who stood next to him. His name was Jorge, and he was probably in his late forties or early fifties. Gray streaked the sides of his black hair. He'd been part of Cas's father's guard since his early twenties, according to Galo. His face was familiar to Cas, though he couldn't remember ever meeting him.

Cas didn't think his father would have bothered to pick his captain of the guard personally, but he'd told Galo he wanted to meet everyone. He trusted very few people these days.

"Where were you usually assigned with my father?" Cas asked.

Jorge sat up straighter in his chair. "For the past few years, I was his personal protection whenever he left the castle, Your Majesty. Here, I swept his rooms every day and stood guard outside."

"What would you change if you became captain of my guard?"

"I would rotate the guards stationed outside your room more often—they've been getting drowsy," Jorge said immediately. "I would form a small, private committee to look into every one of the guards. Some slipped back on your side after you banished Jovita. Anyone who wasn't always loyal to you should go."

"Even if they've changed their minds?" Cas asked. "We don't exactly have a surplus of guards right now."

"A smaller, fiercely loyal group is better than a large group that can be swayed. And the new guards we're recruiting worship you. You have an incredible reputation with the people of Lera, and we have many interested in being guards as a result. We'll have plenty of new guards to train."

Cas leaned forward, resting his chin in his palm. "An incredible reputation? I think you may overestimate the people's love for me. I'm the king trying to convince them that the Ruined aren't dangerous."

"No, Your Majesty. They're scared and confused about the Ruined, but they trust you. They think you're immortal."

Cas let out a short laugh. "Immortal?"

"You've survived numerous attempts on your life."

"True. I hope Jovita hears that rumor." He laughed, though it was tinged with a hint of bitterness. "She'll really never have a shot at the throne if I can't die."

Cas noticed Galo's lips twitching. He'd mostly been serious through the interviews for the new captain of the guard, but he seemed more relaxed with Jorge, who he'd told Cas was his top choice.

"I'm assuming you agree with my Ruined policies?" Cas asked Jorge.

"I do."

"You understand it is my sincere hope that you will have direct contact with Emelina Flores soon, and often, and I'll expect you to protect her the same way you protect me?"

"Yes."

"Good."

Cas asked a few more questions about security, then Galo ushered Jorge out of the room.

"Would you like to talk to a few more guards, or have you made a decision?" Galo asked, standing in front of Cas's desk.

"I think it should be Jorge."

Galo smiled. "I agree."

"Why don't you go change out of your uniform and meet me in the Ocean Room? I have a meeting and I'd like you to attend."

"The meeting with Violet and Franco?" Galo asked, clearly surprised.

"And Danna and Julieta."

"Are you sure?" Galo asked.

"I'm sure." Cas wasn't sure what role Galo should fill now that he wasn't a guard, but he was happy to have another person he could trust. Surely he could find something for Galo to do, and Cas would start by keeping him by his side during important meetings.

Galo hurried out of the office, and Cas ate a few bites of the lunch a staff member brought him. Then he headed to the meeting, guards trailing after him. They stopped at the door of the Ocean Room and he stepped inside.

Everyone was already there, including Galo, now dressed in black pants and a crisp blue shirt. They all stood when Cas entered the room.

"Have a seat," Cas said, sliding into the chair at the head of the table. Violet was on one side of him, Franco on the other. Next to them were Julieta and Danna, and Galo at the end.

"You all look grim," Cas said. "Did Olivia attack another town?"

"No, Your Majesty," Franco said. "She appears to have gone back to Westhaven after killing everyone in Fayburn."

"It's Jovita," Violet said. Her voice was gentle, her eyes worried, and Cas already knew what she was going to say.

"She poisoned me," he said. "You found out for sure."

"Yes. I'm sorry, Cas."

His stomach dropped into his feet. He'd known it, deep down, but maybe a part of him had still hoped she didn't hate him *that* much. She hadn't even had the decency to kill him herself. She'd just sent someone in with poisoned soup.

"How did you find out?" Galo asked after a brief silence.

"We talked to some of the guards," Franco said. "Discreetly. Which led us to some people in the refugee shelters, who spoke to us once we assured them we wouldn't try them for treason as well. None of them actually participated, they just knew of the plan," he added quickly.

"We're recommending a couple of guards be let go, because they didn't come forward with this information earlier," Violet said.

"You should pass the names along to Jorge," Galo said. "He'll take care of it right away."

Violet nodded.

"This is not new information," Julieta said. "Most of us suspected it was Jovita. And as long as Jovita is alive, she poses a threat. We understand that you're not completely opposed to killing her, Your Majesty."

The words were said so bluntly that Cas blinked, surprised. He glanced at Violet, who was chewing on her lip across from him. She must have told them that he'd asked if the soldiers could take care of Jovita.

"I . . . ," he began, before realizing he didn't know what to say.

"No one would blame you," Violet said quietly. "She threatens the safety of everyone here."

"Is there any news of her army?"

"It's growing," Danna said. "Jovita is smart, and determined. We all know what she's capable of. We can't just ignore her. She *will* attack again, Your Majesty."

The words triggered a memory, and Cas suddenly heard his

father's voice in his head. *Imagine if you were alone with him. Look what he's capable of.* He'd said it to Cas the night he'd captured Damian, as they watched the Ruined use his elemental powers as a result of being tortured. Cas remembered asking who Damian was, and what he'd done, and his father only had one answer: he was Ruined.

The situation with Jovita wasn't the same—she'd technically broken Lera law by trying to take the throne. He could sentence her to death for treason and attempted murder and no one could argue.

But this had always been his father's solution. Whether he was scared, or angry, or unsure, he always made the same choice. Kill them before they became a threat. Even if Cas had a better reason than his father, if the outcome still resulted in death, how was Cas any different?

Murmured voices sounded from behind the door, followed by running footsteps. Cas instinctively stiffened, waiting to hear the sounds of Olso attacking. He found himself listening for them at the first sign of trouble. They may have fled when the Ruined came to Lera, but he wasn't convinced they were gone forever.

"Wait here, Your Majesty," Franco said, jumping to his feet and flying out of the room. Galo stood and positioned himself in front of the door.

Franco darted back into the room a few moments later, breathless and eyes wide. "They're saying Emelina Flores is at the gates. Alone."

The guards at the front gate eyed Em warily. She didn't recognize them, but they clearly knew her. She pushed back the hood of her cloak so they wouldn't think she was trying to hide.

The sun was sinking behind one of the towers of the Lera castle, and she was surprised to feel a rush of affection as she looked at the castle. She was hit by a memory of walking down the hallways with Cas, sunlight filtering in through the big windows.

A familiar dark-haired man ran out the door. Galo. "Open the gates!" he called.

The guards obeyed immediately, pulling open the iron gate to let Em walk through. The gate was plain but shiny and new, replaced after the warriors destroyed the last one. She stepped forward.

A whole parade of guards rushed out the front door and Em's face broke into a smile. In the center, flanked by guards on all sides, was Cas.

He darted away from the guards and ran forward, pulling her into his arms. She laughed as she hugged him.

"Why are you here?" he asked without pulling away. "Is something wrong?"

"No, I came to talk. Officially, as the queen of the Ruined."

"Does that mean I should stop hugging you?"

She buried her face in his neck. "No," she said, her voice muffled.

He held her for a few more seconds, and when he finally let her go, she saw that every eye was turned to them. Guards lingered all around them, and Galo, Violet, and several other people were watching from the front door. Behind them, staff members were clustered on the stairs, craning their necks to catch a glimpse.

"Come on," Cas murmured, taking her hand. The guards fell into step beside them as they walked into the castle. She noticed they all had one hand on their swords.

The staff members scurried out of the way as Cas took her upstairs to a room she'd never been to before. Cas opened the door and nodded for her to go in first. It was an office.

"Please wait out here," he said to his guards, and closed the door behind him.

When he turned, Em forgot why she'd come. She forgot about Olivia and the Lerans on the other side of the door. The world narrowed to just Cas, to that smile he was giving her.

She looped her arms around his neck and kissed him with all the pent-up energy of the last couple of weeks. He pulled her body flush against his with a sharp intake of breath. His lips parted. Her fingers closed around his hair. He grabbed a fistful of her shirt. She melted into him.

She hadn't planned to stay even one night in the castle, but being in his arms again made rational thinking difficult. If he'd asked, in that moment, if she'd stay forever, she might have said yes.

He pulled away, just a little, and she took in a breath as she prepared to speak. He shook his head and pressed his lips against hers, then to her cheek, then to her jaw.

"No," he mumbled.

"No?"

He pressed his lips to her neck, making her fingers tighten around his hair again. "Whatever you were going to say, no. Not yet."

She smiled as he kissed her again, and they stayed that way for so long that she was a bit dizzy when they finally broke apart. His hair was mussed from her fingers, and she laughed as she smoothed it down. He caught her hand and kissed the back of her palm.

"I did come here to talk, I swear," she said.

"It was dangerous for you to come here, you know. Now that you're here I may never let you leave."

She laughed. "That's the dangerous thing about coming here, is it?"

"Yes. Keep it in mind for next time." He kissed her once more, then pulled away and led her across the room to the chairs next to the window. He gestured for her to sit and took the chair across from her.

He leaned forward, taking her hands in his. "How is Olivia?"

"The same. I'm sorry about the people in Fayburn. I would have stopped it if I could, but . . ."

She swallowed, unable to meet his eyes.

He squeezed her hands. "I know." He laughed, though it wasn't amused. "I really know."

"What does that mean?"

"Jovita. She's building an army against me. Maybe against you as well. We're keeping an eye on her."

"I guess that was to be expected."

He sat back, letting go of her hands. His expression darkened, and she waited, thinking he was going to share his thoughts with her. But the moment passed, and he smiled and changed the subject.

"Tell me why you're here. Besides to kiss me. I know that's the main reason."

"I came to discuss a way for the Ruined and the people of Lera to live together."

"Are the Ruined open to that?" he asked.

"Are the Lerans?"

His eyes darted away from hers. "I'm working on it."

"I know. I am too. I spoke to the Ruined about what it would take for them to stay here in Lera, to help protect you from Olivia."

"What would it take?"

"We discussed reparations. Money to start rebuilding a life."

"Of course."

She clasped her hands together. She'd never been so nervous speaking to Cas before. Her heart thumped in her chest. "They—we—think it's best to strip the monarchy of some of its power."

Cas didn't respond right away. He just studied her, his expression unreadable.

"How much power?" he finally asked. "What exactly would I do as king, then?"

"We could figure that out together. I'm here to find out if you'd even be open to that discussion. And to plan a way for us to communicate in the future."

"I'm open to it," he said, but there was hesitancy in his voice.

"What?" Em asked.

He turned to look out the window. "When we were in Westhaven, I said I was going to give up the Lera throne and you told me that was the dumbest thing you'd ever heard. You said I had to stay and make things better."

"I know. And you still can, but I don't think their request is completely unreasonable. We're in this situation because your father had unlimited power."

"I'm not my father." He said it sharply, his eyes cutting to hers. "I'm actually working really hard to not be like him."

She leaned forward, reaching for his hand. "*I* know that. But the Ruined don't. They have no reason to trust you, except for my word. And they don't trust me that much. Not yet, anyway."

He laced his fingers through hers with a sigh. "Even if I agree to it, I'm not sure my advisers will. We're in a really delicate place right now."

"Let's get them together and talk about it, then. I need to know if it's completely out of the question so we can . . ." She let her voice trail off. She didn't know what they would do next. Go back to Ruina? Let Olivia take the country from Cas?

He strode to the door and glanced back at her. "I'll gather up some of my advisers. Should I have the staff bring you anything? Are you hungry?"

"No, I'm fine."

He nodded and walked out the door, closing it behind him and leaving her alone.

TEN

GALO LOOKED UP at the sound of a knock on his door. He walked across the bedroom and sitting room and opened the door to find Cas. Galo suppressed a smile. Cas could easily have people fetched for him, but this was the third time he'd come to Galo's room.

"Is Em gone already?" Galo asked, holding the door open for Cas to come inside.

"No." He shut the door behind him and leaned against it. He closed his eyes for a few moments, and the smile slipped off Galo's face. Something was clearly wrong. "I'm pulling a few advisers into a meeting with Em. You should come."

"I should?"

"Yes. I want your opinion."

"I'd be happy to," Galo said, torn between being flattered and dreading the awkwardness of another meeting. Surely Violet and Franco and Julieta and all the rest of them assumed he was only there because he was Cas's friend. He didn't have the experience or the title of any of them.

Cas didn't move from the door.

"Is something wrong?" Galo asked.

"I'm realizing that maybe I was too optimistic."

"About?"

"Everything. The Ruined. My marriage to Em. I think I was being stupid."

"You're not stupid."

"Unrealistic, then."

"Maybe," Galo said after a brief silence. "But I never thought we'd come this far. I think your optimism is an asset, not a liability."

Cas sighed and closed his eyes again. He stayed that way for several seconds, like he was gathering his courage before going back out.

Finally, he opened the door and gestured for Galo to follow him. Cas told Galo he'd meet him in the Ocean Room, and walked in the direction of his office.

Galo walked through the door to the Ocean Room and every head turned to him. It was the same small group from before—Violet, Franco, Julieta, and Danna.

He hadn't been inside this room much, and he'd almost forgotten how impressive it was, with the large windows looking over the ocean. It was sunset, and the room was bathed in warm orange light. The meetings in this room were private, and until today, he was always on the other side of the door.

He walked to the long table in the middle of the room and pulled out a chair next to Julieta. Everyone got to their feet suddenly. Cas and Em walked through the door.

Em smiled at each person in turn, her eyes lingering when they landed on him. They barely knew each other, their only connection their mutual affection for Cas, but he found that he couldn't stir up the discomfort he used to feel every time he saw her. He had liked her when she first arrived in the castle, simply because Cas seemed to like her, and Galo was surprised by that fact. Galo had thought it would take Cas months to warm up to his new wife, but it had been days. Perhaps sped along by Em saving his life, but still. Cas wasn't quick to warm up to people.

Then Galo had hated her when it was revealed who she really was (and she'd punched him in the face on the way out of the castle, which hadn't helped matters). He'd told Cas it seemed like she had feelings for him, but that had been a bit of wishful thinking on his part. He'd disliked her more than he'd let on.

But then Cas trusted her, and she saved his life after he'd been poisoned, and didn't let him give up being king for her. Somewhere along the way he'd stopped hating her.

"Thank you for meeting with me," Em said as she and Cas took their seats. Cas sat at the head of the table, Em next to him.

"Of course," Franco said.

"Em and I were discussing a few things, and I thought it was best if you all be involved," Cas said. He turned to Em expectantly, and she quickly looked away from him. Galo would have been able to tell that things were strained between them even if he hadn't known Cas was upset.

Em sat up a little straighter. "The Ruined would like to stay in Lera. Ruina is destroyed, food and . . . everything is scarce there. I'll be honest with you, Olivia feels the same way. She plans to stay. But she intends to take cities by force."

Danna shifted nervously in her chair.

"She's planning to take over cities one by one, until all the humans have fled here to Royal City. She's already started."

"With Fayburn," Violet said.

"Yes. I couldn't stop her, and I don't think I'll be able to stop her in the future, unless Ruined and Lerans work together. But the Ruined have some conditions before that can happen."

"What are the conditions?" Violet asked.

"Wait," Danna interrupted. "When you say Ruined and Lerans work together, do you mean we'll fight Olivia together?"

"Yes. And the Ruined loyal to her. I didn't want it to come to that, but . . ." Em looked down at the table and let her voice trail off.

"How will we do that?" Danna asked.

"The Ruined will be a major help to you," Em said. "We're working on figuring out how many Ruined will stand with me, but I have thirty for sure, and we think it will be at least sixty when we've finished talking to everyone. Do you have any Weakling?"

"I don't think so," Cas said. He looked at Galo. "Do we?"

"No, we had some in the fortress, but none here."

"There are fields of it in Ruina," Em said. "And there's no one there to stop you from taking it."

"Do we have anyone we could send?" Cas asked Galo.

"I think so. It wouldn't be many, but a smaller group could travel faster."

"Is it worth it?" Cas asked Em. "Does Weakling even work on Olivia?"

"Barely, but it does slow her down. And it certainly hurts the other Ruined. We could line shields with it, put it in necklaces like your mother used to. Even stitch it into clothing. I would recommend it, regardless of our agreement," Em said. "Olivia *will* come after you."

"We'll send someone right away, then," Cas said. "Now tell us your conditions."

"We want reparations," Em said. "Homes to replace the ones that were lost, money to start rebuilding a life."

All heads turned to Cas.

"I think that's reasonable," he said. "But that's not the condition they're going to care about, Em."

"They want to strip the monarchy of some of its power," Em said.

"No," Violet said immediately. Cas looked at her in surprise. "The people love you. Absolutely not."

"I agree," Julieta said. "Jovita has just attempted to take over the throne, and she probably will again. Removing power from the monarchy right now could be disastrous."

"The Ruined won't help you if Cas goes unpunished," Em said.

"You think he should be *punished*?" Violet said.

"I'm not completely innocent here," Cas broke in. "I never even tried to stop my father from attacking the Ruined."

"You'd agree to this?" Violet exclaimed.

He sighed. "Maybe?"

"Jovita will be delighted," Julieta grumbled.

"Why does Cas need to be punished, but you don't?" Violet said to Em. "You destroyed our alliance with Vallos when you murdered their princess. You led the attack that killed half the people in this castle. But it's only Cas who needs to pay for their actions?"

Em stared at Violet solemnly, almost devoid of emotion. Galo didn't think Cas particularly loved Em's ability to push aside emotion to get things done, but Galo admired it.

"We want to open negotiations with you," Em said. "If one of your conditions is that I also need to be stripped of power, then I can take that back to the Ruined."

"I don't think it's much of a negotiation if your starting offer is to make Cas little more than a figurehead," Franco said.

"That wasn't our starting offer. I talked them down. They wanted Cas to give up the throne entirely."

Galo looked at Cas. There was a time, only a few weeks ago, when Cas would have gladly given up the throne. He'd made that offer to Em. But Galo suspected that Cas wasn't so willing anymore. He'd worked hard to take the throne back from Jovita, and he'd earned the respect of his people.

Violet let out a long sigh.

Em turned to Franco. "Didn't you oppose King Salomir's decision to attack the Ruined?"

"Yes," Franco replied.

"But the king didn't care. If we limit the monarchy's power, that won't happen again. Other people will be involved in the decision. Why is that so bad?"

"What other people?"

"We were thinking of elected representatives. Ruined and Leran. They would have certain powers that the monarchy doesn't. They could overrule the king or queen."

"Cas doesn't make unilateral decisions the way his father does," Franco said. "It's not the same."

"Sure, but you can't guarantee that will be the case for the next monarch. Or the one after that. This is bigger than just me and Cas. It's about the future of both our people."

Franco tapped his fingers on the table, like he was considering it. Cas caught Galo's eye. Galo tilted his head with a small shrug. He could see Em's point.

"Give us some time to think it over," Cas said to Em. "Can you come back after we've had time to discuss?"

"I don't know if I can get away again without Olivia getting suspicious," Em said. "We were hoping you could send a messenger. Someone you trust not to just carry messages, but deal with us and make smaller decisions. And to be clear, it will be incredibly dangerous. I'll do my best to protect whomever you send, but I can't always control Olivia. They'll need to do their best to avoid her."

"Not a great pitch," Franco said, scrunching up his face.

"I know. But if we're going to communicate about negotiations and my plan to stop Olivia, we need a way to talk to each other."

"What is your plan to stop Olivia?" Julieta asked.

"I don't have one yet," Em said quietly.

"Great," Violet muttered.

"We can send a messenger," Cas said, shooting Violet a look. "But it has to be a volunteer. I don't feel right assigning this to someone. It would have to be a person we trust, who isn't scared of the Ruined."

Cas's eyes flicked to Galo. He saw the idea occur to Cas at the same time it occurred to him. Cas discreetly shook his head.

"I was thinking we go to the soldiers first, maybe General Amaro might have some thoughts?" Cas said quickly.

Galo didn't hear Danna's reply. It was an insane mission. The chances of getting someone to volunteer were slim at best. Everyone knew Olivia killed any human who came near her, so why would someone volunteer to do it willingly?

"I'll do it," Galo said.

Every head turned to him. Em blinked in surprise.

"I'll do it," he said again.

"No, you can't . . ." Cas's voice trailed off, like he couldn't think of why Galo couldn't.

"It should be me," Galo said. "I already know some of the Ruined. I know Olivia. Some of the soldiers have only seen her from a distance. They won't even know who to avoid." He said the words partly to convince himself. He needed something to make himself useful, a way to prove he was actually good at something besides wielding a sword. This was the perfect opportunity.

"That's a good point," Em said to Cas. "And Aren already knows Galo. Aren is always wary of new humans. He'll appreciate having someone he already knows he can trust."

Galo tried not to make a face. While he had warmed up to Em, the same couldn't be said of Aren. He'd been cold and reserved on the Lera guard, and then cocky and annoying in Vallos.

Cas cracked his knuckles as he considered. He clearly didn't want to let Galo go, and he had the power to order him to stay.

"You're sure you want to go?" he asked Galo quietly.

"Yes."

"Then you should go." Cas let out a sigh, but he smiled at Galo. "Get ready to leave in a few days. Pack light. You'll have to go on foot part of the way."

"I'll draw you a map of where you can wait for us," Em said. "It's a little ways outside of town. Me or Aren will check the spot every evening, to see if you've arrived."

He tried not to grimace. Aren was the best choice, in terms of protecting him. In fact, if he wanted to stay safe in Westhaven, he probably shouldn't leave Aren's side. That was unfortunate.

It occurred to him suddenly that he hadn't asked how long

his trips to Westhaven would be. He didn't even know how long he would be traveling back and forth. It could be months.

I'm worried you're going to leave. Mateo's voice drifted through his mind, and he suddenly realized he hadn't kept his promise.

Everyone was getting up, leaving Cas and Em alone, and he quickly got to his feet.

"Galo," Em said. He turned to face her. "Thank you. Really."

He nodded, and realized there was a bigger reason to do this, more important than him wanting to prove something. The Ruined needed help, and he'd never done anything to help them.

He turned and walked out of the room, down the stairs, and to the guards' quarters. He knocked on Mateo's door, and his roommate, Lawrence, opened the door.

"He's on shift," Lawrence said before he could get a word out. "But it should be almost over." He grabbed his jacket off his bed. "You can wait if you want. I was headed out."

"Thanks," Galo said, stepping inside. Lawrence walked out, pulling the door closed behind him.

Galo sat on Mateo's bed, rehearsing what he was going to say.

They need my help!

There's no one else!

I don't have anything to do anyway!

Mateo really wouldn't appreciate that last one. It was Galo's own fault that he had nothing to do and was free to run around with the Ruined.

The door opened, and Mateo stepped inside. His face broke into a smile when he spotted Galo sitting on his bed.

"Hey. I was going to come find you as soon as I got changed." He leaned down and kissed Galo briefly, then walked to the wardrobe against the wall and began unbuttoning his jacket. "I heard Emelina is here. Did you see her?"

"I saw her. Cas pulled me in to a meeting with her."

Mateo tossed his jacket in the bin in the corner and turned, eyebrows raised. "How was that?"

He swallowed. "Um . . ."

"What? Are you not allowed to tell me?"

"No, it's not that. I just . . ." He took in a breath. "I volunteered to do something."

Mateo's face fell, like he could already tell he wasn't going to like it. "What?"

"They need a messenger, to travel between here and Westhaven. Someone who can stay with the Ruined for days at a time, then come back and relay what's happening there."

"Westhaven," Mateo repeated. "Olivia killed everyone in Westhaven."

"Lots of people made it out."

"Lots of people *didn't*." He threw up his hands. "No sane person would go anywhere near Westhaven right now."

"Em has a plan. She can protect—"

"When has Em ever stopped Olivia from killing someone?" Mateo interrupted.

"That's not fair. Aren will be there as well, and he actually can stop Olivia."

"You seriously trust that jerk to protect you?"

"Yes," Galo said. "He's not my favorite person, but he's proven he'll protect us."

Mateo stared at him for a moment. "Cas is letting you do this?"

Galo didn't try to hide the flash of annoyance he felt. He didn't need Cas to *let* him do anything. Cas was his king, and his friend, but he didn't control what Galo did.

"It was my decision," Galo snapped.

Mateo's cheek twitched, like it always did when he was angry. "For how long?"

"I don't know. Until the Ruined come here. I may be traveling back and forth for a while."

"Why does it have to be you? Why do you have to save everyone?"

"I don't have to save everyone. I saw an opportunity to help and I took it."

Mateo let out a long sigh and leaned one shoulder against the wardrobe. "So why does it have to be *you*?" he asked again.

"It doesn't. But I want to do it."

"And what I want doesn't matter."

Galo reached for Mateo's hand. He really wanted Mateo to understand, to hug him and tell him he was doing the right thing. The brave thing. "Of course it matters. But I'd really like it if you'd support me here."

"I'm not supporting you when you're doing something stupid."

Galo dropped Mateo's hand, looking at the floor to hide his disappointment. "Fine."

"Fine?"

Galo stood and pulled the door open. "I didn't ask your permission." He walked out the door and let it slam behind him.

ELEVEN

IRIA LIFTED A spoonful of oatmeal to her mouth and swallowed it, trying to avoid the stares directed her way. Even the guards working in the kitchen were sneering at her. She was only allowed out of her cell for meals and brief exercise, and the hateful looks the other prisoners gave her left no doubt that they knew who she was.

It had once been her greatest fear, being assigned to duty in one of the prisons. The mediocre warriors became prison guards, the ones who could barely pass training.

The only thing worse was being an inmate. That ranked at number one on the embarrassment scale.

Long wooden tables made up the eating area, with inmates sitting on the benches. The room was a square gray box with no windows, and guards at each wall. Iria sat alone, a few seats down from a loud group of women.

She'd only managed a few bites of the oats, but she pushed them away. She'd barely eaten anything since arriving at Central Prison a week ago. The food wasn't particularly good, but mostly, it was hard to eat with her stomach twisted into knots.

A guard at the door shouted for them to finish. Two minutes until they would be marched back to their cells.

Iria grabbed her bowl and walked to the trash cans outside the kitchen. She scraped what was left of her breakfast into the trash and deposited her bowl and spoon in the bin for dirty dishes.

"What's wrong?" A guard stood just outside the kitchen door, her arms crossed over her chest. "You don't like it?" She gestured to the discarded oatmeal.

"I'm just not hungry," Iria mumbled. She turned away.

A hand roughly grabbed the back of her shirt. She yelped as she flew backward into the chest of the guard. The guard clapped a hand over Iria's mouth.

Fear raced up her spine as the woman dragged her into the kitchen, letting the door swing closed behind them. It was forbidden for the guards to harm prisoners, except in self-defense.

It seemed she was the exception.

Iria twisted against the arms locked around her waist, but the woman held firm, swinging them both around to face into the kitchen. Three other guards stood there, all men. The one directly in front of her sneered.

"The famous Iria Ubino," he said. His front tooth was

chipped, and in any other situation, she might have found it hard not to laugh when he spoke. Today, the pure hatred in his eyes was anything but funny. "Is it true you marched with the Leran king to Royal City?"

She just stared at him, because there was still a hand over her mouth. Everyone knew the answer to that question.

The guard took a step closer to her, spitting on the ground near her feet. "If you love Lera and the Ruined so much, they should have punished you like one. They execute people for treason."

Outside the door, Iria heard the scuffle of feet as the prisoners moved to pile their trays and go back to their cells. The chipped-tooth guard held out a hand. The man next to him put a huge butcher's knife in it.

Iria screamed against the hand over her mouth. She tried to flail out her arms, but another guard joined the woman, holding her wrists tight against her body.

The man held the knife directly in front of her face. "You shouldn't come in the kitchen, you know. Accidents happen here."

He hurled the knife at the ground.

Iria screamed as pain exploded through her right foot. The world turned black.

Iria woke up in a white room. It smelled like disinfectant, and when she turned she found a long row of beds. Her body was heavy, her head swimming. Dull pain pulsed from her right foot.

A man leaned over the woman in the bed next to her. He

caught Iria watching and straightened.

"What . . ." It was hard to form words.

"I gave you something for the pain," the man said, walking to her bed. "Had to take your toes off, but you kept most of the foot. If you change the bandages regularly and keep it clean, should stay that way."

Panic shot down her spine, clearing her head. *Most?* She kept *most* of her foot?

She lifted her head. Dizziness crashed over her, but she squinted at the end of the bed anyway. Her foot was wrapped in white bandages. She couldn't see it.

"You'll walk with a limp, but it's not like you're going anywhere." The doctor chuckled. "Certainly won't be running away."

Iria let her head drop back on the pillow as tears welled in her eyes.

TWELVE

"GALO!"

Galo turned to see Violet racing down the hall, her dark hair flying behind her. She grabbed him by the arm.

"Come with me," she said.

"What?" he asked, breaking into a jog. "Is Cas all right?"

"He's fine. It's Jovita."

The name sent a spark of terror down Galo's spine. He'd wondered often in the past few weeks if he should have killed Jovita when it was obvious Cas wouldn't. She had pulled the rug out from under them so easily in the fortress, when she'd convinced everyone that Cas was insane and then poisoned him. It was impressive, in a horrifying way, and Galo dreaded what she'd do next.

Violet stopped in front of Cas's office, knocking once before opening the door and stepping inside. Cas was alone, sitting at his desk, and he let out a sigh when he caught the look on Violet's face. He was no stranger to bad news these days.

"We have reports that Jovita and her loyalists were seen in Olso," Violet said.

Galo blinked, surprised, but Cas didn't look the least bit alarmed.

"We already knew that, didn't we?" Cas said. "Last we heard she was headed for the border."

"Yes, but there's more. She was joined by Vallos soldiers. We're getting word that the Olso army is organizing, and bringing in troops from Jovita and Vallos to launch an attack."

"Vallos might support Jovita on the throne, but Olso would have no interest in helping her retake Lera," Galo said.

"No, they wouldn't," Violet said. "They may be coming for us, but we think King August wants the Ruined gone as much as Jovita does. They're probably partnering to attack them first."

Galo winced. It was a smart plan, unfortunately. August and Jovita would have a much easier time taking Lera if the Ruined were gone. They could fight among themselves later.

"They're still in Olso right now?" Cas asked.

"Last we heard." She gestured to Galo. "I thought we should have Galo take the news to the Ruined right away. I know we haven't made a decision about Em's request, but this seems more pressing."

"I agree," Cas said. He looked at Galo. "Can you leave right away?"

"Of course."

"Good. In the meantime, I want more soldiers at the border. I need to know the minute they cross into Lera, and the size of their army."

Galo hurried out of the office and headed to his room. He had a bag packed and ready to go, and he grabbed it, along with his jacket.

He ran down the castle hallway, his bag swinging against his back. He stepped around a few staff members as he sprinted through the kitchen and outside.

Mateo stood just next to the kitchen door, on duty and dressed in his guard's uniform. His face fell when he spotted Galo. He knew Galo would never disturb him while he was working, unless it was important.

"I'm being sent right now," Galo said breathlessly.

"What? Why?"

"There's been a development." He wasn't sure how much he was allowed to tell Mateo, so he left it at that.

"You're going right this minute? We can't even talk about it?" Mateo asked, his brow furrowed in frustration.

"There isn't anything to talk about. I need to—"

"I talked to some of the guards, and a few of them are willing to go," Mateo cut in. "There is no good reason for you to—"

"There is a perfectly good reason," Galo interrupted. Angry

words boiled up inside him, and he took a step back. "I can't argue about this right now. They're waiting for me." He turned on his heel. Mateo called his name, but he wasn't allowed to leave his post while on duty. Galo walked faster.

Outside, two soldiers were on horseback, prepared to escort him part of the way. They'd saddled a horse for him as well, and he quickly attached his bag to the saddle and climbed on.

"Let's go," he said, turning the horse away from the castle.

They rode east for several hours, until they reached the spot on Em's map where she said Galo should go by foot. He dismounted his horse and waved good-bye to the soldiers as they rode back in the direction of Royal City.

According to Em's map, he was about an hour's walk from Westhaven, and he hiked slowly through the tall grass, keeping a close watch on his surroundings.

He found the area where he was supposed to wait, in a thick patch of trees, not far from a small stream. Em had written on the back of the map that she'd hidden a sleeping bag beneath a rock, and he found it easily. He pulled it out and plunked down on top of it.

The sun was sinking low in the sky, and it was quiet except for the wind rustling the leaves on the trees. He hadn't been alone in so long—since before becoming a guard—that the quiet immediately caused panic to well up inside him. Maybe Mateo had been right. It was stupid to run straight into danger when he'd just escaped it. Surely there was someone else who could have done this?

It was too late to go back now, but he certainly could have left things better with Mateo. He should have at least hugged him before he left. If Olivia took Galo's head off, Mateo would remember Galo's being a jerk the last time he saw him.

He'd been running through all the things he *should* have said to Mateo for an hour when he heard the sound of footsteps. It was almost dark, but he leaned over to try to see through the trees. Aren. He recognized the broad shoulders and long, quick strides right away. Galo had spent a lot of time watching Aren when he was a guard in the castle. He'd always seemed off, and Galo had spent a lot of time trying to figure out why.

Aren ducked his head under a branch. Surprise lit up his face when he spotted Galo. "You're here."

"I'm here. Just for the last hour or so."

Aren walked closer to him, sliding his hands into his pockets. Galo sometimes forgot how good-looking Aren was, and instead only remembered him suggesting Galo had done a terrible job guarding Cas. But he really was handsome, with his intense dark eyes and a smile that suggested he was far more innocent than he really was.

"Was the trip all right?" Aren asked. "No problems?" His smile faded quickly, and Galo realized Aren seemed exhausted. He had dark circles under his eyes, and his frame was thinner than last time he'd seen him.

"No problems," he said.

Aren stood there awkwardly for a moment, like he was searching for something to say. "Thank you. For offering to do this," he finally said quietly.

He sounded sincere, and Galo felt a tinge of guilt for second-guessing his decision to come. "Don't thank me," he mumbled.

"Why not?"

He just shrugged.

"I heard you quit the guard," Aren said. "To come here?"

"No, I'd already quit."

"Oh. Why?"

"It was the right thing to do." He looked up at Aren, not trying to hide the edge in his voice. "You said it yourself, I wasn't doing a very good job."

"When did I say that?"

"In Vallos."

Aren cocked his head, thinking. "Right. You didn't quit because of what I said, did you?"

"Don't give yourself so much credit."

"I'm sorry. I didn't mean it. No one could have protected Cas from what happened. It's a miracle he's alive, actually."

He eyed Aren warily, unsure how to react to that. This was the longest conversation they'd ever had, and it wasn't going at all how he thought. "You meant it, a little," he countered.

"I didn't, I was just being a jerk. I was scared that night, with you guys arriving and having August and the warriors *and* Olivia in Sacred Rock. I just wanted you all to leave before Em got more attached to Cas."

Galo couldn't blame him for that. He'd also wondered if seeing Em again would just make things even more painful for Cas.

"It is best that you quit, though," Aren said. "Cas would jump in front of a sword for you, and that's the exact opposite of what you want, as a guard."

Galo laughed softly. "True."

"Plus it's really boring."

"You were barely on the Lera guard long enough to get bored," Galo said with an eye roll.

"But I still did. That should tell you something." He smiled at Galo. "Em's with the Ruined right now. Do you have anything urgent to tell her?"

"We're pretty sure Jovita has partnered with Olso *and* Vallos and will be attacking the Ruined soon."

"Wow. Even Vallos this time, huh?"

"You don't seem upset by this news," Galo said with a hint of amusement.

Aren shrugged. "Business as usual. They're not attacking right this minute, are they?"

"We think they're still in Olso. We've set up a pretty good system to get messages back to the castle as quickly as possible, so we should have some notice."

"All right. I'll let Em know. Do you need anything?"

"I'm fine. I may need some food tomorrow, though. I'm going to stay a couple of days, then return to check on everything in the castle."

"I'll grab something for you." He took a step back. "If you need me, I'm in the big blue house on the north side of Market Street. It's far from where Olivia is staying, but still, I'd only come in an emergency."

"Thanks, Aren." Galo watched as Aren disappeared into the trees, the quiet closing in around him again. He leaned his head back with a sigh and tried not to think about Mateo.

THIRTEEN

EM SLOWLY WALKED away from Westhaven, Aren by her side. She glanced over her shoulder several times, squinting in the late-afternoon sun, but no one followed them. She hadn't been able to slip away to see Galo last night, but Olivia had finally gone to the courthouse with Jacobo.

"What are we going to do if Jovita and her army come for us?" Aren asked. He'd relayed his conversation with Galo from last night to her. "Can we fight off a large army ourselves?"

Em swallowed. An idea had started to form, but it was so horrible she wasn't sure she could say it out loud. Once she said it, the betrayal of her sister would be complete. She could never go back.

"I'm surprised August is partnering with Jovita," she said, to avoid answering. "Last time I saw him I got the impression he'd realized that attacking Olivia never goes well."

"He probably took some time to think about it and remembered she murdered his entire family."

"Right," Em said quietly.

They ducked under a low branch and found Galo sitting on his pallet on the grass. He'd clearly heard them coming, and he waved as they approached. "Hi."

"Hi." Aren sat down and crossed his legs. "No problems during the night?"

"No problems. I didn't see anyone."

Em dropped the bag she'd brought to the ground and knelt down to open it. She grabbed the books first, three hardcovers she'd picked from the abundant bookshelves in her house.

"Here," she said, holding them out to him. "I know you're going back tomorrow, but I thought you might be bored."

"Thank you," he said with a hint of surprise.

She pulled out the cloth bundle tucked into the side of the bag and handed that over as well. "It's just some bread and cheese and dried meat."

"Thank you," he said again. "What is your food situation like over there?"

"Good." She sat down across from him and crossed her legs. "There aren't many of us, and the shops were well stocked. Though it turns out we don't have anyone who knows how to make bread. We had a few disasters in the bakery."

Galo grabbed the roll she'd given him. "It looks fine."

"We found some recipes and figured it out, but it's still not quite right," Aren said. "Edible, though."

He tore off a chunk and chewed. "Tastes good to me."

"Galo said Cas has been letting people come into the castle to ask him questions about the Ruined," Em said to Aren.

Aren lifted his eyebrows. "How is that going?"

"Um, I don't know. Everyone in Royal City knows you stopped Olivia from storming the castle the night we took it back, so they're intrigued, at least."

"Barely," she said.

"Barely?" Galo repeated.

"I barely stopped Olivia from storming the castle." She focused on a spot on the ground. "I'm not sure I can stop her again."

"Together we can," Aren said with a confidence Em doubted he actually felt. "It exhausts her to use her powers on me, and she can't use them on Em at all."

"Are you completely sure she can't use her Ruined power on you? She healed you once, didn't she?" Galo asked.

"I let her."

"But has she ever *really* tried to use her power on you against your will?"

"I . . . I guess not." Em glanced at Aren. "Has she?"

"Not that I know of."

"Have *you* ever tried?" Galo asked.

"I haven't." Aren lifted his eyebrows in silent question to Em.

"Sure," she said. "Give it a shot."

Aren focused his gaze on her, and several quiet seconds passed. "I'm trying to move your arm. You don't feel anything?"

"No."

"That's good," Galo said.

Em and Aren exchanged a look. It *was* good, but they were clearly both thinking the same thing—had Olivia already tried to use her powers on Em? The thought made her feel sick to her stomach.

"Do you have any other information from Cas for us?" Em asked, to stall the conversation about Jovita and Olso a bit longer.

"We tossed around some ideas about Olivia I'm supposed to relay to you. Fair warning, some of them might be upsetting," Galo said.

She didn't see how anything could be more upsetting than what was already going on in her head. She reached up to rub her thumb across her necklace and found nothing around her neck. She quickly dropped her hand. "Tell me."

Galo took a deep breath. "Right. First, she needs to see to use her power, right? What if she couldn't see?"

"You mean blind her," Em said.

"Yes."

"It would only slow her down for a while," Aren said. "I've known Ruined who went blind. Eventually they learn to use their other senses. Some of the Ruined who can control the mind don't even need to be able to see the person at all, they just sense them nearby."

"Oh."

"And it would just enrage Olivia. Not to mention she would never forgive Em for trying to weaken her power."

"It's too bad, I was thinking it might be a way for her to live a normal life. If she didn't have her powers anymore, she'd have to, I don't know, start using her words." One side of Galo's mouth lifted.

Em let out a short laugh. "That'll be the day." She leaned back, bracing her hands on the ground behind her. "What else?"

"We could give Olivia Olso."

"It's not really ours to give."

"I just meant we don't do anything to stop her from invading Olso. You step down as queen, let her rule by herself, in exchange for her going back to Olso."

"She would kill a lot of people. And it's only a temporary fix. She'd eventually come back," Em said.

"There's always the option of warning Olso. Their technology is beyond Olivia. If they knew she was coming . . ."

They'd kill her. Em gripped the grass beneath her fingers. Was there a plan that didn't end in Olivia's death?

"What are your other options?" she asked.

"Put her back in a prison. If you're right, and she can't use her powers on you, you can get her inside a cell."

"She'd have to be there indefinitely. And there's the problem of the Ruined loyal to her. You'd have to lock them up too or risk them breaking her out."

"Are there a lot?"

"A good number, yes. And their powers are growing. Anything else?"

He picked a piece of grass and twisted it around his finger. "I had an idea of my own. But can it just be between us?"

Em lifted her eyebrows. "Sure."

"What if you gave her part of Lera? Like we divided it into northern and southern Lera, and Olivia gets the south to rule as she pleases. We'd let any Lerans who want to leave relocate, of course."

"You'd displace thousands of people," Em said.

"It's better than Olivia killing them."

"I don't think it would help. She would eventually attack the north. If not now, then in ten, twenty years. We'd always be waiting for it."

"*We?*" Galo repeated with a smile. "Does that mean you'd stay with Cas in the north?"

Em turned her gaze to the ground. Her immediate response was *yes*. She wanted to stay with Cas. She couldn't bring herself to say it out loud, though. It seemed like a worse betrayal of the Ruined, to actually say it.

"Is Cas as king the only thing Olivia really objects to?" Galo asked. "You said the Ruined siding with you wanted Cas to give up the throne, but would that calm Olivia?"

"She'll never let any human rule over her," Em said. "They're wrong to ask Cas to give up his throne. The Lerans need him."

"Good," Galo said, a little relieved. "I wasn't saying he *should*. Cas will be a much better king than his father. The best king we've ever known, maybe. But I think it's right to remove some of the power from the monarchy." He said the last part quietly.

"You do?"

"It's not that I don't have faith in Cas, I do, but . . ."

"Of course," Em said.

"But I did wonder whether it's right to let Lera continue as they always have, considering all that's happened. The Gallegos committed genocide. It wasn't Cas's decision, but sometimes we pay for the mistakes of our family. You and Cas do, anyway," Galo said.

Em laughed hollowly. "You mean your parents have never started a war or killed a bunch of people just because they didn't like them?"

"Um, no."

"Wow. What must that be like?"

"Less dramatic." He chuckled, but his eyes were sad, and worry seized her chest suddenly. Aren seemed to notice too, and his eyebrows furrowed.

"Are they . . . are they all right?" Aren asked. "Do your parents live in Royal City?"

"A bit north. They're fine. I visited them recently."

Em released a breath. "Good."

"Is capturing Olivia the best option, then?" Galo asked. "It's the only one we seem to have so far."

"We can't," Em said. "We're really going to lock up the Ruined like Cas's father did? Death would be kinder."

Aren looked at her expectantly. He knew she had an idea she wasn't saying.

She ran her hands down her face, Gisela's words ringing in her ears. *Olivia has a long-term plan.* Em still didn't have anything concrete—they were preparing to partner with Cas, and the Lera soldiers were gathering Weakling, but she still didn't have a solid plan to tell the Ruined. She knew they were waiting. She knew she had to make a decision, even if that decision would lead to more death.

"I have an idea," she said quietly, to the ground. "But it's horrible."

"What?" Aren asked.

"If the army is really coming for us, like the Lera spies say it is, then we could tell Olivia. We don't wait for the humans to attack us; we let Olivia lead us into battle. She would jump at the opportunity."

"She would," Aren said, his forehead crinkling in confusion. "But what would that accomplish?"

"We wouldn't actually fight. I think I could get at least half the Ruined to abandon her right when the battle starts. We make a run for it, leaving Olivia and her supporters to fight the army on their own."

"Could you actually make it out?" Galo asked. "Once the battle starts, it might be too intense. You may have no choice but to fight."

"It could happen, but if we position ourselves right, we could make it out. Especially with Aren on our side. And Olivia is always at her most deadly when a battle begins. She's at full strength, and we'll hopefully be surprising the army. It should be possible to slip away if we plan it right."

"But if we left them . . ." Aren let his voice trail off.

"They would all die," Em whispered. Olivia would die.

It was quiet for a moment before Galo spoke. "It would take care of two problems at once. Olivia might kill so many Olso and Vallos soldiers that they simply give up and go home. And Olivia might not make it out alive."

"There's a very good chance Olivia wouldn't make it," Em said. Her throat was starting to close up, and it was hard to talk. "She's powerful, but she can't take on an entire army with only a handful of Ruined. She'd barely be able to do it with all of us." She looked at Aren. "It's horrible, right?"

"It's horrible," he said quietly. "But there's no way this ends without Olivia's death."

Tears burned her eyes, and she tried to blink them away. They fell anyway. Galo looked at the ground.

"Is it a stupid idea?" she asked. "Maybe I should just kill her tonight and save us all the trouble."

"Em, no one would ever ask you to do that," Aren said. "*I* would never do that."

"How is it different? If we do this, we're going to lead her—and dozens of other Ruined—to their deaths. It will be our fault."

"She'll fight them sooner or later," Aren said. "It's a good plan, Em. We have to deal with the army eventually, it might as well be now, when they can help us take care of Olivia."

Em roughly wiped the tears off her cheeks.

"You could present her with an option," Galo said after a few moments of silence. "Tell her the army is coming, and let her decide between going back to Ruina, or fighting them. Maybe the threat of another attack this soon will finally scare her."

She let out a long breath and shook her head. "Never. She'll be delighted to fight them."

"Then . . ." Aren winced. "I hate to say it, but we gave her plenty of chances. We've pleaded with her to go back to Ruina. It'll be her decision, Em."

It would be Olivia's decision, but she'd make it thinking Em would help. Olivia would be devastated by that kind of betrayal from Em. Even if her sister somehow made it out alive, she would never speak to Em again. It would be the end of their relationship.

"This is it, then?" she asked hollowly. "Is this the plan Galo takes back to Cas?"

"I think it is," Aren said.

"Well, there's one more option," Galo said. "You can come back to Royal City with me tonight, and let Olivia do whatever she wants. Jovita is definitely coming for her anyway, regardless of whether Olso decides to help. Cas won't mind if you and some of the other Ruined just want to leave her now. I think he'd be relieved, actually."

Em closed her eyes briefly. It was tempting. But she knew

Olivia—as soon as Em was gone, she'd round up the remaining Ruined and head to the next city. And she'd kill everyone. She'd start with the nearby cities, like she said, then head up north. Galo had just said his parents lived north. He didn't understand what he'd just suggested to Em.

Or maybe he did, but he didn't think Em cared to save a bunch of humans she didn't know. She wouldn't blame him for thinking that. It seemed unlikely that any Ruined would want to save a Leran.

"Too many people will die," she said. Galo didn't look surprised by her answer. Maybe he'd never expected her to take that offer at all.

"Then . . . ?" Aren prompted.

She swallowed and took a step back. She needed this conversation to be over. She needed a few minutes to scream and cry. "How are we going to say we got this information when Olivia asks?" Em asked.

"Me," Aren said. "I'll leave for a couple of days. I'll go with Galo to Royal City, to talk to Cas. Olivia won't think it's strange if I just disappear. She already knows I hate her. I'll come back saying I heard the plan from someone."

"Will she buy that?" Galo asked.

"She might be suspicious, but she's not going to turn down the chance to head off an army. Killing humans is Olivia's favorite pastime."

Em took in a shaky breath. "We may need help from the Lera

army, to get away at the right moment once the battle starts. Will Cas provide assistance?"

"We can ask," Aren said softly.

She nodded and turned away before her eyes filled with tears again. "Do it."

FOURTEEN

"SO WE'D BE sending them to their deaths."

Aren looked at Patricio, who was looking at Em with a horrified expression on his face. Em stared at the floor.

"It's the best idea we have," Aren said. A group of about twenty Ruined were gathered in Mariana's sitting room, squeezed onto couches and spread out on the floor, and they all gawked at him. He sat next to Em on the floor, their backs to the wall.

"If you have any other suggestions, please speak now," Em said quietly.

Patricio pushed two hands through his dark hair. Beside him, Gisela put a hand on his knee. "I think it's a good plan," she said, her tone more gentle than usual.

"There are already so few of us," Selena protested. She was

next to Ivanna on the couch. "The Ruined are going to be completely extinct if we keep dying."

"We're going to be extinct if we let Olivia continue," Aren said. "The Olso and Vallos armies are coming, either way. And Cas will be forced to turn on us eventually, if we let Olivia run wild."

"It's only a matter of time," Ivanna said quietly. "Before Olivia is killed, I mean." She cast a sympathetic look in Em's direction.

Aren swung his arm over Em's shoulders and she leaned against him. She'd stopped talking about Olivia to him, besides their conversation with Galo last night. He couldn't blame her. He didn't know what to say either.

"I'm leaving with Galo tonight," Aren said. "We're going to present the plan to Cas and see if he'll provide Lera troops. Our plan is for them to hang back, to help us escape after we leave Olivia and her supporters to fight the army on their own."

"So we flee," Selena said.

"Yes. We'll go back to Royal City with the troops. We're hoping to get word as soon as they cross the border, so we'll have to travel into the Lera jungle to head them off." They'd probably be almost halfway to Olso by the time they caught up with the troops, if everything went to plan.

Halfway to Iria.

Was he really going to turn around and go back to Royal City, if he was already so close to her?

Em started talking about logistics, and he leaned back against the wall and looked up at the ceiling. Could he leave the Ruined after they defeated Olivia? Maybe she would be weak enough (*or dead*, he thought with a shudder) for him to go to Olso, just for a few days.

The meeting was coming to a close, and Aren stood. A few Ruined surrounded Em to ask more questions about Olivia, and he lifted a hand in good-bye as he stepped away.

Be careful, she mouthed.

He nodded and slipped out the door before any Ruined could corner him. The sun had just completely set, and he and Galo needed to go.

He stopped by his house to grab the bag he'd never unpacked. It was the same bag he'd carried since before all this had started— it was filled with medicine, food, clothes, and extra water. Even as a guard in the Lera castle, he'd never unpacked that bag. It was always ready to go. He couldn't really imagine life without being constantly prepared to run.

He swung the bag onto his back and headed outside. He went quickly, checking over his shoulder to see if he was being followed. He didn't see anyone, but it was dark. He probably should have gone earlier, but it had been hard to get all the Ruined together without Olivia noticing. They'd had to wait until she retreated inside her house.

He ducked under a low branch, headed to the spot where he could sense Galo hiding. He felt the familiar burst of relief when he found Galo in front of him, unharmed. The agreement with Lera was shaky at best, and it certainly wouldn't be helped by the king's best friend getting his head removed by Olivia.

Galo was on his feet, sword drawn, and he let out a sigh as he squinted in the darkness. "Hi, Aren." He sheathed his sword.

"Expecting someone else?"

"I couldn't tell for sure who it was in the dark."

Galo had packed up his bag and pushed his blankets and books beneath a shrub. "We're good to go?" he asked.

"Yes. The Ruined are on board." He turned and started walking east, Galo falling into step beside him. It was too risky to take horses from the barn, so they had to go on foot until they reached the point where soldiers were permanently stationed to transport Galo back to the castle. It would only take a few hours to walk there.

They didn't talk as they left Westhaven behind. Aren was on constant alert, searching the area around him for Jacobo or Olivia.

"You're making me nervous," Galo said as Aren glanced over his shoulder again. "Do you think someone is following us?"

"No. I mean, I hope not. I can't sense when a Ruined is nearby, so I just want to make sure Olivia or Jacobo didn't spot us."

"Can you sense when there's a human nearby?"

Aren nodded. His power had grown stronger recently, and he could sense humans even from great distances. "I can feel lots of them," he said quietly. "There are a bunch to the east, so there must be a town there."

"Yes, but it's pretty far," Galo said with a hint of amazement.

"And I can feel the prisoners back in Westhaven."

"You have human prisoners?"

"Olivia does," Aren replied.

"Right. I'm sorry, I didn't mean to imply you were also part of it."

"I can't save them, so maybe I am."

Galo stared at him, but Aren couldn't read his expression in the darkness. "I was just going to suggest that we don't bring that up."

Aren raised his eyebrows. "You think we should lie about the prisoners?"

"Let's say we omit it. I'll tell Cas, and he can decide what to do with that information. But I don't think we should make it any harder for the advisers to come to your side. They might ask why you're allowing it."

"Fair question."

"I know you're doing what you can to keep Olivia under control."

Aren rubbed the back of his neck with one hand. He'd avoided the prisoners since his one and only visit to them. It was too painful, to be confronted with his own worthlessness.

"Em said she's trying to draw power from them?" Galo asked. "Because you can?"

"Yes. She's still failing, last I heard. I have a theory about that."

"What's that?"

He reached his hand out. "May I have your arm for a second?"

Galo slowly extended his arm out. Aren wrapped his fingers around his wrist.

Energy flowed through him suddenly. His Ruined magic stirred inside of him, almost like it was thanking him for the boost.

Aren let go. "Can you pretend to be afraid of me for a minute?"

"How do you mean?"

"I don't know. Just . . . don't trust me. Don't let me have your arm."

Galo dropped his arm, but he still looked confused. Aren winced. If this test was going to be effective, he probably needed to make Galo *actually* afraid of him.

He spun on his heel so he was facing Galo, and froze him in place. Galo's eyes widened, a twinge of panic crossing his face as he clearly tried to move his limbs and failed. Aren roughly grabbed his arm.

Nothing. The energy was gone.

Aren dropped his arm and released his hold on him. "I'm sorry. I needed to test something."

Galo regarded him suspiciously. His shoulders had stiffened. Aren turned and started to walk again.

"I won't use my Ruined magic on you again, I promise. I just wanted to know for sure why she can't do it and I can."

"Why?" Galo asked.

"You have to give it willingly, it can't be taken."

"Oh." Galo held out his arm. "So you got nothing the second time?"

"Nothing. Don't tell Olivia that."

"We don't have many conversations."

"Lucky you."

"That's why you discovered it with Iria, then," Galo said. "She was the first human who really trusted you."

A lump suddenly formed in Aren's throat. "Yes," he said quietly. "She was."

It felt strange to be headed back to the castle without Iria. They hadn't been very close when they'd been in Lera together, but she'd still been a safe space for him. He'd be surrounded by Lera guards, his heart pounding, when he'd see the flash of her red uniform. They rarely spoke—they weren't supposed to know each other—but she smiled at him often. He hadn't told her how comforting that was.

"Do you have any plans to go to Olso or . . ." Galo let his voice trail off. *Or are you abandoning her?* was what he meant.

"I'm going to Olso," he said immediately. The words were a relief, finally spoken out loud. "As soon as I can, I'm going to Olso."

FIFTEEN

THE CASTLE WAS lonely with Galo gone again. Cas was surrounded by people all day—staff members, guards, advisers—but everyone was rushing in and out, many of them stiff and formal with him.

Mateo came to talk to him a couple of times, but he'd left on a recruitment trip to some of the neighboring cities, and wouldn't be back for a few days. Cas had warned him that he might miss Galo returning briefly with information, but Cas got the feeling that maybe that was the point.

He was alone in his office this morning, listening to the murmured sounds of the castle staff on the other side of the door. He understood his father a little better these days, as much as he hated to admit it. The king had been so outgoing, so friendly, to everyone. Cas had thought it was an act. Now he thought that his father was probably just trying to stave off the loneliness of constantly being surrounded by people who had to obey, not befriend, him.

A knock sounded on the door and he sat up straighter in his chair and tried to appear as if he hadn't just been sulking.

"Come in!" he called.

Violet stepped inside, a smile on her face. "Galo's returned."

Cas jumped to his feet, relief coursing through his veins. "How is he?"

"Great. He's at the gate. He brought Aren with him, and the guards weren't sure he should be allowed in."

"Of course he should," Cas said, though he was surprised Aren had come. "Just Aren? Em didn't come with them?"

"No, I'm afraid not."

He edged around his desk and walked out of the office with Violet. "Let the guards and the staff know that Aren is always welcome here."

"I'll do that right away."

"They probably won't like that, will they? Do the guards hate Aren?"

Violet cocked her head in thought as they descended the stairs. "From what I've heard, he was very reserved when he was part of the guard here. No one really knew him. So they don't hate him any more than they hated Em."

Cas couldn't help but take note that *hated Em* was past tense. He hoped it was intentional.

He walked across the front foyer with Violet, his guards falling into place around him as he stepped outside. Galo and Aren were standing on the other side of the iron gate. Galo waved when he spotted him.

Two guards pulled open the gate. Cas strode across the dirt and embraced Galo for a moment, then turned to Aren.

"Aren. Nice to see you again."

Aren's eyes skipped over the guards, all of whom were staring at him. He shifted uncomfortably, but he managed a small smile for Cas.

Cas led them inside and up to his office. Violet split off from them, taking instructions for lunch to a staff member.

Cas grabbed the door to his office and held it open for Galo and Aren. He stepped inside and started to close the door, when Jorge suddenly grabbed it.

"Your Majesty, may I suggest you go to a dining room, where I can put a few guards with you, out of earshot?"

"You may suggest it, but the answer is no," Cas said. He suppressed a smile as Jorge tried to hide his annoyance.

"You're making his life miserable, aren't you?" Galo asked as Cas shut the door. "That's the new captain of his guard," he explained to Aren.

"I don't know what you mean; I am pleasant and reasonable all the time," Cas said. Aren snorted.

He took a seat in one of the chairs near the window, and gestured for them to sit as well. Aren stared outside as he lowered himself into a chair, his expression unreadable.

"Aren, I didn't expect you," Cas said. "If I'd known you could get away, I might have suggested Galo not go at all."

Aren turned to him. "I didn't expect to come either. But we needed Olivia to see me leave for a day or two."

"Why?" Cas asked.

"We want to tell Olivia about the impending attack from Olso and Vallos," Galo said. "Aren will say he heard about the troops while traveling, and he won't even have to suggest Olivia go after them. She'll insist on it."

"What's the point of that?" Cas asked.

"We've gotten over half of the Ruined to agree to step away from the battle, at a crucial moment," Aren said. "Olivia and her followers will have a very hard time fighting on their own. It will solve two problems at once."

"The army will likely take severe casualties, as will the Ruined," Galo explained quietly.

Cas raised his eyebrows as he looked at Aren. "Are you all right with that? Is Em?"

"It was her idea. It's our only option."

"Has there been any movement spotted at the border?" Galo asked.

"Yes, we got reports yesterday of troops crossing the border. It's a sizable army, over a thousand soldiers, but slow-moving. They have a lot of equipment with them. You should have time to cut them off in the jungle."

Aren scrubbed a hand down his face. "That's good," he said, in a tone that didn't sound like it was good at all. "But we'll need to leave immediately."

"And we could use some Lera troops as backup," Galo said.

"I can't spare many soldiers," Cas said regretfully. "I can't leave the castle unguarded, even with the army supposedly still far away. I won't let my guard down."

"I understand," Aren said. "Our hope is they won't actually have to fight, and if they do, it will be against Vallos and Olso. But we'd mostly need them to bring the Ruined to Royal City after the battle. We don't know if we'll have any horses or supplies. We may just have to run."

"I can spare a few for that. And I'll start making space for the Ruined. I think we still have some room in the guards' quarters, and there are several other empty rooms."

"You want to put them here?" Aren asked in surprise.

"That seems like the safest option, don't you think?"

"What will the people here think? Will they consent to sharing space with Ruined?"

"They'll just have to get used to it," Cas said. "Besides, we'll all be safer with the Ruined in the castle. You'll be close if we're attacked again."

"And if you're not attacked?" Aren asked.

Cas laughed. "I'd be surprised, but that would be nice."

"I meant what happens to the Ruined?"

"We'll find a place for you, of course. I can start negotiations with Em right away, and we'll start settling you into Royal City."

Aren nodded, but his brow was creased, his gaze on the floor.

"Is that not what you want?" Cas asked.

"No, that's . . ." Aren swallowed. "That's fine. That's good."

Cas suspected there was something more Aren wanted to say, but only silence followed his last words.

"We were hoping to stay one night, if that's all right," Galo said.

"Of course," Cas said. "I'll have the staff make up a room for you, Aren."

Galo hopped to his feet and strode across the room. He opened the door and relayed instructions about Aren's room to a staff member.

"Do you mind if I go now?" Aren asked as he stood. "I need to wash up."

"Sure," Cas said. "We'll have some food sent up."

Galo stepped back to allow Aren to walk through the door. "Do you want me to come with you?"

"I'll be fine, thanks."

Cas got to his feet as a thought occurred to him. "Aren."

He was halfway out the door, and he turned to face Cas again. He raised his eyebrows expectantly when Cas hesitated.

"You can come to me if you have any problems. I'd just ask that you don't use your powers here."

"Hadn't planned to."

"Thank you."

Aren turned and walked out of the room. Cas watched him go, wondering if perhaps he'd insulted him. He wished Em were here. He'd gotten used to communicating with the Ruined through her.

Galo closed the door, leaving the two of them alone. "Should I go with him anyway?" he asked Cas.

"No, I don't want him to think we don't trust him."

Galo walked across the room and they both took their seats again. "You do trust him, right?"

"Yes," Cas said quickly. "Mostly. Do you think I insulted him? Why did he suddenly want to leave?"

Galo stared at the door like Aren was still there. "He probably would have told you if you insulted him. I think he's sad, actually."

"Sad," Cas repeated.

"Both he and Em are. They're having a hard time with the decision to betray the Ruined. And Aren lost Iria."

Cas sat back in his chair, his chest suddenly heavy as he thought of Em, alone in Westhaven.

A staff member entered with a tray of food, and Cas waited until she was gone to speak again.

"So," he said. "You got angry at Mateo before you left."

Galo looked up at him quickly. "He told you?"

"Yes. I don't blame him for not wanting you to go. It's just because he cares about you."

Galo let out a long sigh as he pressed his palms to his forehead. "I was a jerk when I left, wasn't I?"

"Yes, you were," Cas said.

"Hey," he said, dropping his hands with a startled laugh. "Whose side are you on?"

"I'm kind of leaning toward Mateo."

Galo laughed again, then slumped back in his chair. "I don't blame you."

"He's not here, you know. He went on a recruitment trip."

"Oh." Galo couldn't hide his disappointment. "Probably because he was still mad, huh?"

"I think so, yes." Cas leaned forward. "I could pass along a message, if you'd like."

Galo was silent for a few moments. "Just tell him I'm sorry."

Galo left the castle with Aren the next morning. A carriage took them halfway, but now they were on foot, still a couple of hours from Westhaven. They mostly walked in silence.

Galo had hoped Mateo might return that morning, but no luck. Galo wasn't sure what he would say to him anyway. He wasn't sorry that he'd gone, but he was sorry about how he'd left things. He wasn't sure how to express either thought.

He glanced at Aren, who was staring at the ground as he walked. He'd barely seen Aren yesterday, after he retreated to his room. He'd come out once, to discuss troops joining the Ruined with Cas's advisers.

Aren stopped suddenly, turning to face the direction they'd just come from. "Why don't you go back?"

"What?" Galo asked, surprised.

"You should stay with the soldiers. I should be able to get away again to pass along our plans."

"Aren, that's ridiculous. We just set up a plan where I need to know all the information about your plan of attack. I need to be there to get that information. And you don't know for sure that you can get away."

"I also don't know for sure if I can protect you. I don't think we should risk it."

Galo stared at him for a moment. Aren seemed genuinely worried, his brow furrowed and his gaze directed east, like he could still see the town where the soldiers were waiting for Galo to return.

He was realizing that he didn't really know Aren at all. He wasn't cocky and rude. Or maybe he had been, but it was certainly gone now. He seemed sad, and tired, and it was hard for Galo to hold on to any of the animosity he'd felt for him before.

"I'll be fine, Aren."

Aren laughed hollowly. "You don't know that."

Galo put a hand on Aren's arm and turned him back in the direction of Westhaven. "I made my choice. I'm sticking to it."

Aren sighed heavily and began walking again. "Fine. But I should tell you something."

"What?"

"I'm not going to go back to Royal City after the battle."

"You're going to go to Olso?" Galo guessed. Aren looked at him in surprise. "Where else would you go?"

"Right," Aren said softly. "Where else would I go?" He was

quiet for a moment before he spoke again. "But, I just thought you should know. I won't be around to protect you—or anyone— when you ride back to Royal City."

"I'm sure we'll be fine. Is Em going to go with you?"

"Oh, no. I'm going alone."

"Alone?" he repeated incredulously.

"There's no one to go with me. Not that anyone would any-way." He laughed, though it wasn't really full of humor.

"You don't have . . . any friends?" Galo asked slowly, unsure if it was a rude question.

"Besides Em? Not really. I know all the Ruined in Westhaven, of course. And I'm friendly with those that are loyal to Em. But I wasn't close to any of them before, and it's the same now." He kicked a rock. "Damian would go with me, if he were still here."

"The Ruined who was executed at the castle?" Galo asked.

"Yeah. He and Em were my best friends. He would go with me, even if he'd never even met Iria. Just because I asked."

Galo stared at the ground, fully understanding for the first time how much Aren had lost. Galo remembered feeling sorry for himself at Fort Victorra and in Vallos, thinking about how much *he'd* lost. A large portion of the guard, gone. The castle almost destroyed. Both his king and queen dead. But his parents were alive and well, as were his best friend and his boyfriend. A lot of his really good friends on the guard had come through fine, because he'd rounded them up and taken care of them when Olso attacked.

"I'm sorry, Aren," he said quietly. "About Damian. And everything."

"It's not your fault. I know you and Cas tried to stop his execution."

They had, but Galo couldn't think of much else he'd ever done to help the Ruined, beside his current mission. While he'd always found the king's policies abhorrent, he hadn't spoken out against them. He didn't want to risk jail. He hadn't even talked to Cas about his opinions, not until after Cas met Em and started to reconsider everything.

"It's better I go by myself anyway," Aren said, his tone a little lighter. "It'll be easier to sneak around. And I'll be surrounded by humans. It'll give my power a boost."

"You can't take what they won't willingly give," Galo said, repeating Aren's own words.

"Well, yes. Let's hope I find some friendly humans. I'll have to talk to some of them, at least. I don't even know what prison she's in." He scrunched up his face. "I've never even been to Olso."

"Me either."

"Hopefully you never will," Aren said with a smile. "I hear it's not very nice there."

"Yeah," Galo said. "Hopefully."

SIXTEEN

EM OPENED THE door to find Aren on the other side. She pulled him into a hug and squeezed him a little tighter than necessary.

"Are you all right?" he asked.

"I'm fine," she said, even though she wasn't. She'd alternated between worrying about him and drowning in guilt over Olivia since he'd left.

"Did—" he began.

"Olivia is here," she whispered before he could finish.

He pulled away, his eyes darting to the kitchen, then the sitting room.

"Do you . . ." Her words were barely a whisper, and she had

AMY TINTERA

to blink back tears before she could finish the sentence. "Do you want to tell her?"

Aren nodded solemnly.

Em took a deep breath. "Olivia! Aren's back!"

Footsteps sounded in the hallway as Olivia walked over. She stopped and leaned against the wall, cocking an eyebrow.

"Had he left?" she asked.

"You know he did," Em said. Olivia had grilled her about him yesterday, actually. *Where is Aren? I know you know where he went. Is he coming back? Did he go to Olso?* Em played dumb, acting like she had no idea where he'd gone.

"I'm sorry I didn't say good-bye," he said. "I was going to Olso, and I was worried Em wouldn't let me."

"Do you take orders from Em?" Olivia asked, eyes narrowed.

"Yes. Sometimes."

"Why'd you come back? Is Iria dead?" Olivia asked, and Em flashed her a dirty look. Olivia had only asked that question to be mean—she knew there was no way Aren could have already traveled to Olso and back to check on Iria.

"I didn't make it to Olso," Aren said. "I heard some news and I had to come back."

Olivia lifted her eyebrows in a silent question.

"There's an attack coming," he said. "An army made up of joint Olso and Vallos forces. And Jovita is with them as well. They're coming for us."

"So?" Olivia scoffed.

"From what I heard, it's a sizable army."

146

"Let me go to Cas," Em said quickly, just as they'd planned. "I'll ask him to help us. With Lera soldiers we can—"

"He knows, Em," Aren interrupted. "I heard this from soldiers. They were told to monitor the troop movements, but not attack. Cas doesn't want to risk his people right now."

"He only cares about himself in the end, after all," Olivia said smugly.

Em swallowed and tried to appear upset. It wasn't difficult. Her stomach was churning as she and Aren lied to Olivia.

"We don't need his help," Olivia said again. She drew in a breath and was quiet for a moment. "By being here, we're protecting Casimir. You see that, right? They're not attacking him because they're attacking us."

"They hate us more at the moment," Aren said.

"Maybe we should go back to Ruina and just let them fight it out," Olivia said.

Em blinked in surprise. She felt a surge of hope for the first time in days.

She grasped Olivia's hand. Her sister reeled back with a startled look on her face. She snatched her hand away.

"Let's go back," Em said, her desperation real. "I think going back to Ruina is the best choice right now."

"We have plenty of horses and supplies," Aren said quickly. "It would be a much easier journey than last time."

Olivia looked between the two of them. Her lip curled. Em could tell they'd made a mistake. She and Aren had been far too eager to take her up on the suggestion of going back home.

"We're not running," Olivia snapped. "The Ruined don't hide anymore. We *fight*."

Em and Aren were silent.

"Do you know where they are? The troops who are coming for us?" Olivia asked Aren.

"Yes. I know the general route they're taking. An army that large shouldn't be hard to find."

"We'll go to them, then," Olivia said. "I'm not going to sit around here and wait for them to make their move."

"Are you sure?" Em asked. "Olso has pretty powerful weapons, you might remember."

Worry flashed across Olivia's face for the first time. She quickly shook it off. "Some of us have been working on plans to get around their weapons. A surprise attack will help."

Em swallowed hard. She'd done just as Galo suggested—she gave Olivia the option of going home. She'd chosen to fight. She would always choose that option, no matter how much Em wanted her to change.

"When should we leave?" Em asked. Her voice shook.

Olivia brushed past her and Aren and walked to the door. "First thing tomorrow morning. I'll start preparing the Ruined. You two get the horses and supplies ready to go. I want as little as possible. Nothing to slow us down."

"Fine," Em said.

"What about the human prisoners?" Aren asked. "Maybe we should let them go before we leave."

"No need," Olivia said. "I killed them all yesterday. They

weren't useful anymore." Olivia stepped outside, letting the door slam behind her.

Em closed her eyes briefly. "I'm sorry," she said, though not really to Aren. "I didn't know."

"It was unavoidable," Aren said quietly.

Em waited until she could see Olivia walking down the road through the window before she spoke again.

"That's it, then."

"I'm sorry, Em," Aren said. "I thought she was going to go back to Ruina for a minute there."

"I did too." The moment of hope still lingered in her chest, making the reality even more painful. She cleared her throat. "What did Cas say?"

"He can send some soldiers, but only a few. They'll follow us, but really far behind. Galo will coordinate with them and travel between us as we head there. We should only have to travel a few days to get to them. We'll probably make it about halfway to the Olso border." He rubbed the back of his neck with his hand. "And I plan to keep going."

"To get Iria?" she guessed.

He nodded, worry in his eyes. "I'll already be on my way, and if everything goes according to plan Olivia will be weakened and everyone will be going back to the Lera castle anyway so—"

"Aren, it's fine," she interrupted gently. "Go. You're right, you'll already be halfway there, and she's imprisoned for helping us. It's the right thing to do."

He let out a breath. "Thank you."

"Of course. Bring her back safe."

"I will."

Olivia snuck out of the house before dawn. She shut the door quietly behind her and stepped onto the dark porch, shifting the bag she'd slung over her shoulder.

A tall figure leaned against a tree by the house. Jacobo.

"Is Em still asleep?" he asked quietly.

"Yes. Did you see anything last night?"

"Not much. A couple of Ruined went in and out of Mariana's house, but there's no way to tell what they're talking about. I spoke to Gisela and got nothing. She just said she's following your and Em's orders."

"Of course she did," Olivia muttered. All the Ruined had readily agreed to chase down the human army.

Even the ones Olivia knew were on Em's side.

If that's what you think is best, Ivanna had said to Olivia. Ivanna had never trusted Olivia.

Olivia expected a fight. She thought Ivanna and a few of the others might flat-out refuse to go.

But they'd all just nodded and agreed with her plan. Mariana had said she'd help get the horses ready. Gisela hadn't met Olivia's eyes once during their conversation.

They were planning something. They all knew about the Olso and Vallos armies before Olivia did, and they *wanted* to go. She just didn't know why.

"Stay here," Olivia said to Jacobo. "I want you to keep an eye on Em as we travel. Never let her out of your sight."

"Are you sure we should do this?" he asked. "If she's planning something, maybe we should stay here."

White-hot fury raced down Olivia's spine. "I don't care what she's planning. Are you really scared of a useless Ruined?"

Jacobo looked properly shamed. "Of course not."

"Good. We'll play along for now, figure out what she's doing, and stop it." She turned on her heel and stalked down the road. She'd briefly considered the same thing—telling Em she'd changed her mind, and she was just going to stay put in Westhaven for now.

But Jacobo's hesitation made her even more determined to go. She didn't care what Em was planning. If Olivia backed down now she'd never win support of the Ruined.

She visited the barn first and saddled the fastest horse, attaching her small bag to his saddle so everyone would know he was hers. Aren was supposed to help get the horses ready in the morning, and he'd certainly give her the slowest one if she left it up to chance.

Aren. He'd lied about going after Iria. He wouldn't have stayed with Em this long just to randomly take off for Olso. They'd concocted the whole plan for Olivia, like she was an idiot who would believe a word they said.

She left the horse and started down the road to Aren's house on foot. Jacobo would keep an eye on Em, and Olivia would take Aren.

There was a flicker of light in the window as she approached his home. She hung back, stepping off the road and sitting on the steps of a deserted house where she'd be hidden from his view.

He emerged from the house as the sun began to rise. He wasn't carrying a bag, which was odd, and he turned and began walking east, which was even more odd. There was nothing east.

She waited until he was a good distance away before she followed. He walked cautiously, occasionally looking over his shoulder, and she almost lost him twice because she was hanging so far back.

She felt the presence of a human suddenly. Maybe more than one. She had no way to tell.

Olivia stopped, fear seizing her chest as she watched Aren walk into a heavily wooded area. Had he and Em plotted something with the humans? Perhaps they were about to attack, and Olivia was stupidly following Aren around instead of preparing.

She darted forward, keeping low to the ground, and crept into the trees.

". . . should be close," she heard an unfamiliar voice say.

She lowered into a crouch and peered around a tree. Aren stood with a human. Just one. They were a good distance away, but he looked a bit familiar.

Aren said something she couldn't hear. She wanted to get closer, but wouldn't risk him discovering her. Not when she didn't know what he was up to with this human. She leaned forward as far as she dared.

The human shifted slightly, his face coming into view. She

dug her fingers into the dirt to keep from screaming.

Galo. The guard who was always with Casimir. He'd been with Casimir in Sacred Rock, when the idiot had let his cousin poison him. Em and Aren were working with the king of Lera.

"I'm always going to be southwest," Galo said to Aren. "Somewhere between you and Lera soldiers."

The *Lera soldiers?* Olivia took a deep breath to calm the Ruined magic boiling in her veins.

"I'll come find you every night, if I can," Aren said. "But I'll definitely come see you at least once, when we're getting close to the Olso and Vallos armies."

Galo nodded, and Aren said something too quiet for Olivia to hear. Galo smiled at him, and then Aren turned and began walking back in the direction of Westhaven. Galo headed in the opposite direction.

She waited until Galo had taken a few steps before she began trailing him. He wasn't as cautious as Aren, only glancing over his shoulder once and even snapping a twig with his boot. He wasn't used to moving stealthily.

The sun was higher in the sky when he slowed and waved at someone in the distance. Olivia stopped, shielding her eyes with her hand.

The Lera troops. They weren't in uniform, instead just wearing black and gray, but she might have known who they were even if she hadn't just overheard that conversation. They had the clean-cut, cocky look of a Lera soldier.

There were only ten of them, all on horseback, and she waited for the rest to catch up. Galo walked to them and said something she couldn't hear.

It became apparent a minute later that there were no more troops. Just these ten men and women. What did Aren and Em think they were going to do with *ten* Lera soldiers?

She frowned, and considered killing them all right now. That would certainly put a damper on Em's plan.

But she didn't know what that plan was. And she couldn't prove that Em knew these Lera soldiers. It was only Aren who had talked to Galo.

She took a step back. No, it was better to let this play out. The Lera soldiers could follow them. Ten humans were no match for her, and when she killed them, it would need to be in front of the Ruined. They would need to see Em's betrayal for themselves.

She walked back to Westhaven, occasionally breaking into a jog, and was gasping for breath when she arrived at her and Em's house. Jacobo was still lurking. Em stepped out of the house as Olivia approached.

"I was looking for you," Em said.

"Here I am." She took in a breath through her nose and tried to appear calm. "I was getting my horse ready."

"We're still leaving this morning, then?" Em asked.

"Of course. Why wouldn't we?" She stared Em down. Em acted like she was so much better than Olivia, but she had no problem looking her sister right in the eye and lying. Even their mother wouldn't have done that, and she was the most vicious

Ruined Olivia had ever known.

"Have *you* changed your mind?" Olivia asked. A tiny part of her, an ugly, weak part, hoped Em would say yes. There was still time to stop whatever plan she'd set in motion with Casimir.

"No," Em said.

"Good." Olivia turned on her heel. She couldn't stand to look Em in the eyes anymore. "Then let's go."

SEVENTEEN

"GET UP."

Iria rolled over in bed to look into the angry face of the guard above her. His blond mustache twitched.

"Now," he barked.

She slowly sat up, scanning the room for the doctor. She'd been in the medical wing for days, and it wasn't a surprise that her time was up. Still, part of her hoped that the doctor would jump in and say she wasn't ready to be moved yet.

"Doctor cleared you for release back into the general population," the guard said, dashing her hopes.

"You mean solitary."

"I mean general population." His lips twisted into a terrible smile and fear seized her chest.

She'd be attacked by the other prisoners. They knew that; it was why she'd been in solitary before. They must have found a way to convince the warden to lock her up with everyone else.

Her knees shook as she stood, and pain rippled through what was left of her foot. She leaned heavier on her good leg as she took a tentative step forward. The doctor appeared from behind a curtain. He looked her up and down.

"She should come every day to get those bandages changed," the doctor said. He grabbed her shoes from the floor and held them out to her. "Just wear one on your good foot." She obeyed, slipping her foot into the flimsy shoe and holding the other one in her hand.

"Fine." The guard jerked his head, indicating for her to walk in front of him.

Iria took a few more steps forward, wincing as she did. She was limping, badly, and panic shot through her body. She couldn't run. She'd barely be able to fight with a sword in this state—she'd stumble after the first attack. Of course, she'd never have access to a sword again, so maybe that didn't matter.

She lowered her chin into her chest and frantically blinked back tears. Crying when she entered the general population would only make things worse. She had to at least pretend to be tough.

The guard unlocked the door leading to the prisoner cells, and she lifted her head as they walked through. The cells were lined up on either side of her on two levels, stretching out a good distance in front of her. They walked past about twenty cells. She kept her head up, but didn't dare to glance to her sides.

The guard stopped. "Against the wall!" he yelled to the inmate inside.

Iria took in a deep breath as she looked up at her new cellmate. It was not good news.

The woman was older than Iria, probably in her thirties or forties, with dirty-blond hair and a body built for hard labor. Her expression mutated into disgust as she stared at Iria. They'd never met, but every prisoner must have known she'd show up here eventually.

She walked to the back wall and leaned against it as the guard opened the door. When Iria didn't move, the guard grabbed her by the shoulder and shoved her inside. Pain splintered through her foot as she landed on it, and she pressed her lips together to keep from yelping in pain.

The door banged shut behind her.

Her new cellmate stared at her, arms crossed over her chest. The cell consisted of a bunk bed, the bottom one clearly in use, and a sink and a toilet in the left corner. It felt too small for one person, much less two.

"I'm Iria," she said, just to prove she wasn't scared. Her voice sounded too weak to be convincing.

The woman took a step forward. "Julia."

Hope ticked in her chest. Maybe this woman wasn't so bad after all. Not everyone was fiercely loyal to Olso—in fact, an imprisoned citizen might not like her home country much at all.

Julia grabbed her by the collar, extinguishing the tiny spark of hope. She yanked Iria's face closer to hers. The fabric pulled tight across her neck, making it difficult to breathe.

"Bit small for a warrior, aren't you?"

Iria tried, and failed, to tug Julia's hand from her shirt collar. "I'm tougher than I look," she wheezed.

Julia barked a laugh and released her. Iria stumbled back and sucked in a breath.

"I'm in for life," Iria said, straightening her shoulders and leveling her gaze at Julia. "You should be careful. I have nothing to lose."

Julia's fist smashed against her cheek suddenly. Iria hadn't seen it coming, hadn't even realized Julia was so fast. The force of the punch hit her so hard her back hit the cell bars. Stars danced in her vision.

"None of us have anything to lose," Julia sneered.

EIGHTEEN

THE RUINED TRAVELED for two days, and Olivia barely spoke to Em during that time.

Em glanced at her sister as she laid a blanket on the grass. Around her, the other Ruined were preparing to sleep. Aren had just disappeared to check on Galo. Mariana stood at the edge of camp, surveying the jungle around them. She was on watch tonight.

Jacobo spread his blanket out not far from Em. Olivia had clearly told him to keep an eye on her. He was her constant shadow.

Ivanna walked to Em, extending a cup to her. "Tea?"

"Thank you." Em took a sip.

"How are you?" Ivanna asked. "You look tired."

"Everyone keeps saying that." Truthfully, she hadn't slept well in days. It was hard to sleep while traveling anyway, but she kept having nightmares about Olivia, lost in the woods and calling for help.

Ivanna squeezed her arm. She looked like she was about to say something, but Olivia strode toward them, hands on her hips. Ivanna slipped away.

"We should ditch the wagons," Olivia said.

"We need the wagons," Em said. "They have food for us and the horses, extra water, weapons, blankets, and all sorts of other things we might need."

"They're slowing us down," she protested.

"It's not about speed. We're going to cut off the troops in a few days anyway. We gain nothing by getting there faster." Em would have preferred to go slower, actually. Put off the inevitable for as long as possible.

Olivia wrinkled her nose, but she didn't protest. She glanced around at the Ruined, who were eating and talking quietly.

"You did a good job, Liv," Em said quietly, honestly.

Olivia regarded her suspiciously. "With what?"

"Getting the Ruined prepared. You're even better at it than our mother was."

Olivia snorted. "What do you want?"

"Nothing!"

"Please."

"Seriously. I was just . . ." Em shrugged, staring at the ground. *Feeling guilty.* "I just thought you should know."

"Thank you," Olivia said shortly. She began walking away, but then abruptly turned back, her lips set in a hard line. "Tell me the truth."

"About what?"

"You went to see Casimir, didn't you? That time you said you were going for feed."

Em considered for a moment. "Yes," she said finally. "I went to see him. He gave me the feed, actually."

Olivia's nostrils flared. "Why'd you come back?"

"I always intended to come back. I just wanted to see him." Em met her sister's gaze. "You said I could have him. We agreed. You do what you want, but you don't harm Cas."

"We did agree to that."

"Have you changed your mind?"

"No."

"I'll give him up if we can go back to Ruina," Em said, even though the thought of never seeing Cas again was horrifying. She had to try one last time. "If we turn now, it won't take us that long. We have plenty of supplies."

Olivia studied her. "You're suddenly so eager to go back to Ruina."

"It seems like the only good option at this point."

"Does it? What's wrong with this option?" Olivia gestured around them. "Aren was the one who suggested all of this. You didn't challenge him."

Em had nothing to say to that.

"Tell me the truth," Olivia said again.

Em looked at her sister. Worry seized her chest. Did Olivia know something?

"About what?" Em asked, her breath getting stuck in her throat. The words sounded strange. It was a terrible attempt at a lie.

Olivia just stared at her. She stared for so long that Em got uncomfortable and had to look anywhere but at her sister.

"I'm ditching the wagons," Olivia finally said. "We should cut off the troops soon anyway. Maybe tomorrow. We can come back for them if we want."

"Someone might take them," Em said.

Olivia shrugged and turned away. "Then we'll kill them, too."

On the third day of travel, the Ruined scout, Ester, informed Olivia that they were close to the Olso army.

"How many?" Olivia asked quietly. She jumped off her horse and walked a few steps away from the rest of the Ruined so she could talk to Ester privately. Em watched them curiously from atop her horse.

"Hundreds, that I could see," Ester said. "A thousand, maybe. I couldn't get a good look, though. I wanted to get back here as soon as I could. They were letting the horses take a break when I spotted them, so we have a little while to get in position."

"Good." Olivia resisted the urge to look at Em. "And did anything seem . . . off?"

"Off?" Ester blinked in confusion.

"Did you spot anything odd?"

"I don't think so." Ester gave her a strange look. "They looked like every other human army I'd ever seen."

"Right." A burst of nerves exploded in her stomach. She thought she'd figure out Em's plan before they encountered the army.

"Olivia?" Em called from behind her. "Has Ester spotted the army?"

"Yes," Olivia said. She turned to face Em and the rest of the Ruined. Her mind raced as she tried to decide what to do next.

"When do you want us in position?" Em asked after several seconds of silence.

Olivia's eyes skipped over the Ruined until she found Aren. He was in the back, slipping off his horse. He looked over his shoulder, in the direction they'd just come from.

"Jacobo, find a tree to keep watch," Olivia said. He took off toward a tall tree and began climbing. "Everyone else, get in position and secure your horses, but stay on the ground for now. Hide when Jacobo gives the word. I'm going to do a quick scout of the immediate area. I need to know where the warriors can hide."

Em nodded and dismounted her horse. She didn't glance back at Olivia.

Olivia stepped away from the Ruined and darted through the trees once she was out of sight. She caught a quick glimpse of Aren as he broke into a run, headed south.

She ran behind him. Her breath caught in her lungs, either from anger or lack of exercise. She'd spent so much time on her magical training she hadn't thought about her physical limitations.

She forced herself forward, almost losing him twice. But he ran in a straight line, and it was easy to keep him in her sights, even at a slower pace.

He finally stopped. She darted behind a tree and watched as he approached Galo, who was on a horse. He said something to Galo and the human nodded.

Aren ran back in the direction he came and Galo turned his horse to ride south. Olivia let out a frustrated breath as she broke into a run again to follow Galo.

She lost sight of him quickly and instead followed the sound of horse hooves pounding the ground. They stopped very quickly, and she skidded to a halt when the Lera soldiers she'd seen before came into view. There were still just ten of them.

Olivia braced her hands against her thighs and took a moment to catch her breath. She couldn't hear what they were saying from this distance, but it didn't matter. She didn't have time to waste. She needed to get back to the Ruined before the Olso army attacked.

She straightened, closing her eyes for a moment as she steadied herself. She stepped out from behind the tree.

Galo spotted her first. His body stiffened and his eyes rounded with fear. He said something to the soldier next to him. The soldier quickly grabbed the bow off her back and pointed an arrow at Olivia.

She waved her hand, throwing Galo and the soldier in

opposite directions. The remaining nine soldiers sprung into action all at once. Several grabbed their swords. One tried to hide behind his horse. Another just started running.

She snapped their necks, one after the other. Each one slumped to the ground as the others screamed. The screams died with the last *thump* of a body hitting the dirt.

Galo was several paces away, slowly getting to his feet. She strode to him.

"Galo, right?" she asked.

If he was scared, he was doing a good job of hiding it, she noted with some disappointment. He just stared at her without a word.

"You should kneel when a queen approaches you, Galo." She waved her hand and he fell face-first to the ground. She crooked her finger to make him slide across the dirt toward her. He yelped as his face collided with a large rock.

"Get on your horse," she said, pointing. "And don't even think of trying to take off. I'll snap your neck."

He didn't move.

"I'll also snap your neck if you don't get on that horse in the next three seconds," she said. "One . . . two . . ."

Galo quickly walked to the horse and swung his leg over the saddle. She would have smiled if she didn't want to tear out his heart so badly.

Blood poured from a cut over Galo's eyebrow and streamed down his face. He kept glancing around, like he thought someone would pop out and save him.

She got on the horse behind him. He leaned forward, like he didn't want her to touch him. The feeling was mutual.

"Go," she said.

"Where?" His voice was quiet, serious. He probably thought he was about to die. He was right.

"To the Ruined. You know where they are."

The horse began moving forward. She grabbed a fistful of his shirt to keep steady behind him.

"Faster," she said. Galo urged the horse forward.

It didn't take long to get back to the Ruined on horseback. She spotted Jacobo still in his tree, his gaze fixed to the west. The rest of the Ruined weren't in position yet. They'd moved the horses somewhere that Olivia couldn't see, and were milling around, anxious looks on their faces. Several turned and spotted Galo and Olivia.

She ordered Galo to stop and slid off the horse. Ester strode out in front of the Ruined, her brow crinkled.

"Is that a human?" she asked.

"Yes it is," Olivia said. "Aren! I found something of yours!"

He pushed through the crowd that was forming in front of her. The annoyance on his face immediately melted into horror. Em appeared next to him. She gasped, her fingers curling around Aren's arm.

Aren took a step forward.

"Stop!" Olivia yelled. He had the good sense to obey. "Take

another step toward him and I'll snap his neck." She glanced at Galo, making him topple off the horse. He landed on the ground with a grunt.

Aren stared at her. She knew he must be weighing his options—he could use his powers on her, but if she resisted just enough, she'd have plenty opportunity to kill Galo.

She smiled at him.

Around them, Ruined stood rooted to the ground, watching.

"Would you like to explain why there's a Lera guard following us?" Olivia asked. "How about the Lera soldiers I just killed?"

"I—I don't know," Aren said, entirely unconvincingly.

"If you don't know him, you won't mind if I kill him, then." She spun on her heel to face Galo and fixed her gaze on his neck. "Bye, Galo."

NINETEEN

GALO'S BODY WENT numb. A scream echoed in his ears, and for a moment, he thought he was the one yelling.

But the scream wasn't his. It was Olivia. She flew through the air and hit a tree with a *thunk*, her scream dissolving into a whimper.

Galo put a hand on his chest. His heart was still in his chest. His head was still connected to his body. He wasn't sure how that was possible, considering the look Olivia had just given him. He thought that her hateful face was the last thing he was going to see before he died.

Olivia pressed a hand to her head as she stumbled to her feet.

Aren shot forward and placed his body in front of Galo's.

Right. Aren. There was no one else who could have tossed Olivia like that and saved him.

Considering the look that Olivia was giving Aren right now, she knew it too. She was breathing heavily, eyebrows lowered, face twisted with rage. Galo thought that maybe he should be the one standing in front of Aren instead.

Blood dripped into Galo's eye. He'd nearly forgotten that Olivia had smashed his head into a rock. His body was still numb with terror, but he could feel a faint pounding beginning to form behind one eye. He wiped at it with the back of his shirtsleeve.

Around them, the Ruined were silent. A few were edging closer to protect Olivia, their eyes fixed on Aren and Galo.

"Don't move," Aren said quietly. He reached back and wrapped one hand around Galo's wrist. Galo was scared to breathe too loudly, much less move.

Olivia turned her furious gaze to Em. Galo had seen Em in some horrible situations—fleeing the Lera castle, finding Cas near death, stumbling injured through the jungle—but he'd never seen her look so upset. He could see her hands shaking, and her lips quivered like she was trying not to cry.

"You knew about him, didn't you?" Olivia spat at Em, pointing in Galo's direction. "You knew he was following us with Lera soldiers."

Aren turned his head over his shoulder. "Did she kill all the Lera soldiers?" he asked quietly.

"One may have survived," Galo said. "I wasn't able to check."

Em didn't reply to Olivia, which appeared to only make her

angrier. She looked at the Ruined around her, still pointing at Galo. He wished she'd stop.

"Don't you see what she's doing? She *betrayed* you," Olivia said.

"No, she didn't," an older Ruined woman said, stepping beside Em.

Olivia's lips parted. She stared at each of the Ruined in turn, her expression growing more furious by the second. "You let this happen? You're helping the people who *murdered* us?"

"Olivia," Em said gently. "It's complicated, and we—"

"It is not complicated!" Olivia yelled. "We do not partner with Lerans! We do not betray our fellow Ruined!"

"We have to make certain alliances to survive," Ivanna said. "If you can't see that, then—"

"Then *what?*" Olivia screamed. "What will you do?"

"Aren!" Em yelled. "Jacobo, behind you!"

Aren let go of Galo's wrist, and they both whirled around. Jacobo charged at Galo with a sword. Galo actually felt a burst of relief. A sword he could handle. He reached for the blade at his waist.

Aren yanked on his shirt suddenly, pulling Galo back and darting in front of him as Jacobo lunged. Galo stumbled, his hand slipping from his sword. Jacobo's eyes widened as he realized he was going to stab Aren, not Galo, and the blade twitched to the right. It sliced across Aren's waist.

Gasps echoed across the forest. Aren's shirt was immediately soaked through with blood.

"They're coming!" someone yelled from the tree. "From the west! We have to get into position now!"

Galo stared at the blood spreading across Aren's shirt. He put a hand out, ready to steady Aren if he was going to fall. "Is it deep?" he asked.

Aren didn't reply. He and Em were communicating with their eyes. He didn't seem the least bit bothered by the wound.

"It's a trap," Jacobo said.

Olivia stared at Em. "I killed all their Lera soldiers."

"That doesn't matter," Em said quietly. "I have no control over the Olso army. You either need to run or prepare to fight."

Olivia's eyes flashed. Em took a step back.

"Let's run," Jacobo said. "They're planning something."

"No," Olivia said sharply. "Get in position."

"But—"

"Get in position!" Olivia screamed. "I don't care what they're planning." She directed her next words at Em. "I can kill all the soldiers myself, if I have to."

Galo took in a sharp breath. He didn't think that was true, but Olivia looked determined enough to make it happen.

"Get in position!" Olivia yelled again.

Em took off first, headed into the trees to find a hiding spot. Aren grabbed Galo's arm and pulled him, frequently looking over his shoulder at Olivia. Galo's gaze was fixed on Aren's bloody shirt.

Aren led him west, away from the Ruined, and in the direction the Olso army would be coming from. The trees were a little thinner this direction, and they had to crouch low behind a mess of vines. It wasn't the best hiding spot, but they'd be the first to see the soldiers as they approached.

"Let me see," Galo said to Aren. He tried to lift Aren's shirt to examine his wound.

"It's just a scratch," Aren said, batting his hand away. "Get down."

Galo obeyed, sinking a little lower to the ground. He looked over his shoulder to see the last few Ruined running into position—climbing trees, disappearing behind bushes, and making gestures to each other. He'd lost sight of Olivia and Em.

The jungle went still and quiet. Galo looked at Aren to find him lifting his shirt, examining the gash on his side. It was more than "just a scratch," and actually looked rather painful.

"Why would you do that?" Galo whispered. "I'm good with a sword, I could have fought him off."

"You're welcome," Aren said wryly.

"I didn't mean—"

"I know. I'm fine. It's just one more scar." He said it easily, without bitterness. Galo's gaze fell to the burn scars on Aren's arms. He'd always tried not to stare at them, afraid it would make Aren uncomfortable, but he couldn't help himself this time. If someone had asked him, an hour ago, if he considered himself vain, he would have immediately said *no*. Now he was thinking about what kind of scar that rock was going to leave on his face, and thinking that he wouldn't want even half the scars that Aren had.

"Thank you," he said. He could tell Aren had noticed him looking at his scars. "For saving me," he added, like it wasn't obvious. He felt the sudden urge to do more for Aren, though he wasn't sure what that would be. He didn't have much to offer a powerful Ruined.

"Sure. I'm probably going to have to do it again in a minute, so don't leave my side no matter what. Got it?"

Galo might have laughed if he weren't still vibrating with terror from his encounter with Olivia. "Got it."

Aren leaned forward, bracing his hand against a thick vine as he looked for the Olso army. Beside him, Galo was on his knees, his hands pressed to the dirt like he was preparing to run at a moment's notice. Aren nodded his approval.

A few horses appeared in the distance. The riders weren't wearing Olso or Vallos uniforms, and Aren leaned forward just slightly, squinting at them. Several more horses appeared behind them.

"It's Jovita," Galo whispered. "The one in front, on the brown horse."

Aren glanced at him. "How can you tell?"

"She's wearing a royal belt. The sun is catching it. See?"

Aren looked again. Sure enough, a large buckle on her silver belt was shining in the sun, announcing her presence to everyone in the area. She wasn't used to traveling discreetly. Or she just didn't care.

There were about two hundred riders in all black around her, and Aren caught a flash of blue on several of their shirts. Ruined pins. They were hunters.

More horses appeared behind her, these wearing red-and-white warrior jackets. There were a few black and yellow Vallos uniforms scattered among them as well.

They kept coming, hundreds of them, probably more than Olivia and her Ruined supporters could handle. That was the plan, but his gut still twisted.

The army advanced in their direction. Some of the people in front were near enough to see now, and it was indeed Jovita. They were on the path directly in front of Aren and Galo, so close that Aren could have taken only a few quick steps to reach them.

The hunters passed, and a familiar blond man appeared behind them. He was on a horse, flanked by two warriors. August. The new king of Olso.

Aren's eyebrows shot up. He hadn't expected August to join the troops.

August's brow was lowered, dark circles beneath his eyes. He looked not just exhausted, but almost like a completely different person. Aren wasn't surprised. He knew what it felt like to lose your entire family in one swoop. He knew the toll it took.

August turned, scratching at a spot on his neck. His eyes met Aren's.

They stared at each other for a moment. August cut his eyes to the left, then the right. His gaze landed on the tree not far ahead, where Jacobo sat in the branches.

Galo took in a sharp breath. Aren curled his fingers around a vine, preparing to shout for the Ruined to attack.

August jerked his head at the men around him and cut his horse to the left. Away from the Ruined.

Jovita and the other hunters looked over their shoulders, frowning in confusion as they watched the Olso and Vallos soldiers take off.

"Is he . . ." Galo let his voice trail off.

"He's leaving her," Aren said. "They're not prepared to fight, so he's abandoning her." It was a smart choice, maybe the only one Aren had ever seen August make. The warriors weren't prepared to fight, their bombs and weapons packed away. By the time they got ready, Olivia would have already killed them all.

Of course, that meant there were only a couple of hundred humans for Olivia to fight off. She could handle a few hundred without a problem. Em's plan had failed.

A loud whistle rang through the forest. The signal from Olivia to attack. Jacobo dropped from the tree right next to Jovita's horse. Jovita's face changed from confusion to horror as she realized what was happening. A couple of hundred hunters were surrounded by Ruined on all sides.

"August!" Jovita yelled, like she'd thought he'd simply made a mistake. She clearly didn't know him very well.

Chaos erupted around Jovita and the hunters. Olivia dropped from her tree, and at least thirty other Ruined emerged from their hiding spots. Jacobo used his magic to shake the ground beneath the hunters and several fell off their horses. The animals darted away in fear.

Olivia killed three men with the flick of her wrist, but she was staring at the retreating army. A warrior fell off his horse as she killed him.

"Cowards!" she screamed after them. She whirled around and pointed at Aren. "Help me stop them!"

Aren stood slowly and shook his head. If August had stayed, he and Em and their Ruined supporters would be running right now. They'd be putting as much space between themselves and the armies as possible. But Aren could see Em, rooted to the ground as she watched the army leave.

Olivia turned left, then right. The Ruined who were supposed to be helping her were moving back, away from the hunters. Davi and Mariana ducked behind trees. Several other Ruined followed.

An arrow whizzed through the air, and Aren gasped as he watched it barely miss Olivia's face. It soared past her ear and found a different target—Jacobo. The arrow pierced his chest, making him stumble backward, blood dripping out of his mouth. He crumpled to the ground.

Olivia whirled around, finding the hunter with the arrow. Blood spurted from his chest and he slumped to the ground. The hunters around him fell as well.

"Why aren't you helping?" Ester screamed at the hiding Ruined. Ivanna and Em were nearby, crouched behind a bush, but neither of them moved. Ruined-made lightning streaked across the sky.

Olivia's face contorted with rage, but her anger at being deserted didn't slow her down. She spun and flung her arms, the hunters around her dropping to the ground as she killed them. Galo, still crouched on the ground near Aren's feet, made a strangled noise as he watched.

The two hundred hunters were fewer than fifty in a matter of minutes. Priscila pulled a tree down with her Ruined magic, crushing several more hunters beneath it. Other Ruined formed a circle around Olivia, guarding her as she surveyed the area. There were about twenty hunters left, all of them running for their lives. They darted through the trees in every direction.

Olivia pointed to each hunter as she killed them. One fell only a few paces from Aren. Another straight ahead of him. A few disappeared into the jungle, but Olivia killed the others.

Aren sucked in a breath. Human bodies littered the ground all around them. Olivia had killed almost every one of the two hundred hunters. And as far as he could tell, they'd only lost one Ruined—Jacobo was slumped on the ground, an arrow still sticking out of his chest.

Priscila collapsed against a tree, and several other Ruined followed suit. Olivia's eyes met Aren's, and he could see the exhaustion there. Blood was splattered across her white shirt. Her hands shook just slightly.

Em stepped out from behind the bush, Ivanna and several other Ruined following her. Mariana appeared next to Aren, looking at the scene in front of Olivia with wide eyes.

"Are the Lera soldiers still there?" Em asked Galo.

"No, she killed them all."

Em closed her eyes briefly. "Right. Of course she did."

"Oh, Em!" Olivia called. Her voice shook with rage.

Em slowly turned to face Olivia. Aren gestured for Galo to get behind Mariana.

Olivia took a step forward. She scanned the area, clearly searching for something. She knelt down and pulled a sword from beneath a dead hunter.

Olivia stood, sword pointed at Em. She lunged.

TWENTY

EM'S SWORD WAS in her hand. She hadn't even thought about it. When someone came at her with a weapon, she grabbed her sword.

But this someone was Olivia. Her sister was racing straight at her, blade pointed in front of her.

Em tightened her fingers around the handle of her sword but didn't lift it. She stood there, motionless, watching as Olivia drew closer. Em waited for her to slow down or lower the sword. She kept coming.

Em raised her sword at the very last minute. Olivia's blade hit hers. It would have been Em's chest if she hadn't reacted in time.

Olivia tried to point her sword at Em again, but Em easily

deflected it. The sword tumbled out of Olivia's hand. Em had told Olivia once that she should spend more time learning to use a sword. *It might be necessary one day*, Em had said.

Olivia glared at her like she could tell what Em was thinking.

"Was this your plan?" Olivia asked, gesturing to the dead bodies around them. "Lead us to a battle, and then refuse to fight? Did you think that would be enough to defeat *me*?"

Em didn't respond. She was still looking at the sword on the ground. Olivia would have killed her if she hadn't stopped it. Her sister would have driven that sword through Em's chest, and she was suddenly rooted to the ground, her body cold.

"Were you hoping they would kill me?" Olivia asked. "Were you hoping they would kill all of us?" She gestured to the Ruined behind her.

Em still had no response. She hadn't been hoping for that, no. Dreading it. Expecting it. She'd spent the last few days feeling sick over her decision, living with a constant rock in her stomach, and she didn't know how to handle the fact that Olivia was both alive and wanted to kill her.

"You're a *traitor*," Olivia said. "You and everyone who helped you."

"I'm sorry," Em finally said quietly. Her voice shook. "You left me no choice."

"You're *sorry*?" Olivia balled her hands into fists. "You're choosing that boy over me, over your *people*, and you're sorry?"

Em couldn't deny that. She had chosen Cas over her sister. She'd chosen a lot of things over her sister.

"It's bigger than that," a voice said. Ivanna was standing a few paces away from Em.

"You're worse than her," Olivia said to Ivanna. "A useless Ruined isn't a Ruined at all. But you should know better."

A rustling noise made them all turn, and Em saw a dark-haired girl jumping over bodies, trying to dart out of sight. Jovita.

Olivia waved her arm, sending Jovita crashing to her feet. "I know that one." She glanced over her shoulder at Ester. "Bring her here."

Ester trudged to Jovita and grabbed her by the shirt collar. Jovita clawed at Ester's hands as she dragged her across the dirt.

"Cas's cousin, right?" Olivia asked. "The one you so desperately didn't want to have the throne?"

"Yes," Em replied. Jovita landed in a heap behind Olivia, breathing heavily.

"Weren't you going to kill her?" Olivia asked. "Failed at that, too, I guess."

"Cas was going to kill her," Em said. "But he didn't need to."

Jovita looked startled, and then insulted, even through her fear.

"Get some rope and tie her up," Olivia ordered.

Jovita threw a panicked look at Em as Ester dragged her away. Em felt sorry for Jovita—she felt sorry for anyone Olivia took hostage—but there was nothing she could do for her. She had to make sure the Ruined made it away from Olivia.

"Let's go, Em," Ivanna said. "We're not leaving without you."

Olivia looked around, like she suddenly realized just how few

Ruined were left with her. She jumped forward and grabbed Em by the collar, bringing their faces close together. A few flecks of blood were spattered across her cheek.

It took Em a moment to realize what Olivia was doing.

Her sister stared at her, eyes wide and wild. Her brow crinkled. She was trying to use her powers on Em.

Em felt a flood of relief when nothing happened. Her body didn't move. It didn't even twinge. Dread quickly followed the relief. Olivia was trying to kill her. Again.

She jerked away. "Did you just try to use your powers on me?"

"You're not Ruined," Olivia snarled. "You're *nothing*."

Part of Em wasn't surprised to hear Olivia say that. Another part of her was devastated, thinking of every time Olivia told her she still had value even though she was useless. Those two words—*you're nothing*—immediately canceled out every kind thing her sister had ever said to her about her lack of Ruined power.

"Whatever I am, you can't control me." Em's words came out a little bitter.

Olivia's expression darkened. The truth hurt, it seemed.

A hand touched Em's arm. She turned to see Ivanna standing next to her.

"It's time to go," Ivanna said softly.

"I'll consider everyone who goes with Em a traitor," Olivia said. "You will not be welcome back."

"You're not our queen," Ivanna said. "She is."

AMY TINTERA

For a moment, it was as if Ivanna had slapped Olivia. The anger melted off her face and she just looked hurt, like the girl Em had once known.

Then Olivia lowered her eyebrows, pure rage in her gaze as she stared at Ivanna.

Ivanna screamed. Blood soaked through her shirt and trickled down her arms. Em pressed a hand to her mouth and squeezed her eyes shut. She heard the body drop a moment later.

Gasps echoed across the forest. When Em opened her eyes, she found even a few of the Ruined behind Olivia were horrified. Priscila stared openmouthed at Ivanna's dead body. Carmen looked like she was going to vomit. Em's stomach churned.

Olivia grabbed a fistful of Em's shirt and yanked her closer. "I'm going to *kill* you."

Em's heart dropped into her feet. Her sister wasn't being dramatic or just speaking in anger. She was dead serious.

Em thought briefly of their mother, of her big plans for Em to rule by Olivia's side. She wondered suddenly if their mother would be horrified by both of them, or if she would have taken Olivia's side. The uncertainty was too much, and Em had to push the thought away.

"Em, let's go," Aren said, his voice strained. He knew Olivia was serious.

Em tried to tug her shirt from her sister's grasp. Olivia held tighter.

"Why do you look so surprised?" Olivia asked. "You led me here hoping I would die, didn't you? You and I are exactly the

184

same. I just have the guts to kill you myself."

Em finally wrenched her shirt from Olivia and took several steps backward. Em was breathing heavily, even though she hadn't done anything strenuous. Tears pricked her eyes.

Olivia was pale, her shoulders sagging. The use of her magic on Ivanna had truly exhausted her. She glanced back at the other Ruined. They looked even worse.

She turned back to Em. Disappointment crossed her face, and Em realized with horror that she was upset she didn't have the strength to kill Em now.

Em quickly turned. Aren took her hand and squeezed it.

"You can run now, sister," Olivia said from behind her. "But I'm coming for you. I promise."

TWENTY-ONE

GALO FOLLOWED AREN and the other Ruined away from Olivia. They were all silent as they hurried through the jungle, to the spot where the Ruined had left the horses and wagons.

"Are we still going to Royal City?" a young woman whispered to Aren. She glanced at Em, who was pale and shaky as she untied a horse from a tree. "Because this plan . . ." *Failed*. She didn't have to say the word.

"We don't have a choice," Em said without looking at them. "We can't stay with Olivia. And we can't stay out here, with the Olso and Vallos armies so close by."

"It's the safest option," Aren said. "We need to get far away before they regain their strength." He looked over his shoulder, his face troubled. Galo knew he had to be thinking about his plan to go to Olso.

"It's fine, Aren," Em said. "You should go." She turned to face a worried girl hovering around her. "Mariana, can you make sure the wagons are ready to go?" Mariana nodded and hurried away.

"I can't go, Em," Aren said as she mounted her horse. "Olivia is livid. She's going to come after all of you."

"She's going to come after *me*," Em corrected. "And I don't need you to protect me from Olivia. We're so close to the Olso border. It would be ridiculous not to go now."

Aren rubbed the back of his neck, his face pained. He clearly wanted to go. "It's too dangerous to go by myself," he said with a sigh. "I'll wait until things settle down."

"When was the last time things settled down for us, Aren?" Em asked. "That may never happen."

"I'll go with you," Galo blurted out. Em and Aren both looked at him in surprise. He shared the emotion. The idea had been in the back of his mind for days, but he wasn't sure he was crazy enough to actually make the offer.

Mateo was going to be really, really mad.

He pushed the thought away and looked at Aren. "You need help, don't you?"

"Sorry?"

"Going to Olso. You just said it was too dangerous to go by yourself, and none of the Ruined can go right now. Wouldn't a human be more help to you anyway? You said we fuel your power."

"Y—yes?" Aren stuttered, unable to believe what Galo was clearly getting at.

"I'll go with you."

"Why?" Aren asked, with growing incredulity.

"You need help. I owe you."

"You don't owe me anything."

"I want to help." He turned to Em before Aren could protest. "If that's all right with you. Can you make it to Royal City by yourselves?"

"We can manage."

"Tell Cas I went with Aren? And tell Mateo . . ." Galo winced. "Um. Tell him I'm sorry. But I had to."

"Sure. I can do that." She traded a look with Aren, raising her eyebrows just slightly, and Aren nodded. If Galo were going to guess, that was a *You better not let him die* look. Nerves exploded in his stomach. Mateo was right. He really did feel the need to save everyone.

Em reached down and squeezed Aren's hand briefly. "Be careful in Olso. I hope you find Iria."

"I will."

Em took off, the Ruined following behind her. Aren strapped his bag to a horse, and Galo mounted another. He'd lost his bag when Olivia attacked, and he certainly didn't have time to look for it now.

"That cut looks bad," Aren said, pointing to his face. "Do

you want to bandage it before we go?"

He gingerly touched the gash above his eyebrow. His fingers came away bloody. "It's fine. I'd rather put some distance between us and Olivia first."

Aren nodded. He looked down at his shirt, which was covered in blood. "Good idea."

They rode west, in the direction of Olso, until it was pitch-black. Galo's head was pounding and he wondered if perhaps he'd hit it so hard that he'd lost his mind.

He was going to *Olso*.

With *Aren*.

There was still time to turn back. He could apologize and say that perhaps the blow to the head had been harder than he thought, because he'd temporarily lost his mind. Aren wouldn't try to make him stay.

Galo let out a long sigh. He wasn't going to back out. As much as the logical part of the brain was screaming at him, he couldn't ignore the little voice that said Aren needed, and deserved, his help.

"Let's stop here," Aren said after they'd been riding at least an hour. "There's a stream over there, and we should let the horses rest."

Galo nodded gratefully. He needed the rest as well. He hadn't slept much the past few days. He'd been busy racing messages between Aren and the Lera soldiers.

Aren dismounted his horse, then took the reins from Galo and led both horses to the stream to drink.

Galo slumped down against a tree, letting out a breath as he pressed his palms against his throbbing forehead.

Aren grabbed his pack off the horses and opened it. He pulled out a clean rag and poured some water on it, then grabbed a jar from the bottom of his bag. He walked to Galo and sat down, lifting the rag to his head.

He stopped suddenly, hand still poised. "Do you mind? We should clean it so it doesn't get infected." He held up the jar. "It's a salve to help heal the wound."

"Sure. Thanks."

Aren pushed Galo's hair back and wiped the cloth across the wound.

"You came prepared," Galo said.

"I had nothing to treat my burns after fleeing the Ruina castle," Aren said. "I'd never needed anything; Wenda Flores or Olivia healed me the few times I was injured. Now I always have a bag packed with medical supplies."

Galo winced as Aren dabbed the salve over the cut above his eyebrow. "Olivia didn't heal your burns after you rescued her?"

"She couldn't. You can't heal an old wound. The window is very short."

"And you can't heal at all?"

"Sadly, no." Aren scooted back and lifted his shirt to examine his own wound.

"Do you want help?" Galo asked.

"I'm fine." He grabbed a fresh rag and began cleaning the cut. "It doesn't seem fair, does it?"

"What?"

"That Olivia can heal and I can't. She has no interest in healing anyone." His next words were quieter. "Your power is a gift, but you have to choose what to do with it. My mother used to say that."

Galo didn't know how to respond, and silence stretched out between them as Aren finished tending to his wound.

"Why did you come with me?" Aren asked softly.

Galo let out a short laugh and leaned his head back against the tree. "Because I'm crazy?"

"That was my first guess." He paused. "You don't really even know Iria, do you?"

"I think we've spoken maybe five words to each other."

"So . . . ?"

Galo stared up at the sky, black in between the tree branches. "Mateo says I have to save everyone."

"Is that true?"

"Maybe. A little. I was a king's guard, it was my job to save people. Or protect them, at least."

"True." Humor crept into Aren's voice. "Are you going to protect me, then?"

"It seems so."

"You should sleep," Aren said, pulling a blanket from his pack. He tossed it to Galo. "I'll watch."

"Are you sure?"

"I'll need to sleep more when we get closer to the Olso border, so my powers are sharp. And you look ready to pass out."

Galo tucked the blanket under his head as he lay down. "Thank you."

"Thank *you*," Aren said quietly. "For coming with me."

"You're welcome," Galo said. "Do you think Iria is expecting you to come?"

It took Aren several seconds to answer. "I don't know. I told her I would, but . . . I don't think she's going to be happy to see me." He said the second part quietly, almost to himself.

"Why not?"

"I was going to leave her in Lera and go with the Ruined. She was really mad."

"You're going to break her out of prison. I think she'll come around."

"Would you?"

"Yes."

Aren looked at him skeptically. "Seriously?"

"Of course. You had a really tough choice to make. You couldn't just abandon the Ruined to Olivia. Not when you're the most powerful one."

"The most powerful one," Aren repeated under his breath, almost like he didn't believe it. "This is crazy, isn't it? Going to Olso right now?"

"Yes. But I'd do the same thing. Obviously."

"I guess that means you're crazy too."

Galo smiled as he closed his eyes. "I guess so."

TWENTY-TWO

CAS BURST OUT of the castle door and ran down the dirt path. The sun was setting, and he shielded his eyes as he squinted at the main gates. Four guards stood in front of them, matching terrified expressions on their faces.

"Open them," Cas said breathlessly.

The guards did as he ordered. Beside him, Jorge tensed. He gestured at a few other guards to surround Cas.

Em stood on the other side of the gates. She wore black pants and a loose gray tunic, both of which were dirty. Her dark hair was pulled back haphazardly, and she had deep circles under her eyes. She was obviously exhausted, her olive skin paler than usual.

Behind her were more Ruined, most of whom Cas had never

even seen before. There were about sixty, most of them just as haggard as Em.

But there was no one else. No Lera soldiers. No Galo.

His heart dropped as he met Em's eyes again. She didn't smile at him. He stepped forward slowly.

"Galo?" he asked, his voice barely a whisper.

"He's fine," Em said quickly. His heart shifted back into place. She closed her eyes briefly, like she was too tired to think. "I'm sorry. I should have said it right away. He went with Aren to Olso. To rescue Iria."

"He went *where?*"

"I know, but he offered. He said to tell Mateo he had to, and he's sorry."

He blinked, his brain still trying to process it. "Olso. With Aren." Mateo was going to love that. He glanced behind him, but Mateo wasn't among the guards. He was probably on duty in a different part of the castle.

"The others, though . . ." Em took in a shaky breath, and he realized she was trying not to cry. "Olivia killed all the Lera soldiers. I'm sorry, Cas. She almost killed Galo, too, but Aren saved him just in time. And the Olso army—" She cut herself off suddenly, glancing at the guards and others around Cas like she'd just realized they were there. She looked so lost, so upset, that he couldn't stop himself. He rushed forward and wrapped his arms around her. He pulled her tight into his chest. She squeezed him in return, but it was a weak effort.

"I failed, I'm sorry," she said into his neck. "The Olso and

Vallos armies took off as soon as they spotted us. Olivia killed all the hunters and captured Jovita."

He started a bit at the information that Olivia had taken Jovita. He wasn't sure what Olivia could possibly want from her.

"I'm just glad you're here," he said softly. He pulled away, lacing his fingers through hers, and looked at the Ruined behind her. Nerves twisted in his stomach. "We have rooms prepared. Will you come inside?"

A stone-faced young woman just stared at him. "Em," she said.

Em pulled her hand out of his and walked to the Ruined, saying something to them that he couldn't hear. Several of the Ruined looked alarmed at the prospect of going into the Lera castle.

"You'll be safe here," Cas called.

The woman leaned to look around Em and rolled her eyes. "Please. We won't be safer here than we are anywhere else."

He opened his mouth to protest, but the look Em shot him made him shut it. The Ruined was right, as much as he hated to admit it. The castle could be attacked tomorrow for all he knew.

Em said something that finally made them all trudge forward. He took her hand again and led them down the dirt path. Several people were gathered in the front entryway to see what the commotion was about, Violet and Franco among them.

"The Lera soldiers?" Violet asked. Cas shook his head.

"I'll set up a meeting right away and Emelina can tell us what happened," Franco said. "Violet, get Julieta from—"

AMY TINTERA

"No," Cas said quickly. Em was staring straight ahead, her eyes dull like she wasn't even listening. "They'll rest first."

Franco seemed like he was going to argue, but Cas gave him a look that meant there was no room for argument.

"I can tell them," Em said. She'd been listening after all.

"It can wait," he said, squeezing her hand.

He led them through the castle and to the west wing, where the guards' quarters were. The rooms had been half empty since they returned anyway, and they'd squeezed an extra cot into each room so it could house three people. Staff members scurried around him, opening doors down the long hallways and ushering the Ruined in. They were visibly nervous, and he watched as one girl quickly darted away from a Ruined to avoid touching him.

"They're bringing some food," he said, to no one in particular. A passing Ruined man looked at him suspiciously. He glanced at Em, who was still by his side. "Is this all right? There are some rooms upstairs as well, if you want to take some Ruined up there."

"I think they'd rather be together."

"Will you stay with me?" he asked quietly. He couldn't imagine leaving her here, not when she looked ready to crack at any moment.

"Just give me a moment," she said, and walked away from him. She stepped into a room and emerged a few minutes later, looking upset.

"It's fine if you need to stay down here with them," he said. "If it will make them feel better."

"Nothing will make them feel better." She said it a little bitterly as she passed him. He turned to follow her, and they went through the corridor and up the stairs. He gently steered her in the direction of his room. She looked over her shoulder at the royal suite, which he still hadn't moved into, but didn't say anything as they went to the room that had always been his.

They walked through his library and into the bedroom. Em looked down at her hands, like she'd just realized something.

"I left my bag on my horse."

"A staff member will bring it in," he said. "Your clothes from before are all still in your old room. I'll have someone bring them over."

She walked across the room and sat on the chest at the end of the bed. She looked down at her arms, which were flecked with dirt. "I need a bath."

Cas knelt down in front of her and took her hands in his. "I'll have them draw one for you." He was quiet for a moment, unsure if he should ask what happened. She looked devastated, and he didn't know if it was about Olivia, or if something was going on with the Ruined. He realized suddenly he knew very little about Em's relationship with her own people.

"Olivia wants to kill me," Em finally said. "She already tried, actually. She and the other Ruined were just too weak to fight me."

He tightened his fingers around her hands. "She can't, though, can she? Kill a useless Ruined?"

"Not with her powers, no. But she can find other ways. She

AMY TINTERA

will. Find other ways." She met his gaze. "It may not be safe for you to be near me."

Cas shook his head. "We're safe here, for now. For tonight, at the very least."

She nodded, closing her eyes briefly. He got the impression that she didn't agree, but she was too tired to argue about it.

He stood and lightly kissed her forehead. She wrapped her arms around his waist, letting out a long sigh as she leaned against his chest.

"We're together now," he said quietly. "Everything will be fine."

TWENTY-THREE

AREN HAD UNDERESTIMATED Olso.

He'd thought their defenses would be weakened, that the border would be less guarded than usual with all the warriors in Lera.

If they were spread thin, Aren had picked the wrong spot to try to cross into Olso. All the border posts were manned, warriors stationed in basic wooden towers placed at strategic points.

Aren and Galo stayed hidden in the trees as they crept along the border, scoping out the posts.

"I think in between these two," Aren said. He looked left, then right, but it was too dark to see either post from this location. It was unlikely they could pass through without being spotted, but if they were fast enough, the warriors might not be able to catch them. "I guess."

"That doesn't instill a lot of confidence," Galo said.

"Do you have a better idea?"

"No," Galo said. "But they're going to aim for the horses."

Aren glanced back at them. "I think we should leave them."

"And go on foot?"

"Like you said, they're going to aim for the horses, whether with arrows or the cannons. We likely won't make it far on them, and I don't want you getting crushed to death under a horse."

"I see your point," Galo said. "So we're going to run fast. And hope their aim with those cannons isn't great?"

"We're going to hope they don't have those ready to go." Aren raised an eyebrow. "Having regrets about this yet?"

"Not yet, but there's still time." He looked back at the horses. "It's going to take us a long time to get to the capital on foot."

"The warriors have horses at every post," Aren said. "They're going to use them to chase after us. We'll grab them after I get rid of the warriors."

"That easy, huh?" Galo asked.

"If the warriors stay on those horses we're dead, so yeah, I'm hoping it's that easy." Aren peered through the trees at the posts. They were still far enough away not to be spotted, but just barely. The element of surprise was the best thing they had going for them.

"What do you want me to do?" Galo asked. "Hold your hand?"

"Yes, actually. Not right away, but as soon as I start using my Ruined magic. Just grab on to me."

"Got it."

"And tell me if you see anyone coming. I want to try to keep them all at a distance. If anyone recognizes me they'll know I'm coming for Iria."

Galo nodded.

Aren stepped forward, Galo close behind him. They kept low to the ground in the darkness.

"Did Olivia get in unnoticed?" Galo asked quietly.

"No. The warriors saw them coming and sent a whole mess of people to greet them, from what I've heard."

"And Olivia killed them all."

"Yes."

"She didn't do us any favors there," Galo grumbled.

Aren straightened as they walked out of the trees. They were in sight now, if the warriors in the tower were paying attention and could see in the dark.

"Now?" Galo asked.

"Now." Aren broke into a run. Galo's shoes pounded the dirt beside him.

They ran in silence for at least a full minute, and Aren wondered if perhaps they'd gotten lucky. Maybe the warriors couldn't see them. The moon was only a sliver tonight.

An arrow whizzed through the air and sailed past his ear. Horse hooves pounded the ground.

"Behind you to your left!" Galo shouted. "And your right! And directly behind us!"

Aren skidded to a halt and grabbed Galo's arm. He stumbled as Aren pulled him to a stop.

Through the dark, he could see two horses to his left, one to his right, and three straight ahead.

He focused on the warriors to his right first. Galo's frantic energy pounded through his body, and he easily lifted the men from the horses and tossed them backward.

Arrows whizzed past his face, and Galo suddenly let out a gasp. Blood trickled down his arm from where an arrow had scraped him.

"Can you do this any faster?" Galo asked. The three warriors in front of them all had arrows pointed in their direction.

Aren took them all out at once, throwing them a little farther than the other warriors. Their landing wouldn't be soft. They wouldn't be able to grab their bows and run after them again.

Aren threw the last warrior off his horse and let go of Galo's arm. "Are you all right?" he asked.

"It's just a scratch."

Aren whirled around and found three of the horses stopped not far away, the other three still galloping even though their riders were gone.

"Get that horse," Aren said, running toward them. He mounted the warrior's horse quickly and urged him forward. "Do you see the tracks?" he yelled to Galo as they rode.

"There!" Galo pointed to the right, where the silver tracks glinted in the moonlight.

Aren glanced behind him. Nothing. The warriors hadn't known they were coming, and it was unlikely they counted on a Ruined being one of the intruders. It would take them a while to ride to the other posts, spread the word, and assemble more warriors to chase them down.

"Let's stick to the tracks as long as we can!" Aren yelled to Galo. Em had told him that the tracks led straight to the capital.

They rode until the sun came up. They abandoned their horses and went on foot since they would draw attention on the warriors' horses, and at the moment, they were trying to blend in.

Aren could tell they were nearing the capital—he could hear the sound of voices on a nearby road, and he could sense the presence of a large number of humans nearby. A carriage passed them, and the coachman cast a curious glance over his shoulder.

Galo stopped, touching Aren's arm. "Do you have something to cover your neck?"

Aren's fingers flew to the Ruined marks there. He'd been stupid to forget about them. He'd gotten used to his scars covering them, but there were plenty that were visible these days. He dropped his bag on the ground and dug through it.

"I don't think I have anything. I could rip up the blanket to make a scarf, I guess. Might look weird, though."

"Here," Galo said, gesturing for him to get up. He adjusted

the collar of Aren's coat so it was standing up, covering his neck. "Keep it like that and no one can see. You'll just have to keep the coat on, even if you get hot."

"Thanks," Aren said. Despite the clear skies and sun, it was much cooler in Olso than in the Lera jungle. He stuck his hands in his pockets. He needed to keep those out of sight too.

They walked until the city came into view. The castle was to the east, its peaks rising high into the sky, visible even from a distance. The city stretched out below it, with buildings bigger than those in Lera, the sidewalks more cramped with people. The streets were dirtier than in Lera, but there were several men dressed in gray jumpsuits scooping up the trash and putting it in bags. One frowned at Aren as he tried to get to an apple core by his foot.

Aren stepped aside, touching his collar. There were more people than he'd expected.

"So what's the plan?" Galo asked. "Are we just strolling into the prison? Do we even know which prison she's in?"

"No. I need to find out which prison she's in, and what it's like. Most likely, it's heavily guarded, and it will be tough for me to take on that many guards by myself. If they manage to corner me and get me in a cell it's all over."

"So we need someone to tell us which prison she's in, and maybe the basic layout."

"Right."

Galo scrunched up his face as he surveyed the crowds around

them. "Got anyone in mind?"

Aren released a breath. "Yeah."

"Who?"

"Iria's parents."

TWENTY-FOUR

EM WOKE TO the sun in her eyes. She blinked, the room around her slowly taking shape. The Lera castle. Cas's bedroom. He hadn't closed a window last night, and the breeze rustled the curtains, letting in streaks of sunlight.

She turned. Cas was dressed but barefoot, standing at the half-open door and speaking softly to someone she couldn't see. He closed the door and turned, his eyes lighting up when they met hers.

"I'm sorry. I was trying to let you sleep."

"What's wrong?" She propped herself up on her elbows.

He crossed the room and climbed onto the bed. "Nothing's wrong. That was just Franco. I asked him to push our morning meeting to later."

She lay back down with a sigh and rubbed her forehead. The sun peeking through the windows was bright. She'd slept late.

Probably because she'd barely slept at all since leaving Olivia. She'd been so foggy-headed yesterday that she barely remembered how she got to Cas's room.

The Ruined were mad at her. And scared. Ivanna was dead, and Em had underestimated what a good job she was doing keeping the Ruined calm. Gisela might have taken Em's head off yesterday, if Em were human.

"I need to go check on the Ruined. Did they eat? We need to find them some clothes, too. And I should probably scout the area around Royal City with a few Ruined tonight, to see if we spot Olivia. Maybe some guards should come with us? Do you think—" She stopped talking suddenly as Cas stretched out beside her and pulled her into his arms. She closed her eyes and buried her face in his chest, losing her train of thought. He smelled like the Cas she'd known when she was here as Mary. The air of the castle clung to him, with scents of fresh flowers and pastries and the ocean.

"A maid brought you some clothes, they're in the wardrobe," he said, his lips brushing the top of her head. "So feel free to dress and see the Ruined whenever you like. I'll see what we can do about getting the Ruined clothes and other essentials. And you can go out looking for Olivia if you want, but I like you better right here."

A smile crossed her lips. She didn't think she'd smiled in days, but the smile came easier than she would have thought. His

words last night—*We're together now. Everything will be fine*—
had seemed so naive at the time, but now, as she wrapped an
arm around his waist and held him tight, they didn't seem so
far-fetched.

Guilt crept into her chest. She couldn't stop thinking about
Olivia's words—*You're choosing that boy over me, over your people.*
She knew her sister was just trying to get under her skin, but the
words still stung.

Because she *had* chosen Cas over her sister. And she would
do it again. Like Ivanna said, it was bigger than that, bigger than
just the two of them, but Em couldn't deny that she was happy to
see him again. She could push thoughts of her sister away when
she was in his arms. She didn't know what kind of person that
made her.

She slowly untangled herself from him. "Can you give me a
few minutes?"

"Of course." He leaned forward and pressed a kiss to her forehead, then climbed out of bed.

He left her to get dressed, and Em found the clothes—her
Princess Mary clothes—in the wardrobe. She pulled on pants
and a soft blue tunic and tied her hair into a braid.

She found Cas waiting for her in his library, perched on the
edge of a chair. They had so much to talk about that she didn't
know where to begin—the Ruined downstairs, Olivia, their marriage, stripping the monarchy of power. But she didn't want to
talk about any of it. So she kissed him instead.

He took in a sharp breath and stood, his fingers finding their way into her hair. She grabbed fistfuls of his shirt and kissed him like she might not get another chance. Maybe she wouldn't. Maybe Olivia would burst through the doors in a minute and kill every last one of them. It happened to Em before. She'd hugged her mother good night and the Lera king broke down the door to the castle not two hours later.

She even considered pushing him back into the bedroom and taking off the clothes they'd just put on. They could lock the door and ignore all the responsibilities waiting on the other side of it for a day.

She pulled back, pressing a soft kiss to his cheek before stepping away from him. She wouldn't do that to the Ruined. And she wasn't even sure she wanted to have sex with Cas for the first time now, with this heaviness pressing down on her chest. She suspected she'd just be doing it to feel something besides sadness, and they both deserved better.

"I'm going downstairs to check on the Ruined," she said. "Am I allowed to wander the castle freely? Are the Ruined?"

"You can go wherever you like. We have Weakling stored in the shed by the stables, so you'll probably want to tell them to steer clear of that."

"How much did they find?"

"You're welcome to go look. The shed is stuffed full of boxes. Floor to ceiling."

She raised her eyebrows, impressed. "I'll let them know. We'll need to get started lining shields and armor with it right away. The other Ruined can't do it, obviously. I'd like a few soldiers and guards to help me, since they'll be the ones using it. Can you spare people?"

"Sure. I'll talk to Jorge and see who's free."

"Do you have guards stationed at the shed now?"

"Yes. Two."

"We may want to take over guarding it."

He studied her for a moment. "We've weeded out everyone who was loyal to Jovita. You can trust my guards."

She almost laughed. *Trust his guards.* How ludicrous. "I'm sorry, Cas, but no. I trust you. I trust several of your advisers, in a way. But I don't trust a large group of humans I don't know."

"They've sworn to protect me, and I made sure they know that means they protect you, too."

"It is way too early to expect that sort of loyalty from them," she said, exasperated. She liked Cas's optimism most of the time, but he couldn't expect blind trust from her, and especially not from the other Ruined. "I'm not saying I think they're going to attack us. But you can't be sure they're all completely on your side. You could very well have a spy from Jovita on your guard right now."

He cracked a knuckle. "I don't care if the Ruined want to guard it. I would think you'd all want to rest for a while, not spend your time standing in front of a shed, but if that makes you happy, be my guest."

Annoyance surged in her chest at his sarcastic tone. "Everything isn't fine now, Cas, and we can't pretend it is."

"I know. I really do. But how do you expect the Ruined to

trust us if their queen doesn't?"

"They won't automatically trust you just because I do. I don't hold that kind of sway with them."

"Really?" He lifted his eyebrows in an almost amused way. "Because you got all of them to betray one of the most powerful Ruined ever and sleep in the castle of their former enemy. I think your opinion means everything to them."

She didn't know how to respond to that. He wasn't wrong. The Ruined had followed her here even though her plan to stop Olivia had failed. They'd been angry last night, but they were still here. There were no reports of them all fleeing the castle last night.

"You know it's not in my nature to trust people. I have no reason to," she said quietly.

He stepped forward, cupping her face in his hands. "Em. Of course you have a reason to."

TWENTY-FIVE

THE UBINOS' HOUSE was listed in the town registry, which Galo found while Aren waited outside City Hall. They walked east, to a neighborhood full of giant houses.

They stopped in front of number twenty-two, an impressive two-story home with a sweeping balcony upstairs.

"Let's pretend I'm from Lera as well," Aren said.

"You don't think they'll be accepting of a Ruined?" Galo asked.

"They're important people in Olso. Their first priority will be protecting Olso. We just attacked them. You, they owe."

"How do you figure?"

"I don't know. They attacked Lera. At the very least, they can feel smug."

"Got it."

Aren walked up the gravel path that led to the large wooden and stained-glass front doors. He tapped the knocker against the door twice.

A young woman in a gray-and-red uniform answered. "May I help you?"

"We're looking for Claude and Veronica Ubino," Aren said. "We're friends of Iria's."

The woman's face fell. "One moment." She closed the door.

It didn't open again for at least a full minute. When it did, a tall, dark-haired woman who looked very much like an older version of Iria stood in front of them.

"What do you want?" she asked.

"I'm Aren, and this is Galo, and we're friends of Iria's. We were hoping to speak with you."

A man appeared behind the woman, his eyes wide.

Iria's mother took a step closer to them. "You shouldn't go around claiming to be friends of Iria's. She's a traitor."

Aren's heart dropped and he slid his hands farther into his pockets, hiding his Ruined marks. He realized suddenly that he'd had high expectations for Iria's parents. He thought they'd start crying and invite him and Galo inside. He thought they'd be relieved to hear Aren's side of the story—that Iria had saved his life when the warriors had betrayed the Ruined.

He'd imagined his own parents. They would have stood by Aren no matter what, and he'd wanted that for Iria.

He had to swallow down the lump in his throat before he was

able to talk. "We were wondering if perhaps her sentence was too harsh," he said carefully. "Maybe—"

"Her sentence fit her crime," Iria's mother spat. "Don't come back here. We have nothing to do with that girl anymore." She slammed the door shut.

Aren and Galo shared a pained look as they turned away from the house. Aren hoped Iria didn't know how her parents felt.

He heard the door open again and he quickly turned back. Iria's father stepped outside and jogged to them.

"The appeals won't work," he said in a hushed tone, his voice cracking just slightly. "But Bethania Artizo is working on one, if you'd like to talk to her."

"Who is that?" Aren asked.

"A friend of Iria's. She's at Fifteen Grundle Place. Don't come back here." He started to turn away.

"Thank you," Aren said quickly. "She did the right thing, you know."

Iria's father took in a shaky breath, nodded once, and strode back toward the house.

Aren watched him go. Maybe Iria's parents would be secretly relieved when he busted her out of prison. They would never see her again, but at least they would know she wasn't rotting away in a cell for the rest of her life.

They walked out of the neighborhood and back to the center of town. Galo asked an old man for directions, and he pointed them to a line of small identical homes at the edge of town. There were rows of them, perhaps housing for warriors or other city workers.

They found number fifteen and Aren knocked. A young woman with wild dark curls and a round, cute face answered the door.

"Bethania?" he asked.

She looked him up and down. "Yes?" she said hesitantly.

"We're friends of Iria's. We—"

Bethania leaped forward, grabbed Aren's hand, and yanked it out of his pocket. Her eyes widened as she stared at his Ruined marks.

"Aren?"

He nodded, swallowing down a sudden wave of emotion. Iria had told her about him.

She nodded at Galo, still holding Aren's hand. "Who is this?"

"Galo. He's from Lera."

"You two are insane," she muttered. She dropped his hand and stepped back. "Come in, come in. Before someone sees you."

Aren and Galo stepped inside, and Bethania closed the door behind them. She ushered them into a small sitting room at the front of the house and gestured for them to sit on the couch. Papers were spread out all over the table in front of it, and Aren leaned forward to study them.

Bethania sat in the chair across from them, reaching over to shuffle the papers into order. "I'm working on Iria's appeal. She's only allowed one, so I'm doing as much research as possible."

"How do you know Iria?" Aren asked.

"We dated a couple of years ago. We're friends now."

Aren blinked, surprised, and wondered if perhaps he'd read Iria completely wrong.

A smile twitched at the edges of Bethania's mouth. "Don't worry, she dates both men and women. She told me all about you, in fact."

Galo made a sound like he was trying not to laugh. Aren felt his face warm.

"You've seen her since she came back?" Aren asked.

"No, only at the trial. But I saw her briefly after she came home from Lera the first time, before heading to Ruina. She told me about her time in the castle and the jungle with you and Em."

A lump formed in Aren's throat. Iria had told Bethania about him even before their time together in Ruina. He'd still been guarded and suspicious of her back then.

"You know I'm not here to help with an appeal, right?" he asked.

Bethania sighed and rubbed her forehead with two fingers. "I was afraid of that."

"Would an appeal work?" Galo asked.

"If I could . . ." She trailed off, then pressed her lips together. "No. It would take a miracle. And Iria's already been attacked once in prison. I'm not sure she has that much time."

"What?" Aren sat up straighter. "Is she all right?"

"I heard she was injured, but not too seriously. Some guards claimed it was an accident, but they didn't even bother trying to hide the truth."

"Then I need to get her out as soon as possible," Aren said. "Do you know anything about the prison? How hard would it be to break in?"

Bethania looked from him to Galo and back again. "It's just you? And a Leran?"

"Yes."

"He's the most powerful Ruined alive," Galo said.

"Still." Bethania appeared skeptical. "She's in the most secure prison in the country."

"I can take out thirty warriors just by looking at them," Aren said. "If I can just get an idea of what the prison is like, I can get her out of there in minutes."

"And take her where?"

"Lera."

Bethania winced slightly. She clearly didn't like the idea of Iria leaving for Lera forever.

"It's her only option," Aren said quietly. "You can't tell me she'd rather stay in a prison in Olso for the rest of her life?"

Bethania shook her head. "No, she wouldn't. And from what I heard, they forced her back to Olso? She'd already decided to stay in Lera?"

Aren nodded.

"Then you should take her back to Lera." She leaned forward, rubbing her palm across her forehead. "You're going to have quite a time getting in. And out. But I think I can get you the general layout."

"Any chance of help on the inside?"

"None."

"Has there been anyone else?" Aren looked around, like they might pop out. "Anyone interested in helping Iria?"

Bethania waved one finger in a circle. "This is it."

"Seriously?" Galo asked. "She must have had friends. They all deserted her?"

"In their opinion, she deserted them first." She met Aren's eyes. "Honestly, I'm glad you're here. I don't think she has anyone else."

Aren blinked to keep back the sudden threat of tears. "Let's get to work, then."

TWENTY-SIX

CAS PUSHED OPEN the door to the north wing of the castle and stopped. A common room stretched out in front of him, and the two guards sitting in faded red chairs scrambled to their feet. It was evening, almost dinnertime, and the guards were out of uniform, in loose, comfortable clothing.

"No, don't get up," he said quickly. The guards didn't sit. He'd never been in the guards' quarters before—he figured they probably needed a space to relax where they didn't have to worry about the royal family—but he wanted to find Mateo without having another guard fetch him.

"Can we help you with something, Your Majesty?" one of the guards asked.

"I'm looking for Mateo. Is he around?"

"I think he's in his room, Your Majesty," the guard said. "I'll take you."

"No, that's fine. Can you just tell me which one it is?"

The guard hesitated, like he wasn't sure if this was a test. He slowly pointed to the hallway to Cas's right. "Down that hallway, last door on the left."

"Thank you," Cas said, turning on his heel and walking down the hall. He stopped at the last door and knocked.

"What?" Mateo's voice called from inside.

"May I come in?" Cas asked.

The door swung open and Mateo's eyes widened when they settled on Cas. "I'm—I'm sorry, I didn't—"

"I know, you weren't expecting me." He bit back a laugh.

"That's an understatement." He stepped back, brow furrowed in confusion. "Do you want to come in? Or should I come out?"

Cas stepped into the small room, which contained only two small beds, a desk, and a wardrobe.

"Did you and Galo share a room?" he asked, realizing suddenly that he'd never been in Galo's room when he lived down here.

"No, rooms are assigned by the captain of the guard. I was assigned to this one months ago, when I first arrived."

Cas perched on the edge of one of the beds. "That must have been tough, trying to have a relationship when you both have roommates."

Mateo let out a breath as he sat on the other bed. "Are you here to tell me bad news?" he asked, his words rushed. "Because I know Galo didn't come back with Em, and someone told me he's not dead, but he's not here."

"It's not bad news," Cas said. "I mean, it's not *good* news, but—" He cut himself off before he terrified Mateo. "He went to Olso with Aren."

Mateo blinked several times. "He went to Olso. With Aren," he repeated slowly.

"Aren is breaking Iria out of prison. From what I understand, Galo offered to help."

"Iria?" Mateo's expression grew even more incredulous. "He doesn't even know Iria! *I* know Iria better than he does—I traveled to the southern province with her and Aren."

"I don't know any more than you do. Galo said to tell you he was sorry, but he had to."

Mateo made an annoyed noise. "He *had* to. Of course he did." He flopped back on the bed with a moan. He quickly sat up again. "I'm sorry, I didn't mean to be rude."

"Mateo, I'm not here as the king. Do whatever you want."

He dropped back on the bed dramatically. "It's just dumb. We were running for our lives for weeks, and now, when we're finally safe, he decides to go back out again. Stupid savior complex."

"Does he have a savior complex?"

"Yes. He'll deny it, but he definitely does. It's how we ended up together."

"I assumed you met on the guard," Cas said.

"We did. He was assigned to some of my training when I

joined. But we didn't really get along until we were both on leave and—" He stopped suddenly, sitting up. "I just realized that maybe I shouldn't tell you this."

"Now you have to tell me."

"It involves us doing something illegal. But for a good reason," he added hastily.

"Unless you're about to tell me you were partnered with Em to kill us all, I really don't care."

"Not quite that bad." He took a breath. "It was my brother. He was caught stealing. He's not a bad guy, it's just that our family was going through a hard time and he's not known for his good decisions." He looked anywhere but at Cas. "And, at that time, all criminals were being sent to join the hunters."

"Oh," Cas said, the shame of being his father's son hitting him full force, once again.

"I didn't think it was right, for him to basically be sentenced to death or become a murderer just for stealing some food," Mateo said quietly.

"It wasn't," Cas agreed.

"So I decided to bust him out of prison, when they were transferring him," Mateo said. "Galo came through town on his way back to the castle, and I was supposed to join him. But I was panicking at the time, and I told him everything, and he stayed and helped me."

"You two were successful, then? You saved your brother?"

"We did. And Galo didn't even know me that well at the time.

If we'd been caught, the two of us would have been sentenced to the hunters as well. But he can't pass up the opportunity to save someone."

"Maybe he already liked you," Cas said.

Mateo ducked his head with a smile. "Maybe."

"Where's your brother now?" Cas asked.

"Um, he was moving around a lot."

"I didn't ask so I can punish him." He reached over and grabbed a pen and a slip of paper from the desk and handed them to Mateo. "Write his name down, along with the town where he committed the crime. I'll send a pardon."

Mateo blinked. "Seriously?"

"Yes. I've pardoned at least a hundred criminals recently who fled instead of joining the hunters. I'm happy to."

Mateo looked like he might cry as he grabbed the paper and scribbled on it. "Thank you."

"You're welcome."

Mateo handed the paper back to Cas. "Galo really didn't say anything else? No hint as to why he's going to save an Olso warrior he barely knows with a Ruined he doesn't even like?"

"I think he and Aren are becoming friends, actually," Cas said.

"Oh, wonderful. That makes me feel better. Galo's becoming friends with the ridiculously attractive all-powerful man."

Cas bit back a laugh. "I don't think it's going to be a romantic trip to Olso."

"It better not be," Mateo muttered. "But Aren will protect him, right? He really is as powerful as they say, so he has to protect him."

"I'm sure he will," Cas said, as much to reassure himself as Mateo. "I don't think Aren would have let Galo go with him if he didn't think he could protect him. And Galo probably has faith Aren can keep him safe, or he wouldn't have gone. He's not stupid."

"No, he's not," Mateo said, almost begrudgingly. "But I wouldn't be surprised if he went just to spite me."

"That seems like a bit of an overreaction."

"I did go on a recruitment trip just to avoid him," Mateo said.

"He didn't seem mad about that. Just sad."

Mateo dropped his eyes. "Oh."

"For what it's worth, I would have been mad at him too, if I were in your shoes. We just got out of danger and he ran right back into it." Cas cocked his head. "I am a little mad at him, actually. Why couldn't he just stay here and save himself for a change?"

"Thank you," Mateo said, spreading his arms wide. "That's exactly what I said."

"Give him a hard time when he comes back," Cas said. "For the both of us."

"Oh, I will." He vigorously ran his hand through his hair, mussing the curls. "How is Emelina? Or, Queen Emelina? I'm sorry, I don't know how to refer to her."

"I don't know how she likes to be addressed, honestly. The Ruined are pretty casual with one another. And she's fine. I'm giving the Ruined some space this morning. Have they come out of their rooms?"

"Not that I've seen."

"I wanted to talk to you about Em, actually. I need someone coordinating the security of the Ruined while they're here. And she wants to get started with the Weakling, so I need someone in charge of getting guards and soldiers to help her. A few staff members, too."

Mateo's eyebrows shot up. "Me?"

"Em is wary of new people, and you're the only guard she knows. Jorge can't do it all, and he already agreed to let you take charge, if you're up for it."

"But . . . you know I'm not actually the best guard, right? I mean, I'm fine, they wouldn't let me stay if I wasn't, but there are certainly better ones. I'm not nearly as good with a sword as Galo is, for example."

"Most people aren't as good as Galo."

"Well that's true."

Cas smiled. "I've seen you fight, Mateo. I'm not worried. But the Ruined are capable of protecting themselves. This is more about making them feel welcome, and safe. I think it would be better if Em has contact with other people in the castle besides me. And I don't have a lot of people I trust a hundred percent."

Mateo blinked, like he was surprised to discover he was one of those people.

"You're welcome to say no. It's a request, not an order," Cas said.

"No, of course," he said quickly. "I'd be happy to."

"Good. Jorge has some information for you, so you should meet with him, and then go to Em. I think she was headed to the shed after speaking with the Ruined."

"I'll go right away."

Cas stood and walked to the door. "Thank you, Mateo." He smiled at him over his shoulder. "And I'm sure Galo will come back safe."

"He better."

Em found the Ruined in their rooms, and recruited Mariana and Gisela to head outside to the stables with her.

"How was last night?" Em asked as they walked down the hallway. A maid saw them coming and quickly ducked out of sight. "Any problems?"

"No problems," Gisela said. Her face was neutral, less angry than it had been last night.

"We're fine," Mariana said. "Uh, some Ruined went . . . exploring this morning." She looked over her shoulder like she might spot them lurking in a corridor.

"Exploring?" Em repeated.

"They're just checking out the castle." Gisela cocked an eyebrow. "Were they supposed to be confined to their rooms?"

"No. They're free to roam." Em pretended not to be nervous about Ruined just wandering the castle alone. They knew the polite thing to do was to wait for a guide to invite them on a tour.

Em pushed a door open and stepped out into the sunlight. She spotted the shed straight ahead, not far from the stables. She'd broken into it once, a few nights after she'd first arrived in the castle. It had been full of cutlery and candlesticks and other boring things that had probably been unwanted gifts.

No one had been protecting it then, but now two guards stood in front of it, watching as Em approached with Mariana and Gisela. Em stopped in front of them and they bowed.

"I'm here to take a look inside," she said. "They told you I was allowed access?"

The female guard nodded and turned to unlock the door. She stepped back to allow Em inside.

A yell sounded from her left. She tensed, reaching for the dagger she'd slipped into her belt, and whirled around to face the stables.

Two young Ruined—Selena and Patricio—stumbled out of the stable, a guard and a stable hand hot on their heels. The guard pointed at them and yelled something. He put a hand on his sword.

Em broke into a run, headed for the stables. Gisela and Mariana followed close behind.

"We weren't doing anything!" Selena yelled, her hands balled into fists at her side.

The guard opened his mouth to reply, but Patricio narrowed his eyes at him. The guard tumbled backward, head over feet, and landed in a clump on the ground.

"Patricio, no!" Em skidded to a stop in front of him, blocking his view of the guards. "You can't use your power on anyone in the castle."

"He had a sword out," Patricio said through gritted teeth. "Why shouldn't I use my power on them?"

Em turned to see the sword on the ground, the guard scrambling to grab it. The stable hand looked utterly terrified. He turned and sprinted toward the castle.

The guard jumped to his feet, sword stretched toward Em. She didn't reach for her dagger.

"Put your weapon away," she said.

"They were snooping through every corner of the castle," the guard said, ignoring her request. "I caught these two in the stable. They scavenged the whole castle. We haven't determined yet if anything is missing."

"If anything is *missing*?" Selena yelled. "Why do you assume we're thieves?" She jumped forward and Em put an arm out, keeping her from the guard.

"You need to put that sword away," Em said. "Now."

The guard didn't move. Dread began winding its way up her stomach. She'd be insane to think the Ruined could stay here. Maybe Olivia was right to think they could never coexist with humans. It hadn't even been a full day and they were about to kill each other. She was right when she said she had no reason to trust—

"Dominic!" a voice yelled. Em turned to see Mateo striding across the castle lawn. "Queen Emelina just told you to sheathe your sword."

Dominic's sword twitched as he turned to look at Mateo. "Jorge said we could use our weapon if a Ruined used their powers on us."

"You drew your sword first!" Patricio sneered at him. "You want to see how well you can hold a sword if I break all your fingers?"

"Patricio," Em said sharply. He rolled his eyes, but he looked away from Dominic.

Mateo said something to Dominic that Em couldn't hear, a hard edge to his voice. "Go. *Now.*" He pointed to the castle. Dominic glared at him, but he sheathed his sword and walked away.

Mateo turned to face him, his eyes flicking to the angry Ruined around her. If he was nervous, he was good at hiding it. His expression was calm, like he encountered this kind of situation often.

"I'm sorry," he said. "We'll have another talk with the guards tonight."

"Is it true the guards were instructed to pull their weapons if a Ruined uses their power on them?" Em asked.

"Yes." Mateo held her gaze. "If they strike first, we were told we could defend ourselves."

"I didn't strike first," Selena protested.

"I'm sure you didn't," Mateo said, and one side of his mouth actually lifted in a smile. Patricio looked from Em to the guard, like this was some sort of trick. "Dominic is jumpy, and frankly, sort of an asshole."

Selena giggled and nodded her agreement.

"The guards will just pull their weapons on us anytime they feel threatened?" Gisela asked.

"No," Mateo said. "We'll talk to them again." He turned to Em. "Cas asked me to coordinate security for you and the Ruined, if that's all right. And help you get the Weakling shields and armor started."

"Security?" she repeated.

"Making sure idiots like Dominic aren't threatening you."

"You're not going to follow her around everywhere like Cas's guards do, are you?" Selena asked.

"Not unless she'd like me to," Mateo said with a smile. Selena blushed.

"I'm fine, thank you," Em said.

Mateo jerked a thumb over his shoulder. "I was going to show you a spot where we could work with the Weakling, if you're free. I still need to recruit a few people to help, but I thought I'd let you choose a working spot first."

"Sure." The panic in Em's stomach started to subside. Cas was still wrong—everything wasn't fine—but maybe she was wrong too. Maybe she needed to have a little more faith in the people around Cas.

"Why don't you two take Patricio and Selena back?" Em asked Mariana and Gisela. "Let everyone know they shouldn't be using their powers unless they absolutely have to. And tell them where the Weakling is, so they can steer clear."

Gisela looked from the guards to Em, her face scrunched up

in confusion. "Are we fine with letting the Lerans guard it?"

Em looked at Mateo. "I'm assuming Dominic won't be assigned to guard it?"

"No, he was never on that list. We're rotating a select few through that post. I can introduce you to all of them, if you want."

"I'd like that, thank you."

Gisela was still looking at Em, like she was waiting for final confirmation. Cas was right, Em realized. They were following her lead.

"We trust them to do this, then?" Mariana asked.

"Yes," Em said. "We trust them."

TWENTY-SEVEN

OLIVIA WOKE TO a growling stomach and an angry face staring down at her. Ester had her hands on her hips, her lip curled.

"What?" Olivia sat up and took a discreet look around. It was midmorning, judging by the sun, and the Ruined around her were still lounging about, or napping, or huddled together eating some berries they'd picked. They were in the middle of the jungle, beneath the shade of thick trees. Jovita sat tied to one, bloodied but still alive. Most likely alive. Her eyes were closed, but Olivia was pretty sure she was just sleeping.

Olivia only had twenty-five Ruined with her. There should have been more, but she'd woken the first morning after Em left to find about ten of them had disappeared. None of the remaining Ruined had a clue where they'd gone. Or they just weren't saying.

"I told you we had to take feed for the horses. I told you we couldn't ride them constantly," Ester snapped.

"Is there something wrong with them?"

"Two of them collapsed," Ester said. "And two more are dead, including yours."

She let out an annoyed breath. "We'll have to get more horses, then."

Ester gestured around wildly, as if to point out that they were in the middle of the jungle. It wasn't like there was a barn full of horses waiting around the corner.

"It's not my fault they couldn't keep up," Olivia snapped. Ester just turned and walked away. She said something to Carmen, who looked at Olivia and then quickly averted her eyes.

The Ruined hadn't looked at her the same since Em left. Olivia had decimated Jovita's hunters—she would have killed the Olso army too if those cowards hadn't run—but it was like they'd decided Olivia had *lost* somehow. She'd *won*. She wanted to scream it at them.

It was all Em's fault. Olivia wished their mother were still alive. She would have been on Olivia's side. She would have rather seen Em dead than partnering with humans.

Or maybe their mother could have talked some sense into Em, and Olivia wouldn't have to kill her at all. The thought made her insides twist painfully.

Olivia got to her feet, folded her blanket, and stuffed it in her pack. She stomped to Jovita and knelt down in front of her, snapping her fingers in her face.

Jovita sucked in a breath as she woke. Her gaze fell on Olivia, and Olivia was pleased to see a spark of fear in her eyes. Jovita had only anger at first. But Ester had been in her mind a few times, making her see terrible things, and she had the good sense to be afraid now. Or perhaps her grasp on reality was slipping.

"Do you have anything useful to tell me yet?" Olivia asked.

Jovita just stared at her.

"I don't understand why you're protecting Casimir. If you can tell me the best way to get into the castle, I'll kill him and my sister. It's a win-win for you."

Jovita turned her face away.

Olivia stood and waved at Ester. "Work harder on her, will you? I think you'll need to break her mind before she tells me anything."

"I'm trying. It turns out her mind is pretty tough." But Ester walked over and sat down across from Jovita.

"I'm going to go check on the Olso army. They didn't move, did they?" Olivia looked up at a tree, where a Ruined had been keeping watch, but there was no one there. She let out an annoyed sigh.

"Calm down," Priscila said in a tone Olivia didn't appreciate. "Someone just climbed up there an hour ago. They're not moving."

Olivia shot her a venomous look and stomped to the tree herself. She grunted as she climbed, her feet and back sore from the endless days of travel.

She reached a high branch, carefully balancing against the

trunk. Priscila was right. The army was still there, hiding in the jungle. There were hundreds of them, and they were surrounded by horses and wagons and carts of weapons. The weapons scared Olivia the most. A human didn't even have to be close to kill them with some of those weapons. That was terrifying, for a Ruined.

She climbed back down the tree.

"We're still waiting?" Ester asked, without turning around to look at her.

"Yes. I think the army is plotting the best way to attack Royal City, and I want to see what they do." They'd been following the army for days. When Olivia had first tracked them down, she'd been excited, ready to jump in and kill them all. But then she'd looked around and considered the powers of the Ruined with her. She didn't have Aren. She didn't have Jacobo. She had twenty-five Ruined, which was no small number, but none with enough power to help her take down an army of that size.

And to be honest, she wasn't sure they would even obey an order from her right now.

So she was waiting. She told herself it was the smart decision. With any luck, the humans would kill each other and she could swoop in and take down the rest.

Jovita screamed, then went silent, her eyes wide. Ester turned away from her to face Olivia.

"If you really want to get into the castle to kill Em, maybe you should help them." She pointed in the direction of the army.

Olivia recoiled and gave Ester a disgusted look.

Ester lifted her eyebrows. "What? Your mother did it. Do you think she entertained Olso warriors at the castle because she *liked* humans? She needed them. You've failed because you could never be strategic in the way your mother and Emelina are."

The word *failed* hung in the air. The Ruined around them were silent, watching.

"I haven't failed at anything," Olivia spat out. "That army ran in fear from me."

"I suppose," Ester said quietly. "But working with humans keeps turning out well for Em, wouldn't you say?"

Olivia balled her fingers into fists. She refused to admit this to Ester, but she had been wondering what would have happened if she'd gone behind Em's back to work with Olso. August would have been happy to kill Casimir. They could have taken care of him in Sacred Rock, and then moved on to Royal City. She'd be ruler of Lera by now.

Instead, she'd attacked the Olso castle, and then run all the warriors out of Lera. She'd helped Casimir, in the end.

And now it was too late. She wasn't dumb enough to waltz up to August and ask for a deal now, not when she'd killed every member of the Olso royal family.

"I don't work with humans," she said. "We don't need them."

Ester turned back to Jovita. "If you say so."

Olivia bit back the urge to scream. "We just have to wait. Lera will fall after I kill Em. I just need to get to Em."

TWENTY-EIGHT

BETHANIA OFFERED TO let Galo and Aren stay the night (begrudgingly, muttering that they were going to get caught wandering the streets of Olso), and they slept on blankets and pillows in the sitting room. Galo tossed and turned most of the night, listening to the sounds of the busy street outside and thinking of what Mateo was doing.

Bethania left in the morning, handing them two hot mugs before rushing out the door. Galo sat on the floor with his back against the couch as he lifted the cup to his lips. Bitter liquid rushed over his tongue. He grimaced as he swallowed.

"Oh, that's disgusting. What is that?"

Aren sniffed his, then took a sip. He wrinkled his nose and put the cup back on the table. "I don't know. Maybe she heated up some dishwater to torture us." He cocked an eyebrow as he looked at Galo. "Maybe to torture you. I think when faced with the choice of Ruined or Leran, I win by a large margin."

"She does glare at me a lot, doesn't she?" Galo had gotten the distinct impression that Bethania had never met anyone from Lera, and she would have preferred to keep it that way.

"Yes, she does."

Galo leaned his head back against the chair. "I did serve the late queen. She didn't even have a good reason to betray Olso, unlike Iria."

"She wasn't in love with the Lera king?"

Galo let out a short, loud laugh. "No. They'd never met before she arrived as a traitor from Olso. If they were ever in love, I never saw it." He lowered his eyebrows in thought. "I'm actually not sure any Gallego has ever married for love. Cas would be the first."

"Assuming your people actually let him marry Em."

"I'd like to see it happen," Galo said quietly. "It feels like the only good thing that could come out of this."

When Bethania returned, she had an envelope full of papers and a basket of food. She ignored Galo and thrust the envelope at Aren.

"Take a look at these. It's the best I can do on short notice."

Aren pulled the papers out and spread them on the table. Galo edged closer, peering over his shoulder. There were some old articles from a local newspaper about the prison as it was built, with a few details about the layout and security. There were also several rough sketches of what he assumed was the inside of the building.

"I'll explain those," Bethania said, removing bread and meat from her basket. "I went and talked to a friend who used to work in the prison."

"Are they going to help us?" Galo asked.

"No. I wasn't direct with my questions. I tried to just keep it a general conversation about how Iria would be housed in the prison. Like I was concerned, as her friend."

Aren looked up from the papers. "There's a chance they'll figure out you were helping us. Won't you also be tried for treason?"

"Possibly, though the case against me would be far less solid than Iria's." She waved her hand like she wasn't concerned.

"You know . . ." Aren glanced at Galo. "I think if you wanted to come with us, back to Lera, that would be fine."

Galo nodded. "King Casimir would welcome you."

"Ugh." Bethania screwed up her face. "No offense, but ugh."

Galo pressed his lips together to keep in a laugh. "I just thought it might be a good alternative to prison."

"No, thank you. Iria's made her choice, and I'm making mine. I'll take my chances here."

"All right," Aren said. "But if you change your mind . . ."

Bethania shook her head and took a seat next to him on the couch. "Let's talk about these plans. I think your best bet is to go in on the east side, because there's no prisoner exit near there. No one has ever tried to break *into* the prison before."

"So we'd hop the fence on the east side, and go in . . . ?" Aren asked.

She pulled a sketch forward and pointed. "North. Here. There's a door that's usually used for bringing in kitchen deliveries. I can't tell you exactly where you'll end up, but let's assume near the dining hall and kitchen. If you go at night, it will be empty."

She grabbed another sketch. "This is a general outline of the prisoner cells, as much as I can guess. One of the articles says there's a long hallway that leads from the dining room to the cells, so I've drawn that here." She ran her finger along the hallway. "She's probably in solitary, which is separate cells to the west. If you head this way, you should find them. The door leading to them will be guarded, and there will probably be guards inside as well. If she's not there, then you'll need to go search for her in the general population. You're going to want to hope that doesn't happen."

"But chances are she's in solitary?" Galo asked.

"Yes. She's unsafe with the general population, given her reputation. But there's a chance they'll put her in with everyone else at some point, if only to torment her. Luckily you're probably here early enough to have avoided that."

"So we should go tonight," Aren said.

"Yes. I'm not going to be able to get any more information than this for you. Not anything that would be particularly helpful, anyway. And they may know a Ruined crossed into Olso, if any of the warriors you attacked at the border survived. It's best you go now, before they have a chance to beef up security or move her."

"Is there a spot Galo can wait where he won't be seen?" Aren asked.

Galo looked up with a start. "What? You don't think you're going in there alone."

"It's incredibly dangerous, and just being with you both has made me plenty strong. If you—"

"You can't do it alone, Aren. Besides, if you don't make it out, what do you think happens to me? They're not going to send me back to Lera."

"It's true. They'll put him in prison," Bethania said. "Maybe have him killed if they decide he's not useful."

"Don't sugarcoat it," Galo said dryly, to hide the burst of panic he'd just felt. King August knew who Galo was, and it hadn't occurred to him that they might use him against Cas, or torture him for information about Lera. Galo knew more about Lera's military, royal family, and castle than maybe anyone else in Lera.

Aren was staring at him like he'd noticed Galo's sudden panic. "Why did you come here?" he asked, his bafflement coming through in his voice.

"Because you asked for help. Why did *you* come here?"

"For Iria, of course. But you don't even like me. Or Iria."

Bethania looked from Galo to Aren, confusion etched across her face.

"I like you," Galo said. "I don't really know Iria."

"You don't know Iria?" Bethania asked.

"Not really."

Bethania exchanged a baffled expression with Aren.

"You needed help," Galo said. "And there's no one left to help you, because my king killed them all. And I sat there and said nothing while it happened. So I figured this is the least I could do now." Saying it aloud helped to lessen his fear. He wouldn't make a different choice, even if he could go back and change it.

Aren blinked. "Oh."

"So I'm going in the prison with you. You'll protect me."

"You say that with such confidence," Aren said.

"You're not confident."

Aren blew out a breath, closing his eyes for a moment. "Have faith, Aren," he said quietly.

"Does he usually talk to himself like that?" Bethania whispered. Galo just chuckled.

"We're going together, then," Aren said with a smile. "Thanks."

"You're welcome."

TWENTY-NINE

EM ROUNDED THE corner and slowed as she spotted two guards stationed outside of Cas's office. She wondered if they were always there, or if this was a new development because the Ruined were there.

One of the guards immediately bowed and opened the door when he spotted her. Cas had asked for her to attend a quick, informal meeting, so he must have given them instructions to let her in. She smiled at them and stepped inside.

Cas looked up from his desk, his eyes lighting up when he spotted her. He stood and edged around the corner of his desk, extending a hand to her. She took it, tilting her head up to kiss him quickly.

"I heard you had some trouble at the stables this morning," he said, his brow furrowed.

"We did, but it worked out. Mateo took me to meet some of the guards."

He looked at her in surprise. "He did?"

"We're all on edge. He thought it would help if we talked to each other. He introduced me to all the guards on duty at the Weakling shed." She smiled at him.

His lips turned up, and he kissed her again, wrapping an arm around her waist. He pulled away sooner than she was expecting, glancing at the clock on the wall.

"We have a few minutes until everyone else arrives," he said. "Can I talk to you about something?"

"Sure." She followed him to the chairs by the window and settled down across from him. He reached for her hand, his eyes on their fingers as they intertwined. His expression had turned serious.

"Jovita is probably dead, isn't she?" he asked quietly.

"Yes. She was alive the last time I saw her, but I can't imagine she still is. Olivia isn't good at keeping humans alive." She said the last sentence apologetically.

"I considered killing her a few weeks ago. I had soldiers following her. They could have gotten to her. It seemed like a pretty good option, considering I failed in killing her at the fortress."

"I thought you decided not to kill her, not that you failed."

"I didn't so much decide not to as . . . chicken out," he said.

"That's not a bad thing."

"It felt like a bad thing. After Jovita left here and started gathering people to fight against me, it felt like I was an idiot." He let go of her hand and sat back in his chair. "This is going to sound terrible."

"I've said plenty of terrible things to you."

He laughed suddenly, some of the weight leaving his expression. "Like what?"

"I think I once told you that I didn't regret killing anyone, that they had it coming."

"You did say that, didn't you?"

"It was a lie."

"I know."

She smiled at him. "What's the terrible thing?"

"I sort of understand my father. And Olivia. Why they chose to just kill instead of negotiating. It's easier, isn't it?"

"Yes." She took in a ragged breath. Just the mention of Olivia's name made her want to curl into a ball and cry. And then flee the castle to search for her.

"It was hard to shake the feeling that I should just have Jovita killed. The law was even on my side."

"The law was on your father's side as well, when he killed the Ruined. It is technically still Lera law that all Ruined have to be exterminated, right?"

Cas nodded solemnly.

"Then clearly you can't always rely on your old laws. They might be wrong. They might need to be changed."

"I didn't do it, obviously," Cas said. "I hesitated until it was too late, and she'd partnered with Olso and Vallos."

"You shouldn't consider your hesitance to kill people a weakness, Cas. When I came here, after I killed Mary, I was horrified to realize I'd become like the king by killing Mary. Olivia has certainly become everything she claims to hate." She swallowed hard. "And I don't want to do that. I imagine you don't, either."

He shook his head. "No. But I was a little surprised by how I felt, after everything settled down and we got word of Jovita still trying to take the throne. I felt weak, like I had never really punished her for convincing everyone I'd lost my mind and poisoning me. I wanted revenge. I wanted to show her that I had the power now."

"I know a little bit about that feeling."

"I know you do." He studied her. "I empathized with you before, but I think it was the first time I really understood you. Once I had somewhere to direct my anger, I wanted to embrace it. It felt better to embrace it."

"Only at first."

"What if I'd been horrible?" he asked. "If you'd come here as Mary and discovered I was just like my father, what would you have done?"

She started to reach for the necklace that no longer hung around her neck. It was upstairs, buried in the bottom of a bag. She dropped her hand into her lap. "I think I would have done it."

"What is *it*? You never told me the details of the plan, the way it was supposed to go."

"Are you sure you want to hear?"

"Yes."

She hesitated for a moment, but she knew that at this point, there was nothing she could say that was going to scare him. He knew everything she'd done, and he didn't judge her for it.

"It was flexible, because we knew we'd have to work around guards and take opportunities as they came up. Ideally, we wanted to kill all or most of the royal family right as Olso was attacking. It would have thrown the castle into total disarray at the exact right moment. I would have killed you in your bed. I wouldn't have needed to talk to you first, to explain. I would have been fine killing you quickly."

He actually looked a little amused by that, and she went on.

"Same with Jovita. I would have tried to sneak up on her in some way. I might have asked Aren to take care of her—he was assigned to protect her a couple of times while we were here. Same with the queen. It would have been Aren, or maybe Iria and the other warriors. The king would have been last, and he would have been mine. I wanted to talk to him first, to tell him who I was." She would not have been kind, or quick, but she didn't think it was right to say that to Cas. He probably knew anyway.

"And do you think it would have made you feel better?" he asked. "If we were all just as horrible as you imagined, and you killed us like that?"

"At first," she said. "I think that night, when you all died and Olso claimed the castle, would have felt like a victory. The feeling probably would have lasted through saving Olivia, and as we traveled back to Ruina. But eventually, I would have had the same realization. That by using the king's violent tactics, I'd become exactly like him. He killed because he was scared. I killed in revenge. Different reasons, but they have the same ending. I like to think of your father as pure evil, but do you really think he felt entirely comfortable with what he'd done?"

Cas shook his head. "No. I think he became even more stubborn because it was too terrifying to consider that he'd made a mistake."

"It's easier not to think about it. To just make the decision and stick with it, no matter who you meet, what new things you learn." She said her next words gently. "Do you think you got so mad at Jovita because you weren't allowed to get mad at me?"

His eyes quickly shifted to hers. "I'm allowed to be mad at you. I *was* mad at you. You remember."

"I remember you forgiving me pretty quickly too."

"I thought you deserved forgiveness. I believed that you really had feelings for me."

"I'm just saying, you lost both your parents and your country was invaded. You forgave me, the Olso warriors retreated as soon as you arrived, and you'd never blame the Ruined as a whole, not after what your father did to them. So all you had left is Jovita. It was easier to put all your anger on her, wasn't it?"

He paused for a moment. "Yes. I hadn't considered that." A small smile crossed his lips. "I don't know what I'd do without you. I was trying to find someone to talk to about this the past few days, and there's no one who . . ."

"Who has killed people in a vengeful rage?" she guessed.

He laughed softly. "No. There's no one who will give me an honest opinion, even if it's uncomfortable. And no one else who can really understand what I'm feeling."

"I'm sorry I can understand what you're feeling. I wouldn't wish it on anyone."

He lifted a shoulder in a small shrug, his gaze shifting to the window. He was different from the boy she'd met months ago, standing silently and sullenly on the castle lawn with his parents. He was even different than the boy she'd known in Vallos, the one who'd tried to give up. He was stronger, but steadier.

She forgot sometimes that he wasn't very far removed from his parents' deaths. She hadn't been nearly as calm as him a few months after her parents died. She'd been angry and difficult, snapping at Aren and Damian, fantasizing about all the ways she could take revenge on the Lerans.

He caught her looking at him, and he cocked his head with a smile, sending butterflies fluttering through her stomach. She held his gaze, watching the way his dark hair fell into his eyes and he tossed it back with a flick of his head.

"What?" he asked with a laugh.

A knock sounded on the door, and Violet stepped inside, followed by Franco. Em stood and greeted them, and Violet managed a small smile when their eyes met. Em knew Violet didn't like her much, and she couldn't blame her. Violet's father had died in the raid on the Lera castle.

But if Em and Violet could smile at each other, maybe there was hope for the rest of them.

Violet and Franco took the other two seats by the window.

"Thank you for meeting with us," Violet said. "We've discussed some things with Cas and the advisers, and we thought it was best if we talked to you alone before doing larger meetings with the Ruined."

"Of course."

"First of all, we'd like to get the Ruined and our soldiers training together. I understand that Olivia was the one in charge of training the Ruined?" Violet asked.

"She was."

"Is there anyone who you would trust to take charge here? Work with General Amaro on some strategies?"

"I think Mariana would be good at that. And one of the Ruined who can manipulate the body. Gisela, maybe."

"Good. Let us know who and we'll set up a meeting."

"Do you know where the Olso and Vallos troops are right now?" Em asked.

"We had reports of them a bit north of where you attacked them, but we haven't heard from a messenger recently. It's possible Olivia got them."

"Entirely possible," Em said with a sigh.

"But we know for sure that Olivia is coming here eventually, because . . ." Violet let her voice trail off.

"Because she wants to kill me," Em finished. She swallowed down a sudden lump in her throat.

"She wants to kill all of us," Cas said. "Let's not blame it all on Em."

"Right. Sorry, I didn't mean that," Violet said.

"It's fine."

"It's just that regardless of what happens with the human troops, Olivia and the other Ruined are coming. We want to be prepared."

"How is the Weakling coming?" Franco asked.

"We set up a workstation and recruited some guards and staff to help," Em said. "We're lining shields and some armor. It shouldn't take long."

"Then the last thing we need to discuss is your marriage," Franco said.

Cas looked at Franco quickly, like he hadn't been expecting that. "I told you I wanted to wait on those discussions."

"I know," Franco said. "But we've been discussing the Ruined request to strip the monarchy of some of its power, and we need to know about your marriage plans. Everyone agrees that your marriage isn't legal, since Em's name isn't on the document. You'll need to draw up new documents if you'd like to marry again."

"We're not even entirely sure you'll have enough support to get married," Violet said carefully. "We don't even know the Ruined's opinion on that matter."

Em didn't know their opinion either. She had carefully avoided asking anyone, afraid of the answer.

"We need to know if this is something we should be fighting for," Franco said. He looked at Cas, and then Em. "Do you want to marry again?"

Heat rose up Em's cheeks. *Yes.* The word was on the tip of

her tongue, but it was too awkward to say it in front of Franco and Violet. This conversation needed to happen in private with Cas first.

"Let's pick up that discussion tomorrow," Cas said, avoiding Em's gaze. Franco looked surprised, but said nothing.

"Let's talk about supplies, then," Violet said. "I'm working on getting some clothing and other things for the Ruined, but we—" She stopped as a knock sounded at the door.

"Come in!" Cas called.

A young man stepped inside, his eyes wide and his breathing a bit heavy. Em tensed and began mapping a route in her head back to Cas's bedroom, where she'd left her sword.

The man stepped inside, extending an envelope to Cas. "The king of Olso was just at the gates. He has a message for you."

THIRTY

"LET US GO with you. We'll stay back. August will never see us."

Cas shook his head as he shrugged into his coat. Em made an exasperated noise and plunked down on the edge of his bed.

"The message said not to bring any Ruined. That he'll consider it an act of war," Cas said. The note from August had been short, but clear:

King Casimir—Meet me after sundown in the clearing by the mill to discuss a peace treaty. If you bring any Ruined to this meeting, I will consider it an act of war.

"It's a trap," Em said.

He turned to face her. "I'm bringing an army of guards with

me. And we already sent people out there to make sure it isn't an ambush. The Olso army isn't anywhere nearby. August came alone."

Em let out a breath, clearly frustrated. "You can't trust him."

"I know. But he's offered peace talks, and I can't decline the invitation."

"The proper thing to do would be for him to come here, to the castle, if he was truly serious about peace talks." She rolled her eyes. "It's so immature, sending you a note to meet him at a secret location."

"Nothing you have ever told me about August makes me think he's mature."

"Good point."

"Besides, the Ruined are here in the castle, and he seems very concerned about that. We could have one of them snap his neck as soon as he walked through the door."

"I considered it. Gisela would be happy to do it." Em couldn't say it with a straight face. August didn't know Em well if that was truly the reason he didn't want to come to the castle. She would never have him killed on sight. She'd at least talk to him for a few minutes first.

He leaned down and kissed her. "This may take a while, so try to get some sleep. I'll fill you in on what happened tomorrow and we can talk about . . . other things."

She nodded. She knew what *other things* he was referring to.

Do you want to marry again? The question had sent an unexpected blast of terror down Cas's spine. He thought he had more time. He thought they'd deal with Olivia first, and the Olso and Vallos armies, and settle into a regular life. He thought there would be hours of negotiations with the Ruined and a few formal dinner parties and plenty of time to show Em that this could work.

Instead, she was supposed to decide the day after arriving in the castle. And he was terrified of the answer. Em had never given him any indication she thought that their marriage was a realistic option, even after deciding to partner with him against Olivia. He'd told her that he loved her, and that he wanted to marry her weeks ago, during Olivia's raid on the castle. She had never given him a response, on either point.

He said good-bye and rushed out of the room. Maybe he was a bit grateful for the timing of August's note. He could delay hearing Em's answer for a little while longer.

Outside, he found his horse saddled and ready to go. Twenty guards were traveling with him, with more spread out in every direction, many of them out of view. If August was indeed trying to lead them into a trap, he would have a very hard time succeeding.

The meeting spot was less than an hour's ride, and it was dark by the time they arrived. They didn't light a torch, instead waiting silently in the darkness. The sliver of moon provided minimal light, but it was so quiet in the open field that it would be near impossible for August to sneak up on them.

Cas didn't dismount his horse, prepared to bolt at the slightest hint of trouble. The minutes ticked by, stretching into hours.

He arched his back, annoyed. Perhaps the trick had been just to make him wait for no reason.

Finally, horses appeared out of the trees. August rode in front, flanked by a dozen warriors on either side. Several carried torches, the fire lighting up their faces as they approached.

Cas let August dismount his horse first, then did the same. Several guards followed him as he walked to the king of Olso, Jorge so close he kept brushing Cas's right arm. August had a warrior on either side of him as he walked forward.

Cas had seen August only from a distance—a few times through the windows of his house in Sacred Rock, and again when he'd kidnapped Em. He was thinner, his cheeks sunken, and dark circles under his eyes. His blond hair looked greasy.

"Hello, Casimir," August said as they both came to a stop. "Nice to see you again."

"Have you seen me before?"

"Yes. You were barely conscious and mumbling Emelina's name, so I suppose you don't remember." Perhaps the words were meant to be light, but Cas detected a trace of bitterness.

"I don't remember, but that does sound like me."

Behind him, he heard a sound like a guard trying not to laugh. August didn't look amused.

"I've come to talk to negotiate peace between our two kingdoms," August said. "Are you open to that?"

"Of course."

"You heard we were ambushed by the Ruined in the jungle?"

"I did. I heard you left my cousin to die."

"She's been trying to take the throne from you. You could say I did you a favor."

Cas just stared at him.

"I was only partnered with Jovita because she agreed to help me kill the Ruined. I don't care who rules Lera, as long as it's not a Ruined." He crossed his arms over his chest. "I know that Em and some of the Ruined are in the castle."

"They are."

"And the rest of them are with Olivia somewhere. They're divided. Together, we could defeat the Ruined for good."

"You mean all the Ruined, don't you?" Cas asked. "Not just Olivia."

"All the Ruined," he confirmed with a nod. "I will allow you to spare only Em, as long as you don't have children. You'll have to produce heirs with a human."

"How kind of you," Cas said dryly.

August's jaw twitched. "They killed my entire family, Casimir. Even the children."

Cas tried to hide the twinge of sympathy he felt for August. "I know that Olivia did that, but you can't blame all of the Ruined for the actions of a few."

"I won't argue with you about this," August said sharply. "There is no greater threat to Olso than the Ruined, and I'm here to destroy them. My offer to you is this: Abandon whatever alliance you're forming with the Ruined and align yourself with me instead. You've heard that the people of Vallos have joined me?"

"I have."

"Join us in standing against the Ruined, and we'll sign a peace treaty immediately. We won't leave until we've completely eliminated the Ruined threat from Lera. After that, no one from Olso will ever set foot in Lera again without your permission. And you may have Vallos."

Cas barked out a laugh. "That is not yours to give."

"I've spoken with the Vallos royal council. They've been in chaos since Mary was murdered. They've agreed that you may rule Vallos, if the Ruined threat is eliminated. You may also take Ruina, if you want it. I'd be willing to work out an agreement for the mines there."

"My father would have liked this deal very much," Cas said quietly. He could almost feel his father standing beside him, staring at Cas with mounting disdain.

"It's a very good deal," August said, like he thought Cas was actually considering it.

"You'll let me have Em, but what makes you think she'd still want me after I betrayed her like this?"

"She won't have anyone else." August shrugged. "Besides, you forgave her once."

August really didn't know Em at all. Cas couldn't help but feel a bit smug about that.

"No," Cas said. "I've formed an alliance with the Ruined, and I won't break it. If you'd like to join us in fighting Olivia and the Ruined standing with her, I'm open to that."

August's eyes flashed. "I won't align myself with *any* Ruined."

"Then we have nothing to talk about."

"I don't think you understand. If you decline this offer, we *will* come after you. I won't allow you to keep Ruined in your castle."

Annoyance flared in Cas's chest. "I didn't ask your permission."

August opened his mouth. Shut it. He took a deep breath, like he was trying to remain calm. "We can easily stamp out the Ruined if we do it together. With your army and Olso technology, they won't stand a chance. I know that you have feelings for Emelina, but you need to think of your people first."

"I am thinking of my people. They include the Ruined, and I won't kill my own people. Not to mention, the Ruined are incredibly powerful allies. You know that. You tried to secure that alliance yourself."

"Em betrayed me," August said through gritted teeth.

She'd betrayed him for Cas. He felt smug again.

"She'll betray you, too," August said with a hint of desperation.

"Are we done, then?" Cas asked.

August stared at him with growing disbelief. He'd actually expected Cas to take the deal, it seemed. Like he would sell out all the Ruined in exchange for Em.

"You'll regret this," August barked. "Warriors are pouring into your country every day to join my army. I will kill the Ruined *and* take your kingdom." He said it with barely contained rage, his eyes shooting daggers at Cas.

Cas was probably supposed to feel fear. That seemed to be what August was going for. But the man shaking with anger in front of him just didn't seem all that scary. In fact, he reminded Cas of his father, all blind hatred and no ability to think strategically.

Cas considered saying something flippant, or mean, to let August know just how much he *didn't* fear him. But he almost felt sad for the man.

"I'm sorry to hear that," Cas said quietly, and stepped back. "I hope you find peace, August, even if it isn't with me." Then he turned and walked away.

THIRTY-ONE

AREN FOLLOWED BETHANIA down the winding dirt road that led to the prison, Galo beside him. It was the middle of the night, and Aren could barely make out her features in the dark.

"Just head that way," Bethania said, pointing straight ahead, though he couldn't see the prison yet in the darkness. The dirt road was flanked by thick, tall trees on either side, and he couldn't see anything at the end of the road.

But Aren would have known where the prison was, even if she hadn't indicated. He could sense the large group of humans, tucked away from the rest of the population of Olso. He was surprised he could tell the difference, since there were homes full of people only a few streets over, but he felt like his power to sense humans was sharpening, the longer he was around them.

"Thank you," Aren said to Bethania. "For all your help."

"I'm not sure I helped much, but you're welcome." She adjusted the bag on her shoulder. "I'll wait at the meeting spot. If you're not there by dawn, I'm leaving. You understand that you can't come to my house with Iria? They'll be all over me after she escapes."

"I understand," Aren said. "We'll be at that meeting spot in less than an hour." He said it with a certainty he wasn't sure he felt. His heart was pounding in his chest, and he kept grabbing Galo's wrist to steady his power.

Bethania turned and quickly walked away. Aren watched her back as she disappeared into the darkness.

"Ready?" Galo asked.

Aren let out a slow breath. "I guess."

"That doesn't instill much confidence."

He glanced at Galo and quickly turned away. He was terrified he wouldn't be able to protect Galo once they got inside. The strength of his terror was surprising—he hadn't realized he cared that much.

"You're sure you don't want to stay here? I've been with you all day, so my power may hold up until I can get to Iria."

"Just come on," Galo said, a hint of amusement in his voice. Apparently he didn't share Aren's fears.

Aren strode ahead of Galo as they walked. The prison came into view a few minutes later. The structure was as Bethania described—a large square building with a tower in the center, surrounded by a courtyard, and three smaller buildings scattered on the grounds. There was an iron fence surrounding the entire property, with tips that would be rather painful if he landed on them.

Bethania had said a lookout was stationed in the center tower, but usually only when the prisoners were outside. Aren couldn't see it clearly enough to confirm that it was empty.

They jogged to the fence. Galo leaned down, letting Aren use his back to hoist himself up. Aren grasped the iron bars and carefully swung one leg, then the other, over the fence, and jumped to the ground. The hard fall reverberated through his legs, and he took a moment to steady himself.

He raised his eyebrows at Galo, asking if he was ready, and Galo nodded. Aren used his Ruined magic to lift Galo off the ground, over the fence, and set him down gently on the other side.

They took off running to the north door. A guard stood in front of it, hands stuffed in his pockets, his back to them.

"*Wall breach!*" a voice shouted from somewhere above Aren. That tower must have been occupied after all.

The guard at the door whirled around. He gasped and reached for the club at his waist.

Aren threw the guard back against the wall, pinning him there with one stare. He grabbed Galo's wrist as they ran closer, though he wasn't even sure he needed to. His power hummed inside of him peacefully, like it wasn't bothered by Aren's sudden use of it.

"Get the keys," Aren said, releasing Galo. "I've got him."

The guard's eyes widened, his body shaking as it remained pinned to the wall.

Galo grabbed the keychain off the guard's belt. There were five or six keys on the chain, all different shapes and sizes.

"Which one?" Aren asked the guard as Galo hurriedly tried a key.

The guard just stared at him wide-eyed, even though he was perfectly capable of talking.

Aren dared a glance over his shoulder. There were no footsteps, but he feared most of the guards were inside. It would be much easier for the guards to face them inside the prison, and they knew it.

"Found it," Galo said as the door swung open. A long, dark hallway stretched out in front of them.

Aren grabbed Galo's arm, pulling him back so he could go in first. He glanced at the guard and tossed him clear across the courtyard, a yelp sounding in the distance as he hit the ground. Aren stepped into the hallway.

"Keep your eyes open," he said quietly to Galo.

They hurried down the pitch-black hallway. Above him, Aren could hear the sound of running footsteps. The guards were coming for them.

Light poured out of a door to his left, and he glanced in. A deserted dining room. To his right was a closet, half open and full of food trays.

Aren slowed as they reached the end of the hallway and

found a door. He pressed his ear to it, trying to hear if there was anyone on the other side. It was quiet.

He pushed on the door. It didn't move. He pushed harder. Nothing. Galo pressed his shoulder to it.

A loud *pop* sounded from behind Aren. He whirled around. Guards stood at the end of the hallway, throwing something that looked like rocks.

Pop-pop-pop. Light exploded from the rocks. Smoke engulfed the area around Aren and Galo, clouding Aren's vision.

Panic crept into his chest. If he couldn't see, he couldn't fight the guards.

He faced the door again and shoved it. It moved slightly, like it was being held by someone or something on the other side.

"Galo, on the count of three!" He counted down and slammed his body against the door as hard as he could. Galo grunted as he pushed.

The door suddenly gave way, and Aren tumbled through, hitting the ground hard on his back. The tip of a sword appeared in front of his face.

He tilted his head back to see the owner of the sword poised at his throat. A woman scowled down at him. He felt cool metal against his skin.

He shot her up to the ceiling, her body hitting it with a *crack*. She tumbled back to the ground, falling on top of another guard. There were at least ten that Aren could see.

Smoke was spilling into the hallway from behind him, and Aren whipped his head to the right to find Galo. He was on his knees, his sword in front of him as he tried to fend off an attack from two guards.

Aren jumped to his feet, shooting the guards down the hallway. He threw the rest overhead, leaving them to hover there above them as he grabbed Galo's arm and took off. He heard the bodies drop as they ran.

He jumped over the guards at the end of the hallway. One man scooted back against the wall, hands raised in surrender.

They exited the hallway and found a large, round room. There were four different doors leading out of it, including the one behind him. If Bethania was right, the door directly to his left led to the solitary cells.

He took a step in that direction. Galo had closed the door to the hallway behind them and was pressing his back against it. Aren gestured for him to step aside.

Aren opened the door. Two guards were getting to their feet. He rooted them in place and crooked his finger at the surrendering guard, still sitting with his back pressed to the wall. Aren didn't give him a chance to come willingly—he pulled him to his feet with his Ruined magic and forced him to walk forward.

"Iria," Aren said once the man was right in front of him. "Where is she?"

The man pressed his lips together, his eyes darting to the right.

"Is she still in solitary?" Aren asked. "Keep in mind I'd be happy to come back and rip your head off if you don't tell me the truth."

The man shook his head vigorously. "Not anymore. They moved her to the general population yesterday. That door." He pointed to the right.

Aren's heart dropped. "Which cell?"

"Umm . . . I don't remember the exact number. Upper level, in the middle."

Aren grabbed the keys off the guard's belt. "Do these open the cell doors?"

He shook his head.

"Does one open the outer door?"

The guard reached out a shaky hand to point at a large, square key. Aren released his hold on the man, shoved him back into the hallway, and pushed the door shut.

Aren turned to find guards flooding the round room from all entrances. He took a step back and let out a breath, trying to steady himself.

He pushed his Ruined magic out with such force that he almost stumbled. The walls shook as bodies slammed against them. Behind him, he heard Galo take in a deep breath. He touched Aren's arm, like he was checking to see if that had weakened him, but Aren felt stronger than ever.

He cleared the guards from in front of the door with one sweep of his hand and stuck the key in the lock. He stepped inside.

THIRTY-TWO

IRIA'S EYES POPPED open. Someone was yelling. Not the usual yelling from the other inmates she'd already grown accustomed to—this was wild, panicked yelling.

She sat up in bed, ducking her head to avoid hitting it on the bunk. Above her, she heard her roommate stir, and she tensed. Her eye seemed to throb a little harder at the sound. A nasty bruise had formed where Julia had socked her.

"We need more smoke bombs! Get the—" The voice cut off with a scream, followed by a loud bang.

"What is going on out there?" Julia mumbled sleepily.

Iria stood and walked to the bars of her cell. Her fingers shook as she wrapped them around the bars.

She was almost scared to hope.

"Iria!" Aren's voice ripped through the yells.

Her body almost collapsed with relief. "Aren!" she yelled, sticking her arm through the bars.

He shouted her name again, excitedly, and she waved, hoping he could see it.

A hand roughly yanked her back. Julia pulled her into the cell, twisting her around and shoving her against the wall. Iria curled her fingers into fists.

"Aren!" Iria yelled.

Julia went to put a hand over Iria's mouth, but Iria batted it away. She threw a punch, hard, and Julia stumbled backward.

Julia regained her balance quickly and slammed her body into Iria's, shoving her forearm into her neck. She gagged.

The arm disappeared from her neck as a loud *crack* echoed through the room. Julia screamed, stumbling backward as she cradled her arm to her chest.

Iria looked up. Aren stood in front of her cell. He appeared even better than she remembered—strong and confident and looking at her like he'd never been so happy to see someone in his entire life.

But worry crossed his features for just a moment as he took in her appearance. He opened his mouth.

"I've got it!" a voice yelled before Aren could speak. A familiar Lera guard ran to Aren, holding up a key. "I think this is it."

Iria gaped at Galo. What was a Lera guard doing in Olso?

Galo stuck the key in the lock. The door swung open.

Iria stared at Aren and completely forgot her disappointment and anger. She limped across the cell as fast as she could and threw her arms around his neck. He wrapped his arms around her waist so tightly he lifted her off the ground.

"I'm sorry," he whispered. "I should have come sooner."

She shook her head, afraid that if she tried to talk she'd burst into tears. She didn't want to tell him she wasn't sure he was going to come at all.

"Aren, to your left," Galo said.

Aren quickly released her and turned. A line of ten guards ran up the stairs.

Aren settled his gaze on them, and they all tumbled back down at once and landed in a heap at the bottom.

Aren took her hand, glancing down at her bandaged foot.

"I . . . I can't run very fast." Her voice shook, and she wished it hadn't.

"That's fine. I can carry you on my back when we get outside." He gripped her hand a little harder, and she could tell he wanted to say something, maybe ask how she was. She looked away.

Aren reached around her and closed the cell door, locking Julia inside. Her roommate glared at them, still cradling her arm to her chest.

Aren pulled on Iria's hand gently as he started running, glancing at her as though to ask if the pace was comfortable. Pain shot through her foot, but it was bearable. Especially if it meant getting out of here.

She let go of Aren's hand to grasp the railing and limp down the stairs. The bodies of guards were scattered across the floor, some of them dead, but most of them with broken arms or legs. A few ran in the other direction when they spotted Aren coming back.

"Can we go out that door?" Galo asked, pointing to the right. Cells stretched out in either direction, and there was a door at both ends of the room. The left door led straight to the front of the prison, right into the laundry and a mess of hallways she hadn't had a chance to figure out yet.

Aren shook his head. "Let's go out the front. Less chance they can trap us."

They took off again, Aren launching guards against cell doors as they went. The prisoners were screaming and shaking the bars of their cells, and Iria felt a blast of panic shoot up her spine. If Aren failed, she'd be dead by tomorrow. Maybe in the next few minutes. The guards could certainly use an escape attempt as an excuse to kill her.

They reached the door that led to the front lobby, and it was locked when Aren tried it the first time. She had to bat down another swell of panic. But he pulled out a chain of keys and easily slid the right one in.

They ran into the big circular lobby and Aren headed straight for the front door. Through the windows, she could see guards lined up, waiting for them.

Aren fixed his gaze on them through the window, tossing

them so far Iria wasn't even sure where the bodies landed. When he opened the door, there was nothing but bare grass in front of them, all the way to the fence.

Aren crouched down in front of her. "Get on my back."

She circled her arms around his neck and he reached back and grabbed her thighs as he stood. He broke into a jog and headed for the fence.

He let her down when they reached it, and Galo gave him a boost over. Aren used his Ruined magic to pull her and Galo over, and offered his back to her again when she was on the ground. She climbed on.

He ran slowly with her on his back, but his breathing was steady. She buried her face in his neck and refused to look back at the prison.

"Do you want me to take her for a while?" Galo asked as they turned a corner onto a tree-lined road.

Aren shook his head. "I'm fine." They jogged in silence for several minutes, Galo often running backward as he checked to see if they were being followed. In the distance, Iria heard shouts, but no one appeared as they turned another corner.

Aren slowed to a walk after a few more minutes, turning to peer behind him.

"I haven't seen anyone," Galo said.

Aren nodded, leaning down to let Iria slide off. They stood in front of a small, unfamiliar house. The front door opened a crack, then a little more. A familiar face stuck her head out. Bethania.

Tears sprang to Iria's eyes as she limped forward. Bethania

eased the door wider and opened her arms, enveloping Iria in a hug as soon as she stepped over the threshold.

Iria couldn't stop the tears now that they'd started, and her shoulders shook as Bethania held her tighter.

"I can't believe they actually did it," Bethania murmured, her tone almost amused.

Iria smiled through her tears. "They had a bit of help from you?"

"Some. But I let those crazy boys go in on their own."

Iria laughed as she pulled away. Her bruised eye stung as she wiped her tears away. "That was probably smart."

Bethania stepped back, waving Aren and Galo in. "Come on. Quickly."

Iria stepped farther into the house. The front two rooms were completely empty, a few pieces of trash scattered on the wooden floors, like someone had just moved out.

"I knew the house was vacant," Bethania said, following her gaze. "We have some clothes for you, and food. We don't think it's smart to stay long in this area, because they'll probably go house to house when they can't find you on the road."

"We're going to wait until they sweep the roads in this area, then we'll go back out," Aren said. "Bethania got us some horses."

"I stole them," Bethania admitted.

"You always were stealthy," Iria said. She slid down the wall and hit the ground heavily.

"Why are you limping?" Bethania asked.

"I was injured," Iria said, closing her eyes briefly. It seemed easier to not look at any of them. All of them had matching worried expressions on their faces. Even Galo, a man she'd barely spoken to, seemed alarmed.

"How?" Aren asked.

"A knife. They had to take off part of my foot."

"Who?" Aren asked sharply. "One of the guards?"

Iria nodded wordlessly.

"Does it hurt?" Bethania asked. "I can maybe find bandages, if you need."

She started to say no, but the bandages hadn't been changed today and the last thing she needed was an infection.

"We should probably change them," she admitted.

"I have some fresh clothes for you too," Bethania said. She ushered Galo and Aren out of the room and sat in front of Iria with new bandages.

Iria leaned her head back against the wall. "Thank you. For asking them to leave. I need a moment."

"I could tell." One side of Bethania's mouth lifted as she unwrapped the old bandages on Iria's foot. "I can also tell you're happy to see Aren."

"Yes, well."

"It's complicated?"

Iria blew her hair out of her face. "Yes."

"I like him. He's crazier than you are, which is saying something."

Iria laughed, her first genuine laugh in weeks. Bethania had thought she was insane to volunteer for the mission to Lera to help Em, and she hadn't been shy about expressing that feeling.

Of course, this whole situation proved her right. Iria decided not to mention that.

"They really took off a substantial portion of your foot," Bethania said as she bandaged it. "Was it that bad of an injury?"

"I don't know, I passed out. It was a very large knife, though they might have decided to amputate instead of treating just to spite me."

"Bastards," Bethania muttered. She finished and sat back, glancing over her shoulder. Aren and Galo were still out of sight, and Iria could hear mumbled conversation from another part of the house. "They're taking you back to Lera. Is that what you want?"

"Do I have any other choice?"

"I'm sure we could come up with something."

"Lera is fine. Is Aren . . ." She trailed off, her eyes darting to the door. "What part of Lera? Is he dropping me somewhere?"

"Let's change your clothes and you can ask him yourself." She tossed Iria brown pants and a white shirt. Iria slowly got to her feet and changed, tossing her prison clothes aside. The new clothes were softer against her skin, and she gratefully shrugged into a warm coat. It wasn't that cold, but she was shivering nonetheless.

Bethania opened the door and called for Aren and Galo as Iria plopped down on the floor again.

"Iria was asking where you're going," Bethania said.

Aren met Iria's gaze. "Em's at the castle with a bunch of other

Ruined. We're going there, if that's all right with you."

"And Olivia?"

"She's on her own. I'm staying with you in the Lera castle. I won't leave you."

She felt more relieved than she wanted to admit. She didn't want to go to Lera by herself, especially not now.

Aren reached into a bag and pulled out a canteen and something wrapped in a cloth. He sat down in front of her, crossing his legs. A piece of the cloth flopped over, revealing a sandwich.

Her fingers brushed his as she took the sandwich. He looked at her as if he had a million things he wanted to say, but he just lowered his eyes. Maybe it was because Bethania and Galo were there, or maybe he just felt too awkward. She'd thought he was going to kiss her that night in the woods, when he'd told her she'd have to go to Royal City without him, and the uncomfortable buzz of that night still lingered between them.

"Thanks, Aren," she said quietly. She was expressing gratitude for more than the sandwich he'd just handed her, and he smiled like he understood.

"You're welcome."

THIRTY-THREE

CAS RETURNED TO the castle just before sunrise, and found Em half asleep in his bed. She jerked awake as he climbed in, and he quietly relayed his conversation with August. She didn't say much as he told her about August's plan to betray the Ruined; she just wrapped her arms around him and squeezed, like she'd never expected a different answer from Cas.

She was gone when he woke up, the sun now high in the sky, and he dressed and headed to his office. He'd recounted the story for Violet and Franco last night, but he was asked to explain it again to General Amaro, which led to a tense discussion on possible Olso plans of attack.

Cas slipped away, leaving a message with a guard to have Em come and find him when she was done working with Weakling today. He retreated to the tallest point of the castle—an attic filled with dusty memories of his grandparents and ancestors he'd never known. There was a loft area above the storage with a tiny round window that looked out all the way to the ocean, and he'd made the space his own years ago. A blanket and a few pillows were scattered on the floor, books stacked in the corners. Only a few guards had known about the spot, before, and he was never disturbed when he came here.

Now, he heard a guard cough on the other side of the door. Two had followed him up here.

He leaned his head against the wall and closed his eyes, pretending for a moment that he was back in the world he'd known a few months ago—when he and Em had just started to get along and his parents were still alive and his biggest worry was his father's approval.

He felt a stab of guilt as he opened his eyes. It was easy for him to think fondly of the way things used to be, when Lera was great, but it meant ignoring the fact that it wasn't great for Em, or the Ruined. Reminiscing about those times was selfish and ignored the pain they'd caused.

Behind him, the door creaked open. It really wasn't a great hiding spot.

"Cas."

He turned at the sound of Em's voice and crawled to the edge of the loft to look down. She stood next to the ladder below him and turned in a circle, surveying the boxes and old furniture around her.

"Is this it? The hidden room?" she asked.

"What?"

"When I was looking for you once, when I lived here before, you said you were in a hidden room. Is this it?"

"Yes." He pointed to the ladder. "Come up."

She climbed the ladder and ducked her head as she stepped into the loft space. He scooted back, leaning his head against the wall and stretching his legs out in front of him. She sat down across from him, glancing briefly out the window.

"I think we should talk about Franco's question," he said, his heart pounding in his chest. "About marriage."

"Yes." She rubbed her hands on her pants. "Can I go first?"

"Please."

"Do you think the Lerans will even let—?" She cut herself off, shaking her head. "Sorry. That's the wrong place to start."

"The wrong place?"

"Everyone else's opinions. That's the wrong place to start this conversation." She met his gaze, a look crossing her face he'd never seen before. She was nervous, maybe. Her cheeks turned pink.

"I love you," she said.

He blinked. His heart hammered in his chest, still expecting the worst. "What?"

"I love you," she said again, like he actually hadn't heard. "Of course I want to marry you. Again."

A smile spread across his face and she laughed, still blushing.

"Is there a 'but'?" he asked.

"No. I want to marry you. I don't think the Ruined will object, but frankly, I don't care if they do."

His eyebrows shot up. "You don't?"

"No. I've sacrificed plenty for them. I don't need to give you up too." Her smile faded a bit, the way it did when she was about to mention her sister. "I told Olivia I would, but it was a lie. I never would have given you up, Cas."

He was trying not to grin, but he was so happy he thought he might burst out of his skin. "I want to marry you, too," he said, even though she already knew.

"And do you think the Lerans will allow it?"

"I don't care."

"I'll be an unpopular queen. I'm used to people looking down on me, hating me. Some Lerans will never accept me, and they'll hate you, too. Are you all right with that?"

"Yes." He said it with absolute confidence.

"When we start negotiations we'll need to make it clear that you get to choose who you marry, even if we strip the monarchy of some of its power. We can't give anyone approval or veto power over your marriage. For your sake and for the sake of your"—her lips twitched up—"our—children."

He leaned forward, reaching for her. She slipped her hand into his and let him tug her closer, scooting across the floor and settling down in his lap with one knee on either side of his thighs. He tilted his head up and kissed her briefly.

"They would be fools to say no," she said. She looped her arms around his neck. "Our children will be Ruined. Every other kingdom will be terrified of Leran royalty, even if we have a limited role in government. August made that clear last night. Tell them that."

He laughed as she leaned down to kiss him again. "They'll like that, actually."

"I know they will."

He pressed his lips to hers again, tightening the arm around her waist. All of this was assuming that Olivia didn't kill them all, or August didn't launch a successful attack and take the country from Cas again. He knew they weren't anywhere close to out of danger yet, but he let himself pretend for a moment, as he kissed Em.

She pulled back just a little and rested her forehead against his. Her fingers were in his hair, gently gripping the too-long strands. He was overdue for a haircut, but he might leave it long if she was going to grab it like that.

"I'm sorry," she whispered. "That I didn't tell you I loved you before, that I didn't believe we could do this the way you did. It's not that I didn't love you, I was just scared."

"I know," he said, even though he was practically still vibrating with relief from her confession. She didn't need to know that a tiny part of him hadn't been sure that she loved him the way he loved her.

She kissed him like he'd been totally insane to doubt her. Her fingers were still in his hair and his hands found their way to her thighs. If he and Em had been somewhere more private, he probably would have started tearing her clothes off. He would have pushed her back on the pillows and finished what they started weeks ago in Vallos.

But he heard the murmured voices of the guards outside and pulled back, letting his lips linger on hers for a moment longer.

"Have dinner with me tonight?" he asked. "The staff has reluctantly agreed to let me make my own meals in the small kitchen off the private dining room."

"You're going to cook the dinner?" she asked, raising her eyebrows.

"Don't look so skeptical. I've gotten pretty good."

Her smile suggested she knew what he had in mind for after dinner. "I'd love to."

THIRTY-FOUR

AFTER THE WARRIORS did a sweep of the street, Aren ushered everyone out of the house. He could still feel the humans in the prison from the house, and he was eager to get as far away as possible.

He carried Iria on his back as they made their way down the street. Galo took over when Aren started to get tired, and he could tell Iria was frustrated with having to be carried—she mentioned several times that she could walk, but her pain was apparent every time her feet hit the ground.

Aren was curious about the full extent of her injury, but she wasn't forthcoming with details and he didn't want to pry. At least she could walk, if she had to. They could worry about the details later.

Warriors spread out through the streets of the city, and Galo suggested they stay not far behind one group as they made their way out. It was easy to stay away from any humans as they ventured farther out of town, since Aren could easily feel them coming.

Bethania had tied up the two stolen horses in trees near the tracks that led back to the border. Iria slid off Galo's back as they approached them.

"I have to leave you here," Bethania said. "I should get home before someone shows up at my door with questions."

Iria walked to Bethania and pulled her into a hug.

"You could come with us?" Iria said it as a question, her face in Bethania's shoulder, and Aren could barely hear the words.

"I know. They offered." Bethania pressed a kiss to Iria's cheek and pulled away. "But this is still my home."

Iria swept a hand across her eyes, but her body was angled away from Aren, so he couldn't see her tears. He had the same feeling he'd had at the house—that Iria was more upset than she was letting on, and there was nothing he could do about it.

Bethania said good-bye to Galo, then smiled at him. "It was nice to meet you, Aren. You better get her to Lera safely."

"I will."

Bethania hugged Iria again, briefly, then quickly turned away. She didn't look back as she jogged down the road.

Aren let Iria watch for a moment, then quietly said, "Ride with me?"

Iria nodded, swallowing hard as she turned around. He

mounted the horse first, then extended his hand to her. Galo helped lift Iria onto the horse, and she settled in behind Aren.

"I'm really tired," she said softly. "I might fall asleep."

"Go ahead. I'll wake you up if there's a problem."

"You're headed to the south section of the border, right? Bethania told you about the abandoned posts?"

"She told us."

Her arms slid around his waist, and he felt her cheek against his shoulder a moment later. "Wake me up if you need help navigating."

He laid his hands on top of hers for a moment. "I will."

Bethania was right—a portion of the Olso border to the south was unguarded, the towers abandoned. Iria was still asleep as they crossed, and Aren sat up straight, alert and waiting for trouble.

It never came, and they easily crossed into the unguarded Lera. Aren found himself breathing a sigh of relief. When had Lera become his safe place?

They rode for a few hours, putting some distance between them and the border. They stopped not long after sunrise, and Galo led the horses to a stream while Iria sank down against a tree. Aren sat across from her and held out her canteen.

"Thanks." She tipped her head back as she drank.

They sat in silence for several long moments. Galo didn't come back, and Aren thought he was probably making himself scarce so they could talk. Aren wasn't sure where to begin.

"The Ruined are really at the Lera castle?" Iria finally asked.

"That's where they were headed when we left," he said.

She jerked her head in the direction Galo had disappeared. "How'd you convince him to come?"

"I didn't. He offered. We . . . became friends?" The statement felt strange, and came out as a question. But the word *friend* seemed the only appropriate way to describe Galo.

Iria laughed softly. "Huh."

"And I think he feels guilty about everything." He didn't expand on what *everything* was, but he knew she understood.

Silence stretched out between them again, and he took in a deep breath, trying to find the right words.

"I'm sorry," he said quietly. "For abandoning you. For not saving you when the warriors took you."

"You tried," she said to the ground.

"If it hadn't been for Olivia, I would have been at full strength and those warriors wouldn't have stood a chance against me. I'm sorry I was too scared to separate myself from her."

"I understand you had to stay with Em."

"Maybe me and Em don't always need to be together anymore. We want the same thing, and we can do it separately occasionally."

She nodded. "It's . . ." Her voice trailed off. "Thank you, Aren. For rescuing me. For everything."

He noticed she didn't say *It's all right*, because maybe it wasn't yet. Still, she didn't seem mad at him. She looked exhausted, and in pain, and he thought that her relationship with him probably wasn't her first priority at the moment.

"You're welcome," he said. "And if you need any help with your foot, don't hesitate to ask." He gestured at his scarred hands. "I have experience treating terrible wounds."

She managed a small smile. "I'll let you know."

THIRTY-FIVE

EM PICKED A familiar pink dress for dinner. It was low-cut in front with a million buttons in back, and something about it appealed to her. It was beautiful, but it was more than that. When she pulled it out of the closest she was sure something great had happened the last time she wore it.

Em stared at the dresses for a long time before making her choice. Cas's mother had picked out every one, and Em could hear the queen's voice in her head—*I have excellent taste*—when she looked at them. She wasn't sure if the queen would be furious or smug that Em still wore them after her death.

But apparently Cas didn't mind her wearing them, since he'd brought them to his room. And she certainly wasn't going to waste a huge wardrobe. Someone had worked hard, and quickly, to make all these dresses for her.

She'd told Cas she'd meet him in the private kitchen on the first floor, and she walked out of his room and through the castle hallway. It was still quieter than usual in the castle, but she spotted Mariana turning a corner to the sparring rooms with Mateo and another guard, Gisela following behind with a deeply suspicious look on her face. Em paused at the top of the stairs, wondering if she should go check on them.

No. She couldn't hover around the Ruined forever, trying to ward off possible conflicts. The best thing she could do right now was to step back and let the Ruined get to know some of the people in the castle.

Two guards stood in front of the door to the dining room, and one opened it as she approached.

"Thank you," she said as she stepped inside.

She'd never been in this room, even when she lived here before. The rectangular table in the center of the room sat eight, but only two places had been set, right across from each other. The curtains were drawn back from the two large windows, letting in the last wisps of sunlight and showing off a view of the side gardens.

Two people Em didn't know stood at the end of the table, a tall, slim man and a pretty older woman, each of them holding a basket. They straightened as she walked into the room.

The door to her right swung open and Cas stepped out,

changed into nicer clothes than the last time she'd seen him, but already rumpled. One side of his shirt stuck out of his pants. She stifled a giggle.

He smiled at her, then looked at the man and woman. "This is Queen Emelina. Em, this is Kenton and Lucinda. They own the largest bakery in Royal City. They made some cheese bread for me, and they brought you a present as well. I asked them to stay to deliver it personally."

Lucinda crossed the room. She held it out to Em. "I made you some berry tarts, Your Majesty."

Em took them slowly. "For me?"

"For you," Lucinda said with a nervous laugh. "My children love them. I thought you might like to try them, since berries don't grow in Ruina."

"I—thank you," Em stuttered. "That's very kind of you."

"They were made in the kitchen here," Lucinda said. "I know there are strict rules about what you and King Casimir can eat."

She didn't know of any rules, but it had already crossed her mind that the tarts could be poisoned. She smiled and thanked them again.

Lucinda and her husband bowed their heads and left the room, a guard shutting the door behind them.

"She made me tarts," Em said to Cas, holding them up.

"I know," he said, his voice full of amusement. He crossed the room and kissed her gently.

"Are there rules about what you can eat?"

"Yes, since I was poisoned my food is strictly monitored. So is yours." He pointed to the basket in her hand. "It was all prepared here, with ingredients from our kitchens, under guard supervision."

"Wonderful." She put the basket on the table and tried to suppress a grin as she looked at him. "Come here."

"What?" He looked down at his clothes.

"You're all rumpled." She tucked the escaped edge of shirt back into his waistband. The first time she'd met him, she'd thought it was strange he was so rumpled and dusty, especially compared to his perfectly pressed parents. It had momentarily distracted her from the rage and terror she'd felt stepping out of that carriage as Mary.

Cas looked her up and down. "I know this dress. I unbuttoned this dress for you once."

Em pressed her hands to the waist of her dress with a laugh. "I thought I remembered something nice about this dress."

"That was back when you still hated me."

"You were already wearing me down, honestly." She rose up on her toes and kissed him. "I hope you'll unbutton it for me again tonight," she whispered against his lips.

His hand tightened on her waist. "I certainly will."

She kissed him again, lingering for a moment. When she pulled away his eyes flicked to her left arm, which bore the scars of the Olso fire.

"Does that still hurt?" he asked.

"No."

"Good." He turned and headed back into the kitchen, and

she followed him. Meat crackled on the stove, and he turned the two pieces over in the pan. A pot of something sat across from the meat, and she peeked inside. It was a white creamy soup.

"I may have had help with the soup," he said. "And the bread. But I did knead it myself. I'll start going down to the kitchen more often and take out my frustration on dough."

She peeked into a bowl on the counter. Rolls. Next to it, a bowl of potatoes.

"You enjoy it?" she asked, sitting at the small table against the wall. "Cooking?"

"Yes. It's relaxing, the chopping and kneading. And it's satisfying, to put it all together and see it make a meal." He turned, bracing his hands against the counter behind him. "You don't like cooking?"

"Not particularly. I prefer it this way. Someone else making me food." She smiled at him.

He leaned down to kiss her quickly, then returned his attention to the meat.

"Do you think you would have been a chef, if you had been born into a different family?" she asked.

He cocked his head. "Maybe. When I was younger I wanted to be a teacher, but that was only because my tutors came and went from the castle every day. I think I just wanted that kind of freedom. And they told me stories about studying in Vallos or living in Gallego City. It seemed very glamorous to me, to be a teacher. Plus, my father—" He stopped suddenly, his shoulders tensing.

"You can talk about your father, Cas," Em said quietly.

He reached into the shelf and pulled out two bowls. He didn't turn to look at her. "It was a nice memory, the thing I was going to say."

"So? Tell me."

"I can't imagine you want to hear nice things about my father."

"Sure I do," she said honestly. "I don't want you to pretend that your father was horrible all the time and you don't have a single good memory of him. I'm not going to pretend that about my mother. Or my father."

Cas glanced at her over his shoulder. "You never talk about your father. You always mention him as an afterthought like that."

"I didn't know him well. He was uncomfortable around all children, including me and Liv. I think he only had children to make my mother happy."

He nodded as he put the meat on plates, then ladled soup into the bowls. She took them from him and walked into the dining room, placing the soup on the table. Cas followed with the rest, filling her plate and then his own.

"What do you think you would have done if you had been born to a different family?" Cas asked as they sat down.

"Tell me the memory of your father first." She took a bite of meat. "This is delicious, by the way."

"Thank you." He slowly cut into a potato, his eyes on his plate. "My father liked to read. He'd always spend some time with my tutors, recommending books and discussing things with them. I mean, he'd insist that his interpretation of a book was the only correct interpretation, so perhaps it was more of a lecture than a discussion." He laughed softly. "But my father had a lot of respect for my tutors, which is perhaps part of the reason I wanted to be one."

"That makes sense."

"Now tell me yours," he said, letting out a breath of air like he was relieved to be changing the subject.

"I would have been an outcast if I'd been born into a different family," she said. "Since I'm useless. I still was, in many ways, but I was afforded a little more respect, since I was a royal."

"Are there any other useless Ruined still alive?"

"No. There was one, before, but he died."

"Were you friends with him?"

"No, he was fifty years older than me. I never even met him, I just heard about him from other people. My mother probably kept him away on purpose. She didn't want me feeling sorry for myself about being useless, and from what I heard, he was very bitter." She chewed a piece of bread. "I think I might have been a seamstress, in a different life. I've always patched up my own clothes, and I've even made a few of my own dresses."

"Really."

"They weren't very good. But I'd like to try again sometime." Her heart dipped, the way it often did when she thought about the future. She knew it was possible that she didn't have one, that Olivia could burst into the castle tonight and kill everyone. She'd lived with the very real possibility of death for so long that the word *sometime* seemed hopelessly optimistic.

"I'll make sure you get some fabric," Cas said. "We should set up a room where . . ." He let his voice trail off, his expression thoughtful. "We should move into the royal suite. There's a lot more room there."

"I wondered why you hadn't already, honestly."

"Memories." He didn't elaborate. She didn't need him to.

"I think it's a great idea," she said. She reached for his hand. "I would love to move into the royal suite with you."

He smiled, tightening his fingers around hers. "Good."

Em slid her arm around Cas's waist as they walked up the stairs after dinner. He pressed a kiss to the top of her head.

They walked through Cas's library and into his bedroom. Her heart picked up its rhythm, and she pressed her hand to it, hoping he couldn't tell. He looked calmer than she felt.

He put his fingers lightly on her neck, tilting her head up with his thumb, and when he kissed her, she realized he wasn't calm at all. She could feel his breath hitch, could feel a little uncertainty when he put a soft hand on her waist.

She leaned into him, her hands against his chest. Some of her nerves settled as she melted into him, breathing into the kiss until her legs felt weak.

She pulled back just enough to talk, his breath warm on her face. "You should unbutton this dress for me."

His fingers were still tangled in her hair, and they closed

around the strands as he kissed her. "I would love to."

He pulled away and she turned around. He gathered her hair and let it loose over her shoulder. She felt him release the first button, at the base of her neck.

"Did you know I wanted to stay?" he asked, freeing more buttons. "The first time I did this?"

"No. You just left without looking at me." She turned her head, but she couldn't see him. "Did you want to stay?"

"I did, a little. I would have stayed if you had asked." He undid a few more buttons and the dress began to slip down her arms. She let it.

"I hope you plan to stay this time," she said.

He chuckled, air sweeping across her back as he undid the last of the buttons. The dress slipped down farther, and she pulled her arms out of the straps, letting it settle around her waist.

His fingers trailed down her spine, and a moment later, she felt his lips against her skin. He burned fire across her back, his fingers slipping down until they met the dress.

He used both hands to push it down, and the dress crumpled to the floor. He slid one hand around her waist until his palm was flat against her stomach. She leaned against him, taking in a sharp breath as he pressed his lips to her shoulder, then her neck.

She turned, her eyes flicking over his body. He was still fully dressed, which she had known, but was suddenly disappointed about.

She reached for the buttons of his shirt and unfastened them. He grabbed her around the waist before she could push it off, picking her clear off the ground. She laughed, wrapping her legs around him as he took a few steps and dropped her on the bed.

He shrugged out of his shirt as he climbed onto the bed, only to reveal another thin white shirt underneath.

"You have on so many more clothes than me," she complained, tugging at the bottom of his shirt. He ducked his head to let her pull it off.

"Better?" he asked with a grin, bracing his hands on the bed as he gazed down at her.

"Not really," she said, tugging on his belt loop.

He was still smiling as he leaned down to kiss her. She ran her fingers through his hair, the lightness of the moment fading as she wrapped her legs around him. Her breath was stuck in her chest, her hands grabbing at him to pull him closer.

He freed himself from her grasp long enough to sit back and reach for his belt. His gaze flicked over her as he did it. She'd never seen that particular look from him before—his lips curving up, a hint of mischief in his eyes—and she wanted to see it every day for the rest of her life.

She sat up, throwing an arm around his neck and kissing him. A few minutes ago she might have laughed about how she hadn't even let him get his pants off, but her heart was pounding too wildly for laughter.

He pulled her into his lap, his hands warm against her back. His fingers curled against her skin, like he was trying to pull all of her closer to him. She wanted to let him.

She let go of him long enough for him to shed the rest of his clothes, and to let him pull off the last of hers. He climbed back on the bed, his lips finding hers again. She closed her eyes as his lips brushed across her cheek, her neck, down her jaw. His breath was against her ear, then he said her name, a whisper so soft she barely heard it.

"Em."

THIRTY-SIX

GALO CAUGHT AREN glancing at him for the tenth time that day. They were in Lera, only an hour or so from Royal City. Aren and Iria rode on the horse next to him, Iria's arm occasionally circling Aren's waist to steady herself.

"What?" Galo asked.

"I didn't say anything," Aren said.

"You keep looking at me."

"You look nervous. Is it because of Mateo?"

"Mateo? The guard?" Iria asked.

"His boyfriend," Aren said. "He didn't tell him he was going to Olso before running off with me."

"What?" Iria let out a laugh, perhaps the first genuine one Galo had heard from her since they'd left Olso several days ago.

"You didn't tell your boyfriend you were crossing enemy lines?"

"It was a last-minute decision. Besides, he wouldn't have liked it."

Aren threw his head back with a laugh. "I'd come up with a better excuse than that."

"Seriously," Iria muttered.

"He's going to be mad," Galo said.

"That goes without saying," Aren said. "But! You're not dead. I bet he's going to be excited that you're not dead."

"That's what I'm hoping." But nerves still swirled in his gut. It was very possible that Mateo was mad enough to want to break up. Perhaps they'd already broken up, and Galo just hadn't been informed yet.

"I'd be happy to see you, then I'd whack you over the head," Iria said.

"I feel like that would be the best-case scenario," Galo said.

Aren stiffened suddenly, his head whipping to the right. He pulled on the reins of his horse, indicating for Galo to do the same. They both came to a stop.

Galo heard the murmured voices a minute later. Aren had warned them of every nearby human the past few days, steering them to a different area if he sensed a large number of people.

Today, he stayed still, which meant he sensed only a small group. Sure enough, Galo spotted a group of four older men through the trees. They carried bags on their backs and traveled by foot. One looked to his right and spotted them, his eyes resting on Galo first. Then he spotted Aren and went completely still. He could clearly see the Ruined marks on Aren's neck and arms.

"It's all right," Galo called, quickly dismounting his horse. He walked to the men with his hands up in the air. "We're on our way to the castle. You've heard there are Ruined there?"

The man with a thick, dark beard stepped out of the first trees. He eyed Aren warily. "I heard it, but I wasn't sure it was true. We just saw Ruined yesterday, killing people."

"You saw Olivia?" Aren asked from behind Galo.

"I guess," the man said. "We took off before anyone spotted us."

The other three men cautiously stepped forward, one of them staring at Galo's arms intently.

"I'm not Ruined," Galo said quietly. "I'm a former Leran guard making sure these two make it to the castle safely."

"We're headed to the castle too," the bearded man said. "The Ruined—" He stole a glance at Aren. "Well, some of the Ruined, I guess, are following the Olso army. We're going to tell the king."

"They're following the army?" Galo repeated. "How do you know?"

"Because we were tracking the army too. They blew through our town not long ago and took whatever they wanted. We'd heard that King Casimir was rebuilding the army in Royal City, so we decided to head that way. We tracked the army until we spotted the Ruined."

Galo looked over his shoulder at Aren. He wasn't sure why Olivia would find a human army and not strike.

"She's waiting for something," Aren said quietly. "The right moment, or . . . I don't know." He looked at the men. "Can you tell us anything else about the Ruined? What they were doing? Where is the army now?"

"I'm—I'm not sure I should say," the bearded man said nervously. "I think there's some information I should only give the king."

"Understood," Galo said. He couldn't fault them for not trusting strangers they'd just met on the road. "Do you want to travel with us? I can't guarantee you access to the king, but I'll make sure you get to an adviser."

The men agreed and walked stiffly next to their horses as they headed to Royal City, always keeping Aren in their sight. Galo noticed that while Aren was far more subtle about it, he also kept a close watch on the men. The distrust was mutual.

Soon, the top of the castle finally came into view. Guards stood at their usual posts, and the castle wall had been fully repaired since the last time Galo had seen it.

One of the guards recognized Galo, and his eyes widened. He looked from Galo to Aren and back again. He rushed to open the gate. Another guard darted away from the others and up the castle steps. He disappeared inside.

Galo pulled his horse to a stop in front of the gate and dismounted. He unhooked his bag and swung it over his shoulder. Beside him, Aren and Iria also dismounted, Iria wincing as she put pressure on her foot.

"Wait here for a minute," Galo said to the four men. He

walked to one of the gate guards—Wade—and lowered his voice. "We just met those four men on the road. They said they have information for the king. They'll need to be searched for weapons and accompanied by guards if they set foot in the castle."

Wade nodded, then smiled broadly. "Welcome back."

Galo returned the smile. "Thank you." He took a step toward the castle, then stopped and glanced back at Aren and Iria. Iria had her head tipped back, staring up at the castle like she hadn't seen it before, hadn't spent weeks here not long ago. Maybe it looked different this time.

"Are you coming?" Galo asked.

Aren offered his arm to Iria. She shook her head and stepped forward. "I'm fine."

Galo turned back to the castle entrance to see Cas flying through the door. His face broke into a grin when he spotted Galo. He sprinted down the steps and pulled Galo into a hug.

Galo laughed as he squeezed Cas. "Nice to see you too."

"You're totally insane." Cas pulled away, keeping his hands on Galo's shoulders. "Did you really go to Olso?" His eyes flicked behind Galo and he seemed to find his answer immediately as he spotted Iria.

"You seem surprised," Aren said with a hint of amusement. "You didn't actually think I'd be able to rescue her?"

Cas laughed, then to Galo's surprise, embraced Aren briefly. Aren appeared even more shocked.

"I never doubted it for a second," Cas said. He turned his attention to Iria. "It's nice to see you again, Iria."

"You too," Iria said quietly.

Galo glanced behind Cas. If Mateo was on duty, he wasn't allowed to leave his post. So it didn't mean anything that he hadn't shown up yet to greet him.

That's what Galo was telling himself, anyway.

Em appeared at the door and rushed out, grabbing Aren for a hug. Galo pulled Cas aside and spoke quietly.

"Those men claim to have seen the Olso army and Olivia," he said. "We just met them an hour ago. They want to give you information directly."

"Let's hear it, then," Cas said, striding toward the men.

"Cas." Galo jogged to catch up with him. "I don't know them; you should have an adviser—"

Cas waved his hand. "It's fine. I'm immortal."

Galo made an exasperated noise, but several guards were already surrounding Cas, shielding him from the men, who looked startled to see the king approaching them.

Galo started to edge forward, hoping to hear what the men had to say, but a flash of blue caught his eye. Mateo ran out of the castle in his guard uniform, skidding to a stop when he saw the crowd at the gate. His eyes were wild as they bounced over each person, until he found Galo.

Galo let his bag slip through his fingers. Mateo ran to him, almost knocking him over as he hugged him.

"You idiot," Mateo said fiercely.

Galo laughed, relief coursing through his veins. He wrapped

his arms around Mateo's waist and dropped his forehead onto his shoulder.

"You idiot," Mateo said again, quieter.

"I'm sorry," Galo whispered.

Mateo pulled away from him, putting his hands on Galo's neck as he examined him. "Are you hurt?" He found the cut on Galo's eyebrow, not yet fully healed. "What happened?"

"Olivia." He touched it gingerly. "It's fine. Aren is well-prepared for injuries." He took Mateo's hand, glancing at the guards around them within earshot. Cas was inviting the men into the castle, gesturing for Em to follow them. Galo would have to hear what the men had said later.

"Come talk to me?" he asked Mateo.

Mateo squeezed his hand and nodded. They walked inside and up the stairs to Jovita's room—or Galo's room. He was still having a hard time thinking of it that way. It was just as Galo had left it, the wardrobe door ajar from when he'd hurriedly grabbed his jacket.

He dropped his bag on the floor and sat down on the edge of the bed. His body felt heavy, his legs sore from days on a horse.

"I'm sorry I left like that," Galo said to Mateo, who was still lingering by the door. "I could have taken a few more minutes to talk to you, but I just left."

"You could have," Mateo said, lifting an eyebrow. Then he smiled, walking forward until his knees brushed Galo's. Mateo took his hand and laced their fingers together. "I didn't really listen, though. You needed to find a way to help. I just wanted you to stay here, where you were safe."

Galo nodded, swallowing down the lump in his throat.

"Did you succeed?" Mateo asked, one side of his mouth turning up. "Or are you planning a second trip to Olso? Or maybe Vallos this time? They've declared war on us too, you know."

"I think I've had my fill of enemy kingdoms for a while." He looked at his hands, intertwined with Mateo's. "But I do want to keep helping. I don't want to rejoin the guard."

"I know."

"I don't know what's going to happen next, or where Cas will need me. Or where Aren will need me."

Mateo lifted his eyebrows. "Are you taking orders from Aren now?"

"Not taking orders, but I support him. He's my friend." It felt strange to say it out loud, even if Galo knew it was true.

"Your friend," Mateo repeated.

"He's not how he seems. He's actually kind of great."

Mateo let out an exaggerated sigh. "I'm sure it doesn't help that he's also very good-looking."

Galo laughed, pulling on Mateo's hands to bring him closer. "Are you jealous of Aren?"

"I wouldn't say jealous. Concerned, maybe." A smile played on his lips. "Annoyed. Slightly worried."

"We went to rescue Iria because Aren is in love with her. You knew that."

"Well, yes. But you're very charming. He might have changed

his mind halfway there."

He grabbed the front of Mateo's shirt and tugged him closer. "I wouldn't have changed *my* mind."

Mateo smiled as he leaned down to kiss him. "Good."

THIRTY-SEVEN

"SO JOVITA'S ALIVE," Em said. "Or she was, a few days ago. Probably not anymore."

Cas watched as the guards escorted the men out of his office. They'd spotted not only Olivia and the Olso army, but Jovita as well. She was a prisoner of the Ruined, and it seemed unlikely she was still alive.

Conflicting emotions warred in his chest. He hadn't wished for Jovita's death, but he'd be lying if he said he hadn't been relieved that the choice had been taken from him.

One of the guards stole a glance at Em before he shut the door. She sat in Cas's chair, at his desk, and the guards had kept glancing between her and Cas, like they'd thought this was strange.

"Should I have moved?" she asked, noticing the guard's stare. The door quickly shut. "Does it look bad, me sitting in the king's chair?"

"No, I think it's best you sat there," he said. "No doubt the men will tell everyone what they saw, and people should know I trust you."

She leaned back, draping her hands across the arms of the chair. "They may say I've taken control. The poor king can't even sit in his own chair."

He shrugged. "Let them say that." Even if the people in the castle were warming up to the Ruined, they certainly didn't see Em as Cas's equal. He could tell by the way they interacted with her, the way some wouldn't bow or would pretend to not see her in the hallways. Perhaps rumors that Em had more power than Cas would do some good.

"Why would Olivia be tracking the army?" Em asked. "Has she ever stumbled across humans and not killed them?"

"Sure, if she wants something from them."

"Do you think she's made a deal with August?"

"No. Never." Em shook her head, her eyebrows furrowed. "On both sides, never. You know August hates Ruined as much as Olivia hates humans."

"Then . . . ?"

"If it were me . . ." She considered it for a moment. "I would be waiting to see what the army was going to do. Olivia has too many goals—she wants to kill me, she wants to kill you, she wants to conquer Lera. But she can't do it all, not with that small group of Ruined. I'd be waiting for the army to attack, and strike then."

"I was hoping there was a chance that August would change his mind after I refused his deal."

"I think that may be a bit too optimistic," she said. She smiled as if he'd said something funny.

"What?"

"The way you say his name. August."

"How do I say it?"

"Like it tastes bad."

"It does." He wrinkled his nose. "August."

She giggled.

"I don't like him."

"I'm shocked."

"He tried to marry you, and then he kidnapped you. I don't like him."

She leaned forward to kiss him. "We have to assume that August is still planning an attack. They're preparing. Waiting for the right moment. Perhaps we shouldn't let them have it. Strike first."

"We're better positioned here in the castle. We have walls and towers and we know the area well."

"He's just sitting out there, waiting, though. And he told you warriors are pouring into the country. If we continue to wait for an attack, we may just be letting them build up their army and weapons."

"They're still weakened after the Ruined attack. He could

very well be exaggerating to bait us into leaving the safety of the castle and striking first."

"True," she said. "It might be what he wants, for us to grow impatient and strike first."

"We'll wait for now, then?"

"Fine. But what about Jovita? There's a possibility that she could provide Olivia with information. It's probably why she's keeping her alive."

"Jovita doesn't have any useful information, not anymore. Especially not that we're redrawing battle plans to include the Ruined."

"Good. But you'll need to decide what to do about her. If someone is able to get to her, what are your orders?"

He paused, thinking. "I'll ask people to bring me any reports of Olivia or Jovita sightings, but other than that, let's just wait." He let out an annoyed sigh. "If somehow Jovita escapes, she should be brought here to the castle."

"Alive?" Em asked.

"Alive," Cas confirmed.

THIRTY-EIGHT

AREN TOOK IRIA up to Em's old room, which was almost exactly the same as the last time Aren had seen it. All of Em's clothes had been removed, but the blue bedding and extravagant furniture were the same.

Iria walked slowly to the bed and sat with a sigh, then pulled off her shoes. She was clearly in pain every time she walked.

"We should have a doctor look at your foot," he said.

"It just needs to heal."

"Are you hungry?" he asked. "I can go find some food for you. Or do you need a bath? I can find a maid to bring up some warm water." He didn't know what to do, and he felt like if he offered everything, maybe something might be the right thing to say.

"I just want to rest," she said, scooting back on the bed. She pulled back the blankets. That was clearly his cue to leave, but he lingered by the door anyway, hesitant to leave her alone.

"Do you mind if I come check on you in a few hours?" he asked. "I know it's uncomfortable, staying in the Lera castle." He almost added *for me, too* to the end of the sentence, but that wasn't really true. His first visit to the castle had been horrible and terrifying, but this one was not. He was relieved to be back.

"Sure, that's fine," she said, pulling the blankets over her. She hadn't changed her clothes, and Aren realized suddenly that she didn't have any. She didn't have anything, except for the clothes on her back.

He almost told her he'd find some, and anything else she wanted, but she'd already closed her eyes. She probably didn't care about her things right now. He hadn't, when they'd all burned. His possessions had been pretty far down the list of worries.

He walked out of the bedroom, then the sitting room, shutting the door quietly behind him. Em was walking down the hallway, and she stopped in front of her old door.

"Did those men have useful information?" Aren asked.

"Not really. They spotted Jovita. Still alive."

Aren winced. Olivia certainly wasn't treating Jovita well. Death might have been kinder.

"I know." Em tilted her head toward Iria's room. "Is she all right?"

"I think she needs some time to . . ." He wasn't sure what she needed time to do. Not just heal, but to adjust.

"Is the injury serious?" Em asked.

Aren glanced over his shoulder at the maids clustered at the end of the hallway. "Come on," he said, leading Em down the hall, to the corner room Violet had just shown him. It was smaller than Iria's, just a single room and bathroom, but it was still impressive, with a huge wardrobe, a large desk, and giant windows that overlooked the south lawn. It was obviously used for important guests, and Aren wasn't sure it suited him.

He shut the door behind Em and sat down in the desk chair. Em perched on top of the trunk at the end of the bed.

"Some of the guards attacked her," Aren said. "She took a knife to the foot. They cut off a good portion of it."

"Can she still put weight on it?" Em asked.

"She can. Or she will, eventually. It's still painful. She'll walk with a limp, though."

"She might have a hard time with a sword as well," Em murmured. "Balance, I mean. It's fine. I'll work with her."

"Galo and I were talking about it, and we think we can make her a boot to wear that will help. It's not a terrible injury, she just needs something to balance out the part of the foot she lost."

"It's lucky you got there so fast," she said. "It could have been much worse."

He'd been trying not to think about that. "How are things here?"

"We haven't started any formal meetings yet. We've been working on armor and putting together battle strategies so the

Ruined can fight with us. Plus, we were hoping you would return soon."

"You were waiting for me?" he asked, surprised.

"There aren't a lot of Ruined leaders left. Everyone looks up to you. And I think it might be better if you and Mariana take the lead in negotiations, considering my relationship with Cas."

"I'd be happy to. I need a day or two to rest, though."

"Of course. The other Ruined are downstairs, if you want to go see them. We offered to put some of them in a few rooms like this one, but they wanted to stay together in the guards' quarters."

Aren nodded. He didn't feel the same, he realized. He wanted to be up here, close to Iria, not back in the tiny guards' quarters.

He wasn't sure how to balance his feelings for her with his responsibilities with the Ruined. He'd never known, but the answer was muddled now. Putting the Ruined first had always been natural, a given, but that wasn't the case anymore.

"I want to see about getting some clothes for Iria," he said. "Is that possible?"

"They provided some basic stuff to the Ruined, so check with Mariana. There are a lot of refugees from Gallego City and Westhaven in Royal City, so they're stretched thin, but Cas is doing his best to get everyone basic necessities."

He realized that the burst of annoyance that used to accompany any mention of Cas's name had disappeared. "And you and Cas? Are you officially staying married?"

"Yes. We'd have to marry again, but we'd like to." Her throat bobbed as she swallowed. "I was hoping I could get your support on that. I think the other Ruined will follow your lead here."

"Em," he said gently. "Of course. It's your choice."

She looked a little surprised. "You're sure? You told me once that he was nothing compared to me."

"I was wrong. He's not as strong as you, he's not the natural leader you are, but he's not nothing. He's a good man, and you deserve to be happy. Everything you've done has been for the Ruined. We can let you have this."

She got to her feet, crossed the room, and circled her arms around his neck. "Thank you, Aren."

He laughed as he embraced her. "You must have known I wasn't going to fight you on Cas. I just went to Olso to rescue a warrior."

She was smiling as she pulled away from him. "I hoped. But I also would have understood if you told me I had certain responsibilities as queen."

"You do, but we're about to upend the entire Lera government, and probably our own as well. I'll fight for you to marry Cas in the meetings, if that's what you want."

"It is, thank you."

THIRTY-NINE

A DOCTOR VISITED Iria and examined her foot. He said she was healing fine, but she needed to stay off of it as much as possible for the next few days. Apparently he relayed this information to Cas, because a staff member showed up in her room with a pile of books, a tray of snacks, and a bell. She told Iria to ring it whenever she needed something.

Iria had pushed the bell across the nightstand. Her new personal goal was to never ring it.

She lay back on the pillows. Her foot hurt a little, but it had healed a lot on the journey from Olso to Lera.

She'd asked the doctor how long it would hurt, and he said not much longer, provided she rested and took care of it. She supposed that was good news, but she was having a hard time getting excited about it.

If the journey from Olso to Lera had taught her anything, it was that she wasn't nearly as strong as she used to be. She couldn't walk without limping, and that wouldn't change once her foot healed. Her balance was off without toes to steady her, and she frequently almost fell on her face just trying to move from one place to another. Aren was constantly catching her, and it was humiliating.

This could have been good timing—she was no longer a warrior anymore—but it didn't really feel like it. She wasn't sure what skill she had if she couldn't fight. Her loyalty to Olso felt thin at best after her time in prison, but it wasn't like she could offer to help Cas. What was she going to do in Lera?

A knock sounded on the bedroom door. She'd left the sitting room door open so she wouldn't have to get up when Aren returned. She called for him to come in.

The door opened to reveal Em, and Iria sat up a little straighter, surprised.

"Hello," Em said. "You look terrible."

"Thanks," Iria said dryly, even though she knew it was true. She'd caught a glimpse of herself in the mirror after bathing. The bruises on her face were an ugly shade of yellow and blue, and she was gaunt and pale.

Em shut the door behind her and crossed the room to perch on the edge of Iria's bed. "Who did that to you?" she asked, gesturing to Iria's face.

"Cellmate."

Em glanced around the room. "This used to be my room, you know."

"I remember. Where are you now?"

"With Cas."

Iria smiled. "Of course."

"You didn't come out for dinner last night. Are you hiding from us?"

"Just from you, actually."

Em gave her a mildly annoyed look, her lips twitching.

"I'm resting." She pointed to her foot. "I'm injured."

"I heard it's healing very nicely." Em walked closer to the bed. "Do you mind if I take a look?"

Iria threw the blankets off to reveal her feet, the right one bandaged. Em perched on the edge of the bed and examined her feet.

"It could have been much worse," Em said.

"That doesn't really make me feel better."

"Sorry."

A knock sounded on the door, and Aren stepped inside a moment later. He wore fresh clothes, all evidence of their journey gone. He looked relaxed and handsome, his eyes lighting up when he looked at her.

"How are you feeling?" Aren asked. He'd visited her last night when the doctor was there, and peppered him with so many questions that the man seemed a bit aggravated by the time he left.

"Fine," she said.

"I was just making her feel worse," Em said.

"She was," Iria confirmed with a laugh. She actually hadn't felt this good in weeks.

"I suspected as much." Aren crossed the room and held out the measuring tape. "Do you mind if I measure your feet? A few staff members are going to help me build boots for you, but I need measurements first."

She nodded, and Em moved away from the bed, letting Aren take her spot.

"We're starting formal talks between the Lerans and the Ruined soon," Em said as Aren held up the measuring tape to Iria's good foot. "I wanted to check to see if there's anything you want."

"Anything I want?"

"In terms of your asylum here. I was thinking I could include you as part of the Ruined, because we'll be asking for housing, reparations, things like that. But you're welcome to negotiate on your own, if you want. Cas will be fair to you."

"Cas won't hold power for much longer, though," Aren said, his eyes flicking to Iria's. "It might be in your best interest to let us include you with the Ruined. We can request whatever you want."

"What am I supposed to want?" Iria asked.

"I don't know, honestly. Queen Fabiana asked to marry King Salomir when she defected from Olso, but I can't imagine you want that."

A laugh burst from her mouth so suddenly she clapped her

hand over it to stifle it. Another one bubbled in her chest. Aren grinned.

"That's a no to marrying Cas, then?" Aren asked.

She lowered her hand, giving in to the smile spreading across her face as she looked at Em. "No. In fact, I think I'll go back to Olso if someone suggests me marrying Cas."

"Hey!" Em exclaimed.

"I would pick prison over marrying Cas too," Aren said.

Iria laughed again, realizing she hadn't done that since last she'd seen him. A lot of people saw Aren as stoic and serious, and she'd always felt secretly smug that she knew the real him.

"You don't need to know what you want right away," Aren said. "Just think about if there's anything you need. Maybe start with a document making you a citizen of Lera. Then Olso can't ever demand your return, or legally take you again. You'll belong to this country."

"Will the Ruined be asking to be citizens of Lera as well?" she asked.

"I think so. We have no plans to go back to Ruina, so someone has to take us," Em said. "I can just include you when we discuss housing and citizenship, and we'll figure out the rest later, if you want."

"Sure," Iria said gratefully.

"Good." Em walked to the door. "I'll see you both later. Iria, you better start practicing with that boot when it's ready, because I expect to start sparring with you again soon."

The thought of sparring with Em was a little terrifying,

considering she was often better than Iria, even when Iria was at her best.

"To the death, right?" Em said.

"What?" Iria asked with a short laugh.

"That's what you always used to say when we sparred in the Ruina castle." Em lifted her hand like she was holding a sword and tilted her head back dramatically. "To the death!"

"I did do that, didn't I?"

"You were very intense." She smiled at Iria. "To the death, then? Later?"

"I look forward to it," she lied.

Em left, shutting the door behind her, leaving Iria alone with Aren. He'd finished measuring her foot but was still perched on the edge of the bed. They hadn't really been alone since before he'd rescued her. She'd sent him away quickly yesterday, feigning exhaustion, when really, she just wanted to be left alone to feel sorry for herself.

They actually hadn't had privacy since she'd deserted her fellow warriors and took off with him in the Lera jungle. If he'd stayed with her, and she hadn't been taken back to Olso, they might already be sharing a bed by now. She might have grabbed him by the collar and pulled him beneath the covers with her.

Instead, he was clasping and unclasping his hands, like she made him nervous. "I should get started on the boot," he said, standing. "Do you need anything?"

"No, I'm fine."

"If you wanted to go to dinner later, I'd be happy to help."

"No, thanks. The doctor said I should stay off the foot for a few days."

He nodded, sliding his hands into his pockets. "I'll come check on you later, then." He turned and walked out, leaving Iria alone again.

FORTY

EM MOVED INTO the royal suite with Cas. All of his parents'
belongings had been removed, and the room that used to be his
father's was mostly bare except for the bed Cas had brought in
from his old room.

She woke up in that bed every day with him. In the mornings,
he would roll over and wrap an arm around her waist, pulling her
close, and the sun would be high in the sky by the time they
emerged from the suite.

Today, she lightly kissed his forehead, then scooted out of
bed. He caught her hand as her feet touched the floor.

"Where are you going?" he asked.

"First Ruined negotiation today," she said. "We have to get
dressed."

He let go of her hand and rolled over to look at her. He attempted a smile, but she could see the nerves all over his face. She probably looked the same way.

They'd spent the last week or so in a bubble—settling into the royal suite, spending every night together, and pretending that there weren't several people who wanted to kill them. Em spent a lot of time trying to ignore the ache in her chest, the reminder that one of the people who wanted to kill her was her own sister. But today was a harsh dose of reality—the Ruined and the Lerans would decide if they could actually get married.

They'd handed the discussions over to other people after telling everyone their intentions. Aren spoke for the Ruined, and several of Cas's advisers were making decisions for the Lerans. They'd yet to have formal discussions since Em had first brought up the idea of stripping the monarchy of some of its power. There was the possibility that everything could fall apart today.

"I want to go down and see the Ruined before we start. Galo was going to stop by this morning," she said. Cas had offered Galo the job of Ruined ambassador, and Galo had accepted. He'd spent the last couple of days discussing smaller things with them and preparing for the meeting.

They dressed mostly in silence, and Em gave Cas a quick kiss before stepping out of the suite. She headed downstairs, to where the Ruined were gathered in the guards' common area. Galo sat with Aren, Mariana, and Davi, and he nodded as he stood. Aren smiled when he spotted Em and waved her over.

"We were just about to go up," Aren said.

"It's a bit early, isn't it?" Em asked, trying to calm the butterflies in her stomach.

"I want to introduce Aren to a few of the advisers. He's never officially met a few of them."

"Will you introduce me as *the bad one*?" Aren asked. "I have a reputation to maintain."

"I'll try to slip it into the conversation." Galo laid a hand on Aren's arm and steered him to the door. Aren laughed at something Galo said as they walked away. Mariana stopped next to Em, following her gaze to where Aren and Galo were disappearing through the door.

"I think they've become friends," Em said.

"I should hope so," Mariana said. "Otherwise I don't know why that human would go to Olso with Aren."

Still, Aren and Galo becoming friends was more than Em would have hoped for just a few weeks ago. Galo had never seemed to have much interest in the Ruined beyond obeying Cas's wishes, and Aren wasn't inclined to like any human, with the exception of Iria.

"How are things going down here?" Em asked.

"Not bad, actually. A few of the guards invited some of us to play cards last night."

"Seriously?"

"Yes. They looked very suspicious when I said I had the power to ruin the mind, like I was going to cheat, but they warmed up. Plus I told them I saved my power for things much worse than cheating at cards."

"How did that go over?"

"Good, actually. I told them some of the things I could do, and we're going to practice together later. They haven't been great at integrating the mind power into the battle plans, so I'm trying to show them how it can help."

Em felt a tiny burst of relief among her nerves. She'd stepped back from the Ruined on purpose lately, hoping they would find their own way in the castle. It appeared to be going better than expected.

Davi and Gisela joined them, and they headed upstairs to the Ocean Room for the meeting. Violet and Franco were already there, as well as Cas's other advisers, Julieta and Danna, and three men who Em had met a few days ago. Aren and Galo were talking to one of them.

Cas was already seated, and he rose as Em entered the room. Everyone else followed suit. He extended his hand to her and she took it, letting him guide her to a spot next to his at the table.

Aren took a seat next to Galo, and Em watched as Mariana took the seat on the other side of Galo. Davi and Gisela sat on the opposite side of the table, next to Julieta. Em couldn't help but think it was a good sign that the Ruined hadn't all lined up on one side of the table, ready to fight the scary humans.

"Thank you for coming," Cas said, addressing the Ruined.

"Thank you for having us, Your Majesty," Aren said. Em didn't think she'd ever heard Aren call Cas "Your Majesty." It didn't even sound like he was making a joke.

"Let's get started, then," Aren said. "We're satisfied with the plan you've laid out for the Lera monarchy. We agree that King Casimir will still be the head of the government, and he will share power with elected representatives. He will still command the army, and will have the power to introduce and veto laws. All treaties with other kingdoms will have to be approved by both the monarchy and the representatives, and he will have to seek approval before declaring war on any other kingdom." He slid a paper across the table to Franco. "We'd like to change the definition of *war*, though. King Salomir never officially declared war on the Ruined. Certain acts should be considered a declaration of war."

Franco glanced at the other advisers, then nodded. "Agreed."

"All the other powers you've laid out for the king are fine." Aren looked at Cas. "You've seen this?"

"Yes."

"And you're fine with it? You understand that you'll require approval from the elected representatives for almost everything? And they will have the power to abolish the monarchy entirely, if the issue is supported by enough citizens."

"I understand."

"Good. In terms of representatives, we don't agree that the number of representatives be determined by the population of the province. That means the Ruined will have one representative to dozens of Lera representatives. Our vote will mean nothing. We need more than one."

"How many more?" Franco asked.

"Six, with the agreement that you need at least three Ruined votes to pass any law."

"But there are so few of you," Danna protested. "Why should you be overrepresented in our government?"

"Because we don't trust you," Aren said. "If you allow us only one seat, what's to stop you from overruling us at every turn? What's to stop you from blocking every policy that benefits the Ruined?"

Danna rubbed her forehead. "I see your point, but I still think it will be a tough sell to the people."

"It wouldn't be permanent. We could revisit the issue in ten, twenty years."

"It's not unreasonable," Galo said. "You can't give them one seat. That's barely symbolic, and you know it."

Julieta shifted, her lips pursed. "Fine. We'll discuss six. What's next?"

Em caught Galo's eye and nodded slightly in gratitude. He smiled.

"Each citizen of Lera has certain rights," Aren said. "We want all those rights, as well as two Ruined amendments. First, that the mere possession of Ruined power is not considered a crime."

The advisers all looked at Cas. He nodded.

"Agreed," Franco said.

"Second, that a human can never attempt to harness or force a Ruined to use their power."

Franco nodded. "We would also have something to add. A Ruined can never use their power on a human without their consent."

"Yes," Aren said. "But I'd want to see what the punishments

for that should be. A Ruined who kills someone shouldn't be punished in the same way as one who, say, made a man slap himself in the face."

"Agreed," Franco said, taking note of something.

They ran through several more points—Ruined service in the royal guard and military, future housing and reparations for lost land and property, and Ruined access to jobs and education. They came back around to elected representatives, and what powers the monarch could still hold.

"And we'd need to determine what power the queen of Lera would hold," Franco said. "If that's going to be Emelina, we can't allow her to hold the same powers as the king."

Beside her, Cas stiffened. "Why not?"

"We can't tell the people that Emelina Flores has the power to command the Lera army," Franco said. His tone was almost apologetic as he looked at Em. "She would be able to veto laws. Dismiss representatives if she saw fit. None of that will sit well with the people. We fear they may riot. Or abolish the monarchy. We'd be giving them the power to do that."

"What power would she have?" Mariana asked, leaning forward, eyebrows drawn together.

"The queen or king consort of Lera has many ceremonial duties, and you'd be free to take up any projects you like here in Royal City. The previous queen ran a program to feed hungry children and worked with the Royal City Watch, which is our local law enforcement in the city. You would be free to attend most meetings with Cas, if you wanted, but you wouldn't be there in any official capacity."

"No," Mariana said.

"No," Gisela echoed.

"Em is the queen of Ruina," Aren said. "You have never had a monarch marry another monarch. It's not the same."

"Princess Mary agreed to these terms," Danna said.

"I don't care what the princess of Vallos did," Gisela said. "Even with most of the Ruined dead, we're more powerful than Vallos ever was."

"Emelina conspired with Olso to attack Lera," Julieta said. "We're stripping the Lera monarchy of power as punishment for King Salomir's actions, but there are no consequences for Emelina."

"We consider the extermination of almost every Ruined alive to be consequence enough," Aren said tightly.

Em glanced at Cas, swallowing down a lump in her throat. On the one hand, she didn't necessarily want to be merely a queen consort. On the other, perhaps they had a point. He slipped his hand into hers and squeezed.

"You should have talked to me about this before," he said, turning to the advisers. "Because I don't agree."

"Your Majesty—"

"Em and I will have the same powers. If that means you remove more powers from the monarchy, then that's what you'll have to do." He looked at her. "If that's all right with Em."

She squeezed his hand in return. "That sounds fair to me." She turned her gaze to the others at the table, narrowing her eyes. "If you don't agree, just remember that if I don't marry Cas, I still remain queen of the Ruined. And I could also run to be a representative of the Ruined in the Lera government. If I did both, some might say I had *more* power than the king."

Aren ducked his head into his chest, obviously trying not to laugh.

"Are you threatening us?" Danna asked tightly.

"I was merely stating a fact," Em said.

"It's scarier than that when she threatens you," Mariana said. "You'll know when it happens."

Danna looked openmouthed from Julieta to Galo, like she was trying to figure out if Mariana was serious.

"Listen," Cas said, his tone almost amused. "We're done comparing. We've all done horrible things. Em's not threatening you; she's simply pointing out the fact that she is a powerful queen who commands the loyalty of her people and strikes fear into the heart of her enemies. No one like that has ever married a member of the Lera royal family. The rules have to change for her. You can either accept this marriage, or you can run in fear from her like everyone else. It's your choice."

FORTY-ONE

OLIVIA STARED AT the spot where two Ruined had been sleeping. They'd left behind the smoking remains of a fire and nothing else—the blankets she'd seen them snuggled into last night were gone.

She blinked and got to her feet. She was still half asleep, and it took a moment for the world to take shape around her.

No horses, no supplies, no food.

No Ruined. They were all gone.

She turned in a circle, her heart pounding in her chest. She found Jovita, bound to a tree, her hair wild and her eyes unfocused.

"They left," a voice said.

Olivia turned to see Ester ducking under a branch, Carmen

and Priscila behind her, bags slung over their shoulders.

"What do you mean, *they left*?" Olivia barked.

"They were scared you'd hurt them if they told you," Ester said. "We decided to do you the courtesy of saying good-bye."

"Good-bye?" Olivia repeated.

"We're going back to Ruina. There's no point to . . . this." She gestured at Jovita when she said it. Ester had done a good job cracking open Jovita's mind. Just last night she'd spilled all the secrets of the royal family, including the various affairs of her aunt, the queen. They hadn't gotten anything useful yet, but it was only a matter of time.

"You're just giving up?" Olivia asked, stunned. First the Ruined followed her useless sister to the Lera castle, of all places, and now the few smart Ruined who'd remained by her side were deserting her. She pointed in the direction of the army they'd been following for days. "They're preparing for an attack! It won't be long now."

"If we go back to Ruina now, we can claim it as ours," Ester said. "If Emelina claims it, that means Lera has it as well. It should stay in Ruined hands."

"Of course it should," Olivia said. "But we can have Lera as well. Then Vallos and Olso after that. We'll take all four kingdoms back. It was the humans who stole them from us." She pointed to the east. "The Vallos and Olso armies are *right there*."

Ester shook her head. "I'm sorry, Olivia. I want that too, but it won't happen. There are too few of us to take Lera. Our best course of action is to go back to Ruina and start rebuilding.

Maybe in a few generations, after we've built up our numbers, we can try again."

"A few *generations?*" Olivia gaped at her. She'd be dead. She'd be remembered as nothing but a disgraced queen who was captured, then defeated by her useless sister. The Flores family probably wouldn't even rule in a few generations, if Olivia failed.

"You can come with us, if you want," Ester said, throwing a bag over her shoulder. She wrinkled her nose at Jovita. "You can't bring her, though. Just put her out of her misery already."

Jovita made no indication that she'd heard Ester talking about killing her. She blinked once, very slowly, then sighed.

Ester started walking, and Priscila and Carmen fell into step behind her. They hadn't waited for Olivia's answer.

"You're just going to let them get away with this?" Olivia yelled at their backs. "Casimir will continue to rule and you don't even care?"

They didn't turn around. They kept walking until they were out of sight.

Olivia swallowed back tears. It was quiet suddenly. Too quiet. She hadn't been alone since . . . since before she was captured. And even then, she was usually around her mother. Or Em.

Fresh anger rolled through her body. She let a scream loose. She didn't care if the coward Ruined heard it.

She'd failed. Olivia, like her mother, had failed to conquer Lera. She had to admit that.

But she could still make Em pay for what she'd done.

Olivia turned to look at Jovita. She took in a breath to steady herself. Jovita didn't respond well to anger. Not anymore. Not in the past few days, when Ester had really destroyed her.

Olivia walked to Jovita and sat down across from her. "Hey," she said gently. "It's time to wake up."

Jovita opened one eye. "Wake up," she repeated. She whispered it twice more.

"Yes. Time to wake up."

Jovita thought about this for a moment. Then she looked at Olivia like she'd just noticed her sitting there. She rounded her shoulders and shrank back, like she was scared.

Olivia grabbed her canteen. "Do you want some water? Here, I'll even untie you."

She reached around Jovita and pulled the ropes loose until she could free her hands. Jovita greedily grabbed the canteen and drank, tipping it back until she got every last drop.

Olivia handed the last of her dried meat to Jovita, who immediately tore off a piece with her teeth.

"I'm going to be honest with you," Olivia said. "Things aren't going so well for me right now."

Jovita snorted. She may have lost her mind, but she hadn't lost her hatred of Olivia.

Olivia gestured around her. "As you can see, everyone has left. I won't be taking over Lera. But there is one thing I can do."

Jovita gnawed on her meat and stared at a point beyond Olivia's head.

"I can sneak into the castle and kill Em. And Cas, if you'd like."

Jovita's eyes snapped to hers, but she said nothing.

"How did you get out of the castle, the night the warriors attacked?"

"I'm not telling you that."

Olivia raised her eyebrows. It seemed Jovita hadn't completely lost her mind after all.

"Why not?" Olivia asked. "If I get in, I'll kill Casimir. Isn't that what you want?"

"They'll kill you," Jovita said. "There are too many guards. Even you won't make it out alive."

That, unfortunately, was true. With Jovita's help, Olivia could get in, and she could probably kill a lot of people, including Em's beloved Cas, but she'd never make it out. Even if she managed to kill everyone in the castle, she'd be so weak she'd barely be able to walk. Guards would get her before she made it over the castle walls.

But it was the only plan that didn't make her want to rip her hair out. She wouldn't join Em in protecting the people who had killed their mother and father. She wouldn't sulk back to Ruina to be queen of nothing. Killing Em would make her immortal. The Ruined would always talk about it, how she fought until the very end, all alone, and defeated the greatest Ruined traitor they'd ever known.

"You know how powerful I am," Olivia said to Jovita. "You don't think I can kill Casimir? I can kill everyone in that castle."

Jovita stared at her as she chewed. She blinked several times, like she was seeing something that wasn't there. It was an aftereffect of a Ruined controlling the mind, especially when the control had gone too far. Jovita would likely see things that weren't there for the rest of her life.

"Not *everyone*," Jovita finally conceded. "I need some guards. And some soldiers."

"Sure," Olivia lied.

"And you have to leave when you're done," Jovita said seriously.

"Of course."

Jovita studied her like she knew Olivia was lying. She shrugged. "You couldn't stay, even if you wanted to. It's just you now." She swept her arms out dramatically, perhaps to display just how alone Olivia was. "Can't run a castle all by yourself, can you?" She laughed.

Olivia swallowed down the urge to take Jovita's head off right then. "Tell me how to get in."

"You have to promise not to kill me after I tell you," Jovita said.

"What's the point? Would you really believe me if I promised?"

Jovita frowned.

"Listen. I'll let you go, because, honestly, this state you're in amuses me more than killing you. But even if I *did* kill you, wouldn't you prefer to tell me how to get to the castle first? Either way, I'm going to go kill Em and Casimir. You're in no shape to take your revenge now, so let me do it for you."

Jovita chewed on her lip, considering.

"Fine, I promise," Olivia said, rolling her eyes.

Jovita still seemed skeptical, but perhaps she had enough reasoning left to know what Olivia said was true—if anyone was going to kill Casimir, it was going to be Olivia.

"There's a secret passageway in the kitchen," Jovita said. "It ends in one of the lookout towers, but it's totally hidden from view. Even the guards stationed in the tower don't know it's there."

"How do I find it?"

"Pull up the floorboards."

"Which tower?"

"Southeast."

Olivia smiled. "Thank you, Jovita. Ester was right about working with you people." She grabbed the ropes and stood to secure Jovita to the tree again.

"Hey! I thought you were going to let me go."

"I will," Olivia said, and she meant it. She turned to walk in the direction of the Olso and Vallos armies. "I just need to wait for the right moment."

FORTY-TWO

IRIA SAT ON the edge of her bed, considering how many more days she could stay in this room without losing her mind, when a knock sounded at the door.

"Come in!" she called.

The door opened to reveal Aren, holding a wad of clothing and a pair of boots. His expression was so bright and hopeful she felt a smile twitching at her lips.

He dropped the clothes on the bed. Sparring clothes. Her smile faded.

"These are for you," he said, holding up the boots. "I worked with a few of the guards to make something that would be good for running and sword fighting. It's just a first attempt, so don't worry if it's uncomfortable. We can adjust it."

He held the boots out to her and she slowly took them. She thought she might feel relief, or hope, at the sight of the boots that were supposed to help her, but all she felt was panic. What if they didn't make anything easier?

"Thanks," she said, putting the boots on the floor. "But I'm not feeling great today. Maybe we can do it another—"

"No," Aren said firmly. "Change into sparring clothes."

Anger flared in her chest. "I can't."

"Of course you can. The doctor said you can start moving around."

"No, I mean there's no point. I'll never need to use a sword again. I'm just going to . . ." She trailed off. She had no idea what she was going to do.

"What? Stay in this room for the rest of your life?" He pointed to the clothes. "I think those will fit you. They're what the guards wear, and a girl about your size helped me pick some out. So put them on."

She crossed her arms over her chest.

"What? Do you want to see if I'll strip you down and put the clothes on you myself? Don't test me."

She eyed him for a moment. He might have been serious.

She let out an annoyed breath. "Are you just going to stand there? Wait outside while I change."

His lips twitched. "Fine, but if you're not out in five minutes I'm coming in again."

She let out an exaggerated sigh just for his benefit. He laughed as he left, closing the door behind him.

She changed her clothes first, and then sat down on the bed to put on the boots. They were plain and black, but inside the right one was padding that formed to the top of her foot. She stood and took a few steps forward. It felt a bit weird, but it was easier to stay balanced with something in the place where her toes used to be.

When she walked out of the bedroom, she found Aren leaning against the back of the chair in the sitting room.

"Do you even use a sword?" she asked.

"Not well, which is why I'm a good person to start with."

"That makes me feel great."

"Do you want me to go get Em? Because I'm sure she'd be happy to spar with you."

Iria made a face at him, because they both knew she didn't want to spar with Em. With the exception of Cas, Em was probably better than anyone in the castle with a sword. That sounded like a good way to humiliate herself.

Aren opened the door, and Iria hesitated for a moment. "You have to leave this room eventually," he said. "No one is going to bite you."

"You sure about that?"

"I've been playing cards with the guards. Trust me, if they've forgiven me, they don't care about you."

She was still skeptical, but she stepped out of the room and closed the door behind her. If Em and Aren and the rest of the Ruined roamed the castle freely, then she could too.

They walked down the hallway and turned a corner to the

sparring rooms. Aren let Iria step into the room first, then he walked in and grabbed two dull sparring swords from the rack.

"No using your powers," she said as he handed her one of the swords.

"Of course not." He paused. "Even if you start to fall? I can stop you before you hit the ground."

"No."

"No powers, then."

She shifted her weight from foot to foot, trying to get a feel for the boots. They were rubbing against her heels, but that would be the case with all new boots.

"We'll start slow." He shrugged. "I'm always slow, compared to you."

She raised her sword. He raised his as well and stepped forward.

It only took two blows for Iria to lose her balance. She stumbled backward and landed on her butt, her sword skittering across the floor.

"Well that was pathetic," she said.

"Then get up and try again."

He said it kindly, and she was reminded of warrior training, four years ago. A trainer had screamed in her face to get up when she'd fallen once after hours of training. They would have immediately dismissed her for her current attitude.

She used her hands to push off the floor.

They went again, Iria almost poking him in the chest with the sword once, just before she stumbled forward. Aren shot his arm out, grabbing her around the waist before she fell. Her head hit his chest.

"You almost got me that time," he said.

She looked up to see he was grinning. She extracted herself from his arms, her face warm. "You really are terrible with a sword."

"I told you.

"Again," he said, getting back into position.

She steadied herself for a moment, then swung her sword. She was a little slow as she tried to find her balance. The boot was better than she thought, the inserts at the toe of the right foot helping to steady her. It was a little painful, but she found herself steady on her feet much faster than expected.

She took a step back after she pointed her sword straight at Aren's chest for a third time. "You want to start trying? You don't have to go so slow."

"Hey! This is me actually trying."

She threw her head back with a genuine laugh. "Really?"

"Yes."

She laughed again.

"I have no use for a sword," he said with a hint of annoyance, but his lips twitched like he was trying not to smile.

"Sorry."

"Sure you are. Do you want me to go get Em? She's not slow."

"Yes, actually." She wasn't going to get anywhere sparring with someone so slow, and the prospect of practicing with Em suddenly didn't seem so scary.

"Really?"

He looked so happy that she couldn't stop herself from laughing. "Yes. I need someone who actually challenges me."

He darted out of the room like he was afraid she'd change her mind, and returned with Em a few minutes later.

"I heard that Aren's so terrible even you can beat him," Em said with a grin.

"Hey! Maybe she's just really good," Aren protested.

Em picked up Aren's discarded sword. "She's not bad, from what I remember." Her eyes darted to Iria's feet. "Should I take it a bit easy on you at first?"

Iria sighed. "Yes, unfortunately."

She thought Em might make fun of her, but she just nodded. "Is he staying?" she asked, gesturing to Aren.

Iria glanced at him, and he shook his head before she had to ask. "No, I'm going. I'll come get you later for dinner?" He said it as a question, and she smiled and nodded.

He left, closing the door behind him, and Iria turned to Em. She had an amused expression on her face.

"What?" Iria asked.

"He's so awkward around you," Em said, swinging her sword in a circle to warm up her arm. "It's cute. Aren's rarely awkward with anyone."

Iria felt herself blush, and she didn't step forward when Em did. Em lowered her sword, looking at her expectantly.

"I was wondering about something," Iria said. "About me and Aren. Ruined only date and marry each other, until you, but you're . . ." She trailed off, wondering if it was rude to say the word.

"Useless," Em finished.

"Right. But Aren's not. He's the most powerful of all of you. I imagine he'll be one of the Ruined representatives?"

Em nodded.

"Will it be a problem, if we . . . if we're together?" Iria asked slowly. "Will they be angry? Will it cause problems for him?"

"No," Em said immediately. "My mother thought that the Ruined should only marry each other, like all the Ruined before her, and all it did was weaken our power and reduce our numbers. I think it's actually preferable that Aren's chosen you. And I know I'm not the only one who will feel that way."

Iria couldn't help the smile that spread across her face. She ducked her head, trying to hide it.

"He did choose you, you know," Em said. "I know you were angry when he said he'd leave you in Lera alone, but he came for you as soon as he could."

"I know," Iria said. She wasn't angry with Aren about that anymore, she realized. She didn't think she'd been angry since she'd heard his voice in the Olso prison. Maybe before that, even. She couldn't blame him for wanting to help his people, or for not wanting to abandon Em.

"Do you remember when we used to come in here and spar on the days when you were particularly full of rage?" Iria asked.

"That was almost every day."

"It was."

"And I beat you almost every day."

Iria lifted her sword and stepped forward. "Want to try to do it again?"

Em grinned. "Gladly."

FORTY-THREE

AFTER HER SPARRING session with Iria, Em changed her clothes and emerged from the royal suite to see Mateo standing outside the door, as usual. He wasn't as formal as Cas's guards, instead leaning against the wall and smiling at her when she stepped into the hallway.

"Do I need to take guards with me if I leave the castle grounds?" she asked him.

"I would recommend it. Take me with you, at the least," Mateo said. "Where do you want to go?"

"I told Mariana we could take a walk to see Royal City. She's never been." Em patted her pocket, where she had a few Lera coins that Cas had given her. "Maybe buy some cheese bread."

"If it's just the two of you, I'd recommend you take me along.

I'll hang back; you'll barely notice I'm there."

"That seems a bit weird, don't you think?" Em asked with a laugh. "I think I'd prefer you just walk with us."

"I can do that, too." Mateo smiled.

"Good." She turned and began walking, Mateo falling into step beside her.

"May I ask you a question?" he asked, a hint of nervousness in his voice.

"Sure."

"Did you have guards in the Ruina castle? Did anyone guard the royal family?"

Em shook her head. "No. It was unnecessary. Most of the time there was no one but the Ruined in Ruina. And there was no danger when an Olso warrior came to visit, because only a few visited at a time. My mother made sure of that." She started down the stairs. "Besides, my parents trusted no one. My mother especially never would have trusted my and Olivia's safety to anyone but herself." She'd failed, of course, and Em wondered if guards would have made a difference when Lera attacked them. In the end, her mother relied only on herself, so there was no one to protect her when King Salomir came for her.

Of course, Em had failed as well. She was no longer able to protect Olivia, and Olivia certainly had no interest in protecting Em.

"Do you mind me asking questions about Ruina and your family?" Mateo asked quietly. "I understand if it's too painful."

It was painful, but she smiled at him anyway. "No, I don't

mind. I would prefer you ask, honestly. There are a lot of misconceptions about us."

"That's true. Someone asked Cas if you all had horns a few weeks ago."

"Horns?"

"Maybe I shouldn't have told you that."

Em laughed as she pushed open the door to the guards' quarters. Mariana was sprawled out on a couch in the guards' common room, and she waved when they walked in. Two female guards sat in the chairs across from her.

"Did you hear someone thought we had horns?" Em asked.

"Yeah, one of the guards told me." She patted her head. "I'd look cute with horns, I think."

"You would," one of the guards confirmed. Mariana smiled at her.

"Do you want to go for that walk?" Em asked. "Mateo's coming with us."

Mariana hopped to her feet. "I'm ready." She followed Em and Mateo out of the castle and into the late-afternoon sunlight. They walked east down the dirt path, in the direction Em had gone once with Galo and Cas, the first time she'd seen Royal City.

"Have they given you a decision about your marriage to Cas yet?" Mariana asked as they walked.

"Not yet. It was just yesterday that I, uh . . ."

"Politely pointed out that a marriage alliance with you is actually a very smart choice?" Mateo guessed.

She laughed. "Is that how Galo described it?"

"He said something like that." Mateo gave her an amused look. "Did you have to convince the other Ruined as well?"

"No, we were fine with it," Mariana said. "As long as she rules equally with Cas."

"We should get some Ruined together tomorrow and do this again," Em said, looking up at the cloudless sky. "They should see the city they'll be living in."

"I can have a few more guards accompany them tomorrow, if you want to bring all of them," Mateo said.

"All the Ruined at once," Mariana said. "That won't terrify people."

"Maybe half," Em said with a laugh. "We'll ease them in."

They were nearing the city, and Em noticed Mariana's shoulders stiffen as they passed a group of women engrossed in conversation. They didn't even glance at the Ruined marks visible on Mariana's arms.

"Or they won't notice us at all," Mariana said happily.

They rounded a corner, the buildings of Royal City now in front of them. Em could hear the bustle of the city as they approached—horse hooves on the road, carts creaking, the sound of people shouting orders to each other. But another sound cut through it all, loud and sharp.

A scream.

Em came to a sudden stop. Mateo drew his sword. Mariana surveyed Em.

"You didn't bring a sword," she said.

"There's a dagger in my boot. I thought a sword might make it appear like I was looking for a fight."

"We may have found one, whether you were looking for it or not," Mariana said as another yell ripped through the air, followed by a crash.

"Let's go see," Em said, breaking into a jog. The logical part of her brain knew it probably wasn't Olivia—there was no fire, and certainly not enough screaming—but her heart pounded anyway.

She ran in the direction of the scream, Mateo picking up his pace to run slightly in front of her. They skidded to a stop as they turned onto Main Street. A fruit cart was overturned, and an elderly woman sat on the ground with a hand pressed to her bloody head. A few people were running down the street, following a person Em couldn't quite make out.

"That can't be Olivia," Mariana said. She'd obviously been thinking the same thing. "She wouldn't run. Not *away* from violence, anyway."

A young man rushed to the side of the elderly woman, and Em grabbed the cart and righted it. Mateo helped her.

"Who was that?" she asked.

"The king's cousin," the young man said, bending down to examine the woman's wound.

"What? Jovita?" Em whirled around, but the end of the street was empty. She turned back to the woman, who was trying to wipe blood from her eyes.

"Do you have a clean rag?" Em asked the man.

He pulled a handkerchief from his pocket and handed it to her. Em grabbed a jug of water from beside the cart and held it up. "Is this yours?" The woman nodded. Em poured some water on it, then knelt down next to the woman, who hesitantly moved her hand from the wound. It was deep, but the bleeding had slowed. Em wiped the blood from her face, then folded the fabric and pressed it to her forehead. The woman winced.

"Just keep pressure on it so it doesn't start bleeding too bad," she said. "And don't try to get up. You might feel woozy if you stand."

The woman nodded, blinking at Em like she'd just realized who she was. The man was staring at Mariana's arms. Em stood, putting her hands on her hips.

"Do you think Jovita went to the castle?" Em asked.

"Maybe, but she'll never get in. We have it totally locked down," Mateo said.

"True," Em murmured. She looked at the woman. "Was she alone? Why did she hit you?"

"I didn't see anyone else. She was trying to grab some fruit, and I didn't recognize her at first. I thought she was a thief. She started screaming when I tried to stop her."

"Let's go see," Em said.

"How about you wait here, and I can go check?" Mateo said.

"Or I can go with you to check," Em countered.

"You don't even have a sword because you want people to think you're nice," Mariana said.

"I do not want people to think I'm nice," Em said. "I was

trying for less scary, but there's no need to get carried away with *nice*."

"I'm not scared of you," the elderly woman said with a hint of a smile.

"Thank you. See? It's working." She started walking backward. "I'm going after her."

Mateo looked like he wanted to protest further, but Em turned and started to jog away. She heard his and Mariana's footsteps behind her a moment later.

She turned a corner to see a small crowd in the street, all of their faces turned upward. Jovita stood on the roof of a three-story building, her body turned to face the castle. "I see you!" she yelled to the castle.

"Jovita!" Em called.

She turned around, losing her balance and almost falling off the roof. She crouched down for a moment to steady herself. She squinted at Em.

"You!" she yelled.

"What's she doing up there?" Mariana asked.

"I don't know."

"That's . . ." Jovita pointed a shaky finger at Em. "Do you people know who that is?"

A few faces turned to Em.

"Emelina Flores!" Jovita yelled, for those who hadn't figured it out. "She's just standing there with you!"

"They know who I am," Em said. "I've been living in the castle for a while now."

"Oh!" Jovita slapped her hands on her thighs. "I'm sorry. You *live* here now."

"What's wrong with her?" Mateo asked quietly.

"Someone has been in her mind," Mariana said. "Olivia must have tortured her."

Em took a quick glance around. Chances were good that Olivia and her Ruined were still lurking somewhere nearby.

"Is Ester powerful enough to do this?" Em asked, gesturing at Jovita.

"Yes."

Em turned back to Jovita with a flicker of sympathy. "Why don't you come down?"

Jovita pulled her sword from her belt. "Yes. I will come down. If you agree to a duel."

"Sure."

Jovita looked confused by this response. "To the death."

"No problem."

Jovita thought about it for a moment, then nodded. "Good." She walked to the edge of the roof, and tried to climb down with her sword still in hand. It took her several tries to realize she was going to have to sheathe it again if she wanted to get down.

"And you still don't have a sword," Mariana muttered.

"Look at her. I don't need one."

A woman edged away from the group of humans watching them. "You're not really going to kill her, are you?" she whispered to Em.

"No," she said. She pointed to the end of the street, where she could see a few of the Royal City Watch riding in their direction. "In fact, if you could go meet them and tell them what's going on so they don't take me away too, that would be great."

The woman scurried away, appearing relieved.

Jovita finally made it to the ground, and she pulled her sword out again, poised to fight.

"Do you want me to . . ." Mariana jerked a thumb at Jovita.

"Would you, please?"

Mariana focused her gaze on Jovita. Her eyes clouded over and she fell straight backward, hitting the ground with a thud.

Em walked to Jovita, scooping the girl's sword up from where it had fallen from her fingers.

"No fair," Jovita mumbled, her gaze fixed on the sky. "No fair."

Em knelt down next to her. "Was it Olivia who did this to you? Olivia and Ester?"

"*You* did this to us," Jovita said.

"But you were with Olivia recently?"

Jovita turned her head to meet Em's eyes. "Yes. We made a deal."

Em's brow creased, but she was momentarily distracted by one of the watchmen dismounting his horse and walking their way. She quickly held out Jovita's sword to Mateo, blade pointed toward her, so the watchman would know she wasn't a threat.

"This is a Gallegos family sword," Em said. "It should go to Cas."

Mateo took it. "Of course." He walked to the watchmen and said something to them.

"We should take her to the castle," Em said. "Cas will want to deal with her himself."

"We can help transport her," one of the watchmen said.

Em nodded, turning back to Jovita. "What kind of deal?" she asked quietly.

"She's going to kill him," Jovita said with a hint of pride. "And you."

"How?"

Jovita giggled. "I know secrets. I know passageways."

Terror zipped up Em's spine. There was a secret passageway out of the castle—it was how Jovita and the queen had escaped when Olso attacked. But Em had never been told about the passageway during her time as Mary, and she hadn't asked Cas about it since. She had no idea where it was.

She looked at Mateo to see a matching horrified expression on his face.

Olivia could be in the castle right now.

"Get her on a horse," she said, pointing to Jovita. "We need to get back to the castle."

FORTY-FOUR

AFTER SHE'D FINISHED sparring, Aren steered Iria in the direction of the kitchen, refusing to let her go back to her room until she'd eaten dinner with him. He grabbed some bread and cheese from the staff kitchen, and then headed into the gardens. He sat down at a table near the middle of the garden.

"This is where I'd always go to avoid Lerans," he said as he broke off a piece of bread and handed it to her. "I thought you'd appreciate it."

She laughed softly. "Thanks, Aren."

"They're not so bad, though. The Lerans. I've made friends with a few."

"I noticed. I'm not opposed to making a few friends." She

smiled at him. "Though I don't mind being alone with you either."

He'd been tearing off a piece of bread when she said that, and he dropped it, feeling heat rush to his face. Her cheeks had turned pink.

"I wanted to let you know that I understand," she said. "When you said you had to leave me here to stay with Em. She wasn't ready to declare all-out war on Olivia. They needed you."

"*You* needed me," Aren said.

"Not so much, at that moment. You came through when I really needed you. And I didn't think you would, honestly."

His eyebrows shot up. "You didn't think I would rescue you from the prison? I told you I would."

"Sure, but no one would have blamed you for breaking that promise. You had to cross into Olso and figure out a way to get into our highest-security prison." She lifted one shoulder. "I'm really grateful, is what I'm saying."

"I would do it again," he said softly.

A smile twitched at her lips. The bruises on her face had healed, the color back in her cheeks, and he found it difficult to look anywhere else. He wanted to lean across the table and brush her hair away from her face and kiss her.

He'd never been so hesitant to kiss a girl before. This used to be easy for him. He'd had plenty of girlfriends in the past, and he'd rarely felt the kind of nerves he was experiencing at the moment. Past Aren would have kissed her several seconds ago. Several weeks ago, actually.

He felt a familiar tug, and he almost ignored it, too wrapped up in Iria to care. It came again, more insistent.

He took in a sharp breath and shot to his feet. He could feel the frenzied excitement of hundreds of humans, their energy different than the constant flow from around Royal City.

"What?" Iria asked, alarmed.

"I feel someone coming. Lots of someones. Enough to be an army."

"You can do that?"

"Yes." He extended his hand to her and pulled her to her feet. It was probably the Olso army, and he wasn't letting her out of his sight this time. They ran inside, Iria moving surprisingly well in her new boot. Her limp was still there, but she was learning to move quickly again.

"Galo!" he yelled as he ran into the castle. "Cas!" He probably shouldn't have been casually shouting for the king in the castle, but it was an emergency, and he didn't have time for formalities.

He sprinted up the stairs to find Cas emerging from his office. Galo and Mateo appeared behind him, along with Franco and Violet.

"What is it?" Cas asked.

"There's an army coming," Aren said.

"What? No. Our lookouts would have seen," Franco said. "I didn't hear them give the signal."

"Aren can sense people farther out than we can see," Galo said.

"Sound the alarm," Cas said. Violet and Franco took off running and disappeared down the stairs. "Where is Em?"

"She and Mariana went into town with Mateo a little while ago," Aren said.

Fear flashed across Cas's face, but he recovered quickly. "Prepare the Ruined. I know you haven't had a chance to get them training with our soldiers, but we need them to help if they're willing."

"They're willing."

"Can you tell exactly where they are?" Cas asked. "And how many?"

"No," Aren said regretfully. "I think they're southwest, but I'm not a hundred percent sure. You'll have to wait until the lookouts can see for an exact number, but I would count on a lot."

"That's fine," Cas said. "Go get the Ruined and coordinate with General Amaro."

Aren nodded, reaching for Iria's hand again, but she was focused on Cas.

"I can tell you the most likely plans of attack, if you'd like," she said. Aren looked at her in surprise.

Cas wore a matching expression. "I would definitely like that, if you're willing."

"I can't say for sure, but there are three strong possibilities. And if I go up to a lookout, I can probably take a good guess."

"I'll get someone to take you to one," Cas said.

Aren wrapped his fingers lightly around Iria's wrist, a silent protest.

"It's fine," she said. "Go get the Ruined ready."

He held on to her wrist a little tighter, reluctant to leave her, but Cas was already walking, calling orders to his guards. Iria pried her arm from his grip with a hint of a smile, and then stood on her toes to kiss his cheek.

"Go do what you're best at, Aren." She took a step back.

"What am I best at?"

She laughed like it was ridiculous that he didn't already know. "Saving everyone."

Cas was trying not to panic about Em. He'd gotten Iria to the lookout, and met with General Amaro, and reassured everyone that *yes, they are actually coming, even though you can't see them yet*, but it was all done with panic bubbling just under the surface.

"—lock down the castle," Jorge was saying, and Cas snapped back to attention. They were standing in the front entryway, Galo at Cas's side. People zipped by them, shouting orders.

"Not until Em and Mariana and Mateo get back," Galo said before Cas could. Jorge clearly wanted to protest.

"We can't even see the army yet," Cas said. "And Mariana is a very powerful Ruined. She's the one who clouded the vision of our lookouts when Olso attacked. We need her here."

"Fine, but as soon as they get back we need to put you in hiding," Jorge said.

"I can't hide. I need to . . ." It occurred to him that he wasn't sure what he needed to do. He'd put Aren in charge of the Ruined. General Amaro was in charge of the soldiers.

"You need to stay safe, because everything will be thrown into chaos if you die," Galo said. His gaze cut to Cas's sword, which Cas had grabbed after parting with Aren. "So don't even think about it."

The castle doors banged open suddenly, and Cas whirled around, hope blooming in his chest. Em charged through the door, her face grim. She was followed by Mariana, Mateo, and several members of the Royal City Watch, and then, to Cas's surprise, Jovita. His cousin had her hands bound in front of her, and her hair was wild and dirty, but she was just as disgusted as ever when her eyes met Cas's.

Cas rushed forward, putting his hands on Em's cheeks. "I'm so glad you're back. Aren—"

"Cas, Jovita told—"

"There's an army coming, and you can't—"

"Cas!" Em said sharply, taking his hands off her cheeks and holding them tightly. "Jovita told Olivia about the secret passageway from the kitchen, the one they took to escape the Olso warriors. She could be in the castle right now."

"It's sealed," Galo and Jorge said together, before Cas could even begin to panic.

Em was clearly surprised. "It is?"

"Of course," Galo said. "I had it sealed off as soon as we took back the castle."

Jovita let out a loud, extremely annoyed sigh. She muttered something Cas couldn't hear.

"The Olso warriors were in here for weeks," Jorge said,

looking a bit insulted. "There's no doubt they discovered it. We'd be fools to leave it open."

"Oh," Em said. Her brow crinkled. "What were you saying about an army?"

Cas quickly relayed Aren's message, and her face grew more serious as she listened.

"That's why Olivia let Jovita go today," Em said. "She was tracking the army, and she knew when they were going to attack. Olivia needs that kind of chaos right now." She took a step back, dropping Cas's hands. "We know where she'll be, then—at the lookout tower, trying to get in the passageway."

"She can get in the passage from the tower," Galo said. "We haven't fully filled it in yet, so it's just blocked off once she gets to the other side. She'll have to turn around and go back."

"I'm going to go find her. She'll start killing people when she can't get in."

Cas shook his head. "No. You have to go beyond the castle walls to get to that lookout, and there's an army coming."

She held her hand out. "I'll need your sword, then."

He made an exasperated noise, but he unsheathed his sword and handed it to her, knowing that arguing would be pointless. She rose up on her toes and kissed him quickly before turning to run out the door.

"Your Majesty?"

Cas turned to find Franco in front of him, out of breath.

"The lookouts have spotted the army."

FORTY-FIVE

AREN RACED DOWN the guards' quarters, where he found half the Ruined lounging in their rooms or in the common area.

"Attack, now," he said, walking down the halls and shouting it several more times. Ruined streamed out of their rooms, shrugging on jackets and lacing up boots. A guard stumbled out of a room with Gisela, blinking in surprise as he buttoned up his shirt.

"Attack? Where? Who?" he asked.

"I assume it's the Olso army," Aren said. "And they're coming here, so I hope you remember your emergency assignments."

"Yes? Yes." The guard blinked at Gisela, who was halfway down the hallway and gathering up the Ruined. Aren turned and jogged toward them.

"You guys must be attacked often," the guard muttered from

behind him. Aren might have laughed, if he wasn't still thinking of Iria's retreating back as she headed to a lookout tower.

Gisela led them out of the guards' quarters. At the end of the hallway, in the room where they'd been working on the Weakling armor, several soldiers raced in and out, grabbing shields and chest plates and piles of clothing.

They walked upstairs and outside, to the east lawn. The sun was sinking lower in the sky, casting an orange glow across the grass. Hundreds of soldiers and guards were already there, with more streaming out from every door of the castle.

About a quarter of the soldiers had Weakling armor or shields. There was no way to know if Olivia or any other Ruined would be attacking with the humans, so they'd been ordered to put it on just in case. Aren thought Em was right—if Olivia had been spotted following the army, she was going to attack at the same time.

He spotted Galo weaving through the soldiers. Three men and two women followed him—the soldiers assigned just to protecting Aren. Behind them, Mariana made her way toward General Amaro.

"Em made it back?" he asked Galo.

"Yes. We think Olivia is going to the southeast tower to try to use an old, closed tunnel into the castle. Em's going to meet her."

Aren's body went cold. "Just Em?"

"Em is going to the tower by herself. We're sending people with Weakling armor to that side, to help if needed. Do you want to go meet her?"

Aren shook his head, even though he desperately wanted to sprint to that tower as fast as possible. It wasn't just that he thought Em was in danger. He worried what she would be forced to do if it were just the two of them. Would Em kill Olivia in an effort to save the rest of them?

But he knew Em would want him to stay here, to protect the castle and help the Lera troops fight off the impending attack. He'd been given instructions, and the soldiers assigned to him were ready. He wasn't deserting them now.

"Let's get in position," Galo said. Aren noticed him cast a glance over his shoulder at Mateo, who was with a group of guards headed back inside the castle.

Aren followed the soldiers around the side of the castle, to the front and out the gates. The area in front of the castle was nothing but grass, the buildings of Royal City to the right and homes in the distance to the left.

"They're coming from that direction," Galo said, pointing south.

The soldiers rushed past him, getting into formation. Galo took a crate from one of them and put it on the ground. Aren stepped onto it, able to see better with the height.

"Anyone operating a cannon first," Galo reminded him. Aren nodded.

They waited. Aren had sensed the army when they were pretty far out, it seemed. August had already lost the element of surprise by threatening Cas, but Aren had given the Lera soldiers a huge head start with the early warning.

Galo stood directly in front of Aren, the other soldiers forming a circle around Aren. The other Ruined were scattered among the soldiers and guards, dressed the same so they were impossible for most to spot. Aren saw Mariana standing behind two women with swords, and Gisela talking to a guard, but he wasn't able to pick out any of the other Ruined. They were lost in the sea of blue and black uniforms.

He looked over his shoulder, to the southeast lookout tower. He could see the tip of it, but the castle hid the bottom from view. Em and Olivia might have been there now.

"Aren," Galo said quietly.

Aren's head snapped forward. The Olso army had just appeared at the top of a small hill. The first wave was all on horseback and from this distance it looked as if many were wearing their battle armor. They didn't slow when they saw the Lera army waiting for them. Maybe Aren had been wrong. Maybe August counted on him warning the Lerans early.

The warriors kept coming over the hill, hundreds of them. Horse hooves pounded the ground. Blasts erupted from either side of their formation. Smoke rose from the spot where Aren had just seen Gisela.

He focused on the warriors with the cannons first, tossing their bodies high into the air. He wasn't close enough to be very accurate, and warriors all around them launched into the air as well.

The warriors reached the Lera soldiers, yells echoing as swords met and bodies crashed together. The ground began shaking and a tree toppled over, crushing several warriors and their cannon. Vallos soldiers flew through the air. Gisela pointed to them as she threw them.

But the warriors kept coming, their red uniforms fighting their way through the Lera soldiers. Aren took in a deep breath and focused his magic on them.

Jorge asked Cas to move out of the castle foyer as the soldiers and guards rushed out to get into formation.

"We think the small library is the safest place for you," Jorge said, lowering his voice so only Cas could hear. "We've just redesigned the closet in that room so that it locks from the inside. You should go there until this is over."

"Will you come get me as soon as there's any word about Em and Olivia?"

"Of course." Jorge looked at Jovita, who still stood glaring with her hands tied. "What would you like to do with her?"

Cas sighed. "Let her have a bath, and then put her in the basement cells."

Jorge nodded, and gestured for the two guards with Jovita to bring her. She shuffled forward, scowling at Cas from behind strands of hair that had fallen in her face.

Cas looked over his shoulder as they turned down a hallway, glancing at the familiar blade one of the guards was holding. "Is that her sword?"

"Yes. Mateo gave it to me to give back to you. He said it was a Gallego family s—"

Jovita whirled around so quickly Cas barely saw her reach for the weapon in her pocket. The ropes flew off her wrists, then she pulled the dagger from her pants and plunged it into the guard's neck. Jorge lunged, but she launched her foot into his chest. He staggered back with a gasp.

Cas reached for the sword slipping from the dead guard's hand, but it was too late. Jovita grabbed it, elbowing the other guard in the face as he tried to grab Cas.

Cas whirled around, preparing to run, but Jovita roughly shoved him through the open door and into the small library. He stumbled but didn't fall, and quickly turned. Jovita slammed the door shut and clicked the lock into place. She pointed the sword at him and smiled.

He took a step back, taking stock of the room out of the corner of his eyes. Shelves of books lined the walls. A sofa and several chairs sat in the middle of the room, around a small table. More chairs were near the windows. But there were no swords in this room, and he'd given his to Em. His heart pounded in his ears as he stared at his cousin.

"They said you could barely hold a sword," he said. "That you were standing on top of a building, ranting and raving."

She moved a little closer to him. "I was. But you don't think a Ruined could break me that easily, did you?" She blinked three times, twitching the last time. They had broken her, at least a little.

Cas closed his fingers around the back of the chair next to him. Outside the door, guards yelled, followed by a heavy *thud*.

The wall rattled. They were breaking down the door.

Jovita held the sword steady, but she was breathing heavily, and she kept glancing to her left, like she saw something there. He was worried that her panic might actually make her *more* dangerous.

She lunged, blade aimed at his chest. He grabbed the chair, holding it up in front of his chest like a shield, and darted out of the way.

"They will never let you be queen," Cas said. Jovita lunged again, aiming for his arm this time. She nicked him, blood seeping from the scratch. He tried to dodge her, but his back hit the wall.

He threw the chair at her head. She ducked, and it sailed over her and crashed into the wall, breaking into several pieces. A chair leg rolled across the floor.

Cas took advantage of the momentary distraction to dart around Jovita. He ran across the sofa, on to the table in the center of the room, and jumped down to grab the chair legs.

He spun around just in time to see her blade swinging at his face. He blocked it with the chair leg, the wood cracking as the sword hit it. He swung the leg as hard as he could, connecting with Jovita's face.

She stumbled backward, blood dripping down her forehead. Cas hurled himself at her, knocking them both to the ground. The sword skittered across the floor.

She twisted beneath him, reaching an arm out to try and grab the sword. He yanked her arm back, holding it tight to the ground.

"They will never let you be queen," he said again, slower. She kicked her legs and let out an annoyed scream. She blew a piece of hair out of her face and glowered at him.

"I wasn't going to ask permission," she said. "That's your problem. You're always asking permission."

A crashing noise came from behind him. *"Again!"* Jorge yelled.

Jovita squirmed, managing to free one of her arms from his grasp. She wriggled away, making a beeline for the sword.

Cas grabbed the edge of her shirt, pulling her back and diving for the blade. His hand closed around the handle.

She grabbed for his ankle, but he barely managed to avoid her fingers. He jumped to his feet, the sword stretched out in front of him. He took several steps back, still breathing heavily. Jovita sat up but didn't bother getting to her feet. There was no point in fighting anymore, now that he had the only sword in the room.

She leaned against the couch, tilting her head back as she let out a humorless laugh. "It was much more theatrical this way, right?"

His brow furrowed. "What?"

"We joked once, after that man tried to kill you at your wedding. I said I wouldn't have used poison. I preferred something more theatrical."

"But you did poison me."

"Well, desperate times called for desperate measures. And that stupid Olivia failed to kill you again, it seems." She waved her hand in disgust.

Cas walked to the door, reaching for the lock. The door shook as something heavy hit it. "I'm fine!" he called. He turned the lock, then looked at Jovita, hand on the doorknob. "You didn't send that man to kill me at my wedding, did you?"

"No." She lowered her head with a frown. "Not that I remember." She blinked twice, pulling her knees to her chest and muttering something he couldn't understand.

Cas opened the door to find the hallway packed with guards. Jorge held an ax, and he quickly lowered it.

"I got it!" a guard yelled, rounding a corner with a key held up in the air. He skidded to a stop when he spotted Cas. "Oh."

"Are you all right, Your Majesty?" Jorge asked.

"I'm fine." He pointed at Jovita. "You'll want to keep several guards on her. She's still plenty capable of wielding a sword."

Jorge ordered a few guards into the room, and Jovita grumbled as they pulled her to her feet.

"I'm sorry, Your Majesty," Jorge said. "I shouldn't have let that happen." His eyes flicked to the sword in Cas's hand. "I was sure you didn't even have a sword."

Cas barked out a laugh. "I didn't. I took this one from her."

Jorge looked from the sword to the pieces of the chair on the floor. "I think perhaps you really are immortal, Your Majesty."

FORTY-SIX

EVEN IF EM hadn't known where Olivia was, she could have just followed the trail of dead bodies.

She spotted them almost as soon as she ventured beyond the outer castle wall, and she could see several in the distance, crumpled and still. Olivia had snapped their necks, a killing style that was much neater and quieter than her usual method. She was trying to be stealthy.

Em carefully stepped around one of the fallen men. From their uniforms, they were part of the watchmen, the humans who policed Royal City. One of them must have recognized Olivia.

She broke into a jog, even though she wanted to stall. The southeast tower loomed in front of her, the door ajar, and she had to force her feet to move forward. She wished the tower was farther away, she wished her sister wasn't in it, she wished they were back in Ruina, cuddled up in bed with their mother.

Em slowed to a stop as she reached the door and tried to shake the thought away. It would do her no good to think about the past. If she'd learned anything from Olivia, it was that obsessing about the past, and trying to get back to some mythical great time, would only lead to more pain and suffering.

She pushed the door open. It caught on something, and Em had to push a little harder. It was a dead body, scooting across the floor as she shoved the door open. The guard who'd been on duty in the tower, from the look of his uniform.

The floorboards right in front of Em had been ripped up, revealing a hole in the ground. She knelt down, craning her neck to get a glimpse inside. She couldn't see Olivia, but the passageway was pretty long. It would take her a while to crawl all the way to the castle and back.

A boom sounded behind her, and Em whirled around, heart pounding. The Olso and Vallos armies had arrived.

Em swallowed as she pressed her back to the door. She couldn't let Olivia run loose, even if it meant leaving the fighting to the Lera army and the Ruined. Olivia would cause more damage if she got out of the tower.

She waited several minutes, the sounds of the attack growing louder behind her. She could hear horses running, people yelling, and cannons firing.

A rustling noise came from the hole, and Em straightened, gripping Cas's sword a little tighter. A dirty hand appeared out of the hole first, gripping the edge of the dirt to pull her body up.

Olivia was a mess. She was covered in dirt, wearing the same clothes she'd had on the last time Em had seen her, her face drawn and pale. She spotted Em when she was halfway out of the hole and paused for a moment, surprise skipping across her features before she rearranged her face into an angry mask.

"Sounds like the army made it," Olivia said, obviously trying to keep her voice casual. Em could hear the edge in it, the disappointment and anger at her failure.

"Aren felt them coming long before the lookouts spotted them," Em said. "Lera has the advantage."

Olivia let out a hollow laugh. "You can always count on Aren."

"Yes, you can," Em said softly.

Olivia's eyes dropped to the sword in Em's hand. "Are you planning on stabbing me with that thing?"

"No."

"Then, what?"

"We're going to wait in here until this is over. Then you're going to leave, and take Ester and Carmen and whoever else came with you."

"They're not here," Olivia said. "I don't need help."

Em raised her eyebrows. "Where'd they go?"

"Back to Ruina, like a bunch of cowards."

"Oh." She felt a flash of sympathy for Olivia. She had no one left. "I think it's best if you join them."

"I don't take orders from you," Olivia spat. She made a waving motion with her hand.

"What does that mean?"

"It means move away from the door."

Em shook her head, trying to keep her face calm. Olivia was sure to lunge at her at any moment. "What were you planning to do when you got into the castle? Kill me?"

"Yes. And Casimir. That's how I got Jovita to tell me about this stupid passageway. I promised to kill him. Though I'm sure she won't cry over your death either."

Em felt a sharp stab of disappointment, even though it was the answer she was expecting. She blew out a breath and nodded.

Olivia stared at her like she was expecting something else. "Is that it?"

"What do you want me to say? You were right. I led you into a battle where I knew you might die. We're not that different. You just don't . . ." She shook her head.

"What? What don't I do?"

She didn't have the ability to see outside herself for even a moment. Em was sure that Olivia would never understand Cas's point of view, or Aren's, or Iria's, and certainly not Em's. She didn't budge, she didn't compromise, and it didn't matter how much Em begged her. She couldn't change who Olivia was, and accepting that made her feel the tiniest bit better.

"Nothing." Em leaned her head back against the door and spoke her next words quietly. "It just makes me really sad that we couldn't find a way to make peace with each other. You're the only family I have left."

Olivia's expression changed, and Em had to turn away. For a moment, she'd appeared startled and upset, and Em was afraid that if she looked for too long, she'd forget that Olivia could no longer be reasoned with.

Another boom sounded from behind her, and Olivia's face snapped back into its angry mask. She took a step forward.

"Move."

Em met her sister's gaze. "Make me."

Olivia lunged, arms outstretched. Her body crashed into Em's and Em easily pushed her away. Olivia stumbled, almost falling into the hole, and made an annoyed noise from deep in her throat.

Em extended her sword in front of her. "I'd rather not use this."

Olivia snorted. "You're not going to use it." She lunged at Em again, darting to the side to avoid the sword. Em slashed it across Olivia's arm.

She'd expected her sister to yelp, or jump back, or at least flinch, but she barely seemed to notice. She grabbed the blade, making Em gasp. Blood trickled from her hand where she held it.

"It goes here," she growled, aiming the sword at her chest.

Em realized too late that Olivia was reaching around her, fumbling for the door handle, and she fell backward as the door swung open. She let go of the sword as she stumbled, afraid it would plunge into Olivia's chest as her sister fell with her.

Olivia's elbow slammed into Em's stomach as they hit the ground, and she wheezed. Olivia had her hands wrapped around Em's throat suddenly, but her body was only half on top of Em's, and she easily threw Olivia off.

Em scrambled to her knees but a hand grabbed her ankle, pulling her back down. Her face hit the dirt. She rolled over onto her back just in time to see Olivia leaping into the air, her eyes on Em's leg.

Her boots slammed into Em's ankle, and Em screamed as the crack reverberated in her ears. She clapped a hand over her mouth to stifle the noise.

"There." Olivia blew a piece of hair out of her face. "That should make you stay put for a minute."

Em sat up, pain screaming down her leg. She gasped at the sight behind Olivia. The Olso army was pushing the Lera soldiers back, advancing closer to the castle gates. Smoke billowed from cannons, and bodies flew through the air, propelled by Ruined magic.

Out of the corner of her eye, Em saw Olivia grab her sword. She snapped her attention back to her sister. Olivia pointed the blade at Em's neck. Em dug her fingers into the dirt, swallowing hard as she looked up at Olivia. Her sister wore an expression Em had never seen before—defeat. Anger, resolve, and resentment, but also defeat.

"You told me once that you didn't really expect to make it out of the Lera castle alive," Olivia said. "So this is fitting, right? This is how it was always supposed to go." She looked from Em to the soldiers and back again, a sad smile on her face. "I don't think I ever really expected to make it out of this alive either. We're not the ones who live, Em. We're the ones who fight alone, so others can live better."

Olivia edged the blade forward so it touched Em's neck. Her sister's breathing was heavy, her chest heaving up and down in short, panicked gasps. Em stared up at her, relief exploding in her chest. Olivia wasn't going to kill her. She couldn't do it.

The blade lowered just a little. Frustration crossed Olivia's face, and Em could have sworn she blinked away tears. She opened her mouth to speak.

Something whizzed through the air from behind Em. It slammed into Olivia's head, sending her stumbling backward. Her face contorted with rage as she touched her bleeding forehead and squinted at the object on the ground. A rock.

Em looked behind her, but she didn't see who had thrown the rock. She couldn't see anyone in the shadows of the castle. All the soldiers were at the front of the castle, not the southeast side.

Em scrambled to her feet, yelping at the pain that seared through her leg, and grabbed for the sword in her sister's hand. Olivia let go of the blade without a fight. Blood poured down her face and into her left eye, but she didn't wipe it away.

Em watched as Olivia looked left, to the dark buildings of Royal City. If her sister ran now, she would certainly make it out alive. Olivia looked right, to the battle raging in front of the castle. Yells rose up from the mess of soldiers, bodies scattered on the ground near the fighting.

Olivia turned right. She strode toward the battle, her coat billowing behind her, arms waving wildly.

Lera soldiers began flying through the air.

FORTY-SEVEN

IRIA DARTED OUT from behind a bush and ran for Em. Her foot protested, but the pain was dull now, only a hint of what it had been.

Em was trying to run, but she was dragging one leg behind her, and Iria easily caught up with her. She laid a hand on Em's shoulder.

"Em," she said.

Em jumped, relief crossing her face when she turned to see Iria standing there. Iria wrapped an arm around Em's waist, letting Em lean against her for support.

"Was that you? With the rock?" Em asked.

"Yes. It was all I could do." She gestured to her clothes. "I don't have Weakling armor. She would have killed me on sight."

Iria followed Em's gaze to where Olivia was headed to the front lawn of the castle. Hundreds of soldiers stretched out in front of the castle, swords, battle-axes, and other weapons flying. A few arrows whizzed over their heads.

The Olso and Vallos armies had clearly taken significant casualties—bodies were strewn about—but they showed no signs of retreating. She spotted several warriors swinging their swords at Lera soldiers.

Olivia was approaching from the east side, running toward the back of oblivious Lera soldiers. A body flew straight up in the air. Screams rippled through the crowd.

Em grabbed Iria around the waist, trying to hobble forward.

"We need to get you inside," Iria said. "You're injured."

"We need to get to Olivia." Em let out a cry as she tried to walk too fast, pain shooting up her leg.

Iria grasped the material of Em's shirt, bringing her to a stop. She knelt down. "Get on my back. It'll be faster."

There was a brief silence, like Em was thinking of protesting, then Iria felt her arms loop around her neck. Iria stood, grabbing underneath Em's thighs to keep her steady.

She'd lost some strength in the last few weeks, but not all of it, and she was able to break into a run with Em on her back. Olivia had disappeared into the mess of soldiers, screams rising up from the crowd. Iria followed them.

An arrow whizzed by, narrowly missing Iria's ear. She felt Em jerk to dodge it.

Iria ran straight into the crush of bodies. She was surrounded by Lera soldiers shouting orders to each other.

"Olivia!" Em yelled at the soldiers. "Did you see Olivia?"

Out of the corner of her eye, Iria saw the glint of a sword, and she darted to the side, clutching Em's legs. An Olso warrior was charging at them, battle-ax lifted above his head. A Lera soldier leaped in front of Iria, slicing his blade across the warrior's chest. He crumpled to the ground.

"She went that way," the Lera soldier said, breathing heavily as he pointed behind Iria.

She whirled around and ran farther into the crowd, ducking around a group of guards protecting a Ruined so exhausted she could barely stand.

To her right, a Lera soldier was fighting off a warrior with a sword, and Iria tried to edge around them. She felt Em take in a sharp breath, her fingers digging into Iria's shoulder.

August appeared out of the crowd. He pulled his blade from the chest of a Lera soldier and pushed him to the ground. His eyes were wild, blood splattered across his uniform, as he searched the faces around him.

He spotted Em first. When he looked at Iria, his eyes went round, his lips parting in shock. Clearly news of her escape hadn't reached him yet.

Em slid off Iria's back. Iria grabbed for her, not wanting to lose Em while she was injured, but she scurried out of sight. August broke into a run. He jumped over a dead soldier, his gaze fixed on Iria.

She drew her sword from her belt, trying to remember how

good August was with one. She didn't think she'd ever had the opportunity to spar with him.

His blade came for her, and she blocked it, bumping into someone behind her as she stepped back. August's sword crashed down again, a snarl on his face. She ducked and weaved, blocking his attacks and barely keeping her balance as the crowd pressed into them.

"*Olivia!*" Em's voice cut through the noise, and August froze. His gaze snapped to the right, where the yell had come from.

Iria took advantage of his distraction to duck behind some soldiers. She ran in the direction of Em's voice, which was still calling Olivia's name.

Several Lera guards turned and bolted, almost knocking her over as they passed by. A hole had opened up in the crowd around her, and she suddenly saw why—Olivia stood a few paces away.

Blood poured down her face from where Iria had hit her with a rock, and she was gasping for breath. She turned in a circle, like she was looking for something.

"*Olivia!*" It was Em's voice again, though Iria still couldn't see her. Soldiers began running from all directions—headed *for* Olivia this time. Shields went up. Iria could smell the Weakling as soldiers closed in with their armor and shields on all sides.

Iria realized suddenly that Em hadn't been calling Olivia's name because she was searching for her sister, or trying to get her to stop. She'd been warning the Lera soldiers so they could get in position.

Olivia spun in a circle as the soldiers closed in. She flung her arms and sent a couple of soldiers flying, but most stood their ground, hidden behind their shields. She lowered her arms, her eyebrows furrowing as she turned. Her anger gave way to pure confusion for a moment.

A hand closed around Iria's arm, and she turned to see Em next to her.

"The shields are working," Iria said. Her eyes darted to where Em was clutching her sword. She was shaking.

None of the soldiers were making a move toward Olivia, Iria realized. A few glanced at Em, obviously waiting for her to charge her sister.

Rage took over Olivia's features as her gaze caught on something. Aren. He was standing a bit above the crowd, elevated by something Iria couldn't see. He was facing away from Olivia, taking care of Olso warriors who had suddenly charged him.

Iria's mind went blank. She pushed Em aside. Her feet moved forward and she was running, shoving aside scared Lera soldiers. She yanked a shield out of a soldier's hand, ignoring his yell of protest. Her hand tightened around her blade. She sprinted forward as fast as she could.

Iria drove the sword into Olivia's back and through her heart.

FORTY-EIGHT

GALO CLAPPED A hand over his mouth as he watched Iria's blade tear through Olivia's chest. Olivia's back arched and she gasped as she fell to her knees. Iria pulled her sword out and took several quick steps back. Olivia crumpled to the ground.

Galo glanced up at Aren, who had his eyes squeezed shut and his face turned away. But Aren allowed himself only a few moments before he opened his eyes again and looked at the second wave of warriors running toward them.

Galo looked back at Olivia, but the crowd had swallowed her up. Iria was pushing her way through, half carrying a sobbing Em.

"Will you make sure Em gets inside?" Aren called to Galo.

He nodded and rushed to Iria, gently removing Em's arm

from around Iria's shoulder. "I've got her," he said. "I'll make sure she gets inside."

"Her leg is injured," Iria said, pointing.

Galo reached down and scooped Em up into his arms. He turned and broke into a run, Em bouncing in his arms. He had to dodge a rush of guards running out of the castle and into the fight.

They crossed over the castle threshold, the sounds of fighting muffling as the doors closed.

"Violet! Is Cas—"

"In hiding," Violet finished, eyes flicking to Em. "What's—"

"She's injured, but fine. Olivia is dead." He said the second sentence quietly.

Galo heard the sound of running footsteps and turned to see Mateo headed toward him. He took Em out of Galo's arms. "I'll take her to Cas. Be careful."

Galo gave him a quick smile before turning to race back out of the castle. Past the gates, hundreds of Lera soldiers fought off the Olso and Vallos troops against the setting sun. Smoke rose from the north corner of the castle, where a cannonball had hit the building, but the damage looked minimal. The southwest tower was on fire, and he watched as a piece of it crashed to the ground.

He found Aren right where he'd left him, standing in front of the castle gates on an old potato crate. He was surrounded by Lera guards and soldiers.

Screams ripped through the air, and a sudden rush of Olso

warriors plowed through the Lera soldiers. They were headed straight for Aren. The attacks directly on Aren were endless. The warriors had clearly been told to make killing Aren a top priority.

"More! We need more!" Galo followed the sound of the voice to see a soldier pointing at Aren. They needed more people to guard him.

Galo raced forward, pushing through the growing crowd of soldiers. He lightly wrapped his hand around Aren's wrist.

"You got Em safely inside?" Aren asked without turning around. Galo wasn't sure how he'd known it was him.

"Yes. Mateo took her to hide with Cas."

Aren focused on the warriors to his left, throwing them all through the air at once. "I need to get somewhere higher."

A body slammed into Galo's, and he let go of Aren's arm. He whirled around, gripping his sword. A warrior charged at him.

Galo lifted his sword, but the warrior was gone suddenly, his scream fading as he shot so far up into the sky he disappeared. The warriors around him shot off the ground as well, flying away one by one.

Aren jumped off the crate and took off in the direction of the castle. "I need to get higher!" he yelled again, shaking off a Lera soldier who tried to make him stay put.

Galo took off after Aren. Arrows whizzed by his head, and struck the soldier next to him. She fell with a gasp.

Aren ran through the castle gate and to the wall. He hooked his fingers onto the stone and began to hoist his body up.

Galo grabbed the edge of his shirt, pulling him back down.

"You'll be too exposed. Too easy a target for an arrow."

"Trust me. I only need a few seconds."

Galo didn't release his shirt. It was too hard to protect him up there. "How do you feel? Are you getting weak?"

"Not even a little."

Galo released his shirt. "Fine." He grabbed the stone wall and began climbing up next to Aren. He could at least try to shield him.

They reached the top and Galo slowly stood, finding his balance on the narrow space.

"Get in position to catch him if he falls," he said to the guards on the ground. He edged closer to Aren, trying to use his body to guard him without blocking Aren's sight.

Aren stared out at the scene in front of him, and Galo followed his gaze. A line of soldiers stood in front of the castle, with Ruined placed at strategic points. He spotted Mariana collapsed in exhaustion, a group of castle guards trying to drag her to safety. It must have been difficult to distinguish between the Lera soldiers and the enemy on the ground, and Galo could see why Aren wanted to stand on the wall. Galo could easily spot the Lera soldiers, with their black long-sleeve shirts, the deep blue stripe on the collar standing out from the crowd.

Two arrows shot out from the crowd and Galo grabbed for Aren, pulling them both into a squat.

Aren shot up, using Galo's arm to steady himself. He stared straight ahead, and warriors began flying backward and into the sky. They went in quick succession, leaving the area in front of the Lera troops completely clear.

The Lera soldiers ran into the now-empty grass, chasing the Olso warriors who were still standing. As Galo watched, several warriors fell, daggers and arrows sticking out of their chest.

Galo's gaze followed a man jumping onto his horse, yelling something as he turned away from the castle. August. The remaining warriors began running away from the castle.

"He's calling for a retreat," he said with a laugh. He pointed, and Aren followed his finger. A smile spread across his face.

Galo turned to look in the other direction, at the warriors on the west side. He saw the warrior, standing with a dead Lera guard at his feet, a split second before she shot the arrow. It hurled straight toward Aren.

Galo threw his arm back, sending Aren off the wall and tumbling to the guards below. He tried to turn his body, to avoid the arrow, but it struck him so hard it sent him flying backward. He flew off the wall and collided with a body. Someone grunted as they broke his fall.

Pain seared through his chest, and there was suddenly a crowd around him. Everyone was shouting.

"Don't pull it out," someone said. "It might bleed too much."

Mateo appeared in front of him, horror on his face as he looked down at the arrow. It was sticking out of his chest on the lower right side, in his ribs. He let out a sigh as he let his head fall back in the grass.

"That's good."

"What?" Mateo was blinking back tears. "How is this good?"

"That seems like an all right place to have an arrow." He winced as pain shot through his chest. "Painful, though."

Aren laughed. "He's not wrong. Thanks for the push, by the way."

"Anytime."

Mateo wiped his eyes. "You idiot," he said with a smile.

Aren watched as guards disappeared into the castle with Galo. He wanted to follow them in, to make sure Galo was all right, but he needed to find Iria first. He'd lost track of her after she killed Olivia and helped Em inside.

The sun was almost completely gone, the last wisps of light shining across the grass in front of the castle. There were bodies scattered everywhere, some of them Lera soldiers, and Aren swallowed down a wave of panic as he scanned the area.

He spotted Olivia, her body still crumpled on the grass where she'd died. A few Ruined stood nearby. He dared a quick glance around the area, trying his best not to look at Olivia as he searched for Iria.

Mariana was trudging slowly toward the castle, Patricio and Gisela on either side of her. She smiled weakly at Aren.

"Did we lose any Ruined?" he asked.

"Not one."

He breathed a sigh of relief.

"What should we tell them to do with Olivia's body?" Mariana asked.

Aren closed his eyes briefly. "Um, I think Em will want to bury it." His throat closed as he said the words. He didn't have much affection left for Olivia, but he knew that Em had to be devastated. All of this had started as a way to get her sister back, and in the end, she'd failed.

Mariana nodded. "I'll let them know."

He scanned the area behind them again, squinting at the soldiers returning to the castle. He purposefully didn't look at the dead bodies on the ground. He didn't want to even consider that she could be there. "Have you seen Iria?"

Mariana shook her head.

"Go rest," he said, putting a hand on her shoulder briefly. He walked farther away from the castle, his heart sinking further with each step. Soldiers and guards passed him, some of them smiling and thanking him, but he didn't see Iria.

He turned back to the castle. Two guards were helping a soldier to her feet a few paces away.

"You were incredible," the woman said to Aren.

"Thank you. Do you know if there was any fighting in the back of the castle?"

One of the guards shook his head. "No, but there was some on the southeast side."

"Thanks." He broke into a jog and headed southeast. There was nothing there but a few dead bodies, many of them killed by Olivia, judging by the state of their necks.

The soldiers around him were celebrating as he walked back

to the front of the castle. Two Ruined passed him, one briefly grabbing his hand and saying something kind. His heart was pounding in his ears so loudly that he couldn't even make out everything she had said.

"Have you seen Iria?" he asked a familiar guard as she passed.

"Not since she brought Em in."

He stopped, bracing a hand against the castle wall. He should have grabbed her after she passed Em off to Galo. He'd wanted to, but he'd had warriors coming at him from all sides at the time. He'd taken his eyes off her for a moment and she was gone.

"I took this shield from a soldier. I'm not sure who it was."

Aren's head snapped up at the sound of the familiar voice. Iria stood not far away, passing a Weakling shield to a guard.

"You're the one who killed Olivia," the guard said. His face broke into a smile. "I'm sure you can keep the shield. I think you can probably have anything you want."

Iria shook her head. "Thanks, but I don't need it." She looked up and spotted Aren watching them, and a tentative smile crossed her face. She lifted her hand in a wave.

He strode forward, reaching her in only a few quick steps. Whatever expression he had on his face, she seemed surprised by it, because her eyes widened a little as he approached.

He put both hands on her cheeks and kissed her. She immediately wrapped her arms around his waist and rose up on her toes, drawing them closer together. His whole body almost collapsed with relief. He might never let her out of his sight again.

"I'm sorry about Olivia," she said as soon as they broke apart.

"She was coming for you. I had to."

"I know," he said softly. He kept his hands on her cheeks, refusing to let her go yet.

"Is Em all right?"

"I haven't seen her yet. But she knows you did it to protect us." Aren thought that Em might have even been a little grateful, deep down. Iria saved Em from having to do it herself.

He leaned down and kissed her again, wrapping both arms around her waist and pulling her tight against him. She pressed both hands to his chest, and he took one as he pulled away, lacing their fingers together.

"Where were you?" he asked. "I lost you after you gave Em to Galo. Did you go into the castle?"

"No, I helped Mariana and a few other Ruined fight off the warriors."

He took in a sharp breath and looked down at her foot. "You really weren't in shape to fight yet. You should have stayed where I could protect you."

"I don't need you to protect me. I did just fine on my own, obviously."

"You're still healing. Once you—"

Iria cut him off with another kiss, a low laugh sounding from the back of her throat. "Are you yelling at me or kissing me?" she asked. Her arms tightened around his waist.

"Both, I think." He smiled and leaned down to kiss her again.

FORTY-NINE

"ARE YOU *EVER* going to die?"

Cas pressed his lips together to keep in a laugh. The words were spoken by Jovita, who glared at him from the other side of her cell. She'd been locked up beneath the castle since the day of the battle, and it seemed she'd assumed he was dead.

"He's immortal," Galo said, stepping off the stairs behind Cas. "I guess you didn't hear."

Jovita looked between the two of them, like she couldn't decide if they were telling the truth. The Ruined had clearly damaged her mind, because he could see the confusion all over her face as she frowned at them. It had been nearly a month since she'd returned to the castle on the day of the battle, and she hadn't improved at all.

He felt a flash of sympathy for Jovita that she didn't deserve. She didn't deserve any of what he was about to do, but he knew it was the right decision. It was the first time he'd felt at peace about Jovita since his mother had died.

"I'm sending you to the fortress," Cas said, stepping forward and pulling out the key to the cell. "There are guards waiting at the top of the stairs. They'll escort you to a carriage, and then south, to the fortress."

She regarded him suspiciously as he pulled the door open. "And then what?"

"And then you may do whatever you want, in the confines of the fortress. You'll be given a room, not a cell, and you'll have full access to the grounds. But you'll be guarded at all times."

She laughed. It was short and loud, and not at all amused. "You're lying. You're going to send me away so you can kill me without getting your hands dirty."

"No, that's what you would have done. The guards have been ordered not to harm you." He swept his arm toward the stairs. "Go. We may come up with a different arrangement in the future, but for now, you will live in the fortress, and I will live here, and with a little luck, we will never see each other again."

She stood slowly, never taking her eyes off him as she walked to the cell door. She stepped out of the cell and darted quickly past Cas, like she was afraid he was going to grab her. She ran up the stairs at full speed.

"No good-bye, then," Galo said as he watched her go.

"I'm heartbroken," Cas said dryly. He walked up the stairs, Galo following behind him, and watched as guards escorted Jovita down the hallway. It was strange that he'd been so scared of her a few months ago that he'd agonized over killing her. Now she just seemed like a sad reminder of the past.

Aren rounded the corner, and Jovita shrank toward one of the guards as soon as she spotted him. He laughed as he came to a stop next to Galo.

"At least I still scare some people," he said. "My reputation has taken a hit recently. No one refers to me as 'the bad one' anymore."

"I'm sure there are still a few people in Olso who call you that," Galo said.

"Thank you. That makes me feel better." Aren bumped his shoulder against Galo's. "Come on. I think most of the Ruined are already waiting."

"We have a meeting," Galo explained as he stepped away from Cas. "We have a few things to discuss before the Vallos king arrives tomorrow."

Cas sighed. The new king of Vallos had reached out to start peace talks, and Cas didn't look forward to his visit. The kingdoms of Vallos and Olso had made it clear that they did not support Lera's decision to let Ruined participate in government. He'd yet to hear from August at all on the subject of a peace treaty. Violet said he was probably too embarrassed after their humiliating defeat at the Lera castle. Rumor had it that everyone had heard that Iria, the most notorious traitor in Olso, had been the one to defeat Olivia Flores. There had even been a movement to pardon her and let her return home. She'd told Cas that August would never agree to that, and even if he did, she had no interest in returning to Olso.

"Iria's waiting for you in one of the sparring rooms," Aren said.

"I know, I'm headed up there now," Cas said.

Galo winced. "You're sparring with Iria? Poor girl." Cas laughed.

Aren whacked him on the shoulder as they began walking away from Cas. "Hey."

"Have you ever sparred with Cas? It's a humbling experience."

"I have no use for a sword."

"How do you always manage to say that so smugly?"

Aren laughed, and their voices faded as they disappeared around the corner. Cas walked to the stairs and started up them, smiling at a maid as he passed her. The castle buzzed with noise around him. They were back to full staff, and new guards came in every week. The castle was almost back to how it used to be.

It felt empty without Em, though. She'd been gone for almost three weeks.

She'd actually laughed when he suggested burying Olivia in Lera. Olivia would come back from the dead just to kill them both if she buried her in Lera, Em had said. Cas couldn't argue with that.

Em decided that Olivia would probably want to be with her mother, so she decided to take Olivia's ashes back to Ruina. Cas had protested, pointing out that Em had a broken ankle, and the Ruined who had been loyal to Olivia had gone back to Ruina, but she wouldn't be swayed. Ten Ruined went with her, including Mariana, who assured Cas they'd be fine. *We made it this far*, she'd said. *We're certainly not dying now.*

That hadn't completely eased his worries, but he did have to admit that she was right. The Olso warriors had retreated, and it looked like they had no plans to invade again. The new Vallos government was too scared of angering Lerans united with Ruined to make a move against Em. And Aren said that the war between Ruined died with Olivia.

Cas reached the top of the stairs and headed in the direction of the sparring room. He found Iria waiting in the middle of the room, sword already in hand.

"Sorry I'm late," he said. "I was seeing Jovita off."

"Was she grateful? To be going to the fortress?"

Cas pulled on his sparring jacket and grabbed a sword. "I don't think *grateful* is the word. She might have lost her mind, but she remembers her hatred for me just fine."

"I'd take that as a compliment. It would have been worse if she hadn't thought of you at all."

"Excellent point."

"Thank you for doing this with me," Iria said.

"I enjoy it," he said. "Besides, Galo is busy and important these days, and most of the guard lets me win. You never let me win. I mean, I always do, but I have to actually work for it."

"There is never any danger of me letting you win at anything."

He laughed as he raised his sword. Iria stepped forward and they sparred in silence for several minutes, Cas tagging Iria twice. She moved smoothly now, her foot healed and her limp slight when she was wearing the boot. She hadn't chosen a specific post in the Lera government yet, but General Amaro had suggested that she might start a program similar to the warrior program in Olso, to train elite Leran fighters.

She stepped back suddenly, nodding at something behind him. He turned to find Mateo standing at the door.

"I'm sorry to interrupt, Your Majesty," Mateo said, a smile spreading across his face. "But the queen has returned."

Em tilted her head back and closed her eyes, the sun warm on her face. She rode in the open-air wagon pulled by horses, her legs stretched out in front of her, the left one still bandaged at the ankle.

She was alone in the wagon, Mariana and Patricio on horseback on either side of her, the other Ruined riding just ahead. Royal City stretched out to her left, and the castle was so close it was hard not to jump out of the wagon and run to it.

Instead, she sat up a little straighter and looked at the place that had become her home. She was glad she'd returned to Ruina one last time, if only because it confirmed it wasn't home anymore. It was right to take Olivia's ashes to the remains of the castle, and it was right to leave them there.

The Ruined who had returned after abandoning Olivia didn't seem surprised by Olivia's death, though Ester had told Em in no uncertain terms that Em had Olivia's blood on her hands. Em had plenty of blood on her hands, but she knew Olivia's didn't belong there. She could tell Ester knew it too.

Even though Em didn't blame herself for what happened to Olivia, she hadn't been able to stop imagining how it could have been. If they'd never left Ruina, if August had never come with the warriors, if Olivia had gone back with Ester and the others instead of coming to the castle. Em imagined a different future for her sister, one where she grew old and learned from her mistakes. A future where she took her power to heal—a power that no Ruined possessed now—and helped people. A future where she learned that the satisfaction she felt from her rage wasn't happiness. The future that Em imagined for her sister was probably much better than any one Olivia would have actually lived, and she tried not to think about that too often.

"On your right," Mariana said quietly, and Patricio and Em both turned their heads. A group of humans stood not far away, staring at them with contemptuous expressions on their faces. One woman put her arm out, like she was shielding the girl next to her.

Em lifted her hand in a wave. One of the men looked insulted.

"Don't antagonize them," Mariana said, her voice amused.

"I wasn't!" Em shrugged. "They can hate us, but I don't have to feel the same."

The castle gates were opening, and the Ruined at the front dismounted their horses. Mariana smiled at Em.

"I think they're excited we're back, Your Majesty."

Em leaned to the side to see past the horses and spotted people streaming out of the castle. Guards were lined up on either side of the front path, which Em thought was the standard way to greet a royal returning to the castle. She had signed the new marriage document before she left for Ruina. There'd been a surge of goodwill toward the Ruined after they'd helped Lera defeat Olso and Vallos, and the advisers decided there would be no better time for Em and Cas to announce their marriage. She was, officially, the queen of Lera, and held all the same powers as Cas.

The wagon stopped just outside the castle gates and Em carefully got to her feet, trying to balance on her good leg. She looked up to find Cas jogging down the dirt path, his face breaking into a grin when he spotted her.

He stopped next to the wagon and held his hands out to help her down. He grabbed her around the waist as she stepped off, sweeping her clear off her feet. She wrapped her arms around his neck and buried her face in his neck. He let out a sigh so big she could feel his chest move.

"I missed you," he said into her hair.

"Every day," she agreed.

He gently put her on the ground, his eyes on her feet. "How is your ankle?"

"Getting better. I could use an arm for walking, though."

"Gladly," he said, holding his out for her. She slipped her arm through. "How was Ruina? Any problems?"

She shook her head. There wasn't much else to say about her journey, nothing that she was able to express right now anyway, and Cas gave her a look like he understood. He did. If there was anyone who understood Em, who understood everything, it was him.

She heard running footsteps, and turned to find Aren and Iria rushing toward her. Iria slowed as they drew closer, her expression a little uncertain. Em dropped Cas's arm, stepping forward to embrace Iria first. Em smiled at Iria as she pulled away. She had assured Iria before she left that she blamed no one for Olivia's death.

She turned to Aren next and squeezed him tightly until he let her go. He appeared a little worried as he pulled away, but he returned the smile she gave him. They'd both agreed it was best if he stayed in Lera while she went to Ruina. He didn't want to leave Iria, and Em didn't want him to leave Lera unprotected, not so soon after the attack from Olso and Vallos.

Aren hugged her again. Neither of them said anything as they pulled away and Aren turned to greet Cas. Aren didn't seem to have words about Olivia any more than Em did. She preferred it that way. Maybe they'd find a way to talk about her one day.

She took Cas's arm again, leaning on him as they began to walk down the path.

Cas turned his head, brushing a kiss to her forehead. "Did you encounter any problems traveling in Lera?"

He must have known about the hostile humans not far from

the castle. Cas and his guards were aware of everything that went on in Royal City these days.

"No one attacked us," she said.

He laughed softly. "That's your bar for things going well, isn't it? No one tried to kill you."

"It's always a good day when no one tries to kill me." She smiled up at him. She knew he wished for more. He wished everyone in Lera could see what he saw in her, that they could love her the way he did, or at least respect her. He was impatient, but Em was not. Many of the people in Lera didn't accept her as their queen. They didn't understand her, or respect her, not the way Cas did.

But they would.

Amy Tintera is the *New York Times* bestselling author of *Ruined* and *Avenged,* as well as the duology *Reboot* and *Rebel.* She has degrees in journalism and film and can usually be found staring into space, dreaming up ways to make her characters run for their lives. She lives in Austin, Texas. You can visit her online at www.amytintera.com.